Life Unseen

CAMERON WOLFE

Life Unseen

HarperCollins*Publishers*

HarperCollins*Publishers*
77–85 Fulham Palace Road
Hammersmith, London W6 8JB

First published in Great Britain in 1999 by
HarperCollins*Publishers*

© 1999 Cameron Wolfe

1 3 5 7 9 10 8 6 4 2

Cameron Wolfe asserts the moral right to
be identified as the author of this work

Portions of the Prologue have been published previously.

A catalogue record for this book
is available from the British Library

ISBN 000 274994 4

Printed and bound in Great Britain by
Caledonian International Book Manufacturing Ltd, Glasgow

CONDITIONS OF SALE
This book is sold subject to the condition that it
shall not, by way of trade or otherwise, be lent, re-sold,
hired out or otherwise circulated without the publisher's
prior consent in any form of binding or cover other
than that in which it is published and without a similar
condition including this condition being imposed on
the subsequent purchaser.

All rights reserved. No part of this publication may be
reproduced, stored in a retrieval system, or transmitted,
in any form or by any means, electronic, mechanical,
photocopying, recording or otherwise, without the prior
permission of the publishers.

Life can only be understood backwards;
but it must be lived forwards.
Søren Kierkegaard

PROLOGUE

He turned away from the tragic sight of his slumbering daughter and resumed the quietest argument in the history of Russian science.

"I am not leaving without you," his wife softly repeated.

Alexis examined her through the ashes of fading anger. Alena's blonde hair framed a face that looked perpetually hungry. Months of fear and worry had turned her cheeks cavernous and drawn her eyes back into dark-ringed sockets. A single glance at his sleeping child, whose features had been aged by the same burdens, was enough to assure him that he had no choice. None.

"Professor Philippa Laremy," he repeated, the words a familiar chant. "San Diego. University of California. As soon as you arrive in Vienna, you must contact her."

"Do you not hear me any longer?" But there was no anger left in his wife either. She knew the time had come. Despite her strongest efforts, despite all the pleas she could muster, she had lost. Defeat hollowed mournful depths into her gaze. "I cannot –"

"If they catch me, they kill me. It is that simple." Alexis wore his newest lab coat and his best cloth-soled shoes. His remaining clothes and all the dollars they had saved were stuffed into a battered leather grip. Two more satchels contained all his wife and daughter had for the journey ahead.

"Is that what you want?"

"I want our daughter to have a father." Her voice was a faint wail. "I want a future together with my husband."

They crouched behind the particle analyzer, which like most of the other lab machinery did not work. His daughter slept peacefully in his arms. Their cramped alcove was carpeted with litter and dust. The cleaners had not ventured back here since the downfall of the Soviet Empire. Why should they, when their pay had slipped to twelve dollars a month and their families were slowly starving?

Despite exterior walls over two feet thick, the wind held such force that the central lab building shook like a huge bass drum. The wind did not bother their daughter, however, for she was a child of the Russian steppes. Alexis glanced at the face made peaceful by slumber, but directed his words at his wife. "This also do I want. It is for this and only this that we risk all."

"But together, Alexis," she pleaded, and the wind rose to wail along with her.

He made a soft shushing sound. His daughter hated it when they quarreled. This departure was hard enough without her squalling. So his voice remained soothed by the pain of his heart as he replied, "I cannot stay. They know what we have discovered, or they think they know, which is even worse. And they expect what we are about to do."

"How can you be so sure? You do not even know who they are!"

The child stirred fretfully. He lowered his face and nuzzled the clean softness of her hair, her cheek, and ached anew at the parting to come. His daughter was three days from her fourth birthday, and shared her mother's fair coloring and almost Oriental features. A glorious mixture of Scandinavian and Mongol marauders, a tragic history of his beloved land etched into the two faces he cherished more than life itself.

"I know enough," Alexis said softly, raising back up to meet his wife's gaze. Showing her the resolve which left no room for doubt. "I know they exist, I know they are coming. I know if I stay, I die. And you. And our daughter. So we must flee. Finished. The discussion is now finished."

"But why alone?" Frantically she clutched at whatever thread remained. "Four thousand kilometers you send us, to a refugee camp we have heard of but never seen."

"Safety lies only in making my and Philippa Laremy's discovery known." Again a chant, one he had spoken to himself a hundred thousand times. "Safety, and if we are lucky, prosperity."

"Luck." Alena spat the word as she would a curse. "When have we ever known such a myth?"

"I know it every time I look in your eyes," he said, emptied and forlorn by what was soon to come. "Every time I see my daughter smile."

Failure forced a single tear from her eye. "And in America? They do not shoot scientists in America?"

"Professor Laremy is still alive. Or she was the day before yesterday." He caressed away the trace of wetness from his wife's cheek, squeezed his fist tight, willing his heart to be firm as well. "I would take you with me if I could. But I cannot. My greatest hope lies in knowing you both are well. Call her as soon as you arrive in Vienna. Use the name we agreed. I will contact you as swiftly as I can."

The chamber was a hundred feet wide and sixty feet high. It had been constructed in the great Soviet tradition, where smaller labs posed the risk of unsupervised activity. A steel-banded corridor ran around the top like a menacing crown, from which their masters had once stood and observed their every step. Three hundred of Russia's finest had worked in this room alone; an entire city had been constructed to service seventeen such labs, all erected to stretch the limits of military science. Those assigned here had received the best of everything, their stores the envy of all who had known of this place. It had been a town with neither name nor road; mail had been addressed to a post-box in Moscow, supplies had come by military transport.

But now the military was bankrupt, and pay was slower in coming than supplies. Six months earlier they had even played host to the enemy, American corporations seeking anything that might be useful, the former masters selling whatever might bring hard cash. Deals were in the making, and attention paid to Alexis Vilnieff's work for the first time in over a year. Which had been both good and bad; good because it meant the chance to travel and granted his family almost enough to eat. Bad because the attention was now focusing down to a rifle scope, and pressure was tightening on the trigger. Of that Alexis was certain.

The lab's outer door squeaked on rusting hinges, and they froze into terrified stillness. Footsteps scrunched across the grimy floor, and when the guard's battered cap came into view they heaved vast sighs of relief. He demanded in a vodka-harshened voice, "You are ready?"

"We are."

"Loading is almost finished. I will come for you soon."

"Thank you, Ivan Ivanovichu. You are a good friend."

"I am a man with four starving children, and for ten roubles more I would flee with you." He inspected them worriedly, then withdrew, adding, "Be on guard. They are a strange lot, these gypsies of the road."

When the door had creaked closed, Alena grasped his arm. "Answer me," she hissed. "For once you will speak of the risks in America or I will return to our quarters."

"And do what?" he replied calmly. Alexis could not respond to her ire. Not now. His entire world began and ended with these two precious ones. He would never have started on this scientific course had he even dreamed of reaching this point. "Wait for them to come and kill us all?"

"Who are they, Alexis? Give them a name and I might share your fears."

"They are the ones who stand to lose power and wealth by what I think we have discovered." He gave to his words determined strength, as firm and unyielding as the Siberian soil in winter. "They are the ones we would see once only, and only for a short while."

"Then come with us," she pleaded, her fingers digging into the flesh of his arm. "Without you I am nothing, have nothing. I beg you, come!"

"I have the passport, the exit pass, the American visa. You have none of this." He brushed a feather of light hair from his daughter's sleeping face and felt his heart squeezed by the impossible beauty of her. "I have the conference in Boston. I have the permission to travel because the authorities think you are here and trapped. My train leaves for Helsinki within the hour. Ivan has promised to hide your absence until I transfer to the foreign aircraft. After that, we are safe."

The door creaked open once more. Alena glanced over as Ivan entered, then moaned the word, "Safe."

"It is time," the guard rasped.

"We come," Alexis called back.

"Tell me again," she pleaded desperately, rising with him. "Let me know of your hope since I have none of my own."

"Kiev," he soothed, saying the word as he would an intimacy. "You will arrive in three days. From there you travel via Lvov and Debrecen and Budapest and on to Vienna. Processing at the detention camp takes six weeks. You will be kept and protected at least that long. Use the name we agreed on so I know how to find you." With both arms now supporting his daughter, he leaned forward and stroked Alena's cheek with his own. He drank in the scent of her, willing himself to etch the memory deep. "Go. Await my word. I will contact you. I *will*."

"Come now or they go without you," the guard hissed.

"Take the satchels," Alexis said in reply, and slipped out from behind the machine, giving silent thanks that his daughter still slept. "We are ready."

As with all personnel in these days of want and misery, the guard's uniform was little more than rags. His cap was battered and sweat-stained, his coat lacked buttons. His shoes flip-flapped as he walked out and scanned the corridor, then returned to wave them forward. "All clear."

The four of them hustled down the long central hall. Mildew and ancient spider webs clustered in the ceiling corners. Their footsteps rang overloud as they hurried past what once had been the centerpiece of Soviet scientific achievement, now as desolate as a forgotten mausoleum.

They turned the final corner, and the wind grew so loud that it covered the sounds of Alena's weeping. They pushed through the inner doors, and instantly the noise became a ferocious howl.

His daughter stirred sleepily in his arms. "Papa?"

"Sha, little one, all is well. We must go outside." He turned to his wife's tear-streaked face. "The towel, Alena."

His daughter was indeed a child of the wind and the wild country. At four years of age she knew enough to remain still as the dampened towel was tucked in around her eyes and nose and mouth and ears. He gripped his daughter more firmly, and nodded to the guard. "Let us go."

As soon as they opened the outer doors, the wind sought to rip them apart.

Russians called their steppes the earthen sea. There in the Siberian borderlands it lay flat and featureless, running thus from the Arctic forests to the southern mountains, three thousand kilometers of aching emptiness. In such early summer days, winds came shrieking down from the land of eternal snows with nothing to slow their blasts until they struck the Caucasus Mountains another thousand kilometers farther south. This time of year, the soil was dry and bare of snow to hold it in place. The wind plucked up giant fistfuls and flung it with a ferocity that stripped paint from a car in a matter of hours. It was a maddening wind, a blinding force that lifted entire trees and sent them whipping unseen onto houses and trucks and people.

Only today, for the first time since his arrival in Siberia eleven years earlier, did Alexis count the wind a good omen.

Arms interlocked for added strength, together they fought their way across the laboratory compound to the outer loading platforms. It was impossible to check their progress visually. Around them swirled impenetrable clouds of yellow-black dust. They walked by memory alone.

Suddenly above the wind's blast came the roar of great diesel engines, and Alena wailed in her husband's ear. He forced her forward until the first dark beast appeared up ahead. The guard shouted words that were lost in the wind, but his signals were clear – this was Alena's truck.

Alexis felt the child in his arms stiffen with fear from the strange roaring shape in front of them. He bent over and buried his closed eyes in the towel that protected her face. Then he straightened and allowed his sobbing wife to clasp his neck. He placed his lips upon her ear and shouted as loud as he was able, "I am ever with you, Alena!"

Together with the guard he forced his wife up into the truck's open door, then lifted his daughter up to her. The satchels came next. He climbed up the step, and in the cabin's relative calm he embraced them once more. Then he stepped back and slammed the door, searching through the yellow storm for a final glimpse of his world.

He saw as his daughter pulled the towel free, as she realized that she was on the inside and her father on the outside. She flung herself at the closed window and screamed at the top of her voice, "*Papa!*"

He stepped down from the truck and watched his daughter claw at the glass, shrieking the single word over and over. "*Papa!*"

The truck bellowed its defiance of the storm and pulled away. Alexis stood and faced the tumult until his daughter's screams had faded to meld with the wind's shrill blast.

The guard gripped Alexis' arm and pulled him along the road. The wind lulled, as though wounded by the same departure which had torn Alexis' heart in two. A smaller shape emerged from the gloom, a passenger car assigned to take him to the train. They embraced in the way of friends in the Orient, a swift hug to either shoulder, and Alexis was surprised to find tears streaking the guard's seamed features. In order to keep the moment untainted, Alexis did not place the final payment into his hand, but rather shoved it deep into the man's pocket, then gripped him by the neck. He shouted, "You are indeed a friend, Ivan Ivanovichu."

"My world collapses and sweeps away all of value, even friends." The guard shoved him brusquely toward the car. "Go while the portal is open. And when your way is clear, remember me."

Alexis climbed in, slammed the door, and looked out at his friend. The man stood defiantly as the wind returned, a power so fierce it threatened to blast him from the earth's surface. The guard shouted out a single word of farewell. *Remember.*

The driver was a mere lad, one of the assistants who had nowhere else to go. He drove with squint-eyed concentration, holding to the road's edge not in fear of what approached but rather because the road's roughened border helped him steer. The first half-hour was the hardest, both men intent upon what swept in and out of focus through swirling masses of grit and dust. Even the car's interior became coated with grime so fine it pushed through the closed windows and frosted every surface.

Then the road began a downward spiral, curving ever more tightly to the right. Both men sighed with relief when shadows took form in the swirling tempest and closed in to either side. The road straightened as they reached the valley's floor and began following the course of a long-dead river. Their route was hemmed in now by steep cliffs which cut the maelstrom to a rain of yellow silt. Overhead the storm bellowed its frustration.

Alexis reached to the back seat for the canteen, an essential part of any journey this time of year. He drank deep, for the storm had a way of sucking the moisture from every pore. He handed the driver the canteen, dug in his pocket, extracted a relatively clean handkerchief, and when the canteen was handed back he doused the cloth and wiped his face, digging into the crevices around his eyes. The cloth came off stained a rich yellow-black. He bent over, doused the handkerchief a second time, and repeated the process. Another drenching, and he handed the cloth to the driver.

It was while Alexis was leaning over that they struck.

He thought at first it was stones dislodged from the cliffs and hurled by the storm. Only these stones were not satisfied with merely shattering the windscreen. They pierced the glass and continued straight on through the driver's body.

Alexis reacted instinctively, reaching forward and grabbing the wheel. Yet as he did so another metal stone rammed its way through the glass and through his chest as well. It hammered him backwards, tossing him halfway into the back seat, ripping the wheel from his grasp and slewing the car into the cliff face.

He sprawled in a position which seemed at first impossibly uncomfortable, gasping for a breath which would not come. Then the light began to dim, as though the storm was reaching down through the shattered windscreen and into his head. And gradually his position and his lack of breath began to matter less and less.

So it was that he lay and gasped and greeted the men who ripped open the driver's door. Then the back door opened, and someone reached down to jab his neck and curse, "You bloody idiot! You weren't supposed to shoot the scientist!"

"He must have leaned across. Look at the bullet holes. All over the driver's side. A correct strike."

The man released Alexis' neck, gripped the fabric of his lab coat and hauled him from the car. Alexis could not move at all. He had become a sack of useless flesh to be dragged out and dumped on the roadside. He heard the first man groan, "What a bloody mess. How are we to find the wife and kid?"

"They must be at the compound."

"And if they're not?" A hand slapped his face, and a shadow-form moved closer. Though his eyes were open he could not focus upon the shape. The man's words seemed shouted from a thousand kilometers away. "What did you discover, you meddling fool? What did you tell the American scientist?" A hand dropped him, a foot kicked a body which was no longer his own. "Put him and the driver in the rear; we will take them back to base."

The final satisfaction was a small one, that his theory had been proven correct after all. His last clinical observation was the borders of his vision closing in around him. His final thoughts were of his child, then Alena, then nothing at all.

* * *

The guy wore a T-shirt from the '78 Smirnoff Pro, his last big win. Thirty years of surfing the world's best waves had left him as handsomely scarred as a water-born tomcat. Age and bulk held him to the longboard set these days, and there were some nasty pre-cancerous patches to his leathery skin. But his eyes were clear and his life untrammeled by any of the ambitions or pressures that so harried Philippa Laremy. He also made the best espresso in San Diego County.

"So what can you do with the thing?" He jammed the metal cup into the machine, slapped it tight, then heaved down on the steam handle. "I mean, an Oscar, sure, I could handle that one easy. Five hundred million people watch you smile, you take the little dingus home, use it for a doorstop." Another load of coffee was wedged into place, the steam pressed through. "A Nobel Prize, though, I don't even know what it looks like."

"It's a medal, actually." Philippa Laremy leaned over the counter so she could watch the black goo trickle into the cup. It kept her from staring at her own picture framed and hung behind the bar. A few months earlier she had been written up by the local San Diego rag, the Englishwoman turned local who was both surfer and physics professor. The grizzled old beast who headed her department had predicted she would someday win the Nobel Prize, provided she didn't first drown surfing Baja. The photographer had caught her toasting the world with a steaming mug, seated just outside this shop. Philippa loathed that picture. Every time she saw it she felt stabbed by the lie of her smug confidence. If only she had known then what she knew now. She went on, "I believe I've read somewhere that it's solid gold."

"A medal, what can you do with that?" His name was Ben and he was still famous in the tight circle of big-wave riders. There beside her own clipping was a yellowed photograph from Surfer magazine, one catching him halfway down the face of a thirty-foot Makaha monster. "They make you wear it to dinner or something?"

"I'm fairly certain there's some banquet. And quite a hefty check. But the big thing's the honor."

Thoroughly unimpressed, he spooned in a single teaspoon of white froth. "You and milk, it reminds me of my old man and the way he mixed drinks. His idea of the perfect martini was a quart of Stoli, two handfuls of ice and an eyedropper of vermouth. Used the same bottle of red vermouth the whole time I was growing up. And my old man, he drank a lot of martinis." He handed over the cup. "Quadruple espresso with half a teaspoon of milk foam, you want me to set up the IV drip?"

"This is too good not to taste, thank you." She took the first sip, felt the bitter warmth slide down slow and smooth. She had just spent seven tense and lonely hours prepping the lab. The clock behind the counter read three-fifteen in the morning. She could not stop the faint quiver of nerves. Another ten minutes and the vacuum chamber would be primed and cooled to within twenty degrees of absolute zero. Then she would go back and run the experiment and know. One way or the other, she would know.

Ben started on her second cup and returned to the topic at hand. "So this Nobel Prize thing. You really think it's worth the hours?"

"Winning the Nobel is a ticket to eternity." She needed this chatter, even if it was with an aging surfer working the late shift at La Jolla's North Shore Coffee Shop. It was remarkable how this week had reshaped her. Pressure of discovery, pressure of nearing the finish, pressure of fear. And there was a lot of fear. Especially now, two weeks since Alexis' last contact. With every silent day his early warnings grew louder.

She caught a fleeting glimpse of herself in the coffee machine's mirrored side. Her wind-tossed curls were red by nature but lightened by sun and sea. Her face was far too lean and angular to be beautiful, her eyes too intense. They were large eyes, green as the rain-clad meadows of her native Devon, encircled now by sleepless shadows, filled with electric anticipation. And loneliness. And fear.

This silence was not like Alexis. He had never been late before, not once in the nine months they had struggled over the problems together. The distance separating them had never seemed to be much of a factor, until the moment he did not respond. Now the dark side of the moon appeared closer.

Philippa looked up and realized Ben was waiting. She had to search her memory to recall what they had been speaking of. "A Nobel Prize winner is renowned throughout the world. Your work becomes a byword in new developments." When that failed to elicit a response, she added, "They carve your name on this ruddy big marble plaque, right there beside Newton and Einstein."

He pushed a bit of foam onto the top of the second cup. "Sure, like a tombstone."

"No, not like that at all."

He began wiping the coffee-maker clean. Eyes clear as the borderland sky regarded her with new concern. "You've gotten yourself so strung out lately your tan looks painted on.

You ever think about getting away for a while, taking time to unwind?"

Philippa nodded acknowledgment of the truth. No chance of getting away, though. "I'd love to get back to Baja. It's been, well, months." Six months to be precise, since the week before she had last seen the ex-man in her ex-life.

Philippa used an impatient hand to push her hair and the memories back and away. "I even went down to Cabo San Lucas once. Some huge conference with SRC and Northstar, my research sponsors. They had this load of government bigwigs over from Washington, senators and congressmen and generals with about a thousand stars between them. All connected somehow with the new shuttle project."

"That's what you're working on, Northstar's new spaceship?"

"The XLS-1 experimental reusable launch vehicle, future replacement for the space shuttle," she corrected. "I suppose you could say I've been involved in a very distant sense."

He played at wiping down the counter-top, staying close. "I got buddies who work over there, that's all they talk about."

"Yes, it's all very exciting." She realized she was prattling, but needed the space to recover from the withering memory. "As I was saying, I loved Cabo. The sky and the sea were incredible shades of blue, and the desert made such a lovely contrast. Two adjacent universes, always touching, never joining. I stayed in this huge place called the Valencia. Grand buffets by the pool every evening, I could sit and eat and watch the sun go down. Marvelous."

"Cabo's too heavy on the tourist trade for my taste." Ben snapped a lid on the second cup. "And I've never been one for big hotels."

"Neither have I, but this was quite extraordinary. The hotel gardens ended only a few steps from Zippers, that's a lovely little right-hand break down –"

"I know Zippers and I've seen the Valencia. It reminded me of a blockhouse by the sea." When she started to reach for the cup, he settled a large hand on her arm. "Haven't seen your guy around for a while. The one with the Hollywood looks."

"Hale," she said quietly, staring at his hand on her arm. "His name is Hale."

"Right. Whatever." He pressed his bulk against the marble counter-top. He was so close she could smell the olive oil he used to keep his grey-blond hair from doing a total frizz. "I've got a place of my own down Baja way, not far from Ensenada. We could make a run south, you and me. Catch some great waves, unwind, have the ocean and the desert to ourselves."

"It's a grand offer, and I'm terribly grateful." Just saying his name had scalded her heart. Hale. She still could not meet the other man's eyes. "But I couldn't possibly get away just now."

"Fresh-caught Mexican lobster cooked on the open fire, man, there's nothing better in the whole world."

"Ben, please."

His hand kneaded her arm. "Think about it, all right?"

"Yes. Perhaps. But not now." Gently she worked her arm free. She spent more time here than in her own living room. No sense in upsetting the help. "I really must go."

Philippa left the coffee shop and unfastened her bike, scouting the darkness all the while. As she set the cup in the special gimbaled holder designed by a lab assistant, she reflected that another week of living life from the wrong end of the clock would kill her stone dead.

She crossed the five-lane road leading to the Scripps Oceanographic Institute and headed up the hill to the university. The weather was typical for San Diego – dry and crisp and lit by a billion stars. La Jolla's empty streets and blind-eyed houses and shadow palmettos all mocked her passage. Even the soft hiss of her bicycle tires along the pavement carried a ghostly taint. A faint wind whispered up from the Pacific, ruffling the threads of her unraveled life. The islands of yellow streetlight did not relieve the gloom she carried along inside. Lost and lonely and chased by phantoms, too many of her own making. Where was Alexis?

She was not a night person, nor was she made for solitude – both of which were considered requisite qualities for a physicist. She had been informed in grad school that experimental physicists were expected to do without either sleep or human company. Lab-rats, certainly, she could always mingle with them, but most lab-rats occupied the same subspecies as undergrads.

In front of the physics lab Philippa gave the empty street a final inspection. The enemy was out there. They did not need naming beyond that, at least not until the current experiment was completed and the results documented. Then she could focus upon this threat, identify the source, and exterminate them all. For now, it would do to simply know the enemy was there, and watching. She was fairly certain they had planted a spy in her lab. Which was why she had spent the past week claiming illness and doing her calculations at home. It had been a tortuous route, robbing herself of the lab computer and most of her notes. Even so, she had managed to identify the solution.

It was said that Einstein came up with the theory of relativity almost a year before he worked out *how* it was true. Philippa's own discovery had held the sense of approaching an answer she had not even been seeking. Yet with it had come a constant echoing to Alexis' fears, that following the course to its end would finish *them* off as well.

That week the nightly terrors had coalesced into a gnawing knot, feeding upon the dark hours. Which was strange, because if her theory was proven true Philippa and Alexis would make headlines around the globe.

All her life she had wanted to see her name established alongside the other greats. Isaac Newton, Albert Einstein, Philippa Laremy. It had a nice ring. She unlocked the lab building's outer doors and shivered at the worry. Up to now, she had put Alexis' prattling down to typical Russian paranoia. Now it cloaked her heart like a shroud.

Philippa entered her lab and walked to the corner where the high-amp transformer sat in its tightly padded cage. The gauge read half-way over the redline, steady and holding, exactly where she wanted. Their energy supply had not been designed for what she had in mind. Even so, the equipment was top-rate and should remain intact for the time required. Static electricity raised the hairs on her arms, amplifying the fear which whispered through the veil of night. She forced herself to move, to act, to carry this through to the bitter end. She pushed the transformer's control lever right to the wall.

The ceiling lights dimmed slightly as the transformer's hum rose to a warning rumble.

She moved to the central lab table, a heavy granite slab supported by twin titanium-alloy I-beams. The vacuum chamber's external base was frosted with water molecules. She checked the control panel, saw the interior was chilled to minus two hundred and fifty-three degrees Celsius, twenty degrees above the point whereby all molecular activity ceased. She bent over and checked the softly sighing pump beneath the table, then straightened and inspected the monitor. The chamber held steady at ten to the minus eleventh torr – one hundred trillionth of normal atmospheric pressure, as close to total vacuum as could be attained in their lab.

She returned her attention to the vacuum chamber's interior. A series of pancaked segments hung suspended at the chamber's center. Taken together, the six innocuous black flat disks were the thickness and shape of a nickel. But these wafers did not even exist under normal conditions. They were composed of a lithium-barium-carbide superconducting compound, and she had managed to lay her hands on almost a gram of the stuff. They were attached to wires thin as microfilaments, a gossamer web of twenty-four carat gold.

Philippa returned to the transformer amp. The gauge lay

flat against the back of the redline, and the air held the a
stench of overly concentrated power.

She walked to a portable slate-topped table stored in the far corner, and tipped it over. The heavy stone lid crashed to the floor. Philippa moved to the door, opened it, and listened carefully. The building remained dark and silent. She went back and crouched behind the table. Her hands were so slick with nerves and sweat she could not grasp the amp's remote.

She dragged her palms down the front of her lab-coat. Then she hefted the remote a second time, took a final breath, and hit the trigger.

She was answered with quite a delicious bang.

The explosion did not dissipate as would happen with a bomb. Instead the roar built for a long moment, rising higher and higher above where she crouched with her hands wrapped around her head. The entire chamber shook with the force. It sounded, Philippa decided, as though a volcano were erupting a few feet away. The heavy slate table felt as insubstantial as cardboard.

Gradually the noise seared away. Philippa emerged an inch at a time. Besides a few ceiling panels and a great deal of dust, nothing touched her. Rising to her feet, she inspected the central lab table. Of the vacuum chamber nothing remained except a charred circle. The three-inch-thick granite slab was cracked clear through. Then Philippa glanced up, and laughed aloud.

She stood there a long moment, hands on her hips, a smile stretching every tired muscle of her face. Despite the almost overwhelming fear which had stalked her through the discovery process, she was safe and the experiment was a success. It felt as though all the ones who had come before her, the Newtons and the Einsteins and the Fermis were gathered around her, applauding and welcoming her into their ranks. The *illustrious* Dr. Philippa Laremy.

But as the applause died and the room returned to the silent dusty present, the worries and the whispers drew into a tight band encircling her brain. Squeezing and constricting until the smile disappeared, and she was forced to see what had eluded her until now.

She caught sight of her reflection in the shattered front window. Her eyes stared fearfully back at a face streaked with grime. Outside, the first traces of dawn turned nearby buildings into dark silhouettes. In the distance rose faint shouts of alarm. She heard a pair of approaching sirens.

Philippa glanced once more at the damage overhead, and announced quietly, "I am thoroughly and utterly dead."

1

Thursday was Ryan's first time home before midnight in a week, her first evening out of a business suit in what seemed like months. This from a woman whose entire college wardrobe had consisted of jeans, T-shirts, sweats, Rainbow sandals, and a Navajo silver-and-turquoise clasp for her hair. Ryan sprawled out in front of the television half-watching an old Star Trek rerun. From the coffee table beckoned a hand-held meal – bacon and pastrami and Havarti cheese and fresh asparagus tips with Dijon mustard and ranch dressing on Ukrainian rye. Friends who tortured themselves through semi-permanent diets observed Ryan's eating habits with deep loathing. Ryan hated frozen yogurt, avoided everything claiming a reduced fat content, never put on an ounce, stood a fraction under five-two and weighed in just over a wet breeze.

The picture window to her right was splashed with a riot of sunset colors. Florida had the ability to astonish with its daily pyrotechnics. The coastlands were utterly flat and permanently humid, the summers suffocating. But the sunsets could stop traffic sure as a shuttle launch.

Their home was situated on a tiny needle of land called Merritt Island, which was in truth not an island at all. To the east lay the true barrier chain of Cocoa Beach. To the west stretched the vast and swampy Florida mainland. Three miles north, however, stood the only reason Ryan could ever be happy with her frantic lifestyle; Cape Canaveral and the Kennedy Space Center.

Ryan worked her mouth around the sandwich, wished she could feel the sense of blissful release such evenings used to represent. She found herself recalling her first year in Florida – not any happier a time, maybe, but from this distance it seemed far easier. Ryan had spent three frenzied weeks finding a kindergarten for Kitty and a school for Jeff and a housekeeper she could trust. She had spent another month mired in guilt from having abandoned her babies for the sake of her career. Then one evening Kitty had repeated something from school, how the Florida soil and climate were perfect for growing anything. She had promptly gone out and dug three very neat holes, and buried a pencil, a slice of Wonder bread, and an old ring. She explained she was growing a pencil tree, breadfruit, and a gold bush. Two weeks had passed before Kitty finally accepted that the things were not going to sprout no matter how much she watered them and mashed the ground flat. Kitty was that stubborn. It had marked a turning point for Ryan; if this was the biggest problem her little girl faced adjusting to Florida and a full-time career mom, then things were going to work out fine.

It was not the first time Ryan had been proven wrong.

Kitty was an incredibly independent ten now, and was upstairs zapping the bad guys with her computer playstation. These days Kitty's world revolved around school and friends and beach and MTV and all things electronic. Her classmates were pretty much the same – over eighty percent of them orphaned by the NASA grind. Kennedy and related industries were by far the largest employers east of Disney.

Her son was in the front hallway phoning somebody about waves. Talk of shredding came up a lot, the rest was mostly teenage gibberish. The waves were the reason Jeff had finally made peace with Florida. Jeff had been seven when they had moved and had loathed that first putridly hot summer almost as much as he had Ryan's succession of housekeepers. In desperation Ryan had taken him surfing one Saturday, despite the fact that her son had never been a strong swimmer. He had whined and complained until he had caught his first wave. After that he had shouted and grinned and shown such joy it was as though he had never known the meaning of misery. Ryan still remembered that smile, his astonished glee over the whitewater carrying him to shore, her own feeling of pride over having gotten something so incredibly right.

Her husband was seated at the tiny desk in the corner, the one normally holding the phone and fax and a vase of flowers. The fax was on the floor and the vase was in the kitchen, standing empty since their last housekeeper had left five days ago. No replacement had been found because Ryan had been too busy to look.

Harry had set the fax aside to give him more room for his documents. It was Harry's way of declaring silent war. Harry liked to say he never started arguments, only finished them. As though his code of battle was the important thing here.

The room's gathering tension drew her around with bands of glassine steel. Harry knew she was watching him but refused to look up. Drawing out the moment, letting the tension ripen. Harry was good at games like that.

She watched him pretend to concentrate on the company papers. Harry was chief accountant for the Kennedy facility of OrionSat, a medium-sized NASA supplier trying to keep from being demolished by the changing times. Ryan sat there looking at her husband, trying to figure out just exactly what it was she was feeling. With his pushed-out lips and his half-moon glasses and his balding head and his sloping shoulders, Harry looked twenty-five years older than her instead of six. Ryan decided what she felt most of all was ready.

She had married too young, had known it at the time. Met the last month of her sophomore year, pregnant by July, married in September. Too young. Decisions taken under impossible pressure, mistakes carried a lifetime. But she did not regret keeping Jeff. At the time, marrying the father had seemed the only alternative. And if they had not wed she would have robbed her life of Kitty. She could not regret that either. Not ever.

Besides, Harry had made her laugh. And he had been so eager, so desperately frantic to marry. He had been a MBA student with a savage wit and a hungry determination to rise from a poor South Baltimore background. He was a small man, only two inches taller than she, sort of a red-headed Danny DeVito. He hated exercise, called it a twentieth-century folly. One of his favorite party conversations was to describe how a hundred years from now people would read about it and say, what the hell was a jog, something they did with animals? Every day? For fun?

When they had started dating Harry's wit had sparkled and his body had been bulky but solid. A nice balance to Ryan's fanaticism over sports, particularly surfing. But time and gravity had long since redrawn Harry, pulling everything downwards – his cheeks, neck, shoulders, chest, belly – everything. When she held him now Ryan was reminded of unbaked dough. They had not held each other very much lately.

Harry finally lifted his head, showed her the flinty accountant's gaze. "Yes?"

"I was just wondering," she said. "When it was we decided to abolish the rule about never bring work home."

"I guess it must have been about the same time," he replied, "you stopped coming home at all."

Ryan used the remote to cut off the television's sound. "I've just gotten a promotion, Harry. A major one. The second in eighteen months. It takes time to adjust."

"Tell that to our kids. Explain why their mom can't even be bothered to replace the housekeeper. So now I get home nights and find the twelve-year-old cooking dinner for the ten-year-old."

"They're good kids. They'll do fine." It sounded lame even to her. "Another few weeks, then things will cool down and I can get back to normal life."

"Then you'll be up for the next slot."

"That could take years, Harry. Maybe never." The next rung was a deputy-directorship, one of only three at the Kennedy Space Center and as close as anyone not politically appointed could ever come to running the nation's manned space program. The mere thought of approaching her lifelong goal was enough to justify almost anything, including Ryan's impossible schedule.

Harry shook his head. Once. The accountant negating an impossible deal. "I know the drill. You've made it out of the cast of thousands. They're watching you."

The problem was, he *did* know. Companies like Harry's survived by being super-sensitive to every breath NASA took. When Kennedy sneezed, companies like Harry's contracted double pneumonia.

Ryan had helped land him the job, a frantic ploy which at the time had eased their move down from Washington. Now it was just one more source of venom. "You knew what I was after when we married, Harry. I never hid any of this from you. Not ever."

"Take the girl, take the dreams." The words were softly bitter. "It sounded nice at the time."

"I haven't changed." Which was true, but small comfort. Her goal had always been the same, ever since she had realized at age fourteen that she would never grow to the height required for an astronaut. If she couldn't fly to the stars herself, she would run the operation that put them there. "You could try to get home a little earlier, help out some."

"I *am* coming home early. I *am* helping out. You're just not around enough to know it."

"What, I'm not supposed to have my own career, not supposed to –"

"This isn't about having a career any more. You've abandoned your own family. You're nothing but a slave to that place."

"That's not true and you know –"

"What about the day before yesterday?" His face blotched red, signaling his arrival at where he had been headed all along. "Kitty got sick and you wouldn't even take the time to go see if she was all right!"

"I called the school, Harry. I talked to the nurse and the principal and her teacher."

"But you couldn't be bothered to go see for yourself. Not even to make sure our daughter wasn't desperately ill and the school was just covering things up!" Numbers on the page, everything down in black and white. No grey areas at all. That was Harry's view of the world. And their relationship. "You've got the most screwed up priorities of anybody I've ever met."

"That's not true, Harry. I also called you six times –"

"We're talking about you, not me! You're their *mother*, dammit!"

"We had a crisis on the launchpad. I couldn't –" Ryan stopped at the sound of Jeff slamming down the phone. She calmed her features as their son did a teenager's boneless slouch into the living room. Nothing she could do about her churning gut. Nothing at all.

Jeff was tanned and solid from surfing and already three inches taller than his dad. Jeff also possessed a remarkable antenna for picking up the unspoken. A swift glance at each parent was enough to reveal all. His face took on a nonchalant air as he draped himself on the sofa's corner, directly between the two adults. He pointed at the television and demanded, "So what's this one about?"

Ryan had to think hard. "The alien that looks like refrigerator slime picks up a piece of hair and transmutes into a Drew Barrymore look-alike."

"You've seen that one a billion times already."

Ryan watched Jeff prepare for a vulture swoop on her sandwich and warned, "My phasers are locked on full."

Jeff gave her a doubtful glance. "You wouldn't fry your only son."

Ryan pointed at the kitchen door. "You know where the fridge is."

"That's right," Harry agreed, angrily banging his papers into order. "Why the hell should your mother be expected to fix you anything to eat."

A pained expression passed over Jeff's features, on and off like a strobe. Ryan fought down the urge to snap back. But the acid remained hot behind her eyes, filling her throat with all she wanted to shriek at Harry, all the regrets.

Jeff rose from the sofa and pulled their attention with him as he moved to the kitchen. "Hey Dad, has Mom told you about the new housekeeper she's lined up? She's a French au pair called Nanette. Nineteen years old. She wears a little black cap and black stockings and these short frilly little –"

"Enough already," Ryan said.

"No, no, I'm beginning to think this has potential," Harry said. Clearly liking the idea.

The refrigerator door opened and closed and he called out, "Mom, how about going surfing with me this weekend?"

It was the perfect ploy. This from the kid who refused to let her even cross the dunes to the beach with him these days. It would be their first time in the water together in over a year.

Ryan made a quick mental review of her calendar. The next shuttle launch was not for nine days. The military had the other pad reserved for a top secret launch. Her boss was in Washington for the week, schmoozing with senators responsible for the interim budget. Ryan's desk was as clear as it had been since the promotion.

Jeff's head appeared in the doorway, a knife in one hand, mayonnaise jar in the other. "Mom?"

"How would you like," Ryan answered, "if we made a dawn run down to Sebastian Inlet on Saturday?"

"You mean it?"

Ryan made the glance at Harry a peace offering. "Maybe we'd even let the second team come along, if they promise to behave."

"Rise while it's still dark, drive forty-five minutes to a beach almost as nice as the one straight out in front of us," Harry replied, but the heat was gone. Probably still thinking about Nanette. "Coming back wet and cold and sunburned. Not my idea of a good time."

Jeff rewarded her with a grin only possible on someone wearing twenty-seven hundred dollars' worth of orthodontic braces. "Better and better."

Ryan reached for her sandwich, diverted the hand when the phone rang. She picked up the mobile and thumbed the switch. "Ryan Reeves."

"Ms. Reeves, this is Clay East, Chief of Staff for Senator Townsend. We met a while back."

"Of course." Senator Townsend was the top man on the subcommittee responsible for NASA's budget. She recalled meeting a tall bulky figure at the same Washington conference where she had met Philippa Laremy. The man had spent most of the day doing a Fred Astaire soft-shoe in wingtips behind the Senator's chair. A man who lived for the Washington powerline, who schmoozed as naturally as he breathed. "How are you, sir?"

"Fine, just fine." He did not sound fine. He sounded taut as a pre-launch team with the clock ticking. "Listen, have you been watching CNN tonight?"

"No, but I believe Fuller Glenn is up in Washington at this time." Fuller was Deputy Director of Kennedy's Manned Space Flight program, and her boss. Such calls should normally have been fielded by the politicos, since they were on the same bureaucratic bandwidth. Senators on the budget committee tended to treat Kennedy as their own personal fiefdom.

"Fuller happens to be in the next room having dinner with the Senator. Turn on your set, Ms. Reeves. It's coming up to the half-hour and, okay, they're running it again. Are you watching?"

"Hang on." She fumbled for the remote, flipped the channel. Beside the newscaster's smiling face was the picture of a building Ryan instantly recognized. Almost all of the upper-floor windows were shattered and gaping. A wide crack ran up the front wall and disappeared beneath the roof.

The phone barked, "Were you aware of this?"

"Wait just a second please." She hit the sound key, heard the announcer say, "For the viewers who wonder about the sanity of our westernmost citizens, here's an item of interest from San Diego."

"California's not the farthest state west," Jeff pointed out, sliding through the kitchen door and moving to where he could see the screen. "Hawaii is."

The newscaster went on, "There's been an explosion of the strangest kind at a University of California physics laboratory. We're taking you to San Diego now, where Ditta Deems is there live for CNN."

Jeff moved a step closer. "San Diego, Mom, isn't that where –"

"Hold that thought," she snapped.

The voice on the phone was saying, "This is the third time they've run it, their little joke to end the half-hour news. What we have here is a potential disaster in the making, Ms. Reeves. It is absolutely vital to our nation's –"

"Let me hear what they're saying," Ryan told him, impatient now.

"There are more questions than answers right now at the lab, here in the hills above fashionable La Jolla," the reporter enthused. "But it appears that there has been a mysterious explosion inside the building behind me. With me are two students who live in a nearby dormitory and who heard the blast."

The camera followed the microphone over to where two students stood, trying to appear unfazed by the publicity. One said, "Sure, we heard it. Felt it, too."

The newscaster demanded, "Do you think it was a bomb?"

"Not a chance." They gave a knowing smirk. "Too long."

"More like a giant freight train," the second offered. "Ghost riders in the sky, that kinda thing."

The first offered, "They're into some really weird gigs over there. Bending time, stuff like that."

"Everybody knows the stories about that place," the second student confirmed. "I bet it was aliens. They crawled through the time holes and blasted their way –"

Hastily the reporter plucked the microphone away, and gave the camera a sickly smile as the phone groaned in Ryan's other ear. The newscaster moved to a uniformed guard and continued, "Officer Henricks of the university security squad was first on the scene. Can you describe for us what you found?"

Clay East said, "The Senator has asked me to instruct you to take whatever steps are necessary to contain this."

"I'll get on this immediately," Ryan agreed. "But we can't be sure Dr. Laremy is in any way –"

"Listen, Ms. Reeves, it is absolutely essential that this be kept utterly secret."

Ryan asked, "Keep what secret?" Thinking that was a pretty bizarre request, even for Washington, while CNN was broadcasting live pictures of a shattered lab.

"Just get over there and take care of it." East cut the connection.

Ryan sat cradling the phone with both hands and listened to the university guard say, "Well, it's pretty strange in there. We've definitely had an explosion. Everybody living around here either heard it or felt it or both."

Ryan punched in a number from memory, grimaced as the newscaster demanded, "Are you thinking it might be terrorist activity?"

"No, this was definitely not a bomb."

Ryan told the room, "There's no answer at Philippa's." She cut the connection, dialed San Diego information, asked for the university's main number. She paused before dialing as the newscaster asked, "How can you be so certain?"

"No fire damage. Not even any smoke." He permitted his bafflement to show through. "Damnedest thing I ever saw."

"Can you describe what you found for our viewers?"

"Looks like somebody screwed a giant hole inside that building," the guard replied. "One with razor-sharp edges."

"You mean –"

The guard glanced off camera, stiffened, and cut her off with, "That's all I can say at this time."

The university operator did not even let Ryan finish explaining who she was. Harried by a hundred previous calls, she read off impatiently, "Yes, there has been an incident at one of the university's laboratories. None of our students have been injured in any way. The authorities are ascertaining the full extent of the damage. The university has nothing further to report at this time." She clicked off so fast Ryan found herself asking the dial tone if any faculty had been wounded.

The television switched to ads; she cut it off, then asked the empty screen, "Can anybody tell me why a Senator's aide would take such an interest in a NASA scientist blowing up a lab?"

Jeff demanded, "It was Dr. Laremy, wasn't it. The explosion they're talking about. She did it."

"I guess she might have." Ryan tossed the control aside. "I'll know more once I get out there."

"Great, just great," Harry sneered. "You think you can spare two minutes before you pop off again, maybe explain to your son about his mother's priorities?"

She sat and watched Harry stomp from the room, a great exit even for him. She then dialed a second number from memory. A crisp military voice broke off the first ring. "Patrick's."

Located four miles south of Cocoa Beach, Patrick's was one of the country's largest air bases and official residence for all military personnel attached to Canaveral. "This is

Ryan Reeves, deputy assistant administrator at KSC. My ID number is, hang on, I set my purse down somewhere."

Jeff walked over, his shoulders slumped dejectedly. He tossed her leather bag onto the sofa and slouched away.

"Ma'am, are you there?"

"Yes, wait, here it is." She read the number off her laminated card. When the NCO had checked it off his book, Ryan went on, "Let me speak to your officer of the watch, please."

When the more senior man came on, Ryan went through the identification process a second time, then continued, "I need a plane readied to fly me to San Diego. Priority One. Authorization Seven Zero Alpha Emma."

"Authorization noted and confirmed," the officer intoned. "A plane will be ready in one hour."

"I'll be there." Ryan cut the connection, rose from her sofa, found Jeff kicking the doorframe leading to the front hall. "Sweetheart, I can't tell you how sorry I am. We'll go surfing next..." She checked herself, determined not to lie. "Next free day I have."

Jeff remained intent on kicking the wall. "Sure. Like the middle of the next millennium."

"No. Soon. I promise." Ryan gave him a swift hug, stung by the way he pulled back. She released him and raced upstairs. She pulled the emergency case she kept readied these days from underneath the bed. Inside were two changes of clothes, underwear, tights, basic make-up, one jogging outfit – enough to see her through a three-day journey. These days she rarely had the chance to stay anywhere longer. Even home.

She raced into her daughter's room and gave her a kiss and a quick explanation, one probably not heard as Kitty's gaze never left the computer screen. Ryan tumbled back down the stairs to find Harry standing in the front hall, his arm draped possessively around his son's shoulders. Glaring at her. Giving her the full beam.

She smiled at the two faces, one glum, the other furious. Determined to hold to as much cheer as she could, not to make things worse with more last-minute skirmishing. "I'll call you as soon as I know something about Philippa."

"You do that." Harry drew the kid closer still, his look raising blisters. He said to their son, "Say, maybe you and me could make that trip down to Sebastian."

Ryan clung grimly to her smile. Knew Harry was drawing lines in the sand, pushing her out. The misery in Jeff's eyes telling her he knew it too. She leaned forward, tried to plant a kiss on the boy's cheek, but he jerked away from both of them. Harry's glare said not even to try one on him. Like she really wanted.

As she started for the door another thought rose unbidden, only adding to her woes. Ryan was going to have to make the call she had been avoiding for six months. There was no putting it off. She was definitely going to need Hale's help on this one.

2

Rain struck Hale's window like windswept cymbals. June was lost somewhere behind an endless storm, one strong enough to sweep away Richmond's sultry summer heat. Not that he minded. Good weather would have only meant one more reason to feel caught by the corporate hurricane, trapped behind a city desk far from the waves and the only life he had ever really loved. He lay in bed listening to the rain's rapid-fire countdown to dawn, and wished there was some way to stretch the night, just pull it over his head and hide there forever.

The phone's ringing came as a welcome relief. But the pre-dawn hour needed to be addressed, which was why he reached over and picked up the receiver and answered with, "This had better be good."

The quietly familiar voice instantly reached across the miles and months since their last raging argument. "I hope I'm not interrupting anything important."

Hale slid up until his back hit the headboard. "Ryan?"

"I mean, if you've got a trio of starlets in there and it's hard to find breath, I could always call back."

"No." Hale rubbed his face, not from sleep, but surprise. "No, I'm alone."

"That's good. Everybody needs a night off now and then. I wouldn't mind one myself." There was a new edge to the throaty tones. "What time is it over there?"

"Same time as it is in Cocoa Beach." Of all the things he had expected to have happened on this night, a casual conversation with his oldest ex-friend would not have made even the bottom of the list. Hale glanced at the side table. The clock read a few minutes after five. "Early. Late. Take your pick. Where are you?"

"San Diego."

Hale rose to his feet and carried the portable phone with him down the hall and into the kitchen. He reached for the coffee pot and filled it with water. Pretending to sleep was over for the night. San Diego meant Philippa. Hale opened the canister, spooned coffee into the machine, and fought against the desire to know more.

"Hale?"

"I'm here."

"I was afraid I had lost you." Ryan had a voice both throaty and too deep for her body. A tiny ballerina with a sex-phone voice. "I've been this tired before, but I'm too weary to remember when."

He watched the coffee drip and compared this almost normal conversation with their last shouting match, the one that had transformed this soft-spoken NASA exec into a raging maniac. But that was not why Hale hesitated. Defeat lay in speaking. Even so, he had to ask. "What's taken you out to the Left Coast?"

"Trouble. I've landed in it with both feet."

"Excuse me." Hale pulled the pot from beneath the drip, poured the first half-cup. "For a while there I thought I was talking to somebody I knew."

"I'm serious, Hale. We're talking critical mass here."

He took his first sip, said what he had known since hearing Ryan's first words. "Something's happened to Philippa."

"You got that right. She's gone. Vanished into thin air." Her normal quietness sounded filed down with a metal rasp. "Look, why don't you take a couple of days off, fly out and give me a hand? The company's treat."

"NASA is going to pay me to fly across the country?"

"Get real. I'd have to lay a paper trail from coast to coast to fly a non-employee to California. Northstar Avionics offered to foot the bill."

Northstar had been a major funder of Philippa Laremy's research for almost a year. Hale had attended several receptions over their time together, shaken a lot of hands, drunk too much, almost learned to accept standing in the shadow of his girl. Northstar and their parent, the Space Research Consortium, were also names in the news recently. They were the major contractors for the new experimental NASA craft, the one intended to replace the current space shuttle. Philippa's work with superconductors was somehow tied to this. His lack of further knowledge was due only slightly to secrecy, and mostly to his unwillingness to listen.

"It's bad, isn't it." Hale felt the familiar stab of guilt, something he had learned to live with since his last fight with Philippa. "Whatever's happened to her must be really bad."

"Time for that when you arrive. Will you come?"

Hale started to describe what he was facing, tell why he had endured the first sleepless night in years. But the temptation of just leaving it all behind was too great. "If Philippa needs me."

"Better get a move on, Studley. Your flight to San Diego leaves in less than two hours. Flight UA1114, change in Denver. Ticket's waiting for you at the United counter. I'll meet you at the airport."

Hale punched off the phone, set it down, finished his mug. The routine of mentally preparing for another trip was highly comforting. There was no need to ask himself why he was flying across the country for a woman he supposedly didn't care about any more. The situation he was facing here was borderline lethal. He had always preferred to meet calamity from a distance.

Besides, as Philippa had told him at their last farewell, he had a lifetime's experience in running away.

* * *

The Richmond streets appeared more alien than ever, lost behind rain and wind and a reluctant dawn. He had lived here for almost five years and never felt anything but a stranger. Comfortable grooves had been worn along the avenues taking him to the office, the airport, the few restaurants and nightspots he had claimed for himself. Otherwise the city was just another place to skim over, passing like a stone tossed by life's careless hand.

The journey's strangeness entered the airport with him. As though someone else picked up the ticket and smiled at the check-in girl's blatant invitation. He watched from a distance, played the role of the young handsome executive on the prowl. Gave her the grand grin. Flashed the blue eyes. Looked down at the world from his six-foot-five tower. And felt nothing but tired and worried and defeated. It was a strange sensation for him, a man who had lived by the rule of taking the easy way out. But today, this morning, he found everything looked back at him with a question mark.

Even his reflection mocked him that stormy morning. The business travelers waited to have tickets and carry-ons examined like dull-eyed beasts in thousand-dollar pelts. Hale moved with the others, walking alongside a one-way mirror and the image of a man with few questions worth asking and no answers at all.

Even with his once-permanent tan bleached by city dwelling, Hale remained tall and angular, his face sharp-featured, his grin electric. Or so he had been told, often enough to accept it as his due. Though surfing had slipped into memory and his thirtieth year breathed heavy on that rainy morning, his body remained hard and solid. Hale inched along with the rest of the weary tide and wondered how none of the internal battles seemed to show.

He endured the take-off and the plastic breakfast, read a paper he could not bring into focus, and felt as though he was fighting against a reluctant tide. When his watch finally showed nine o'clock, he used the plane's cell-phone to call his office.

But it was his deputy who answered, not his secretary. Hale asked, "Where's Betsy?"

"She's gone." Jerry was a forty-something father of four who favored moon-shaped reading spectacles, alpaca sweaters, and a quietly nervous air. He did the designs, Hale did the selling. Together they had made New Products the most profitable of all Keebler Plastics' divisions. "Happened before I got here."

"What do you mean, gone?"

"Exactly what I said. Kaput. Out the door." The guy's voice was actually shaking. "Don't ask me more than that 'cause I don't know. All I do is work here. I come in, I sweat blood for this company, do my basic seventy-five hour week, but do I get told anything?"

"Get a hold of yourself." Words spoken as much to himself as to Jerry.

"You gotta be kidding. I show up, the rest of the girls around here are crying and worrying about what happens to them tomorrow. Betsy was here eleven years, Hale. Two years more than me. They gave her two weeks severance pay, booted her out on the spot."

The woman in the center seat was flipping through her magazine and pretending not to listen. Hale turned his face to the window and asked quietly, "What have you heard since?"

The whine heightened. "Word is, we're all on the way out. New Products is to be dumped like yesterday's garbage. What am I going to do, Hale? Rose starts university next year, I've got mortgage payments, my car is on its last legs. And I've been called in to see our new boss this morning."

The new boss. Even though he had known it was coming, Hale's gut did a swoop from thirty thousand feet to ocean depths. He pushed out the words, "So they gave the position to Mack."

"You don't sound surprised."

He rubbed a defeated hand down the side of his face. "I was working late last night and passed Keebler's office. He and Mack were in there having a drink. Keebler had his arm around Mack's shoulders."

"I'd rather hug a pit viper."

"You and me both." Don MacRuthers, office alias Mack the Knife, had been brought in as an outside consultant to trim Keebler Plastics to the bone, a painful duty the chairman did not have the guts to do himself. Hale had made an enemy of the man early on, walking unannounced into a board meeting to complain that nobody from the outside could know which employees were essential, and MacRuthers' ax was slashing away some of their top people. The board had heard him out, thanked him for his opinion, then ordered him from the room.

Mack's reward for front-line surgery had been a position as assistant sales manager, the same level as Hale. This ten days after Mack had fired the senior Vice President for sales, and the position remained vacant. A position Hale deserved. One he had been certain was his. Until the night before.

"They planned to give him the vice presidency all along," Jerry muttered. "They just started him in the lower slot just for appearances, slide him in easy."

"Sounds that way to me." Hale wondered why he couldn't say it didn't really matter, why he didn't have the ability to speak the words even to himself. His infamous protective cloak had been stripped away.

Hale searched for something that would postpone the inevitable, could only come up with, "Tell Mack I've been invited out to San Diego to make a presentation to Northstar."

Jerry was instantly agog. "Northstar Avionics? You've got to be kidding."

"I'm calling you from the plane." He checked his watch. "I arrive in Denver in less than an hour. Transfer to a flight to San Diego."

"Northstar is huge with NASA and Defense. You know how long Keebler's been trying to get on the government gravy train?" Jerry's tone lightened by ten years. "You got anything that'll show Mack this is more than just smoke?"

"Tell him they're paying my way out."

"This is great news, just great. How'd you get a foot in the door? Aeronautics is a totally new direction for us."

"But it fits, right?"

"Absolutely. We've got a state-of-the-art production line. And design team. At least, we did yesterday."

Keebler Plastics was a medium-size firm specializing in precision molding. Their bread and butter was the chemicals industry – atomizers for perfumes, mouthsprays, asthma inhalers. The business was cutthroat, and most of the sales force remained caught in the same old rut – going after what was easy, servicing existing contacts, living off expense accounts, banking their commissions – taking advantage of Keebler's easy-going chairman, the son of the founder. Hale had no argument with the need for corporate pruning, but there was a difference between careful pruning and Mack's form of amputation by grenade.

Jerry went on, "Just get them to hand you the specifications, I'll start on it personally. How did you get in the door, Hale? Mack is gonna ask."

"I've got a friend who's doing research for them. She's a physicist at UC-San Diego." Another stab to the heart over that one. "Look, I was thinking of taking a couple of days off after seeing Northstar. Can you cover for me?"

"I guess so." Another whiff of the gloominess. "That is, if I'm still around."

"If you hear anything more call me on my cell-phone. I'll keep it permanently turned on."

* * *

Ryan stopped by the airport Starbucks on her way to the bank of telephones, ordered a double cappuccino with a splash of extra cream. Started to turn away, then spotted the fresh-made cinnamon rolls with icing slathered all over the top. "I'll have one of those too. Yeah, the big one. Oh, and can you give me one of those plastic cups of cream cheese on the side? Great. I'll need a knife too. No, no bag. Just a couple of napkins. Thanks."

She paid and started to turn away, only to be stopped by a look of utter disgust from the woman behind her. "Haven't you ever heard of hardened arteries?"

"Absolutely." Nothing to be gained from mentioning the eleven-mile run at dawn. Ryan decided this one deserved the full treatment, made a lascivious sound as she slowly bit her way through the roll. "Want a bite?"

The woman gave her look of choleric disapproval. "I have far too much respect for my body to destroy it with garbage like that."

"Oh, me too." Another bite, the taste sweetened by the woman's disgust. Ryan turned toward the telephones, said as she departed, "I personally avoid all food groups that rust."

Ryan used the time waiting for Hale to arrive to make a few futile calls. The first was to her home, the results no better than they had been all week. She spoke to a daughter who had no idea where Jeff or Harry were and who barely seemed aware that Ryan had been absent. Ryan then made voice-mail contact with her boss, checking in for the sixth day in a row. She left a summary of all the dead ends she had followed trying to track down Philippa, then wondered aloud why she had not heard anything back from him.

She then placed a call to the Senator's office, not finding Clay East there either. Ryan spoke to a secretary clearly used to fielding frantic demands, and received neither respect nor answers. She hung up as people started filing through the flight's exit, wishing there was somebody around who deserved a good solid scream.

Ryan had always preferred to charge ahead. Identify the problem, find a solution, act. She liked to start with a single calm moment, studying the terrain. Then it was time to commit and attack. Today, however, she stood on the airport concourse trapped by present worries and past angers. Her indecision in the face of so much she did not understand was maddening.

The hunt for Philippa had led nowhere. Six days in San Diego, working around the clock, and she did not even have a clue as to why her best friend had run away. But run she had. That was one of the few things they knew for certain now. Philippa had vanished without a trace.

Ryan watched the file of exiting passengers, wondering what she would say when she saw Hale. This to the guy she had been easiest with all her adult life. Even more so than Harry, in some ways. But Hale had redefined everything when he broke up with Philippa. Everything.

Ryan recalled the first time she had ever seen him, the blond giant who had appeared in the doorway to the freshman lounge. Impossibly broad shoulders for such tiny hips, his muscular legs form-fitted into faded jeans. Leathery skin and sandals and faded T-shirt and shoulder-length hair. Standard issue freshie, except for the looks and the poise. It had seemed as though every light in the house swiveled around and settled upon him. The girl seated beside her at the table signing up freshies for various school activities had looked one look and offered a long variety of astonishing acts in a sweet southern drawl. The girl's tirade of fantasies had ended only when Hale had walked over, smiled down at Ryan and pointed at the sign on her table, saying, "A surfing team? You've got to be kidding."

"I never kid about waves," she had responded, glad her voice sounded calmer than her heart. A married woman three months pregnant, acting like she was about to be bedded by the stud of her dreams. "Where are you from?"

"Norfolk," he replied, and she liked him instantly for that. A lot. At the University of Virginia, it took a serious dose of honesty to admit to being from Norfolk. Virginia Beach was next door, handy, and a lot more up-market. "You?"

"Wilmington, Delaware," she confessed publicly for the first time since arriving at campus, and made a face. "Armpit of the east."

"Only reason you say that is because you've never been to Norfolk." Incredibly easy for a guy of eighteen years, ignoring everything in the room except for her and their little island of sea-soaked talk. Pretending he couldn't see the girl seated next to Ryan, the one with the hungry eyes and the invitation tattooed to her forehead, or the dozen other estrogen-charged gazes going off like silent strobes. "The only thing that makes Norfolk bearable is knowing nothing will ever be that bad, not ever again."

Hale had his dark side, a brooding menace that she had only seen in the ocean. As though here was a place whose power matched his own. A place where he could let loose all the tension and the fury and whatever else it was that gripped the dark corners of his soul.

He also had his enigmas, a mountainside of shadowy crevices and a past seldom mentioned. Occasionally, over the campfires and laughter of sea-scented evenings, with warm nightwinds to offer the myth of eternal comfort, Hale spoke a sentence. One. Harry and Ryan and Hale's choice for the weekend would sit and hear him offer a sliver of where he had come from and what had shaped him. Just a hint. Then there would come the sudden tension to his features, as though the few words might unlatch his internal cage and release all the bat-winged mysteries. One such utterance had been about his father, first a policeman and then a detective, and how Hale had worked three summers and after school and weekends with his old man. How he had learned the tricks of the trade, the night photography and the eavesdropping and the legal stalking. Just that, nothing more. Such admissions were treasured because they were rare as unblemished emeralds. She remembered them all.

Ryan spotted him then, stepping through the portal and entering the airport terminal. He had such a hesitant step, such a look of tired worry about him. He hated flying, she had long known that. But this was something new. As though Hale had battled his worst enemy and lost.

He came out smiling at her, a tired smile, but a hint of the old grin just the same. Ryan felt like the look slapped her in the heart. She uncoiled, uncertain how to greet him or what to say. Knowing only that their old argument had not died after all.

* * *

Hale found the La Jolla freeway familiar enough to squeeze out a few pangs. Experiences woven into memory, ones he had colored determinedly as never to be seen again, were unwillingly brought into the focus of now. Hale had not truly realized what he was doing, or where he was, until this moment.

Ryan's silent treatment did not help at all. She sat beside him, no smile, no chatter, no trace of the long weekends spent surfing and laughing and chatting together. Ryan was dressed in a tailored suit and silk blouse, her jet-black hair pulled severely back, her dark eyes sparked by a tight fire. Somewhere along the way her face had grown new lines. A new wall that kept him from seeing what was beneath the gaze. Only now when he was seated beside her could he realize how much he had lost.

She felt his gaze, and the struggle to find words showed on her face. "Sorry about the silent treatment. Got a lot on my mind."

"Don't worry about it, Ryan. Silence is fine with me."

"Still, it's a strange way to greet somebody who used to be an old pal."

He grimaced both at the words and the onslaught of memories. More bizarre still was how he suddenly felt a need to speak the thoughts. "My dad was a great one for public scenes. Every time he got a tankful he put on another display. My job through high school was tracking him down. He'd greet me with these huge hello's, turning the entire bar around so they could all have a good look at his boy. I spent too many nights wrestling my dad away from a spotlight only he could see. I've got no problem with silence, Ryan. None at all."

She gave him as long a glance as the freeway allowed. "In all the years I've known you, that's the first time you've ever told me about your father."

"It's not exactly something I'm proud of." Hale could not help but wonder why he had spoken at all. "Want to tell me why I'm here?"

She gave her head a decisive shake. "Better to wait and show you."

He nodded acceptance. Now that he was here, he found himself uneasy over what was to come. He sat and watched Ryan handle the car with focused ease, untouched by the frenetic freeway hassle. They headed north through rough-cut desert hills, every surface dotted with sparkling new housing developments. Only when they took the La Jolla exit did he say, "Ryan, I'm in a jam."

She stopped at the first juncture, showed Hale little signals within those cautious eyes. "What's up?"

Hale related the previous night's discovery, the conversation with Jerry, the coming changes at Keebler Plastics. "Any chance you could get me into Northstar, see someone in purchasing?"

Ryan gave her head a grave shake. "You don't know what it's like, old son. Trying to become a supplier to a defense contractor is a whole new ballgame."

"We're talking NASA, not military."

"Same thing in spades. They'll check you out six ways from Sunday. Nowadays it's pretty much a closed shop. Business is shunted to folks already in the loop."

Hale let a little of his worry show. "I need your help on this."

Another glance. "This is new. The unshakable Hale Andrews worried?"

Frightened for his future. Worried about tomorrow. All new sensations. None of them pleasant. "Can you do something?"

Again there was the flicker beneath the surface, his friend saying one thing but meaning another. "I'll see what I can do. But you owe me big time on this one."

Relief, Hale decided. That was what Ryan was trying to hide. As though she had been hoping for a way to tie Hale down. "I really appreciate this."

Ryan gunned down the four-lane road leading to the university. "You sure better."

Ryan tightly banked the car into the UCSD campus. Modern structures seized hold of hard-scrabble hills, the surrounding grounds kept green by constant tending and astronomical amounts of imported water. Hale asked, "How long have you been out here?"

"Six days."

"You've known about this for six days and you just get around to calling me? Great move, Ryan."

"There's more involved than just picking up the phone," Ryan replied grimly. "A lot more."

Then the news had to be seriously bad. "So tell me what happened to Philippa."

"Just wait, okay? Let me show what we're facing here."

"I've come all the way across the country, I think I've got a right to know what happened to our friend."

The tone turned bitter. "You've sure got a strange way of treating friends."

"You don't want to fight that battle all over again. You really don't."

Ryan spun into the physics building's parking lot and cut the motor. "Okay, let's go."

The building was an early eighties structure of brick and glass, surrounded by a throng of milling students. A number of broken windows were covered with cardboard. The crack running from the front door to the roof had definitely not been there the last time Hale had visited. "Does this have anything to do with Philippa?"

But Ryan was already headed towards the doors. "Come on, Hale. Stay close."

He had to push his way through the crowd in order to make the entrance. Inside the central foyer the noise of construction was deafening. They took the stairs to the third floor, where Hale's breath caught at the sight of a policeman standing guard by crisscrossed yellow warning-tapes. "What is this?"

"Follow me." Ryan lifted the tape for Hale to step through, then pushed open the hall doors leading to Philippa's office and lab.

A pair of somber men filled the hallway. Their eyes rested on Hale as the taller one said, "Afternoon, Mrs. Reeves."

"He's with me," Ryan replied.

"Name?"

"Hale Andrews."

The second man was black and built like a middle-weight wrestler. He raised a clipboard, checked carefully. "I'm sorry, Mrs. Reeves. His name's not down."

"I told you. He's with me."

"Ma'am, I can't just –"

"Tell you what," Ryan snapped. "Why don't you go check with your people downtown and find out just exactly *who is in charge here*."

The men gave her a hard glance before turning to Hale and asking stonily, "Do you have some ID?"

"Don't show him a thing." Ryan bit off the words.

"It's not a problem." Hale reached for his wallet. "Always like to stay on the right side of the law."

The black man took his driver's license, copied the details, then grudgingly moved aside. "Try not to move anything. Our lab boys aren't finished in there yet."

Hale waited until they had turned the far corner before hissing, "Are you out of your tiny mind?"

"The university's security joes have been crawling all over me. Tried to make out that NASA had cooked this mess up and were behind it from the beginning."

"Behind *what*?"

Ryan stopped beside the entrance to Philippa's lab. The heavy door was canted slightly, hanging free of the top hinge. "I don't have to tell you that what you're seeing here is classified. I mean, not a breath to a soul."

"I've already gotten that message."

"Give me a hand here." Together they hefted the door and slid it open. Ryan stepped back. "Go ahead."

Cautiously he stepped over the doorway, and stopped cold.

"It's okay. The floor is safe. Just watch where you step."

"Ryan ..."

"I know." She moved up alongside him. "I couldn't believe it either."

"What *happened*?"

"Here, step this way." Ryan guided Hale forward. The rubble was everywhere.

"Was it a bomb?"

"The experts say no. Look around, Hale. Nothing in the lab's been touched."

"You're crazy, the place is a wreck."

"No, look around, will you? There couldn't have been an explosion. No fire damage, no smoke, the walls are clean; look, even the generator's intact."

She guided Hale forward until they were standing alongside the central lab table. The cracked granite top was coated with debris and dust and ceiling tiles and wires. Ryan pointed straight up. "Take a look here."

Hale stared up through six or seven floors, maybe more. The hole started about six feet across, and sheered off a perfect circle through the overhead layers. The edges were razored in precision lines.

"They're pretty sure it was a projectile of some sort," Ryan said. "Everything that wasn't nailed down on the floors above was blasted all over the place."

Hale craned and inspected what he could see of the next floor. "The hole gets smaller."

"A perfect cone." The tension in Ryan's voice was fading to a tone of exhausted worry. "Goes up six stories, then disappears."

"What did this?"

"We don't have a clue. The bomb guys have been all over this place, taken fragments from each hole, and not found a thing. Nothing at all."

Hale kept his gaze pointed upwards. "Philippa's dead, isn't she."

"That," Ryan replied, "is exactly what I need you to find out."

3

"A university cop was patrolling a couple of buildings away when it happened. He radioed it in as a possible pipe leak. Most labs use natural gas for the burners. The guard said it sounded like an eruption, this great roar of sound. At first he couldn't get a fix on where it took place because of the echoes. The canyons and cliffs make for perfect baffles. But the time of his radio contact was exactly four forty-one in the morning."

Hale walked around the demolished lab as Ryan gave her summary, his footsteps scrunching over the grit-encrusted floor. He glanced over occasionally, studying his friend as much as the lab. Ryan's quiet voice sounded as though she was reading from invisible notes. The diminutive body was able to contain so much energy only because it was so tightly focused. So *determined*.

Two fingers tapped time on the central table's dusty surface as Ryan continued, "We know Philippa went back to her apartment after the explosion. Her neighbors heard her come in around five-fifteen. They timed it precisely, she was making enough racket to wake them both up. She was in there maybe twenty minutes, then they heard a cab honking outside the window. They know it was a cab because they looked, and watched Philippa come racing out the door dragging a case in each hand. She went back, and this time returned with a surfboard and a briefcase. They strapped the board on the top, she piled in the back, and they took off."

"But why –"

"Let me just walk you through what we know, Hale. Okay, so we found the cab. The driver remembers her vividly. He took Philippa to the airport."

When she stopped there, Hale demanded, "And?"

"She vanished into thin air."

"Ryan, she had to go somewhere."

"That's right." Her dark gaze fastened on Hale with bleak intensity. "Which is why you're here."

"Ryan," Hale backed away, his feet scrunching over scattered debris. "Think of what you're saying. You've got everybody but the National Guard on this case as it is."

"They're not going to find her," Ryan said impatiently. "Hale, Philippa is *gone*."

"Ryan, I can't take off work to come help you. It's not possible. Especially right now." He scanned the demolished lab. "Besides, I wouldn't know how to begin looking for her."

"Your dad was a private investigator, right?" Ryan was pushing hard now. "You worked for him."

Another set of memories crowded up, unpleasant as the ones drifting through the lab's dusty air. His father had been fired from the Norfolk police force for drinking. Hale had been fourteen at the time. He had watched his father shrug off twenty-five years on the force with the casualness of a man who cared more for the bottle than life itself. A friend on the force had slipped Hale's dad a private investigator's license, others had sent him referrals – drinking buddies to a man.

Hale had spent the next three years working nights and summers for his dad. Not with him, *for* him. Doing what the old man was usually incapable of. Filling in the gaps. Losing a place on the football team in the process. Resigned to how his father loved the long lonely hours of surveillance not because it was quiet time with his son, but because the bottle was there to keep him company and his son was there to do the work. The year before Hale left for college, his father had drifted away. Out one night doing his public spectacle routine, then taking off, never to return. By that point Hale had gained a lot of experience in pretending not to care.

Hale followed Ryan from the lab. She ignored the two grey suits, waited until they were on the stairs and their words were covered by the construction racket to continue, "You know Philippa better than anybody alive. You know how she thinks. The police are following the tried and true routine. They're going around, visiting her house and her haunts, showing her picture, putting out an APB."

"Philippa has a warrant out on her?"

Ryan pushed through the outer doors. The setting sun and lack of further excitement was dwindling the number of onlookers. "Take a look around. She blows the roof off a university building, demolishes maybe a million dollars worth of equipment, then disappears. They've got her down for willful destruction of university property, but it's just a ruse. A missing persons doesn't get as much attention as a criminal act. Northstar and SRC are pushing hard for results."

Ryan opened her car door, slid inside, waited for Hale to join her before asking, "You hungry?"

"Starving. Far as I'm concerned, airplane food is about as appealing as bad Chinese."

"There's a bar down near the hotel, the receptionist said they serve a great steak. That okay with you?"

Hale stared at her, wondering who was seated beside him. "A bar?"

She made a slow procedure of fitting her key into the ignition. "I think maybe I'd like to drink my dinner tonight."

Throughout college Ryan had been fanatic about sports, eating, her kids, her career. In all the time they had been together, Hale had never seen her drink. To anyone who pressed, Ryan had always replied that binges and dawn runs were a lethal mix. "Isn't this the girl who never finished a glass of wine?"

Ryan started the car, gripped the wheel, then just sat staring at the sun-dappled windshield. When she finally spoke, the words came out a quiet drone. "All my life, I've had friends tell me, this is it. I'm so happy I'm scared, they say. I love my life just exactly like it is and I never want anything to change, stuff like that. Not me. I used to think, okay, I'll get this promotion, I'll see the kids through whatever it is we've got on now. Then okay, the happy times will start for me. I used to think that. It was sort of a mantra I'd use to get through the day."

She squinted at him, as though piercing a deep fog. "Now I wonder if maybe I missed it somewhere. I shut my eyes for a minute, whoosh, the good fifteen minutes flew by. Or the good hour came, but I was tied up in a meeting with Washington 'crats. Or the really great day, it hit everybody in Cocoa but me, I was tied to the clock, watching the countdown and hoping nothing went wrong. Or the great week ..." She turned back to the windshield, shook her head slowly. "No, I'm pretty sure I would have noticed a whole week that great."

"I'm really sorry, Ryan." It was all he could think to say. "I thought things were going really well for you."

"They are." She flipped the car into drive, pulled from the parking space with grim determination. "Just great."

* * *

Hale rolled down his window, smelled the dry desert and the eucalyptus and the sea. A heady mixture that almost always worked its magic on him. But not today.

He had a hundred more questions for Ryan. But a single glance at her tightly bunched form told him she had said all she wanted to about that topic. So he ran his mind over what she had said about Philippa, and came up with,

"Northstar I know. But what does SRC have to do with this?"

"They're the biggest backers of Philippa's work." She visibly relaxed, now that they were talking about something other than her own internal state. "Northstar's gone conglomerate, like the rest of the defense and space industries. Space Research Consortium is Northstar's new parent. From what I've heard, which is not a lot, the SRC biggies went absolutely berserk the moment they heard she had disappeared. I mean, totally off the wall. Apparently they pressured Washington, and NASA responded by sending me here."

"Northstar's new parent company called Washington about Philippa?"

"I know. It sounded crazy to me as well. I mean, how many scientists have we got on NASA's payroll, thirty thousand? So why is it I get a call from Washington three seconds after the blast, telling me to drop everything and get out here? Northstar must have hit the panic button with the money men in Washington. But I can't get confirmation. I can't get anything. Nobody's around to answer my calls. Either that or they're avoiding further contact." She stopped at a light, gave him a look that was equal parts anxiety and slow-burning rage. "Now there's a launch in three days and I've got to get back. I need somebody to help us out here. Somebody I can trust."

"I've got a job to worry about."

The light turned green. Ryan bolted through the intersection, said to the empty road ahead, "What if I can get you a deal from Northstar?"

Ryan's voice held the same flickering mystery as earlier. He was hearing one thing, missing another. "Land me a sales contract? You can do that?"

"I told you. Northstar are big hitters here and Washington both, and they're hot on getting Philippa back. If I can convince them you're the one they need, we might be able to work something out."

He should have felt pleasure at the news. But the same hollow chord struck at heart level, empty and dull. This is what friendship had come to, striking deals over the loss of his one-time girl. "Do it and I'm your man."

"You're sure about that?" Closing the bargain, hard as nails, not even giving thought to the miles and the changes now between them. "No backing out at the last moment."

"Land me a genuine sales contract with Northstar Avionics," Hale replied. Spelling it out just like he would with any other negotiation between strangers. "Make it clear to my bosses that it's contingent upon me staying on this case personally."

"Done." Ryan pulled into the motel parking lot, stopped before the lobby entrance. It was a renovated sixties structure, located midway between the university and the beach, on the main thoroughfare leading to downtown La Jolla. She cut the engine, asked, "So what does all that back there tell you?"

"She's frightened."

Ryan opened her door. "That's an original thought?"

"Philippa has never run from anything in her entire life." Hale stared through the front windshield, but saw only a fractured lab building with a crack running from the front doorway to the roof. "Find out what scared her so bad she had to disappear, you find the lady herself."

* * *

"Why are you smiling?"

Hale slid onto the barstool next to hers. "Oh, no reason."

"Yes there is." She examined him with a keenness that penetrated the bar's dim light. "This is the second time today you've done that thing."

He found it easier to slide his eye down the length of the bar than meet her gaze. "What thing is that?"

"Your smile used to be like a flashgun, all or nothing. When we walked in here, you gave the same smile you used on me at the airport. Like Hale wasn't really home behind the grin."

"This place reminds me of days gone by, that's all." His eyes were adjusting now, giving him the ability to search the shadows for long-lost memories. "I spent a lot of time in places like this. Fridays were payday, when Pop was able to find work, so around midnight I'd get home from my date and go look. When I found him I'd stick around a while, hang there on the edge of the circle surrounded by all of Pop's cop friends, wait 'till he was ready to let me take him home. No good telling him I was tired or it was late or he'd had a bagfull already. It only made him angry. And you didn't want to get my dad angry when he'd been drinking."

The memories were gathering around him now, driven out of hiding by the place. And the smells. AC on high to keep the smoke and the spilled-drink odors to a minimum. Kitchen in the back, big steaks and home fries and fresh salads. Generous drinks, soft sultry jazz, lights making walls of dark between the booths. The kind of place where tourists looked one look and skulked off in search of ferns and top-forty tunes and low-fat salsa.

"I never knew any of this."

"It's not something I talk about much." Hale spotted the bartender making his way down the crowded bar towards them, so he asked, "What are you going to have?"

"Let me think." Ryan leaned on the bar's padded rail, squinted at the long array of bottles lining the mirrored back wall. "I'd like to try a martini. I've never had one. How can I go through life without trying a martini?"

"People do it all the time." Somehow sitting on the stools seemed to even out their heights. Or perhaps it was just the bar made it matter less. "Have you ever even tried hard liquor before?"

"I don't remember and it doesn't matter. Here he is. Order me a really special one."

Hale asked the bartender, "You got those fancy martini glasses that look like giant champagne goblets?"

"This for the lady?"

"Yes."

He gave Ryan a bartender's smile, stretching the midnight lines of his face. "Steuben crystal, gold rim, the works."

"What about chilled Stoli?"

The gaze and the smile still for Ryan. "Stuff pours slower than syrup."

"Okay, a Stoli martini, double portion of sweet vermouth. Five olives, chilled glass."

"Sweet?"

Hale nodded. "First-time flyer."

"Right. And for you?"

"Beer."

"You will not." Ryan glared at the pair of them. "If I'm going to sit here and get tanked the least you can do is keep the lady company."

Hale turned back, resigned himself to, "Double Jack Daniels in a lowball glass with a light draft chaser."

"You got it."

"And a plate of baby ribs, home fries, slaw, the works." He looked at Ryan. "You want anything to eat?"

"The olives will do me fine. How did you know what to order?"

"You come to know these places. Get hammered and leave your wallet with the waitress, she'll take out the tab, a tip, and leave the rest. Strictly locals-only sort of crowd."

She examined him, the dark eyes reaching deep, searching for this man she once knew. "This is the most you've ever talked about yourself. I want to know more."

Hale found he didn't mind. "Norfolk cops were a tough bunch. They had the navy guys coming in off the ships and they had the beach crowds, all the kids there for a thrill and a drink and a fight. When I was about nine Pop's precinct started a boxing club for the kids, said if we were going to grow up around the navy wildcats we had to know how to take care of ourselves.

"They had two coaches. This guy from the Y, he'd come in and dance us around, make us use the twelve-ounce gloves. On a nine year-old kid those gloves turned our strongest punch into marshmallows. Felt like you were wearing a mattress on each arm." He waited as the bartender walked over and set down the draft and the shooter for Hale, unloaded a beaded martini glass in front of Ryan, then walked off in trained silence. Just another couple out to navigate the alcoholic fog.

Ryan took a tentative sip, made a face suitable for a Japanese kabuki mask. "This tastes *awful*."

"I know."

"I mean, it ranks right up there with used brake fluid."

Hale sipped his shooter, chased the fire with foam from the beer. Sensed the past sidle up to the bar beside him, whisper companionable pain. JD and draft had been his father's poison of choice. He hadn't touched the stuff since college. "The second one is better."

"Oh." She took a breath, dipped her head like a blackhaired flamingo, then drained the glass with one fell swoop. Ryan clenched her eyes closed and gave a choke that came up from somewhere deep.

"Steady now." He patted her back, the first time he had touched his former best friend in six months. Turned to the bartender and said, "A glass of water, please."

"No." Hoarser than usual. "No, I'm okay. I want another."

"Ryan, take it easy. Those things are lethal."

"I'm all right, I tell you." She pushed away the water-glass the bartender offered, said, "That was very nice, thank you. I'll have the same again, please."

The guy gave Hale a bartender's smile, the eyes ancient and void. Ryan leaned over so she could watch him pick up the mixer, start pouring in the stuff, the movements fluid from a billion forgotten drinks. "And the other guy?"

"What?"

"You said there were two coaches. Who was the other one?"

"Oh. The station sergeant, man, was he ever something." The words coming as easy as the memories. Things he hadn't thought of for years, much less talked about. "Marine, golden gloves, the works. Cauliflower ears, nose broken so often he could shift the cartilage around with his fingers, eyes packed in scar tissue. Talked real hoarse from collecting punches in the voice-box."

Ryan smiled for the bartender when he brought the second round, plucked out the olives from the glass he was replacing, pulled them from the plastic sword with tiny white teeth. "Sounds like just the kind of influence I'd like to have for my children."

"I thought he was the neatest guy I'd ever seen in my whole life. This man had been everywhere, done everything. He taught us the art of fighting dirty. He knew all the tricks in the book. Then if we gave him a hundred percent that day, he'd tell us stories about places he'd been. Things he'd done. Only trouble was, giving him a hundred percent usually meant spraying blood all over the place."

She gave a tentative sip, nodded. "You're right, this is a *lot* better. Why couldn't he make the first one to taste like this?"

But Hale was busy living the memories. "I fought a lot. Got to be friends with the ring. Went all the way to the state finals the year I turned seventeen."

"You're kidding."

"Might have even won. Only I got busted my semifinal round. Kicked out, never allowed to compete again."

The look was back, the one that said she wasn't sure who he was any more. "What did you do?"

"Exactly what Coach told me to. Had a guy on the ropes, the ref stopped the fight to let him recover, but I knew one more punch would end things for good." Hale gave an easy shrug. "Hit the kid so hard I split his helmet and fractured his jaw. Knocked him out of the ring. He fell on the judges' table and broke his collarbone. After the ref and the judges had finished chewing me out, all Coach said was, Bad fall, bad call."

The bartender returned with his food, did not need to ask to refill both his glasses. Hale ate in silence, kept company by Ryan's slow steady drinking and the memories. Crowding in, watching him with the patience that had kept them there and ready for all those years, just waiting for his guard to drop.

Ryan said, "I remember back at school, getting you to talk about anything but surfing was like pulling teeth. Hale Andrews, the mystery man." She drained her second glass with a good deal more pleasure than the first. Ryan signaled the bartender by tinging her glass with one fingernail. Smiled at the sound. Then, "How come you never told me any of this before?"

"I don't know." But he did. Said the words so easy it sounded even to him as though he had been saying them inside for years, instead of just realizing it himself. "I guess I went off to college determined to reinvent myself."

Hale knew Ryan was watching him. But he didn't want to meet her gaze. He lifted his shot glass, examined the bewitching elixir, accepted the arrival of the other memory. The one he would never disconnect. A memory so vivid it felt as though he was speaking the words, but inwardly this time, telling himself. Yeah, the reason why he had hit that guy so hard? It was because of the last time he had gone to collect Pop, three nights before leaving for the finals. This time his father had started jeering at him in front of all his barroom buddies.

Scrawny kid, all balls and hair, that's the way his father had described him. Nothing to him, not down where it counts. First sign of trouble, this kid's gonna fold up his tent and steal away with the night. On and on it went, the other drunks laughing and egging his dad on, seventeen-year-old Hale standing there growing tighter and smaller and hotter by the instant. Until his old man pushed himself off the bar, put up his fists, started shadow-boxing. C'mon, kid. Gimme your best shot. Couldn't hit his way out of a paper bag, this kid. Watch me now, I'm gonna lay him low with one shot.

Hale saw nothing but red. He stepped under his father's first roundhouse and buried his left almost to his elbow in his father's doughy middle. Letting the old man fold in around him, just like the ex-marine had taught him. Then putting seventeen years of frustration and rage into his right, feeling the head-punch all the way to his shoulder.

The old man keeled back, did a bounce off the bar, and went down. Hale turned through the silent throng and left the bar. He never saw his old man again.

"Hale?"

He drained the smoky liquid, set down the shot glass, drank the rest of his beer, tasted nothing but ashes. He pushed away the remnants of his meal. "I'm here."

"You coulda fooled me. All of a sudden you changed to stone." Ryan smiled as the bartender set down her new glass, waited as he collected the pair of glasses Hale silently pushed towards him. "You used to do that at the beach, you know. All of a sudden it's not just a surf, it's a war, and you're gonna take on the whole ocean."

A beauty in black chose that moment to walk over, all long legs and disheveled blonde hair. She leaned a substantial chest on the bar beside Hale's chair, glanced over to make sure she had his attention. Asked the bartender for a glass of champagne. Turned back, ready to receive a look or a word from Hale, only to draw away as Ryan swooped in from the other side. Ryan wearing her game face, the voice cutting as a metal rasp. "He's busy tonight, darling. So why don't you just turn back around and undulate yourself on out of here."

Hale waited until their stretch of the bar had been reclaimed, glad for the reason to smile, then said, "Undulate?"

She took a healthy sip. "One night you can go without. It'll do you good."

Hale let that one slide, content simply to have something else to talk about but himself.

Ryan finished her glass, set it down carefully, straightened her napkin with a careful motion. But try as she might to hold onto normalcy, the cold liquid was working its oily magic. She blinked slowly. "Wow. Where did that hammer come from?"

The bartender was there almost before she lifted her hand, which was good. Her coordination was slipping though her voice stayed steady. "These are pretty powerful, you know? Another Novocain frosty, if you please, barkeep."

The guy asked Hale, "You taking responsibility for the lady?"

"Are you sure you want to do this to yourself, Ryan? How about a sandwich or something?"

"Thanks, I'm all full up. Just got room for one little olive more." Her voice remained remarkably clear, even as her eyes had become as frosted as the glass.

Hale sampled the bourbon, then the beer, wiped the foam from his lip. When the bartender had deposited her next glass, he said, "You've changed."

Ryan might have nodded, or it could have been just lowering her head for a sip from the too-full glass. Hale asked, "Is it this trouble over Philippa?"

"That and a lot of other stuff besides." Another slow sip, taking it easy now, enjoying the delicate flavor and the liquid fire. Sighing to release the smoke. Then she asked in a hazy whisper, "Why'd you do it, Hale?"

Hale found it easy to follow her thoughts. Early practice still served him well. But he had no desire to follow this one through. "You're drunk."

"Maybe. No. Yes. Definitely. I am severely novocained. But it doesn't change a thing." She sipped, taking it delicate, leaning her head back, eyes half-closed, letting it roll down slow and smooth. "I think the bartender's finally learned how to do this right."

"Maybe we better hold off on the talk until tomorrow."

"That's silly. I won't remember what I was going to say." She took another sip, found it so good she didn't want to set down the glass, just held it there with eyes closed and drank it dry. Found the napkin by Braille.

When she seemed unable to get her eyes open, Hale turned and signaled for the check. "I think it's time I take you to the hotel."

"A while back he tells me he's done with that scene." She made no protest as he slipped one hand under her arm, half-lifted her to her feet. She made it upright, her arm cocked so he could keep a solid grip, her head straight and erect and her voice clear. "I thought, okay, why not. No reason why the automatic screwing machine can't grow up before wearing down. What he needs is a woman who's on his level. So I introduce him to the finest woman I've ever met. I bring my two best friends together, my good deed of the year. And what happens? He uses her, then drops her so hard she shatters."

Hale handed the bartender some bills, told him to add fifteen percent for the damage, accepted his change. He bid the bar at large a grand goodnight, swiveled her around, nudged her into walking. Understanding through silent communication that she wanted to walk unaided. All the hidden talents coming back into play.

She was out the door, still moving by osmosis with the eyes slitted or closed, he couldn't tell from his height. But her voice remained crystal clear as she went on, "Philippa was pretty good, wasn't she? I don't mean in bed. I mean, good like a person."

"She was great," Hale said. Moving slow down the sidewalk, the hotel sign a beacon up ahead. "Just great."

"'Course she was." Ryan held to a fairly steady pace, leaning only once in a while on him. Mostly just needing his guidance, trusting him to find the way home. They turned into the hotel drive before she repeated, "Why did you do it, Hale?"

"Here, let me have your key."

"Purse. You find it. I can't see so well."

"Can you make the stairs?"

"Sure. Watch this."

"Okay. Lean here on the wall, let me open the door."

She did as she was told. "She really loved you, Hale. I mean, heart and soul."

Inside now, keeping the lights on low. Never could tell when he'd find himself struck in the face with his own reflection. A major danger in strange rooms. Better to do this with just the light through the window. "I know she did."

"Then why did you do it?" Ryan surprised him by managing her clothes on her own. Slow steady movements, dropping them piece by piece as she moved for the bathroom. "Why did you have to go and break her heart?"

Hale pulled back the bedcovers, listened to the water running, knew he had to wait it out and make sure she was okay. She did not take long. Ryan opened the door wearing her blouse, and somehow navigated back to the bed without ever raising an eyelid. Falling into bed, fumbling for the covers, for the pillow, finding neither. The hand dropping down in defeat.

Hale moved over, pulled up the covers around her neck. Lifted her head and settled the pillow underneath. Was rewarded with a murmur, what might have been the word *why*. It was enough to push him away, out the door and back to his own empty room.

4

The worst thing about the whole ordeal was how a Mexican surf trip had somehow been transformed into a prison sentence.

Philippa sat on her balcony and tried to enjoy the sun completing its crimson ride into the sea. But it was impossible. She was too full of loathing for what was about to come. The nights enfolded her with whispered threats and terrors that stalked her dreams. Every light poised below her balcony became pinpoint beams of laser-tracking scopes, and the only question was which one would shoot her first.

Perhaps this was what happened to people who wished to be gods. Either the earthly powers they threatened would grind them down to dust, or nature herself sought revenge through unnamed fears. Philippa had no doubt whatsoever that she was playing with all the earth-bound rules. Reshaping the world and everything upon it. She was not distracted by all the work yet to be done, all the unanswered questions and unsolved mysteries. She was reshaping reality. Perhaps she deserved such a fate.

Not that Philippa had much right to call a five-star seaside hotel an ordeal. She didn't even know why she was staying there, except that she was alone and she was frightened and at some level below thought she felt that surrounding herself with luxury might protect her. Plus it was so far removed from her normal ambience that anyone who knew her would not believe she was staying in such a place.

The evening's daily orchestration was marred by the sounds of street traffic and the mariachi band playing at the poolside bar. It had become a daily ritual, struggling to focus upon the glory of another ocean-desert twilight and push aside the tourists and the noise and the smell of suntan oil and pina coladas and diesel fumes. Futilely believing if she could succeed, then on another level she would be able to push aside the internal disquiet and find the solutions. Shut out the fear and the frustration and the doubts, and identify the puzzle's missing pieces. In the scarce moments when the wind carried the arid fragrance of desert flowers, when the street noise faded and the light was a tide of impossible golds, she almost felt she could.

Philippa took pride in remaining an exception to most rules others lived by. This was especially true when comparing herself to her scientific colleagues. She was a physicist who wanted tangible results. She was a scientist who surfed. She was a female success in the male-dominated scientific universe. She was a feminist who loved a man. Who ached for him. Who felt as though her entire being had been tuned to his frequency, and now searched the heavens for his vibrant essence.

Philippa stood and left the balcony. Her room was a canvas for the day's final light, painted now by soft washes of rose and ochre and violet. She walked to the desk covered by all her toys and switched them on, taking her time, making a ritual of the process.

She flipped open the phone's hook-up, watched it scan the sky for whichever Inmarsat or MiniM satellite was closest. Iridium and a couple of other major players were now advertising linkup connections from anywhere on earth, but that simply was not true. Linkups were possible from places where population density justified hanging a communications satellite overhead. The southernmost tip of Baja did not fall into that category. Philippa's radar link was a hundred times more powerful than any handheld unit, however. It was also designed to look like a CD player to escape attention from anyone who might be suspicious of someone walking around with a long-range mobile communicator. She plugged in her phone to the link, and connected the transponder to the phone and the computer to the transponder.

The number she typed was to an electronic post-office service in Finland, the most highly wired country on earth. The service was unique, offering automatic anonymization to all subscribers. This meant anyone seeking to back-trace a communiqué would arrive in Helsinki and hit an impenetrable wall. She had checked this out carefully. The wall was so tight that not even a search of company records would show who or where she was. Payment was routed through a Swiss bank, her mobile number and dual codes were the only IDs on record, and any communication they had with her was sent via the same e-box. Messages could only be left or received if the sender knew both her voice code and the sender's own assigned code. Direct hook-ups could only be initiated from her end, and only after she had first listened to an audible request and made personal confirmation.

She fitted the earpiece into place as the screen moved through the entrance routine. The screen flickered, then cleared to show the pristine image of a log cabin in the forest by the edge of a vast blue lake. Through her earpiece she heard birdsong and a waterfall.

She was led up the stairs to where a brass plaque on the door requested her ID. She typed in her communicator's number, then the ID codenumber. The door opened, and she entered the antechamber. This was designed like a Finnish sauna, right down to the gleaming coals and the birch branches and the steam and the wooden water bucket. No doubt their way of saying to relax and sit a spell.

The voice in her ear was cool, slightly accented, very feminine. "Please state your codename for voice confirmation."

She drew the flexible microphone up closer to her lips and replied, "My codename is Filly."

A moment's pause, then, "Voice ID is confirmed. Welcome, Filly."

The antechamber's inner door opened, and she entered a long office hallway. The doors she passed were blank steel vaults, the designer's way of silently assuring visitors of their safety. Before her door she watched the dial spin, the vault open, and she was ushered into a stylish office setting. Everything there was of her choosing. Two Degas watercolors hung from the side walls. The view through the great picture window was of the ocean at dawn. The wallpaper was rose and coral, shades she never in her wildest dreams would have considered using anywhere but here.

"You have no messages," the voice announced coolly.

"Bloody hell." Alexis should have been back to her before now. Something was wrong. Three weeks was far too long, even given the state of Russian communications. She typed out the words, *Have my messages been accepted?*

"One moment." Only the slightest hesitation between words indicated the voice was computer generated. These Finns were very, very good. "You have two uncollected voice messages."

"Double damn." Though it was probably futile, she typed, *Prepare voice message.*

"Multiple or single recipient?"

Single.

"Codename?"

Rasputin. It had been her idea, the code name. The one time they had met they had spent most of their brief safe-time together planning this communication. At that point, Philippa had simply put it down to diehard fears of a paranoid Russian. Now she was not so sure.

"One moment."

Alexis Vilnieff had the same wild eyes as the bearded prophet of old, eyes that did not belong to a human face.

Eyes which bombarded everything they touched with subatomic particles and multidimensional energies. Those eyes searched beyond space and time while his mind simply followed along, giving verbal interpretations to things only he could see.

Alexis had been one of the most brilliant people she had ever met – this she had known long before they had actually laid eyes upon one another. Some months earlier, he had written in response to an article she had co-authored. In his haphazard scrawl he had challenged her to go further than she had ever dreamed possible, drawing her along upon his unbridled enthusiasm, an exhilarating ride through uncharted territories.

She would never forget that first contact with Alexis, standing there in her office, her hands shaking as the words on the paper came clear to her mind, feeling the man's incredible energy drive through her fingertips and race down her spine. Simply from reading her article he had seen what she had only caught shadow-glimpses of, and had willingly offered his insights. No request for joint authorship, nothing except this joyous shout of discovery leaping from the pages.

In the darkness of her lonely nights she liked to think she would have arrived there herself, taken the next logical step and the one after that and arrived at the same point he had fashioned with his burst of intuitive power. But she would never know.

The man had been as bizarre as his letter. Philippa had arrived at a Washington conference with three suitcases, two and a half of them filled with notes and printouts and her initial prototype. But Alexis Vilnieff had already been certain he was being watched, and spent the entire lunch time talking about his wife and child. Over dessert he had drawn a photograph from his breast pocket, and presented it with the pride of one showing off his life's work.

Philippa had smiled as best she could over blurred images of a tired-looking woman and a young girl with blonde hair and bright, bright eyes. Philippa's confession that she was not married had been met with the pity of one hearing that a dear friend suffered from some fatal disease.

"Filly, you may begin your voice message to Rasputin now."

"It's Friday evening, the fifteenth of June, and I'm terribly worried." Normally she thought things out carefully, and began with prepared notes and reams of questions. Alexis always came back with shouted excitement and questions of his own. Never answers. He had never given her an answer to anything. But his questions, her brain felt like it was going to explode from the sheer *potential* of his questions. "Alexis, where are you? I'm so afraid. I wish there was some way..."

She took a long breath, and straightened in her chair. "All right. I ran the experiment along the lines I described to you in the *first* message you didn't pick up. And it blew the roof off like I told you in the *second* message, and now I'm sitting in the lap of luxury in Cabo San Lucas. That's the town at the southernmost tip of the Baja peninsula. At least, I am until my money runs out.

"Alexis, the first stage has been achieved. The field was established. But the effective result was to destroy both platform and projectile. I have no idea if the field is stable."

She tried not to think of the futility of her discussion. Or the hollowness of her words. She needed to talk this out, push back the suffocating loneliness for at least a moment of myth and pretend that one friend still remained to her. One connection to a world beyond the walls of her darkening room. "At this point, if I were to enlarge the unit and strap humans on board, all I'd have is blood sausage in spacesuit wrappings. What I need to establish here is *control*."

The thought brought out a sad smile. "As though anything in my life is under control just now. Please contact me, Alexis. Please."

She cut off the machine and sat there, surrounded by darkness and night noises and a loneliness stronger than gravity.

5

Hale knocked on the office door, pushed it open, asked, "Professor Digby?"

The grizzled head rose from behind its cloud of pipe smoke. "Who wants to know?"

"My name is Hale Andrews. Are you Dr. Warner Digby?"

"All the lab technician slots have been filled." The head dropped back down. "Leave your application with the secretary out front."

Hale was dressed in the same clothes he had worn the day before, the pant cuffs grey with dust from the lab. The view through the professor's window showed a typical San Diego afternoon – clear and mild, a comfortable seventy degrees and low humidity. It mocked the slow steady thumping in his head.

He had awoken after noon, only to be greeted by a note under the door. Ryan had left with the dawn, taking the first flight back to Florida. Something about an emergency. The keys to her rental car had been in the envelope, along with instructions not to ding it up. Apparently not even a ride on the martini express could slow Ryan down.

Hale said to the top of Digby's head, "I'm not looking for work."

"All I need, is some fella with Hollywood looks doing a number on my staff, taking the ladies' minds off their data. Mess up a lifetime's work in a week, fella like you."

"I'm not after a job." Hale watched the smoke swirl about the room in lazy drifts. "I'd like to speak with you about Philippa Laremy."

Greying eyebrows lifted and bunched into a single bushy line. "You with the confounded press? I don't have a thing to say."

"I'm not with the press." Hale took that as the only invitation he would receive and stepped inside. "Confounded or otherwise."

"Shut the door. Easier nowadays to own a gun than smoke a pipe. You ever seen anybody hold up a bank with a pipe?"

"You've got a point there."

"Got tobacco vigilantes on the prowl all the time. Well, being head of the department has brought me enough headaches, least I can do is declare this one office no longer a part of state property." He jutted his chin out aggressively, daring Hale to object. "Don't remember seeing you around before."

"I live in Richmond," Hale hedged. "I was wondering –"

"You seen what she's done to my building?"

"Ryan showed me the lab."

"Oh, you know that Reeves gal, do you. You with the government as well?"

"Industry." He decided shorter answers had a better chance of being heard. "Plastics."

"That's good. I've got as much time for those empty grey suits as I do for the press. Ryan Reeves is one exception to the bureaucratic rule. Only one not walking around and shouting orders like there's a million-dollar grant on the line." The pipe started sending up quick angry bursts. "Nobody tells me how to do my job. Right now my job is to get these alien hunters out of my building, find space for my classes, collect my equipment, and rebuild my lab."

"You mean Philippa's lab."

"It's hers if she's still around. Otherwise I've just got another vacancy to fill. I devoted twenty-five years of my life to erecting this department. I'm not about to let it vanish with Dr. Laremy." He glared a challenge across the desk. When Hale remained silent, he grumbled, "Ought to have stuck around and taken her medicine. Got no business heading for the hills just because her experiment went haywire."

"Can you tell me what her experiment was?"

"Had no right to endanger university property, whatever scatterbrained idea she was tracking down." He aimed his pipe at the papers in front of him. "Done nothing but bury me in more work. I've got experiments too, you know. May not be Nobel Prize material, but I know my stuff. And I'm running this department with or without Laremy."

Hale rose from his seat. "Thanks for your time."

* * *

Hale followed the construction clamor upstairs. The noise came from higher still, echoing down the stairwell from three or four floors at once. The security tape and the goons in suits were gone. He walked down the hall to Philippa's lab, saw the door was now sealed with a padlock. An official notice had been attached at eye-level, declaring the lab off-limits unless prior authorization was obtained from the security office. He started to turn back when he heard a noise from farther down the hall, and noticed the door to Philippa's office was slightly ajar. Quietly he walked over and pushed on the hand-scrolled poster covering the door.

He knew bitter disappointment when the door swung open to reveal a younger version of his one-time lover.

The girl was in her mid-twenties, and looked suprisingly like Philippa. Same taut form and loose sun-washed curls, same disregard for fashion. This version was dressed in jeans and an ancient sweater with threads unfurling around the edge. Hale stood in the doorway and watched her fiddle with the equipment scattered over the desk and the floor and stacked along two walls, making notes in a battered pad, muttering to herself as she squinted over dials and read-outs.

The sight was so familiar it speared him with times lost and gone forever.

Which was why Hale announced his presence with a quiet, "How's it going?"

The girl yelped and jumped a full two feet in the air. She landed with one hand clenching the pad to her chest, the other trying to hold glasses to her terrified eyes. "Who are *you*?"

Hale grinned at the memory of other times, when he had enjoyed scaring another girl, one who also lost contact with the world when working. "Hale Andrews. A friend of Philippa."

"Oh, man, don't *ever* do that." The hand stayed in place, wrinkling the pad in an attempt to massage her heart. "I don't think I'd survive a second dose."

"I saw the door was open and came to see if she was back."

"Not a chance." A tense hand-motion took in the equipment stacked along the side wall and piled in the center of the room. "I'm doing postdoc research under Professor Laremy. I've got to recalibrate all this equipment recovered from the lab and get on with my experiments. With or without her."

Hale nodded easily, giving her a chance to recover. "I just spoke with Doctor Digby. Or tried to. The guy was, how should I put it."

"Too busy playing head of department. Like they say, theoretical physicists should be embalmed at forty and save grad students a world of grief."

He took in the clutter of dusty instruments with a wave of his hand. "Any idea what caused the explosion?"

"She was working on superconductors."

"That's all?"

"Far as I know. But Professor Laremy had a totally nonlinear mind."

The past tense referral ground like sand under his eyelids, but he let it pass. "Come again?"

"Most people move logically step by step, life or experiments, it's all the same." She possessed a little of Philippa in her actions, the lilt she gave to certain words, the way one hand rose to carve a diagram in the air. As though she had been studying Philippa, unconsciously copying her attitude. "Point A to B and so on. Professor Laremy, though, she might go from point A to the square root of fifty, then wind up with a totally new concept while the rest of us are still setting up our experiments." Her eyes looked bewildered by the thought. "She had the most amazing mind I've ever known."

"Yeah, Philippa is something." The grad student clearly didn't know anything more than he did. He nodded at the equipment. "Hope you can salvage your work."

"Oh, this won't take too much time. I've seen lab experiments gone wrong before. The equipment seems to be okay."

He started for the door, only to stop and say, "This poster is new."

"Oh, right. Professor Laremy called the list Hokum's Laws. She wanted to remind undergrads that theories aren't necessarily true just because they've been around for a while."

The grad student moved around the clutter of equipment to stand beside him. "Like the first one, 'The universe revolves around the earth', that comes to us care of the Greeks, and lasted over two thousand years. It wasn't until the middle of the sixteenth century that Galileo faced excommunication and public disgrace for saying it was wrong."

Hale read the second, "'An object's natural state is to be at rest.'"

"Another late great mistake, care of Aristotle's gang. Then there's one from Copernicus, he claimed that the planets make perfect circles around the sun. Only now we know orbits are elliptical and imperfect ones at that, since they're also affected by the pull of other planets."

Hale skipped down to the bottom of the sheet. He read what a shaky hand had scrawled on the right-hand corner, "'$F = ma$.' I never was any good at math."

The student stared in open surprise. "I haven't seen that one before."

"What does it mean?"

"It's Newton's second law." Her pad rose back to chest level, arms crossed protectively. "Force equals mass times acceleration."

Hale studied the woman. "Has that been disproved as well?"

"Not that I'm aware of."

"But what does it mean?"

"It was the first formula to describe the law of gravity."

Hale nodded, as though the words meant something. "Sorry for the shock."

"That's okay." Clearly she was relieved to see him leave. "Are you going to be looking for Professor Laremy?"

"I might scout around a little."

"If you find her, tell her Jennifer said to come home quick. I still want to publish my results this spring." She waited until Hale was through the doorway to say, "Oh, hey, the cops haven't said anything to you about finding a purse, have they?"

Hale turned back. "You lost a purse?"

"I thought I left it in my lab drawer. We all have a space in there for stuff. But when they let me in to check it wasn't there."

"Did you ask the cops?"

"Sure." She tried for a casual smile. "I don't think they even heard me. You know, linear minds at work. They've got a bombing, they're looking for a scientist. No room to worry about anything else."

* * *

Driving to Philippa's house was a hard business. Her absence shouted to Hale, mocking all his defenses and well-timed arguments. He turned the corner to her street and was struck hard by the memory of their first dinner together. Ryan had called him to say a dear friend of hers was attending a Washington conference. She had begged Hale to drive up from Richmond and take Philippa out, keep her company. Hale had complained loud and long that the last thing he needed in his life was another woman, particularly one who lived three thousand miles away. Do it for me, Ryan had begged. You won't be sorry.

Hale had been instantly taken by Philippa's sheer *presence*. Exercise and intelligence had honed the physicist's features to passionate dimensions. Her creamy sun-flecked skin had appeared never to have been touched by make-up. Nor needed any. Not to mention the fact that she had possessed the most incredible British accent. Listening to Philippa order a meal had been a free-form poetry performance.

Towards midnight he had spoken what he thought was the truth of his heart, that he was searching for something big enough to be worth caring for. She had watched him with those big green eyes, like jade washed by an impossibly fresh rain, letting him fall and fall and never want to rise to the surface again. He had even believed the words himself for a time.

Now Hale pulled into her driveway and sat thinking of all the times and the laughter that had taken place inside those walls. And the anger. That could not be forgotten or ignored. How he had stormed from the house, swearing never to return. Driving away, sick and yet somehow glad at the same time. Taking pleasure in closing a chapter, almost convincing himself that the move freed him for something new and better. Almost.

The house shouted sixties California, a low-slung wooden ranchstyle with tall redwood-framed windows and a cedar-shingled roof. The entire subdivision had been erected to meet a rapid spate of university expansion. Nowadays the views and the encroaching city were pushing prices beyond reach of most incoming faculty.

Hale used the key he had never bothered to return and let himself into the house. The house rang with Philippa's absence and silent accusations that Hale should have been there when she had needed him.

He grimaced as usual at the orange shag carpet Philippa had kept as homage to the past. He walked along the hallway with its weird sculptures, gifts from an arts faculty friend, and entered the sunken living room. A single sweeping glance was enough to know that whatever he sought would not be found there. If at all.

Philippa had embraced the essence of California life with a fierceness that went far beyond relishing the waves at Windandsea and Scripp's and Black's. She lined the house exterior with aloe plants, harvesting the sticky syrup and making her own natural sunscreen. She owned a car, but went almost everywhere on a four-thousand-dollar titanium-framed custom bike. She was ecologically conscious to the point of separating her kitchen garbage and fertilizing home-grown vegetables from her own mulch pit.

He steeled himself before opening the door to her bedroom, but even so it was agony. The vacant bed and her vague scent attacked with quiet vengeance. The bedside table was empty of their photograph, the one taken on the beach at Blacks after a perfect day of sunlight and pristine waves and a picnic on the sand. Philippa had run down the beach and dragged over some gay guy to take their picture. Hale had hugged her and smiled not for the camera but for the thrill of the day, the shared freedom and the love so clear between them that the guy had cooed and clucked and pretended not to know how to work the camera just so he could sit there a little longer, and be a part of all they were. Now the table's empty space mocked him and his perfectly logical reasons for leaving.

The mirror over her vanity table reflected a man who was exactly as she had described him once, too handsome for his own good. Tall and rangy and athletic, the looks and the strength and the intelligence all leaving him convinced he could slide through life without getting ripped by the thorns, so long as he managed not to care too much or for too long. Only the eyes betrayed him now, the sorrow shadows and the confused look telling him what she was not around to say. He should have been there for her.

The second bedroom had been converted into an office. The blackboard contained its usual scrawl of hieroglyphics, the filing cabinets were unlocked, the floor scattered with papers as always. Only her laptop computer was missing.

Hale was halted halfway down the hallway by a noise at the edge of his range, a soft scratching, then nothing. He was in so much of a hurry to leave he had to force himself to stand and listen to his breathing, jagged in his ears, and try to figure out what wasn't right. Nothing beyond the refrigerator clicking in and his own vague undertones of remorse. He continued on through the kitchen and attached dining alcove with its wall of glass overlooking a green and vacant garden.

By the time he entered the garage he was impatient to leave it all behind. He reached over and punched the electric door opener, using the sunlight to help him see more clearly. Hale stared at the collection of boards, his among them. Silent admonitions from a more-than-friend who had long hoped Hale would move over, or at least come more often.

He stored his wetsuit in the rental car. He went inside, pulled down his favorite board, swiped off six months of dust, walked outside and slid it through the car's side window.

He started back into the house, but the silence was too great a barrier, the reminders of his own mistakes too raw. He shut the garage door then walked around the house to lock the front door. He walked back to the car, sat listening to the still air ring with the arguments and the accusations until he could stand it no longer. He started the car and reached for his mobile phone, then put the car into reverse. Anything to outrun his regret.

* * *

"Hale, good, I needed to call you." Ryan sounded borderline frantic. "You got something for me?"

He backed out of Philippa's drive, the phone cradled on his shoulder. Wishing he could leave all the regrets behind as easily as her home. "Maybe. Where are you?"

"Office. Kennedy. But not for long. What've you got?"

"I could call back."

"No, no." Ryan was tight, clenched hard. "It's not going to get any better. They've scrubbed the launch about an hour ago. And tomorrow I've got to go to Washington. My two least favorite nightmares."

"Right." Hale decided he couldn't drive and keep up with Ryan when she was like this. He pulled over to the curb and stopped, saying, "Philippa was here, just like the neighbors said. And she knew she was leaving."

"What makes you say that?"

"Her board is gone."

"Come on, Hale. She's got how many, twelve boards? Fifteen? Her garage looks like a museum of prehistoric planks. All part of Philippa making the California dream her own."

"Listen to what I'm saying. *Her board*. The eight-foot spoon, the Brewer special. The one she wants to be buried with."

Ryan thought it over. "She knew she was leaving, then."

"More than that." Hale glanced through the rearview mirror. Had he just seen a shadow round the house? "It's like she was leaving us a message."

"Who?"

"Whoever knew her well enough to understand."

"What's it saying to you?"

Hale felt hollowed by the words to come. As though an unseen opportunity had been forever lost. "That she's not coming back."

Ryan did not mock him. Instead, the voice remained taut, searching hard. "Anything else?"

He had to sigh his way around the ache. "At least she didn't throw out my wetsuits and board."

"More than you deserve."

"Thanks a lot."

"Excuse me, Hale. In case you hadn't noticed I'm facing a crisis situation here. You got any smoking guns at your end?"

"Maybe. I went by the lab again. Spoke with Digby."

"Waste of time."

"Probably. But I found Philippa's lab assistant in her office. Jennifer something. She asked me if I had seen her purse. Said she left it in the lab and nobody would let her in to get it. Remember how we had trouble getting in? And she looked like a younger version of Philippa. A lot."

A long pause, then, "You're telling me Philippa might have used the assistant's ID to buy an airline ticket?"

Hearing Ryan say it made the concept sound unworkable. "It's probably nothing."

"I don't know." Turned quiet by the intensity of thinking fast. "It's more than the cops have come up with so far. Let me check around and see if I can find anything about this Jennifer. You didn't get a last name?"

"No."

"Doesn't matter. I can dig that up through university security. Good work, Studley. Okay, you got a pen?"

"Yes."

"You've got a two o'clock appointment with Zack Conway at Northstar." Ryan read off the address and phone number.

"This Conway can work me a contract?"

"I've done what I could. Give it your best shot for a couple of days and see what happens."

"Wait a second. Yesterday you said something I didn't understand." Trying to draw the world into tighter focus brought a soft throbbing to his temples. "Something about people in Washington and pressure about Philippa. Sorry, my head feels scrambled."

"You and me both, Studley." Weariness crept in. "I don't *know* anything. But I'll tell you just as soon as I do."

"There's nothing else you can tell me now?"

"Nothing about the 'crats in Washington. They're a total mystery, far as I'm concerned." A lingering sigh developed into the words, "But Philippa had been calling me on and off. It started about a month after your breakup. She'd pushed aside her stuff on superconductors for a while, SRC had dumped some propulsion problem in her lap. That was, oh, five months ago. Then she starts in on this work she'd been doing with the Russian scientist, did she mention that to you?"

"I think so." Back towards the end. When he had already started the separation routine, going through the well-trod motions, paying less and less attention in the process.

"I'm mixing this up. Never mind. So she's zinging around, you know what she's like, starting in one direction and suddenly she's got this other idea and off she flies. Tangents only she can understand. Anyway, the week before all this happened she called me again, so excited she can hardly get the words out. She asks me what was at the top of my wish list."

"Your what?"

"Just listen and let me tell it, okay? She knew about the budget pressure we've been under at NASA. So out of the blue she calls and asks me what I would like more than anything in the whole world. I figure she's talking business and not personal, so I tell her, a gold-laying goose that Congress doesn't know about. She just laughed and said, Wrong answer, try again. I couldn't come up with anything, so she said, Think about it. Think hard." Ryan paused for a breath, then said, "That was the first time I'd heard her laugh since you two split up. And the last time we talked."

"What does that mean to you?"

"I'm afraid to take it too far." The tension was there in her voice, that and a flickering mystery. "Look, I've –"

Ryan's words were lost in a great *whoosh* of sound, like a giant train racing past and pushing a fist of wind. The car rocked so hard Hale thought he had been struck from behind. And he had, but not by another vehicle. A single glance in his rearview mirror and he was out and running. Racing back up the street, shouting without even knowing that he was speaking at all. "Oh no! No, it can't be happening!"

Philippa's house was already gone. Flames poured from every window. The roof was lost beyond great billowing clouds of smoke. Hale dashed up the driveway, was halted by the garage door beginning to waver and blacken with the heat. He turned back toward the empty street, shouted, "Help, somebody *help me*!"

A door opened further down the road, a woman looked out, screamed a shrill note, and disappeared. He shouted anyway, "Call 911!"

Then he realized he was still holding his phone. He lifted it up, heard Ryan shouting, "*Hale!*"

"Her house, Ryan, they've torched Philippa's home!" He ran around the side, saw more flames melting the remaining glass in the two windows, pouring out with the smoke. The blaze flickered up around the edges of the roof, consuming, devouring. "It's gone, everything, just –"

"*Listen to me.* Are you all right?"

"Yes. Sure. I was in the car. But the house –"

"Is there anybody else there?"

"I don't ... A woman, but she's not ..." He glanced around, saw a street void of life, was drawn back to the inferno like a moth to its own destruction.

"*Get out of there.*"

"What?" He felt as though the words were being spoken to someone else. "Ryan, I can't –"

"Get away from there *now*." Her normally husky voice had taken on a piercing tone. "Hale, the police will tie you up for *days*."

"Ryan ..." Almost against his will he started back toward his car.

"Your job is to *find Philippa*. Do you hear me? I'll deal with the cops, see what they find. Just get out of there, Hale. *Fly.*"

6

Northstar Avionics lined Pacific Highway near the San Diego port. The offices were four-story concrete structures in the grimly squat Pentagon style of architecture. Their lack of adornment shouted accountability to a skeptical visitor. Hale sat in his car listening to the flags ripple and the halyards ring from the dozen towering poles encircling the central structure. Trying to draw the world back within the lines of logic.

Ryan had helped as much as she could from the other side of the country. She had stayed with him on the drive back to the hotel, talking him down. Maybe this was something they taught all would-be Kennedy administrators, part of the crisis control package. Whatever it was, Ryan had steadied him. Explained how the police were desperate for somebody to hang this on. How they would link him to the unwanted encounter at the lab. How he could do nothing for nobody if he was locked up. On and on she went, until his heartrate began to slow and his hands had stopped their manic gyrations. Then she had reminded him of the Northstar appointment, told him to stay in touch, and gone off to fight another fire.

Now he sat with windows open to the sultry afternoon breeze, wondering if he was ready for whatever lay inside those doors. Between him and the entrance rose a display of Northstar's latest government prize, the XLS-1, or experimental space launch. Even at one-fifth true size, it was a lofty concept.

The phone pinged from the seat beside him. When he answered, the relief in his product designer's voice rang over the three thousand miles between them. "Hale, oh man, finally, I've been calling you every twenty minutes." Jerry sounded ready to weep. "First it's busy, then there's no answer. Where the hell have you been?"

"I must have left the mobile in the car. I went in to change after –"

"Things are falling apart." The words came tumbling out. "I got called up to Mack's office a couple of hours ago. He was sharpening his knife, ready to lop me off. At first he didn't want to believe what you'd said about Northstar. It's true, isn't it?"

"I'm sitting in their parking lot as we speak."

"That's good news. Real good. I've got orders to pass you up as soon as you check in."

"Mack wants to talk with me?"

"He's got that vulture look on today. You know the one. Good luck."

"Wait –" But Jerry had put him on hold before the word was out.

A click, and the brassy tones came down the wire. "Hale, good afternoon! How are things in sunny California?"

"Fine." No push behind the word. "How're things with you?"

"Couldn't be better." The man could not have sounded more false if he had been reading from a script. "Say, Jerry told me about your coup with Northstar. Good work, Andrews. This is what we like to hear from our employees."

"Yeah, it just shows how important it is to keep our New Products team intact." He let that hang a minute, then, "So what's this about you firing our secretary behind my back?"

The false cheeriness was not phased. Don MacRuthers was in his mid-thirties and possessed an ability to decimate corporate ranks without a twinge. His slash and burn techniques had earned him a fearsome reputation at Keebler Plastics. "If you'd check by the office more often, these things wouldn't slip up on you."

"I'd be happy to, Don." Holding to calm in his voice was tough. His head felt clamped inside a solid steel brace. "Only new customers aren't found hanging around our lobby."

"In case you hadn't noticed, the firm has encountered some serious trouble. Cuts like these are inevitable."

"She was one of the finest people on our staff," Hale shot back. "Moving around so much makes it essential to have someone trustworthy back at home office."

"Sure, hey, speaking of travel, those expenses are really racking up. Management has been growing concerned about these costs of yours."

"Try hitting a half-dozen cities each week for less."

"I might have to do that."

"Meaning what, Don?"

The cool tones were intended to cut deep. "Meaning I'm not sure how much longer we're going to have a position for you."

Hale smiled a rictus grin at the cars sparkling under the late afternoon sun. "Just when I've finally managed to break us into a new market, this is the way I'm rewarded?"

"A preliminary meeting is a long way from landing a contract, Andrews."

"So what happens if I score?"

"Well, sure, hey, if you can bring home the bacon, we'd have to reconsider our options." Scurrying now to avoid being pinned down. "So do your best out there, Andrews. And keep me posted. Personally."

Hale cut the connection, cradled the phone in his arms as he sat and recovered from the latest shockwave. For once his contact with Don MacRuthers had not been all bad. At least the man had helped him assemble what remained of his spirits and energy for the meeting ahead.

Hale pushed through the main doors, gave his name to the receptionist, did a slow sweep of the flagstoned chamber. A smaller experimental shuttle mock-up rose from the center of the hall, and the side wall was adorned with a series of backlit photographs. Hale knew only what had been reported in the press. Northstar had won the half-billion-dollar initial contract to build an experimental version, the first trial had gone without a hitch, and the company was now negotiating for the contract to build and operate the real thing.

"Mr. Andrews? Zack Conway. Good of you to join us."

Hale turned to face a senior executive of the interchangeable variety. Standard grooming, greying hair, polished manner. A rigid posture all but masked the middle-aged spread. He examined Hale with a careful eye, but said only, "Those pictures sure are something, aren't they."

"Yes, sir. Thank you very much for –"

"No problem." The stare remained fastened upon him as one hand dipped into his jacket pocket and came out holding a business card. "We had to go back to the drawing boards for that baby. Right to square one. Newest of everything, those were our orders. Design a totally reusable launch vehicle. No disposable parts, nothing jettisoned, not even the fuel tanks. Which meant we had to come up with a totally new propulsion system."

Hale examined the card, read, "Vice President for Engineering."

"That's what they call me today. Tomorrow it might be official dogsbody if we don't win the contract for building the shuttles themselves." He offered Hale a visitor's ID. "Clip that onto your lapel. Yessir, the XLS was one for the record books. Designed and built in just twenty-two months. That's a robot-driven version you see there, required a miniaturized Cray supercomputer for navigation. Get a load of this take-off, will you. Damn near perfect performance."

Hale offered a card of his own. "It certainly is good of you to see me like –"

"Don't mention it." The man took the card and stuffed it in his pocket without a glance. He pointed them towards the bank of elevators. "But all that's history now. The engineering boys did their job, now it's back to business as usual."

"I'm not sure I follow you."

"Politics, son. Politics. We're fighting tooth and nail to build the real thing. You'd think having made the trial version we'd be shoo-ins for the contract. But Congress is getting pressure thrown at it from every possible angle. The current shuttles have been in use for almost a quarter of a century, they're to be phased out over the next decade. Whoever builds the replacement gets to run them. In this world of diminishing budgets, far as we're concerned it's win this contract or face the rubbish heap of history."

He led Hale into the elevator, stabbed the button. "The days when we could just sit back and live off the government gravy train are over. Lot of people out there like to think otherwise, but I know. I spent a lot of time in Washington on this one. That's where I met Ryan Reeves, understand she's a pal of yours."

"We go back a long way," Hale agreed.

"Fine lady. Good performer. Honest as the day is long. Wish there were more like her." Conway studied the elevator's closed doors for a moment, his jaw muscle flexing, then he went on, "But tough times require tough methods. Isn't that what they say?"

Hale struggled with the impression that he was missing the main message. "I suppose it is."

"Right." Conway shouldered his way out of the elevator and entered an office over an acre wide. "Northstar Avionics has been hit by military spending cutbacks just like the rest of the industry. Over the past two years we've undergone serious retrenchment, cutting back orders to outside contractors by almost thirty percent, laying off five thousand employees at this facility alone."

He led Hale down one identical passage after another, past thousands of grey metal filing cabinets. Nothing else he saw matched. Individual office spaces were formed by particle-board partitions. No two chairs were alike, or desks or trash cans or sofas or lamps. Hale felt he had to ask, "So where does that leave me?"

"We haven't accepted tenders from new suppliers for over a year. We hardly have enough business to justify work we are doing with our current group." Conway held to an impatient pace, twisting and turning his way through the maze. Horrible acoustics were aggravated by low paneled ceilings. The atmosphere was very military, very male-dominated. Few women, most of the men overweight but tough. Sexist pin-up calendars. Loud crude voices. Greying crew-cuts and numerous tattoos. "Many suppliers lost money on recent business. But they keep on with these relatively small orders in hopes that we can do bigger things in the future. We owe them for this loyalty."

"I see." And he did. Purchasing had refused to see him outright, so he had been foisted on one of Ryan's corporate allies. Hale grew grimly despondent over being deposited into one of these cubicles, offered a brutally uncomfortable chair, given a carefully measured fifteen minutes, then swept back on the street. There to await Don MacRuthers' next phone call, and the end of his corporate life.

To Hale's surprise, Conway continued past the last line of cubicles and into a corner executive suite. The secretary looked up at their arrival and presented them a smile. "Ms. Durrant just arrived downstairs."

"No getting around it, then." The words came out hard, metallic. "Might as well tell her to come on up."

The secretary cast him a worried glance, then resumed her smile for Hale. "How will you take your coffee, Mr. Andrews?"

"Black is fine, thank you." He followed Conway into a office lined with mock-oak paneling. Green carpeting and olive drapes tainted the sunlight and gave the room the feel of an aquarium.

"Have a seat over there." Conway walked around the oversized desk, eased himself down, gripped the chair-arms, said, "Understand from Ms. Reeves you're the man to locate Professor Laremy."

"I wish I could be so sure."

"How much do you know about her work on superconductors?"

"Not much at all."

"Been forced to take an interest myself, though it hasn't been easy." He halted at a knock on the door. "Coffee for our guest, Gladys?"

"Yessir, can I get you some more?"

"No thanks, I've had my quota." He leaned back in his chair, watched impassively as Hale lifted the cup.

He sipped, then struggled not to gag.

Conway's mood lightened perceptibly. "Pretty awful, isn't it."

Hale felt grit coat the inside of his throat like scalding sandpaper. He nodded once, tried to swallow again, felt the load shift another inch or so.

"Gladys is the best doggoned secretary I've ever had. But I swear, she makes a cup of coffee that'd do a cement truck justice. Tried to tell her, but she's proud of that stuff, believe it or not. Decided it wasn't worth hurting her feelings." He spun his chair around, pointed at the potted palm in the window-corner. "Dump your cup in there. Don't know what I'd do if she ever found out why we're losing so many bushes. Now where were we?"

Hale resumed his seat and swished his tongue from side to side, trying to dislodge the granules trapped underneath. "Superconductors."

"Right. It's the coming thing, you mark my words. The next century, there's a good chance it will power a revolution as great as the one we're seeing with computers right now.

Already the first signs are becoming evident. Magnetic resonance imaging in hospitals, particle accelerators, even geological sensors for oil prospecting."

Conway's head jerked up at the sound of muffled voices in the outer office. The momentary lightening of his mood vanished. "I guess that must be Ms. Durrant now."

Hale rose with the older man, turned at the sound of the door opening, and took the next blow at gut level.

* * *

"The Space Research Consortium links together the activities of several companies," the newcomer told him. "We specialize in new projects, new directions for our company members."

Hale's glance at Conway must have shown how helplessly at sea he felt, for the older guy cleared his throat and said, "It was the brainchild of some of the Northstar board. Got under way, oh, must be four years back." Conway held to the same metallic tone he had used to greet the woman, his gaze as flat as his voice. "Other companies joined because they had to."

"Consolidation is the only hope these days," Natalie Durrant agreed helpfully.

"Our competitors are being forced to do the same thing." Conway waved a vague hand towards the woman seated alongside Hale. "Plus they joined all the R&D operations together, make our research dollars go further. Get us out of the rut of current aging products, they said, look for new ventures."

"We won you the experimental space launch contract," Natalie Durrant replied, cheerfully buoyant in the face of Conway's sourness. "I'd say that's a pretty good example of what we can do for our member companies, wouldn't you, Zack?"

"Hard to tell what we would have done on our own," he said, his gaze locked on Hale. "Since we didn't have a chance."

"Oh, you." She leaned across the distance separating her from Hale. "Our dear Mr. Conway is a hold-out for bygone days."

Hale turned to her then, willing himself to keep his eyes fastened on her face. But it was hard. Very hard.

The woman seated beside him was at direct odds to everything else about this place. Dark good looks, flowing raven hair, perfect complexion, impossibly long legs disappearing into a tight navy skirt. Trim form barely concealed beneath matching jacket and ivory blouse. Natalie Durrant had a predator's sureness to her poise, a magnetic power to her smile and flashing eyes. "Consolidation under the SRC umbrella means we now have factories in thirty-one states. That's a tremendous amount of political clout to bring to bear when we're pushing for a new contract." A single warning glance at Conway, an added, "Like now."

Hale knew he'd been blindsided, tried to hide behind company-driven enthusiasm. "We at Keebler Plastics would certainly like to have the chance to work with your group, Ms. Durrant."

"Call me Natalie." The gaze returned to him, lingered. "Northstar is definitely working with high-caliber suppliers these days."

Natalie Durrant was the image of a true California girl, far more than the pin-up blonde. Her features displayed a *mélange* of nations and bloods. Eyes the shape and color of roasting almonds were set within sculpted cheek-bones. She was aware of her splendor, ready to use it at a moment's notice. Totally *on*. "We have been funding an increasing proportion of Professor Laremy's research budget. We were particularly interested in working with her on new forms of propulsion."

"Propulsion," Hale repeated slowly, his gaze flicking back to Conway. But this time the man refused to meet his eye. "I thought Philippa was working on superconductors."

"Professor Laremy worked on what we asked her to," Natalie replied, and took the sting from her voice with a grand smile. "We had several new avenues which opened up recently, and all of them needed to be checked out. She didn't mention this to you?"

"Not that I'm aware."

"Well, we never meant to take her from the principal course of her research, of course. She probably thought it was incidental." But Natalie seemed disappointed in him.

"Or maybe she was respecting SRC's rigid stance on confidentiality," Conway muttered toward the window.

Natalie shot him another glance, then rose slowly to her feet, blocking Hale's view of the older guy. "Why don't you and I go have a look at the supplier's protocol, Mr. Andrews?"

"Call me Hale." He stood with her, offered his hand across the desk. "Thanks for seeing me like this, Mr. Conway. I certainly do hope we –"

"Right." The older man briefly returned Hale's grip while keeping to his blank gaze and his seat. Conway looked around him and said loudly, "Sure would be nice to know what the status of the new shuttle contract is."

"SRC will inform you when it is appropriate." She almost sang her reply as she walked away.

"Seems like it'd make sense for the guy who's supposed to build the damn thing to know what's happening."

Natalie was already at the door. "This way, Hale."

* * *

"Professor Laremy loves the challenge of solving problems. That, more than any future potential of superconductors, has held our interest."

Natalie's voice was like the rest of her, honeyed and sharp. She led him back through the maze of cubicles, walking just far enough ahead for him to appreciate her movements. Her bulky filofax bounced enticingly off one hip with each step. Where everything else surrounding him was faded and drab and old-fashioned military, this woman flashed like a Times Square billboard. "Defense spending is being cut to the bone. Anything more and we're talking amputation. We can't concern ourselves with research projects that might show results five years ahead. Those days are dead and gone."

She turned down an aisle leading towards the grimy side windows. "Professor Laremy took on problems outside her particular field because we asked her. Every time she gave our request her number-one attention. None of this disdainful attitude because it wasn't her field. As a result we funded her semiconductor research even as we've dropped a lot of our other external researchers by the wayside."

She swung into a cubicle like all the others. Irritation flashed when she saw it was empty. "Where's he gotten to now? I specifically ordered him to wait for me."

Hale stepped up beside her, caught a whiff of some exotic scent. "Something wrong?"

"Oh, these former military guys really get up my nose." She slid into the seat behind the metal desk, motioned him into the cubicle's other chair. "The whole defense industry is basically the same. There's tremendous resistance to any form of improvement or managerial change. These old-style macho Marine jocks see it as a gimmick. Look at this place, he doesn't even have his forms on computer." She pointed at a long row of massive binders above the desk, all identical save for a series of letters and numbers stamped on each spine. "Guys like this are *terrified* of change. They know an enormous amount about a tiny sliver of defense purchasing. That's where they gain their importance. It's a mentality imported from the military, along with all the other macho crap you see around this place."

He watched as she ran her finger along the line of several dozen binders, picked one out, let it drop with a clatter to the desk. The motions caused her skirt to hike up and reveal more stockinged thigh. Hale struggled to focus on the business at hand. "You're saying a new supplier like me isn't welcome because I might disturb the status quo?"

"See, I knew you were a fast learner." She opened the notebook to reveal reams of flimsy pages. "FAR's. Ever seen these before?"

"I don't think so."

"Federal Acquisition Regulations. Volumes of the things. All computerized now, accessible on the internet, you'd think this guy might save himself some time and leave the Stone Age behind. As it is, every time the Department Of Defense institutes a change, he's got to go through, take out the old specs, insert the new."

She had a tiny mole just above and to the left of her upper lip. Hale fought down a sudden impulse to lean over, lick it off. "We need to get a set of these?"

"No, I just told you, it's all available electronically. I'll give you the listings for your product range later." She flipped the pages. "It gives you all the hoops you've got to jump through. Look here for example. Descriptions of your production line, air quality control, machine specifications, minority employment percentages, the works. You've got to supply us all of this, and fast."

Hale leaned closer, pretending to study the page. Her perfume was a heady mixture of scents, a lot of it her own. He took a long breath, felt like he was taking a hit of olfactory sex. "I'll get someone on it tomorrow."

"Then there's the company inspection, but we can wait on that for a while. Think you're up to it?"

He forced himself back in his seat. "Absolutely."

"Do you know, I really believe you are." Natalie reached for the phone, dialed a number from memory. "While you're here, we might as well try to get you in to see SRC's chief of procurement. Buzz is super-busy, but he might squeeze you in if I ask nice. Let's see, he has a board meeting in the morning, how about three o'clock tomorrow afternoon?"

He caught the shift in tone, knew he was being given the

polite dismissal. Hale rose to his feet, said, "Three o'clock works for me."

Natalie said into the phone, "Buzz Cobb, please." Then she lifted her gaze to where he stood, gave him the hundred-watt smile, said, "I've just remembered, I have an opening in my book. Why don't we do a dinner tomorrow night?"

"Sounds great."

"Yeah, it does, doesn't it." She pulled a card from the sleeve of her filofax, scribbled a number, passed it over. "That's my direct line. Call me tomorrow morning, I'll confirm everything."

"Thanks a lot, Natalie. We're really grateful for the chance to bid on any ..." Hale let his voice drop off as she turned and started on the phone with a quick little wave of dismissal.

7

Philippa stared at the reams of paper piled upon her desk, strewn over her floor, and pinned to the wall in front of her. The answer was so bloody close, the odor of success was stronger than the diesel fumes floating in through her balcony doors. The solution was right there, and she couldn't bring it together.

Eight days and nights of calculations and theoretical arguments were spread like a snowfall of ink-dappled paper about her room. Every surface was decorated with arguments between herself and the experiment that had blown up her lab and her future. She knew she was near the answer. But she could not find the doorway. Philippa rose from her chair, raised both arms and clawed through her rat's nest of auburn curls. She was tired, and not just from another day of endless searching. This forced segregation from life was wearing her down.

She stepped out onto the balcony, stood listening to the Baja din drifting up from below. Road noise and drunken revelry and street musicians and a band playing by the pool – the cacophony melted with the desert heat and became a single mocking note. Taunting her. Telling her to give up, admit defeat, accept that she could not do anything right. Especially now.

The sense of overwhelming defeat was not because she was alone. She had been solitary most of her life. Her family had treated her fascination with science as an illness, some grave problem that needed treatment and a spell of recovery. School had been the same, only worse. Philippa Laremy had dared enter the hallowed halls of physics and beat the assertive nerds on their own turf. Her colleagues were slow to forgive, and never to forget.

Philippa pushed herself off the railing and walked back inside, resigning herself to the tumult of attempted slumber in an empty bed. Strange that here and now, six months and a thousand miles from her last encounter with the man she still loved, she would feel his absence most of all. She did not need him as much as hunger for him. She could almost taste Hale, feel his supple strength under her empty hands, her lack was that great.

While she was preparing for bed, a sudden memory halted her with her nightdress half-way over her head. Well, nightdress was perhaps too grand a word for an oversized T-shirt commemorating the fourth international surf festival in Lacanau, France. The memory was of Hale's mother, and the first and only time he had taken her home.

Hale had always been very closed about his past. Not secretive; if she asked him a question, he would answer. But the responses were given in the sandpaper dryness of a person discussing someone else. Someone who meant little, someone unimportant. When she asked about his reticence he would simply say, I prefer to reinvent myself with each new day. Perhaps that should have warned her off. But by then she was already lost.

Sometimes she felt as though she had been vanquished since before they even met, as though on some cosmic dimension where time was a long spiral viewed as a unity, their lives and fates had always been intertwined. And Hale's departure threatened the entire universe with destruction.

Her memory swirled and coalesced with the force of boundless universal strands. That particular summer weekend they had traveled down to Virginia Beach, enduring the crowds and the drinkers and the paltry waves. Hale had watched her as they walked the beach, waiting to pounce on her for criticizing his home surfspot. But she had remained silent, content to be with him and let the place speak for itself. He knew she was desperate for him to move to California. Talking about it here would be overkill.

Towards sunset they had taken their boards and paddled to the horizon, so far from shore the condos became lost in the golden haze. Dolphins had come to share the evening, trilling their squeaky song and turning the world to magic. She had thought her heart would explode from the challenge of cramming so much happiness inside.

The next morning he had taken her to his parents' home.

They had driven through a section of Norfolk which had reminded her of paper dolls she had cut out as a child: house after bleak rundown house. The forty-block section was a product of the post-war construction boom, nine hundred houses thrown up in less than two years, accommodation for naval and civilian personnel brought in to staff the shipyards and naval base.

Vague attempts at individualization marked some of the houses with shutters and shrub borders and glassed-in sunrooms. Others were scarred by hard use and disregard and boarded-up windows. Hale's voice was metallic as he drove and recounted the story of his father drinking and getting fired and working as a detective and finally vanishing.

The bungalow was a little more pristine than its neighbors, surrounded by a matchbox of a lawn and a chain-link fence. Hale explained that he had stopped asking his mother to move; she was determined to stay there till she died, so he paid a local kid to keep the place looking as nice as possible.

The woman who stood in the door smoking a cigarette and watching them approach lived off a policeman's pension and what Hale sent her. She did not seem to have any life of her own. Philippa spent the ninety longest minutes of her entire existence struggling to converse with a woman who seemed utterly emptied of life. Doing it for Hale, enduring this impossible stretching of time because of the hollow sadness she saw every time she looked in his direction.

* * *

Philippa sighed her way down into the bed, aching for what might have been. She had always thought Hale to be incredibly strong. It was only now, when his energy was not there to fill the night with the thrill of being together, that she recognized his strength to be as fatally flawed as his mother's. He had been weakened by life's experiences as well, only in a different direction.

Philippa turned off her light and tried to pound her pillow into comfortable submission. If only she could bring herself to hate the man.

* * *

The dream was there waiting for her.

She was stolen away with such ease it felt as though all the tension of the past few weeks propelled her forward and into sweet release. One moment she was trying hard not to cry into her pillow, the next she was drifting through clouds flecked with bits and pieces of emotional rain.

She drifted through dream clouds for one blissful instant, and then she found herself seated at a conference luncheon. She recognized it instantly as the Washington conference where she had met Alexis Vilnieff.

The international physicists' symposium had taken place in the huge new Marriott attached to the Georgetown University campus. Alexis had been impossible to pin down before then; he was a person in demand, author of a dozen seminal papers and known as someone with a far-reaching mind. Which was precisely why Philippa had wanted to speak with him privately, that and their mathematical-laced correspondence of the previous eight months. But there was no privacy. Their single moment of confidential talk had been while walking together to lunch, down a hall crowded with the chattering multinational delegations. There he had simply said, I am being watched.

The shock of that statement had stayed with her until they were seated at the round table for twelve, and Alexis had pulled out the pictures of his wife and child. Granting her the space to collect herself, to smile and lower her head over the pictures, and then realizing that he really did want to introduce them through this series of blurred photographs.

Showing off the photographs was his way of saying Philippa was a new friend. This friendship required that she know about this most precious aspect of his life. Not just about his work. Not more about his incredible mind. His family. Philippa sat beside a man whose eyes danced with an almost uncontrollable energy, his thoughts scattering gamma rays even when he was eating. Alexis possessed the most phenomenal ability to associate random aspects of the universe and come up with new concepts that she had ever encountered. Yet he was desperate for her to understand who he truly was by seeing his wife and child.

Only now she was dreaming. And somehow, even as she sat there and leaned over the photographs this second time, she realized that it was indeed a dream and not a return to the shock of that earlier reality.

In the dream she watched herself lay a photograph out beside that of Alexis' family. Only hers was blank.

She gripped her picture with fierce need, this glossy white square with nothing to show, nothing at all, only she insisted on making Alexis look. Which he did, slowly and carefully. Forcing her to look with him as well.

Then Alexis turned his gaze back to his own photographs. He stroked the picture of his smiling child with one tobacco-stained finger and said, "You need a family of your own. It is the way for you to become whole."

"I thought I was going to have that with Hale." Able to speak his name now, muffled from the pain by knowing it was nothing more than a dream.

"No." Alexis gave her a knowing smile, one that showed a wisdom of heart almost as great as his wisdom of mind. "No. You wanted to possess this man and hold to all else as well. How can this be? Your life is already so full, how could you treat him as a new component, a new factor to add to life's experiment only when it suited you?"

"It wasn't like that at all." But the protest lacked force, and the little girl in Alexis' photograph mocked her.

"Sure, sure, you give what is comfortable. What *should* be enough. But what does the man need? What does he *require*?"

"I don't understand," she said, and wished it was true.

"He ran because you *let* him," Alexis said, no longer smiling.

Philippa knew she was dreaming. She knew she could twist the dream hard and wrench herself free. And she should do that. Should depart because it was no longer nice being there in this dream. No longer safe.

"Here." He reached back into his pocket, as though going for a second photograph.

And suddenly the room was empty.

Only the two of them were seated there now, in a hall decked out for a thousand. Empty and echoing with the sudden force of Alexis and his enigmatic smile. "I have something else for you."

But it was not a photograph he pulled from his pocket. It was a ball of light.

He held a shimmering globe about eighteen inches in diameter. He set it between them, and left it hanging in mid-air. The light was so brilliant it made her want to cry. She forced herself to reach out, touch the cold surface, and ask, "What is it?"

The expression changed then. The light made his smile as sad as his eyes. The room echoed like a great cavern as he leaned forward and whispered, "A consolation prize."

She woke up then. The force of waking blasted her from the bed so swiftly she was on her feet before she realized she had moved. She walked to the window and swept back the drapes and stepped onto the balcony.

A salt-laden sea breeze tugged at her T-shirt, warm and enveloping. She stood there and sobbed. Her tears clung like they were draped there by the breeze. She cried so hard she could scarcely draw breath.

She did not weep over sorrow from the loss of Hale, nor the truth in what the dream had told her. Nor was it the realization that the next step of her experiments was suddenly clear. No.

She wept because in her heart of hearts she knew that a very good man was dead.

8

Before departing Friday for the Orlando airport and Washington DC, Ryan called Harry's office. When she got his voice-mail, she left a terse message that she was off for a one-day trip and should be back that night. Not that she was especially eager to see Harry again. She still felt singed by the previous evening's argument.

After seven days in California, she had arrived back the previous afternoon and driven directly to Kennedy; a crisis had erupted in conjunction with the cancelled launch. She had finally arrived home after eleven, only to be confronted by Harry in premium fight mode – so what if a friend was missing, if it wasn't that plus a launch emergency it would have been something else, what about her family – that sort of thing. Ryan had endured his tirade in silence because Harry was keeping his voice down. Harry tended to amp himself through stages when she argued back. Ryan wanted to let the kids sleep.

That morning the home routine had held a poignant flavor, as she had sipped her coffee and watched her two kids prepare for their summer adventures. Jeff had pretended that all was well, trying hard to put some enthusiasm into his voice over his mom being home. Kitty had noticed only because she wanted to have her ears pierced. And her navel. Ryan had held to her smile as Kitty exclaimed over how all her ten-year-old friends were doing it, and felt another few threads of her life blown to tatters by the storm.

As she departed, Ryan stopped by her secretary's desk to ask if she had found out anything about Philippa's lab assistant. Gloria was shared by all four assistant deputies but made her impossible job more personal by giving Ryan preferential treatment. Gloria informed her, "According to the registrar's office, the lady's full name is Jennifer Velasquez. Final year of post-doc studies. Dr. Laremy is her supervisor."

"Anything on a Ms. Velasquez flying somewhere last week?"

"I'm having a little more trouble on that one. The airlines want to know why we don't go through proper channels."

"Can't." Terseness was her only defense against unanswerable questions. "Washington."

Gloria accepted the reasoning as only a civil servant could. "I've located someone with the airport authorities who seems suitably impressed that NASA is calling."

"Great. Call me on my cell-phone soon as you hear anything." Ryan turned towards the door, and said to the engineer blocking her path, "Chuck, your timing is worse than awful."

The engineer was nervous but held his ground. "Something's come up that can't wait."

"You'll have to talk as I walk, then." She was tempted to brush him off until Monday, but knew that Chuck Evans would never bother her without a real reason. "Come on."

Over the past few years, NASA had been busy redefining itself. Back in the Apollo days, Congress had thrown fistfuls of money at the space authority and said, do whatever it takes, spend whatever you need, just get us to the moon. Now everything was governed by results, getting the biggest bang for each buck spent. As a result, NASA was shedding personnel and missions like never before.

Nowadays, almost everything was subcontracted out to private companies. There were only twelve hundred NASA employees remaining at the Kennedy Space Center, down from a high of over thirty thousand. The remaining personnel were employed by these new private contractors.

Chuck Evans worked for United Space Alliance, one of only four Prime Contractors operating at Kennedy, or primes for short. The others were Boeing, Lockheed-Martin, and the newest kid on the megacorporate block, SRC. These four primes contracted directly with NASA-Kennedy to supply equipment and services. The United Space Alliance was contracted to prepare the shuttles for launch and deliver them on schedule. They were going head-to-head with the Space Research Consortium for the construction and launching of the new shuttle fleet. The ground was already littered with bodies and smoke from the struggle for the experimental launch. Now that the trial run had gone off well, SRC should have held the lead. But the USA corporation was a far older and more experienced fighter on the federal battlefield, and was using every weapon in its arsenal to win this prize. Ryan had seen bets being laid up and down the halls over who would win this contest. She felt the outcome remained too close to call.

Chuck Evans headed several teams, including those responsible for the orbiter launch pads. Orbiter was the term generally used around NASA for the space shuttle. He also supervised all non-destructive materials testing – checking the shuttles' vulnerable points prior to each mission. This covered everything from the nose ceramic heat-shielding plates to the aft-skirting – the points where the orbiter was connected to the solid fuel boosters and the external fuel tank. In NASA-speak, Chuck's team was tasked with examining how exposed materials reacted within their load envelope.

Like most of the people Ryan worked with on the engineering side, Chuck found administration as baffling as Arabic. Early on he had decided he could trust Ryan, and now came to her with every major problem.

Ryan marched down the hallway and demanded, "So what's the matter now?"

"It's the payload bay connector on launch pad 39B. The seal has cracked again."

She stabbed the elevator button. "You have got to be kidding me."

"I wish I was." Chuck was tall, overweight, tired and graying. Like most of the engineers, he lived and breathed his work. Ryan classed the astronauts with the engineers, only amped and focused to an unthinkably higher degree.

Ryan vastly preferred the engineers to the admin paper-pushers with their bureaucratic connections and blatant self-importance. "That's the third time it's happened this launch, Chuck. It can't go on."

"I know, I know. It's been keeping me up nights." He had a nervous habit of pushing his glasses up tight against his forehead. On days when things weren't going right, the frame made a distinct imprint on the space between his eyebrows. Today the spot was bright red. "But I think maybe I've come up with an idea."

The elevator doors opened. "Ride with me."

Ryan stepped in, did a hurried mental calculation, forced her lungs to take a normal breath. The energy and time pressure upon which Kennedy ran was a palpable force. It held everyone in its grip, from the tourist-bus driver to the visiting Washington politico. Most of the time Ryan loved the high, adored the thrill of pushing for impossible goals. But sometimes the feeling of being yanked in a dozen different directions left her chest pounding like an erratic jackhammer.

The shuttle's payload bay was kept tightly sealed while the orbiter was grounded. The seal connected the bay doors to the launchpad's retractable arm, which worked like a giant rubber accordion. Payload referred to whatever the shuttle was scheduled to deliver into orbit. These satellites and experiments contained highly sensitive instruments designed to operate in a vacuum. Kennedy's salt air and dust and sand would have a disastrous effect. Which meant that on earth the payload had to be kept as sterile as a hospital operating room, and as dust-free as a computer chip lab. The connecting seal between the launchpad gantry and the orbiter had to be airtight.

But the seals were not holding. The problem was the Florida atmosphere. Salt was one of the most corrosive elements in the natural world.

"I'll authorize another seal. I have to. But we've got to find a way around this. Three seals blown on one orbiter, you can't imagine the cost overruns we're facing here."

"Yes I can. And that's what I wanted to talk with you about." Another jamming of the glasses up tight, then, "What would you say if I came up with an answer that ended the sealing problem once and for all?"

Ryan started forward before the elevator doors had fully retracted. "I don't know what I'd say. But I'd sure be interested."

"I thought you would." Chuck's smile momentarily rearranged his fatigue-lines. "It's going to cost you, though."

"Anything you engineers come up with is expensive. It's some rule they teach you at MIT." Ryan pushed through the outer doors and scampered for her car. "Do it right, but make it cost a kazillion bucks."

Chuck decided not to try and keep up. "I'll have something for you as quick as I can."

* * *

Heat and humidity blanketed the road to Orlando.

One almost always came with the other in Florida, especially when June started building towards the hurricane season. The drive to the Orlando airport was a forty-minute straight shot down the Bee-Line Expressway, almost empty this time of year. During the winter tourist season, driving somewhere in a hurry was the stuff of nightmares. The coastal routes grew full of elderly tourists down to visit their parents. Getting stuck behind a lumbering vehicle with out-of-state plates left Ryan feeling like she was trying to drive through cream of broccoli soup.

Flat green wetlands stretched out in both directions under a solid blue dome. Heat shimmered off the highway like a mirror to her jangled thoughts. Her mind spun through the problems at home, the situation at Kennedy, the time with Hale, the mystery surrounding Philippa. It always came back to that.

The fire at Philippa's had alarmed Ryan less than having it happen while Hale was there. At the time he had been too rattled for her to discuss the deeper questions, and yesterday evening he had been torn between worry over Philippa and anxiety about his job. The San Diego police had nothing to report, could not either confirm or deny that the fire was deliberate. Ryan tried hard not to worry over having thrown Hale headfirst into the lion's den. She should be out there herself, she knew it for a fact. But the crisis at Kennedy and now this call from Washington could not be put off.

Yesterday a leak had developed in one of the shuttle's inboard oxygen tanks at T minus 46 hours. Despite the engineers' best efforts, repairs could not be completed in time to hold to the launch window. Two days prior to lift-off wasn't so bad. The year before, computerized systems had chopped down one second *into* the launch. That had been a terrible moment, really terrible. The most dangerous time of all for halting a launch was the instant of ignition, when the slightest mishap would have spelled disaster.

The orbiter's liquid fuel was highly pressurized, feeding in constantly to replenish what was being burned off. The danger came not only from the shuttle itself, but also from the feedlines, any of which could have torn loose and transformed the shuttle into a stationary ball of fire.

Ryan and several thousand other launch specialists had held a single unified breath as emergency systems had doused the entire shuttle with a liquid-gas flame retardant, supercooling the smoking engines. The seconds had ticked down, the shuttle had remained intact, the fuel had been drained, and finally her heart had restarted. That had been awful. Two days prior to launch was nothing.

* * *

Ryan spent the taxi drive in from Washington's National Airport worrying over the summons. The call from Senator Townsend's office the day before was as strange as it was urgent. NASA's new Lead Center Concept meant that Kennedy no longer answered directly to headquarters in Washington. For most operations, the Kennedy staff reported to Johnson Space Center in Texas. The stated objective was to eliminate the duplication of activities and expertise. In truth, Johnson had fought Kennedy over the headquarters connection for years. Johnson took over control of the shuttle once it was cleared for earth orbit. Johnson wanted administrative control of the launch as well. In fact, Johnson would have closed Kennedy down entirely, if a suitable launch pad could be erected in Texas. Johnson remained extremely jealous over all the public attention paid to the Kennedy Space Center. Dangerously jealous.

The blackest rumors associated with the new XLS-1 shuttle-replacement vehicle was that Johnson had insisted on a design which would make closing Kennedy a genuine possibility. Ryan seriously doubted this would ever happen. A dozen surveys had shown that not even the vast Texan deserts compared with the Atlantic Ocean's latitude of safety in case of an aborted launch.

Johnson fiercely guarded their connection with Washington power and Washington money. Ryan did not mind this in the least. She had little love for Washington. The primary difficulty she faced was Johnson's natural inclination to take care of home first.

Today's summons was cause for a bureaucratic red alert. Any contact Kennedy had with Washington was routed through Ryan's boss. Ryan had pointed this out to Senator

Townsend's stone-voiced secretary. The secretary had ignored this as she had Ryan's statement that she had been trying to contact Clay East, the senator's chief aide, for over a week. The secretary had simply repeated that Ryan was ordered to appear. As the senator was Minority Chief of the NASA oversight committee, Ryan had no choice but to obey.

When her taxi started across the Fourteenth Street Bridge, she rolled down her window and allowed her attention to be drawn outwards. The day was almost enough to make her like Washington. Sky of endless blue. Breeze from April, not late June, cool and dry. Half the town on vacation, the other half filling the outdoor cafes. Wide-eyed tourists sharing sidewalks with strolling locals. Smiles in abundance. Monuments and buildings sparkling pristine as the American dream. The Washington myth alive and well. At least for today.

Senator Townsend's office was in the Russell Building, one of the older structures along Independence Avenue. The lobby was vast and pillared and marbled and loud. Ryan gave her name to the security guard and was directed toward one of the brass-doored elevators. She exited on the fourth floor, walked down the marble-tiled hall, entered the senator's outer office, and stopped cold. Fuller Glenn, Deputy Chief Administrator of NASA's Kennedy Space Center and Ryan's boss, was seated in the cramped reception area.

The man was every inch the political appointee. Silver hair was sleeked back from a cosmetic tan. His suit was as tailored as his habitual smile, the one there to greet Ryan when he turned away from the receptionist. "How was your trip?"

"Fine." Ryan set her briefcase down on the center table. "I didn't know you were joining me."

The senator's offices were an overcrowded warren of hyperactivity. Staffers hustled about bearing papers and cellphones. Ryan and Fuller were isolated by the clamor. Fuller waved her into a neighboring chair and replied, "I was over at headquarters this morning, told them you were called up for a meeting with Townsend. It was like I'd poked a stick into a beehive."

No surprise there. Any unauthorized contact between NASA staffers and the Washington money machine was a reason for high-octane panic. "Any idea what this is about?"

A hesitation, then, "Better leave that for the Senator to discuss."

"I've been trying to reach you all week."

"I've gotten your messages." The smile assured all who glanced their way that everything was cool, calm, totally under control. "Didn't seem like you were making much headway in locating that scientist pal of yours."

"I'm working on it." Ryan tried to see beneath the man's mask. "What's so special about this one scientist doing NASA-related research?"

"Anything that has captured Senator Townsend's eye is special. It defines the word." A gaze hard as iron turned her way. "We clear on that point?"

"Perfectly."

"Good." He smoothed his jacket. "Anything else we need to discuss?"

"You mean, like the scrubbed launch?"

"I know all about that. The news caught me in the final throes of our interim budget meeting. You can't imagine how well that went down." Fuller touched the knot of his tie, continued softly, "The Johnson boys jumped all over that launch problem. They always do. Anything to make us look bad, emphasize how they handle us better than Washington ever could, keep us on a tight leash." Fuller smiled at a passing face he probably did not even see. "I could have throttled the pair of them with my bare hands."

A pair of trousered legs halted in front of her. "Ms. Reeves, so glad you could make it up."

She rose to her feet, looked up at a vaguely familiar face. "Mr. East?"

"The one and only." The senator's chief aide was as bulky as she recalled. And as polished. He swallowed her hand in his, nodded to her boss. "Hello, Fuller. Good of you to join us."

"Anything we can do for the Senator, right, Ryan?"

"Absolutely."

"Come on in. The Senator is most anxious to meet you, Ms. Reeves." For a man carrying the vestiges of too many years on the Washington political meal ticket, Clay East moved with a light grace. He ushered them past the receptionist and back into the senator's private sanctum. "Got somebody for you to meet, Senator."

"This must be the young lady I've been hearing so much about." The senator moved around his desk, hand outstretched. "Ryan Reeves, do I have that right?"

"Yes sir, Senator."

"An honor. A genuine honor. Always nice to meet our allies down at Kennedy, right, Clay?"

"I've been briefing the senator on your fine work," the aide told the room.

"Indeed he has. Why don't you have a seat right over there." He kept hold of Ryan's hand until she had started her descent. Then he turned and nodded. "Afternoon, Fuller. Good to see you again."

"My pleasure as always, Senator."

Townsend settled into the chair next to Ryan's. His jowls spread in relief, almost covering his collar. The senator was midway through his fourth term, and twenty-one years of the Washington highlife had been deeply imprinted. "Now then. We of the NASA oversight committee have had our eye on several local admin personnel. Been trying to identify people who've taken our changes to heart. The ones doing their best to draw NASA into the twenty-first century, right, Clay?"

"While the rest of them kick and scream and do their damnedest to slow down progress," his aide intoned. "Throwing a wrench in the works every chance they get."

"Exactly. From the way some of your colleagues have reacted to our budget-reducing drive, you'd think they were being asked to part with their eye teeth."

Ryan felt a mild defense was called for. "I find our team at Kennedy to be behind the changes one hundred percent. We all recognize that efficiency and cost-effectiveness are watchwords for the future."

Clay East leaned forward. "Then let's just say some of your team recognize the need more than others."

"Clay has brought a couple of your reports to my attention. The ones suggesting further ways to coordinate tasks and streamline operations. That is exceptional work. And that is why I insisted Clay here bring you up, so I could personally be the one to convey our thanks."

"I'm just part of a team." Ryan glanced at her boss, but was met by the same dimpled smile. All fine, all under control. "If any praise is due, it should really include us all."

"We're well aware of the fine work Fuller and his group are putting in," East responded. "But this meeting is about you."

"Exactly. Being a team player is an important part of the Washington ballgame."

The leather chair squeaked as Townsend shifted his bulk forward. "Ms. Reeves, I asked you up here today to offer you a position as chief liaison to NASA's Oversight Committee."

A lightening bolt through the ceiling could not have shocked her more. "Science or Appropriations?"

The Senator cast an approving eye towards his aide. Clay responded with, "Just like I told you, Senator."

"A lady after my own heart, goes straight to the center of the target." Townsend beamed at her. "The answer, Ryan, is both. We generally have one key person who looks after NASA's interests with both subcommittees."

Clay East added, "You would act as the unofficial go-between on all key issues."

Ryan was unable to respond. There were two key Senate subcommittees responsible for NASA. The Space-Science

Subcommittee was under the Commerce, Science and Transportation Committee, and handled such decisions as long-range project planning and scientific oversight. All financial and funding issues were covered by the Independent Agencies Subcommittee, under Appropriations.

Three or four senior staff members served any Senate committee. Those assigned to the two subcommittees shaped the entire paperwork structure of NASA. Wrangling and rivalry between the two subcommittees was constant, bitter, and typical for the Washington power scene. The go-between would be linked to every critical issue including agenda, budget, future commitments, major purchase decisions. The connections would be fantastic, the opportunities limitless.

The Senator interjected, "Of course, this would mean lifting you to SES rank."

"Pending final approval," his aide added.

Townsend snorted. "I doubt seriously that anyone would throw up roadblocks if this is what we want to see happen."

Ryan knew she needed to respond, but could not find the words. She was currently a GS-11, a high ranking civil servant. SES status, or Senior Executive Service, was limited to those people at the very pinnacle of bureaucratic service. It was not just a matter of time and effort. For every successful SES candidate, more than two thousand were passed over.

Clay East interrupted the clamor in her head with, "I take it your silence means yes."

"Let the lady catch her breath," the Senator chided. "Get used to the altitude."

Ryan glanced at her superior. Fuller Glenn's mask told her nothing. She could not help but think that this was the kind of job he would have expected to land upon his return to Camelot. Not Ryan. Her boss.

Senator Townsend rose to his feet, drawing the others with him. "I imagine you'll want to go home and think over our little offer."

"Doubt if it'll take her that long," his aide replied.

"Nonsense. A move like this she'll want to discuss with the husband and family, am I right?"

The thought of breaking this news to Harry was enough to bring her back to earth. Ryan offered the Senator her hand and said, "I can't thank you enough for the honor, sir."

"Just do your job, remember your benefactors, make sure our needs are well met. Right, Clay?"

"I'll speak to her about all that right now, Senator."

"Excellent. Good to meet you, Ryan. Welcome on board."

She heard the words but did not understand their meaning. Ryan allowed East to usher her from the room and into a small alcove in the corner of the outer office. She looked around, saw Fuller fill the entrance, felt imprisoned by the men's combined bulk. "Mr. East, I've tried to call you several –"

"Call me Clay. We tend towards the informal up here. I've gotten your messages. We're after results, not progress reports."

She scanned from one face to the other. "I'm not sure I understand."

"We remain very concerned about Dr. Laremy's disappearance. I fail to see what is so elusive about that."

Ryan hesitated. "It's just, well, I'm not clear on why she's so important."

"That's simple enough." East continued to press down upon her. "It is vital for us to have NASA developments we can point to as leading towards a better life for Ma and Pa Citizen. This research of Dr. Laremy's into superconductors has really caught the committee's eye. There's a chance of some powerful PR here. Vital technological spin-off, creating a huge industry booster, leaping ahead of our international competitors, producing new jobs. All the things Senator Townsend and his fellow committee members need to justify the NASA budget."

Fuller Glenn added, "Playing on the home team means accepting that certain items take on more importance than you might think they deserve. That's the nature of politics."

"Exactly. It doesn't look good for us to lose a key scientist just when the committee intends to hold their research up to the public spotlight. That clear enough?"

"Yessir." She backed a half-step away, would have moved farther but she was pressed up against a filing cabinet. "I have someone looking into that. He's already turned up what might be our first real lead."

"Somebody who can be trusted to keep all this secret, I hope." East exchanged a sharp glance with Fuller. "And act on this immediately. We're after swift results here."

Ryan started to ask why secrecy was such an issue, decided it was more important to escape East's attempt to trap her in the corner. She ducked and slid between them, gained a fraction of pleasure at their surprise over the speed of her movement. "I'll be in touch with you first thing Monday morning."

9

Friday morning Hale emerged from his first surf in six months feeling frustrated and fatigued, with muscles like cotton and blood like champagne. Sensations only a long absence from the sea could generate, and only in a lifelong surfer. Incredible disappointment that he had ever let anything come between him and the waves. Amazement that fighting for his corporate life had ever seemed a decent excuse for staying away.

The day held a happy-sad cast, as all the homesickness he had refused to permit himself before, all the banked-up yearnings to be back in the sea were coming out. They flooded his empty soul, pouring like perfumed unguent over his tired and satisfied body.

He stripped off his wetsuit, feeling anew the pinprick residue of frigid Southern California water. Dawn's pastel greeting to a new day had brightened as the sun cleared the cliffs beyond the Scripps Oceanographic Institute. The La Jolla Shores parking lot was already full, both of cars and attitude. Surfers dotted the ocean like black water beetles, silent and semi-hostile, jostling and scrambling for the chest-high waves.

The beach scene was cranking. Joggers were so plentiful they outnumbered the gulls. Early beach-goers styled in proper Californians fashion – titanium shades, silver lycra suits, rainbow headbands, razored hairstyles. Warming temperatures had already brought out the first sun goddesses, blonde hair and meager bikinis and wash-off tattoos. Young chatter, young smirks, young life. Ten o'clock and the invasion was total.

As he made his way up to the lifeguard station, he passed a trio of teen beauties who danced prone on their towels to a thousand-dollar B&O portable CD player, playing some pump-and-grind wail, demanding to know how anything that felt so good could be anything but totally righteous. The music was bright spanking new, the message so repetitious it left Hale feeling ten thousand years old.

The La Jolla lifeguard stations were throwbacks to a bygone era, wooden shacks on stilts with peeling paint and ramshackle balconies. A blonde woman stood there now, watching him approach with hands on hips and expression hidden behind wrap-around shades.

He stopped at the foot of the platform, set down his board, and made no move to climb the ramp. "Hello, Margo."

"Decided to come back and recapture your youth?"

"That's not it at all."

"Well, it sure wasn't to make up with Philippa, now, was it?"

"Do you know where she's gone?"

Margo was a taut five-eight, evenly tanned and naturally blonde. She was also Philippa's best surfing pal and once enjoyed a mildly flirtatious friendship with Hale. But there was no welcome now, nothing but flinty refusal. "If I knew the least little bit of anything, which I don't, you would be the absolute last person in the entire universe I'd tell."

Maybe the water had washed away his anger. Whatever the reason, he stood there at the foot of the ramp, utterly defenseless. "Margo, Philippa may be brilliant, but she's not right about everything."

"Maybe not. But she was right to call you a shit, now, wasn't she?"

"Just because Philippa and I argued isn't any reason for you to be mad at me too."

"What a perfectly macho idiotic thing to say."

He sighed his agreement. "So give me a chance to apologize."

"You're too late for either one of us. By six months." She stared down at him a moment longer, then turned and spoke to the guard inside the shack. She walked down the ramp, stopped directly in front of him. The sunglasses were too much of a barrier. Margo stripped them off, revealing eyes of robin's egg blue. Cold eyes. Cold and hard as her words. "The last time we were out, she told me she was pretty sure somebody was after her."

"Where is she?" Hale asked, trying not to flinch under her gaze. "I just want to help."

"That's exactly what she said they were hiding behind." She crossed her arms. "All these offers of help. Help her do what, Hale? Name me one thing you could do for her she couldn't do better for herself."

"Something's made her run away, Margo. Something she couldn't handle. By herself, anyway."

"How utterly nauseating." She held her arms clenched tight to her chest. "I hope you never find her, Hale. It'd hurt her too much to learn they sent you."

"Who is 'they', Margo?"

"You know that better than I ever could." She started back up the ramp, tossing over her shoulder as she climbed, "First the police come around asking all sorts of questions, none of them the right ones. Now you." She reached the balcony, glared down at him, snapped out, "Go home, Hale. You're not welcome here. Any bridges you once had were burned down long ago."

* * *

He walked north, beneath the Scripps pier, then climbed the concrete ramp used by the Institute for its boatloads of scuba gear and measuring equipment. He had learned this habit from Philippa, parking above the Institute, avoiding the worst of the La Jolla Shores pressure-cooker beach scene. The road was a tight alley climbing up between classrooms and dorms. The eight parking spaces at the top of the alley were an early morning secret. Hale arrived at his car and went through the motions, greeting a couple of others returning from dawn patrol, opening his car's windows and turning on his radio before stowing his board. He wrapped the big towel around his waist, peeled off the boardshorts, stowed them in the trunk with his wetsuit. Pulled on his shorts and T-shirt, combed his salt-sticky hair, leaned on the car, looked out over the brilliant shoreline vista. Usually it was enough to return him to the sea-perfumed buzz of a good surf, standing there and looking out over the ocean and the day. Today the emptiness rang with the power of Margo's words. And the truth.

Below him, the wall lining the beach-ramp shouted distorted graffiti curses and claims to local gang power. Surfers in beetle-eyed shades, baggy streetwear and backward-mounted caps lined the wall like sullen vultures. Farther north jutted the first tongue of stone, marking the end of the beach and the rise of sheer cliffs. The bluffs ascended in crumbling height for three long miles, where they grudgingly permitted another tiny elbow of beach. Because this next shore was accessible only by a slippery-steep cliff-walk, Black's Beach remained the domain of nudists and surfers. It had been their favorite break, his and Philippa's. Hale stretched and scouted the horizon, as though searching for a line of white and the signal of a rising swell. As though Philippa was there and they were debating a second surf. As though it mattered.

A cherry-red GTO idled by, blasting chainsaw rock through four open windows, a trio of locals giving Hale the bug-eye before cruising away. It was only after they had turned the corner that he heard his phone.

He pulled it from the glove box and thumbed the switch. "Andrews."

"It's getting worse." A very tense Jerry sweated over the phone. "Mack the Knife's just moved into the office beside the chairman's."

The sun's warmth no longer reached his bones. "This," Hale admitted, "is not good."

"You're telling me. He came sauntering in here this morning wearing that Teflon smile of his. You know the one. Said he hoped for all our sakes you were successful in your endeavors out west."

Hale gave the sea and the sky a grim nod. Overhead the breeze rustled through the California pines, and their whispers were doom-laden. MacRuthers expected him to fail, which was natural for any first visit to a new client. Then Mack was going to use this as the excuse to give them all the boot. The only reason why Hale did not say the words out loud was because Jerry was already close to weeping.

"You're lucky you don't have kids," his assistant was saying. "I sat at the breakfast table this morning wondering how I was going to feed them."

There was no choice but to get as much mileage as he could from what he had. "Look, Jerry, I want –"

"You got any idea how tough it is to land a decent job these days?" Jerry's voice was pitched one note below a full wail. "It's a feeding frenzy out there."

"I want you to go spread some rumors of your own," Hale persisted. Refusing to give in to the fear which clenched his own gut. "Tell them how I met with Northstar's vice-president of engineering and design yesterday. Not only that, how I also met with a senior person from the Space Research Consortium. Are you taking this down?"

"Hale, for heaven's sake –"

"Write this down, Jerry. Make sure you get it right. SRC is currently negotiating to build the new space shuttle. Do you have any idea what that means?"

A long pause, then, "You think we've got any chance?"

"Maybe. But at this point, who cares? What's important is that they *think* we do." Wishing he was not here, knowing he needed to be doing this himself. Jerry was a solid number-two, nothing more, hated the limelight and was useless when it came to sales. Which was precisely what was needed here, a heavy dose of selling their department. Setting the rumors and the excitement and the energy in place, locking them both into jobs, keeping the sharks at bay. "The first meetings went so well I'm set for a conference today with the SRC director of purchasing. And dinner tonight with the senior person I met yesterday." When there was no response, Hale demanded, "Are you taking it all down?"

"I got it, I got it. Mack is gonna hate this." A touch of new power to the voice. "I mean, it's gonna be like gravel in that bastard's gut."

What was really needed here was for Jerry to carry that sense of excitement with him. "Go up to the director's floor. Talk to their assistants, tell them how tremendous this all looks. Millions of dollars in new business. A new lease on life for the old company."

"I got it, old buddy." Worry fought with hope in the guy's voice. "You can count on me."

Hale wished it was true. "Spread it on thick, Jerry. We want these guys to spend the weekend getting used to the idea that we're carrying the company's future on our backs."

* * *

After showering and changing Hale joined the coagulated Friday freeway crawl. He spent the drive rehearsing his spiel, going over the major points he needed to cover in making a presentation on Keebler Plastics. Highly efficient design capability, experience working with a variety of industries, latest production technology, long history of on-time deliveries, competitive pricing. Mumbling to himself, the radio a distant hum, the other cars blurs of passing color. The dry desert scenery, the new houses crawling up nearby hills, the occasional gasp of distant seaside blue, all ignored. No space for anything but the pressure ahead, the pressure behind. He had to land this deal.

The Space Research Consortium was located in northern San Diego, just off Camino Del Rio. The building was modern and imposing, all white marble and copper-colored reflective glass. The lobby was full of quiet tension and vast self-importance. People in lab coats and clip-on ID tags hustled about, talking in low tones and grabbing the air with frantic motions.

"Well, what a lovely way to dress up a Friday!" Natalie did her dancing walk towards him, in a lime-green skirt, ivory stockings, a silky top. Her look showed no interest in anyone's reaction but his own.

Hale kept his attention locked on her face, gave his smile top effort. "I should say the same about you."

"Oh, stop." She moved up, entrapping him within the veil of her perfume, and clipped a visitor's tag onto his jacket pocket. "We'll have to hurry, Buzz is ready and waiting."

He followed a half-step beside and behind. Eyes around the chamber tracked her passage, drawn like puppets on a string. She demanded, "Are we still on for tonight?"

"Absolutely." Struggling to hold to the business at hand. "You say this guy is your boss?"

"Not exactly. I'm Technical Support Manager, Buzz is Director of Procurement." She stepped into the elevator, punched the top button. "But we're a close-knit group here. Titles are like that tag on your lapel. Clip them on, take them off, it doesn't mean a lot. What matters is that we get the job done."

He checked his tie in the door's reflection. What mattered was that this Buzz decided which supplier got the cheese.

"Buzz likes to think he's a tough guy. Really cynical, smokes cigars, married four times. Former jet-fighter pilot. Talks a big game. Lives over on Coronado in Taco Towers. Drives a sixties vintage baby Benz. Goes down to Mazatlan every weekend, plays poker for big stakes."

Hale felt his hopes plummet at the news. He had nothing in common with this guy, nothing to build on.

The doors opened and he followed her into the vast reception area. The difference from the Northstar office corral could not have been greater. No expense had been spared in making this an elitist lair – silk carpet, grainy hand-loomed tapestries, marble reception desk, suede sofas, a back wall of glass and an awesome view of Mission Bay. Natalie traded hellos with the secretary and led Hale straight into an office larger than his own chairman's. "Buzz, got a minute?"

"Sure, come on in." The guy bounced from his chair like a fighter readying for a punch. "You're Andrews, right? Buzz Cobb." His hand stabbed the air. "Put 'er there, sport."

Hale endured the bone-grinding handshake with a poker face. "Thanks for seeing me, Mr. Cobb."

"Don't mention it. Take a seat, why doncha." Buzz Cobb had eyes like glacier ice – old, cold, and hard as iron. "Got a card for me?"

"Certainly." Hale accepted one in return, seated himself, leaned over to open his briefcase. He set the card on the desk in front of him, pulled out a binder and set of company brochures, and began, "Keebler Plastics is extremely interested in working with SRC and Northstar, Mr. Cobb. While we're new to the aerospace industry, we do have an astonishing track record with a variety of other high-tech –"

"Yeah, well, like Natalie's probably told you, we're real keen to see Professor Laremy back at work."

Hale stopped, his hand and a corporate brochure midway across Buzz's desk. "I thought I was here to talk with you about Keebler becoming a new supplier."

The stubby man glanced at Natalie, who had taken a chair by the side wall, far from the line of fire. "What, you think we're gonna reopen a door that's been welded shut for over a year, invite your dinky firm in, sign you up?"

"Well, that's –"

"You got any idea how many suppliers dream of working with us?" Buzz inspected him as he peeled a plastic wrapper from a stogie. "Thousands, that's how many. All of 'em hungry enough to serve the heart of their first-born up on a silver platter if I ask 'em to."

"Buzz," Natalie said quietly.

"What, you think I gotta bandy words with this guy? I don't have the time to waste, Natalie. I gotta tell it like it is. If this guy thinks we're gonna work with his two-bit company outta the kindness of our hearts, we're done here."

Hale protested, "Keebler Plastics is a first-rate firm, Mr. Cobb."

"You know what, sport? That don't mean dick to me." He pulled out a gold-plated Zippo, lit the cigar, puffed until the flame almost covered his eyes. He snapped the lid shut, said, "Hope you don't mind a little smoke."

Hale wondered if he could manage to get up, walk out, show a calm front as he left his career in shreds on the floor. He glanced over to Natalie, was as surprised by her beaming smile as by anything else this entire confusing trip. He said to her beckoning look, "I'm not clear on what I'm doing here."

Buzz targeted Natalie as well. "I thought you told me you brought this guy up to speed."

"There's nothing wrong in having pride in his company," Natalie said, her smile and her look for Hale and Hale alone. "He knows what he wants, just like us. Nothing wrong at all."

"Right. Then let's see if we're running along parallel lines here." Cobb's tracked back, aimed his cigar at Hale like a glowing gun barrel. "We're in the final stages of grabbing the new shuttle contract. Seven billion dollars in new business in the first four years alone. You hear what I'm saying? Seven billion makes for a lotta everything, including room for a coupla new suppliers."

"You're telling me," Hale said, "I go look for Philippa, and my company does business with your group."

"I told you he was sharp," Natalie said. "No need to repeat things with this guy."

"This is sharp?" Cobb shook his head like a bull tossing flies. "This horseshit is second-rate crash and burn stuff."

He leaned beefy forearms on his desk. "I don't know what the lady's told you, sport, but we're not in the practice of giving out prizes for second place around here. You want the trophy, you win the race."

"I understand," Hale said.

"You don't *look*. You don't go run around in tight little circles throwing up dust. You *find*."

"Hale's our man," Natalie said from her corner, her voice honeyed and soothing. "He's the one we need."

Cobb glanced at her, took a puff from his cigar, swiveled his gaze back to Hale. His face pulled into a tight little smile. He leaned back in his chair, still smirking. "Laremy's done some primo work on propulsion for us. I met her a coupla times, just to see what we were getting for our money. Laremy struck me as a stand-up lady, you know what I mean? Don't make sense, her just vanishing like that."

When Hale did not respond, Cobb breathed a long plume, inspected his cigar, said casually, "When you find her, I want you to deliver a message from me. Tell her it's time for her to come work with the pros."

Hale struggled to ignore his future mawing like a dark pit at his feet. "Philippa is pretty independent."

"Tough. We're done messing around with that university lab stuff." Cobb rose to his feet, stalked around his desk, waited until Hale rose to meet him. Then he gripped Hale's upper arm with fingers of stone. "You know what? I bet Natalie's right about you, sport. I bet you can get that professor lady to do just about anything you want her to."

"I'll give it my best shot, Mr. Cobb." The words tasted like dust in his mouth. "You can count on me."

"You put it right, she'll show up here with bells on, I just know it." The fingers bit deep, kneading his muscles. "So we need to make sure you sing the right song. What I'm gonna do here is put my money where my mouth is."

Cobb released Hale's arm, stood smoking and staring up at him, his eyes glinting with savage humor. "There's a hundred-thousand-dollar signing bonus waiting for the Prof. We're gonna pay it to you the day she signs our new contract. You settle up with the lady however you want. You catch my meaning?"

He stabbed Hale's chest with the pair of fingers holding his cigar. The smoke reached out and encircled him. "Now go out there and do your job."

"My job," Hale repeated.

Cobb offered his hand. "Great to meet you, sport. Natalie, you got the paperwork started on this company of his?"

"Absolutely. The documents have been expressed to Keebler's home office."

Cobb flung open the door, pointed Hale out. "Keep in touch."

Natalie led him back to the elevator, where she bestowed another smile. "That went well, don't you think?"

Hale stared at her. "Natalie, that guy did everything but light a fire and fricassee my gizzard."

"Oh, you." Her smile was brilliant. "You're up for a contract on the new shuttle, I'm assigned to help get your company up to speed, you even get the chance to work in a big bonus. What are you moaning about?"

"Nothing," he agreed, as the steel doors opened like the mouth of a shark. "Absolutely nothing at all. Things are just swell."

"You're tired, that's all." With the doors closed, she moved up close, replacing the lingering smoke with a scent all her own. "You meet me at a restaurant in La Jolla called the Top O' The Cove. Seven o'clock. We'll have a nice meal, put everything right. How does that sound?"

"Swell," he said, watching the floors count down to the bottom of the earth. "Just swell."

* * *

Friday five o'clock and he was locked up tight. The air above the freeway frizzled with engine fumes and tempers.

The phone pinged. He plucked it from his pocket, thumbed the switch, said, "Rush hour. What a hoot. Nobody's rushing anywhere, far as I can tell."

It was Ryan who answered. "Sounds like life's got you on the run, Studley."

"No running today. I feel like a bug caught in amber. Where are you?"

"My taxi just passed the Reflecting Pool, we're turning onto Seventh."

"You're in Washington?"

"Came up this morning." Ryan sounded tired herself. Drained of all but sound. "Been a strange day, Studley. Strange even for Washington. How are things your end?"

He didn't want to talk about the weirdness at his end. "Strange how?"

Exasperation was released with an explosive breath. "Well, let's see. I've got a son who's borderline frantic about his parents' marriage falling apart, a daughter of ten shopping for tattoos, and a husband who's heavy into substance abuse. Oh, and I've just been offered the job of a lifetime, if only I can keep Harry from doing his imitation of a Trident missile in our living room. Again."

"Doesn't sound like stuff we should talk about while you're in a public place."

"This is a Washington taxi, Hale. The driver is from lower Uluwatu. His last name has seventeen syllables and a letter

I've never seen before. He's giving me severe whiplash driving ninety-seven miles an hour between stoplights. All the windows are open. The radio is playing music that sounds like the singer is choking on a prune. This is as private as it gets."

He had trouble deciding which question to ask first. "Harry's taking drugs?"

"Not unless they outlawed caramel-coated popcorn while I wasn't looking. Hang on, we're there. I've got to pay and escape."

Hale managed another three feet of progress during the wait. Ryan finally returned with, "Harry is not doing drugs, Hale. Harry abuses his body with every junk food known to man. Harry's idea of a good workout is opening a new jar of Skippy's and demolishing it with a box of Wheat-thins."

"Where are you now?"

"Outside NASA headquarters, next to a bench under the last cherry blossom in all of Washington."

"I didn't know you and Harry were having troubles, Ryan."

"I don't want to talk about it any more." Tight even over the airwaves. "How did it go at Northstar?"

"Today was SRC. Northstar was yesterday. Horrible is how it went. Guy by the name of Buzz Cobb, head of purchasing, tore my career to shreds. Ever heard of him?"

"SRC is the newest prime at Kennedy. They got in by acquiring a couple of local boys. I don't know anybody from the new parent yet. Northstar has been in and out a lot recently, or their engineers have, working on the new launch vehicle. SRC does most of their work with Johnson, Huntsville, JPL, Goddard. They're a name on the rise, from what I hear. But never mind that. You were telling me this guy reamed you?"

"Did it and loved doing it. Just before I get there I hear from head office there's an ax poised over my neck. So I go in there ready to lay my life on the line. What happens, he tosses my brochures in the garbage, tells me point blank the only way they'll work with me is if I find Philippa."

"So? You were going to do that anyway, right?"

Traffic crawled forward another eighteen inches, stopped. "What about competitive bidding, product quality, all those things we were taught meant something?"

"Excuse me, Hale." Exasperation filed down her normal throaty rasp. "In case you haven't noticed, things are way beyond tough in the federal procurement field. You get a chance to muscle in, no matter what the reason, take it. You won't get another."

"Even if it means bribes?"

She hardened further. "SRC demanded a bribe?"

"They offered me one. Sort of." He related Cobb's final comments. "What was Philippa doing for them that was so critical they'd offer me a hundred thousand dollars just to have her come work for them full time?"

Ryan hesitated, then thought out loud, "Legally their offer is clean. At least as far as SRC's involvement is concerned. But that doesn't make it the tiniest bit right." Focusing on work tightened the defeat and the fatigue away. "Okay, to answer your question we've got to go back a ways. The original space shuttle concept was drawn up in 1957, a week after the Sputnik launch. They called it Dyna-Soar. They wanted to make spaceflight routine. To do that the craft had to be reusable. NASA picked the concept up in sixty-six, made three different lifting body designs. The M-2, the HL-10, and finally the X-24. In seventy-two they decided to go with the North American Rockwell design, a partially reusable vehicle."

"You're telling me," Hale said, "that the current shuttle's based on an old design."

"Not just design. Think back to where computer technology was in the early seventies. We were just emerging from the caves. Same with materials. The rate of progress over the past twenty-five years has been staggering. We need a new shuttle that incorporates where we are today."

He thought about what he had heard of Philippa's work, asked, "And propulsion?"

"A different story. No way to apply solid-fuel rocket technology to the family car. Since it doesn't have consumer applications, it can't make a profit unless the government buys in. And the government wasn't buying. So not a lot has been done."

"That's why SRC took Philippa off superconductors and put her on propulsion?"

"She wasn't being redirected." Ryan said, her voice slowing further as she worked through the response. "At least, that's what she told me. She was asked to check experimental results from several field teams."

Hale switched lanes, managed to slightly increase the velocity of his crawl. "Checking somebody else's results isn't much of a reason for her to vanish."

"Or for a senatorial committee to show a personal interest," Ryan replied, speaking to herself. "Or insist I keep it secret."

"Can you ask around, find out which teams' work she was checking up on?"

"It's not a bad idea, Studley. Might stir up the hive a little." She seemed pleased by the thought. "Speaking of nosing around, the reason I called, my secretary managed to track down your lab-rat."

"Who?"

"Philippa's assistant. Jennifer, last name Velasquez. She bought a ticket for Cabo San Lucas. That's down at the tip of Baja Mexico."

"I know where Cabo is, Ryan. And Philippa's lab assistant is exactly where she's always been." He increased his speed another notch. "Can your people spring for a weekend trip to Cabo?"

"There's no way to go through channels with this on a Friday afternoon. But everybody's so all-fired hot to see you get some results, I'm sure I can work it out one way or the other. Got a pen handy?"

"Yes."

"Here's my official MasterCard. Expiry date next December. Put your expenses down to that." She read off a series of numbers, then went on, "I've also spoken with the La Jolla police. They still don't have anything solid on the fire at Philippa's. I'll keep pushing hard as I can from over here."

"Right." The fire seemed shoved into the distance by concern over so much else. More than the traffic surrounded him, held him in place, kept him from opening his door and fleeing from the car and the phone and all the thoughts that swirled and tumbled and threatened. "I tell you what it's like. I've got all these people telling me things, but they're really speaking some secret language. What I'm hearing and what they're saying are totally different."

"I know," she said slowly, "just exactly what you mean."

10

Before entering NASA headquarters, Ryan scooted around the corner to the one place in the neighborhood she recalled with affection. Her time at NASA headquarters had been served like a sentence, chafing at the chains which held her trapped in bureaucratic folds. The thrill of space had been utterly lost beneath the daily flood of paper and petty intrigue. She had endured three years of anguished yearning before finally grabbing the Kennedy assignment.

The basement-level grocery was in different hands these days, the bright old man with his cockatoo tuft of white hair long gone. The place was now run by a morose Lebanese and his severely overweight daughter. Yet they had maintained the same Aladdin's cave appeal which she recalled from bygone days. Cramped aisles were stocked to the ceiling with overpriced delicacies. The rear counter contained a jewel-like display of homemade specialties – everything from fresh tuna sashimi to tiramisu.

Ryan made her purchases and returned to the front entrance. As she pushed through the doors her phone rang. She carefully set her purchases on the guard's central table and pulled the phone from her purse. "Ryan Reeves."

"It's Chuck Evans, Ryan. Did I catch you at a good time?"

"There's no such thing in Washington. But I guess this is

okay, long as you talk fast. Otherwise my stash will get all gloppy."

"Your what?"

"Never mind. What do you need now?"

"I've sketched out the preliminaries of a solution to our problem."

She had to think hard to recall what problem he meant. The morning meeting seemed years ago. "The seals for the payload bay doors."

"Right. We need to meet."

Ryan ran her schedule through her mind. "I had to move some stuff back because of today's trip."

"Yeah, your secretary said I couldn't have a slot until the week after next. This is urgent, Ryan."

Everything was when dealing with engineers. "Then we've got to get it done before the barrage starts. Monday, six-thirty, my office."

A pause. "Six-thirty in the morning?"

"Bring coffee and doughnuts. And be on time."

* * *

Ryan took the elevator to the fourth floor of NASA Headquarters. Tourists and gawkers were drawn by the National Air and Space Museum, the most visited site in all of Washington. Headquarters was nondescript by Washington standards, intended to be missed by all but those with a genuine purpose.

The appointment was with her first NASA mentor. Mentoring was a critical component of every NASA employee's rise from the ranks of thousands. The organization was such a bizarre mixture of science and military and industry and politics, the only way to learn how to swim the treacherous currents was alongside a pro.

Since the end of their first week together, Ryan had held Florence Avery in awe.

Florence Avery was straight-speaking, honest, extremely intelligent and immensely dedicated. Once she had been the right woman in the right place at the right time. Now she was seen by most as just another thwarted bureaucrat with no chance of further promotion.

Though in her late fifties, Florence Avery remained a handsome woman. She chose soft-toned suits to ease her angular features and tenderize her professional toughness. But nothing could be done about her gaze, hard and bitter as old iron.

She had a musician's ability to read notes on a score and hear music, only with Florence it was numbers on a page. In Florence Avery's hands a ledger made better reading than a novel. In bygone days her abilities had marked her for great things. When NASA faced accusations of being a white male-dominated microculture, Florence Avery had been tagged as someone headed for great heights.

Disaster had struck in the form of a certain Major Jack Stone. Ryan had met him on two occasions. Tall for an astronaut. Incredibly fit. A dedication to NASA and a focus on his work that had matched Florence's own. Their affair had ignited like a Saturn behemoth rising from the pad, only to self-destruct in mid-flight.

Both Florence and the astronaut had been married. Both spouses sued for divorce. Florence gave up her husband and their children and a house in old-town Alexandria without a backward glance. Not so Major Stone.

The director of Johnson Space Center, the man directly responsible for the astronaut corps, had personally told the major in no uncertain terms that if he did away with his marriage he could kiss his career good-bye. No scandal that public would ever be permitted to taint the astronauts' image.

The gallant Major Stone had dumped Florence Avery that very same afternoon.

Major Stone went on to command a further five shuttle missions. Florence Avery's career remained frozen in the amber of public shame. She had once confessed to Ryan that it was a good thing the shuttles never carried just one man. Otherwise she might find herself trying to arrange a second Challenger disaster.

Ryan passed through the empty outer office, knocked on Florence's open door and declared, "I need a clean cup and two spoons."

Florence looked up from her spread sheets and eyed the sack in Ryan's hand through the top half of her glasses. "What is it this time?"

Ryan made a show of opening the bag and unfolding a pair of napkins. On them she placed wafer-thin circles of dark chocolate covered with glazed almond slices. "Homemade Florentine cookies, one for you, four for me." She reached back into the sack, drew out the frosted container. "Ben and Jerry's old-style vanilla."

Florence watched her spoon a healthy portion into a coffee cup. "It's a good thing you moved to Florida. Otherwise I'd be the size of a Titan second-stage by now."

Ryan pulled a chair up close to the desk's other side, seated herself, and dipped directly into the ice-cream container. "Actually, living in Washington is part of what I wanted to talk with you about."

"So I heard."

Her spoon halted in mid-flight. "You know about the offer?"

"Since this morning." Florence canted her cup and spooned out the last bite. "Don't look so surprised. Rumors fly around here at nine-tenths the speed of light." She upended the cup, drained the liquid. "I should know."

Ryan nodded sympathy. Washington abounded with bitter jokes of power players who learned of their demise in the press. Like the reporter who called a certain senator and asked for his reaction to his own daughter's suicide before the police arrived. Or the presidential aide whose court summons was delivered with the same Washington Post which announced his wife's filing for divorce. Or the lobbyist who managed to escape the country because she heard a certain radio talk-show host discuss how the IRS was checking out her supposedly secret accounts. "I never thought my goings-on would be the stuff of rumors."

"Clout like that would move you to center stage." Florence eyed her across the desk. "So did they find your number?"

"Which number is that?"

"The one that would suddenly make the despised city become desirable."

"I don't know." Ryan made a process of selecting her first cookie. "I feel like I'm on a seesaw. One moment ready to go zinging off into orbit, I'm so excited. The next and I'm wondering whether Harry and I can talk this through without turning our house into a war zone. He might see this as the chance he's been looking for to go on the attack."

"Things are bad, then."

"Things," Ryan replied, setting the cookie back down, "are horrible. I'm worried Harry will sell it to the kids as Mommy letting her job jerk the family around. Again."

"I'm so sorry, Ryan."

"Thanks." And said with a grimace that she wanted this door closed.

Florence nodded her understanding, then tasted her cookie while shielding the spreadsheets with her free hand. She reached over and picked up a card by the telephone. "Had a salesman stop in this morning. J. Baker Flowers. What a name. What do you imagine the J could stand for that Baker sounds better than?"

Ryan found herself immensely grateful for the change of subject. "Why are you seeing salesmen? You haven't done any purchasing in years."

"Junior, maybe. No. To hang the double-barrel of Junior Baker around somebody's neck would require a daddy with the IQ of a turtle, and this guy had to inherit his smarts from somewhere. Don't have many dumb people trying to sell things around NASA." Florence finished her cookie, wiped her hands on the napkin and tossed it in the wastebasket. "I asked to see the guy. He's closing in on his company's first NASA contract. I hoped maybe drawing close to the brass ring might make him loquacious."

"I've got a friend who's going for his first NASA contract. Matter of fact, from what he says his job may depend on him getting it."

"Lotsa luck." Florence's gaze signaled that she feared Ryan might ask for a favor. "Tough time to be out hunting. Not much going on these days."

"But your guy Flowers will make it, right?"

"Flowers is a back-door jobber. Long-time defense contractor. Now his firm has been acquired by one of NASA's major primes, and they're pulling every political string within reach to have us use him as well."

The number of major prime contractors used by NASA were shrinking daily, through acquisition and budget attrition. A number of smaller fish scavenged for what remained, among them Harry's firm. Many were hanging on by the skin of one contract alone. "Which one? Prime, I mean."

Florence hesitated, her tone hardening to match her eyes. "And just who am I talking with here, Ryan Reeves my old understudy, or Ryan Reeves the power broker on Capitol Hill?"

Ryan straightened, her alarm bells ringing. "You're talking to a friend."

A tiny nod. "Go shut the door."

Ryan did so, returned and demanded, "So tell."

"You first."

"I'm not trading in secrets. Not yet."

"No?" The head cocked to one side. "Who's the friend you're trying to place in the NASA supply fold?"

"Hale? He's, well, a friend. That's all." The older woman's gaze felt like a laser. "No, maybe not. It's all so tangled.

I actually didn't come over to talk about him at all. Well, not directly."

"This is not," Florence observed, "the Ryan Reeves I remembered. Focused, tight, solid on delivery."

"Things have gotten very confusing," she replied.

Florence did not appear surprised by the admission. She repeated, quieter this time, "So tell."

Which she did. From the beginning. The explosion and the call and the journey and the disappearance and the mystery upon mystery, Hale arriving and searching and perhaps Philippa having fled to Cabo, the whys as confusing as her present visit to Washington. "Townsend's aide gave me this spiel about how I had to accept the subcommittee's directives, and how Philippa's work in superconductors is vital. That was the word he used. Vital. Over and over. On the surface, everything sounds fine. Maybe I'm just frightened by the offer, and I'm trying to poke holes in it."

Ryan hesitated, almost hoping Florence would agree with her, soothe her fears and free her to prepare a strategy for confronting Harry. But Florence remained motionless, watchful. Ryan pushed out the words, "What bothers me most, I feel like this is too high a leap. Like the job should have been offered to my *boss*. Not me. This is the kind of plum that'd bring him back from Kennedy with bells on. Instead, he's just standing there, smiling and urging me on, like it's perfectly natural for me to jump over his head and land in his spot."

Florence gave a slow nod, then surprised Ryan by simply saying, "So you introduced your friend to a contact at Northstar. I'm sorry, what was his name?"

"Hale. Hale Andrews. But he's –"

"And what company is he with?"

"Keebler Plastics."

"Out of ..."

"Richmond. But I'm not –"

"Do you know who he spoke with at Northstar?"

"No. That is, I know the person I set him up with, but he got shunted upstairs. And they sent him over to SRC."

"Ah. Now we're getting somewhere." Florence made swift notes. "Who did he see there?"

"I have no idea." Ryan cocked her head. "What is going on here, Florence?"

A couple more notes, then the page was torn from the pad and slipped into her top drawer. Eyes suddenly busy elsewhere. "Have you ever met Congressman Lassard?"

"You've got to be kidding." Congressman Lester Lassard was a throwback to the days of porkbarrel politics. Representative from the nineteenth district, which abutted Brevard County and the Kennedy Space Center to the northwest, Congressman Lassard had made a long and bitter career out of railing against federal overspending. His favorite two targets were NASA and Defense. His own inland district did not attract many tourist dollars, was bereft of any major city, and contained the two poorest counties in the state. Kicking NASA did wonders for his popularity. He was also a womanhater in the extreme Southern tradition. "I've met him. Once. Didn't I tell you about that little encounter?"

"I don't think so."

"Probably too ashamed. It was my second year with NASA." But the memory was still fresh enough to throw out smoke and cinders. "I applied for a committee aide position. It was a big jump, could have given my career a major push. Lassard was the top dog on appointments. He was a shavetail Congressman then, his first year in Washington. He shot me down. I met the Lizard a couple of days later and told him that with all due respect I felt I was the best person for the job. He just stood there, smug as only a southern politician can be. So I asked him why he had voted against me. The bastard leaned up real close and said he preferred his men to wear balls."

Florence looked genuinely dismayed. "Lassard told you that?"

"He was very careful to make sure nobody was in hearing range. But yeah, he actually said it. I'll never forget it as long as I live." Ryan gave her a smile of old cold fury. "I wouldn't get within ten feet of Lizard Lassard without a bubble suit and a flame thrower. I might catch a permanent case of slime mold."

Florence put her pen down. "Then I'll have to get back to you on this."

Ryan stared at the older woman. "On what?"

"On whatever it is I might have to tell you." Choosing her words carefully. "So nice of you to have stopped by."

Ryan knew a closure when she heard one. She folded her napkin around the untouched cookies, stowed them in her purse, and rose to her feet. "Thanks for nothing."

She was almost to the door when Florence stopped her with, "Ryan."

"What?"

A long pause, then, "A word to the wise. When you're hit by the chance of a lifetime, and all it will cost you is everything you have, turn it down."

Ryan found herself looking beyond the bitter tone, seeing the unhealed tragedy beneath. It was enough to send a shiver of apprehension up her own spine. "Why did you hang around here after Jack shot you down? Why didn't you leave?"

"Simple. I loved NASA too much." Her face tightened around the edges. "I can't think of a more terrible curse for anyone to have to bear."

11

Philippa fought off the silent hounds of solitude with the only weapon she had left. Her work.

She longed for simple things – her blackboard, a friendly face in the water, talk with another soul whose life extended beyond the next tequila shooter. She festooned her hotel-room walls with yet more computations, each page another tiny tread along the path to discovery. She hoped.

Whenever she stopped and looked at them, she felt she was looking not at another theoretical examination, but her entire life there upon display. All her existence bound and defined by the battle. And make no mistake, a battle it had always been.

When the school authorities had first spoken with her family about Philippa showing signs of genius-level ability, her parents had gone into shock. Her father's lament was a wish for a normal child. Philippa had come to loathe the word as much as she had her bland home existence. Normal. It defined everything that had sought to trap her and pin her within the confines of society's prison. She had never felt a desire to slip into drugs and music the culture vultures claimed was hot; for her, going with the puerile flow was as imprisoning as her parents' home. She did not want to rebel. She wanted to transform. She wanted to bend the rules of space and time, and stamp her name upon the universe. She wanted to *redefine* normal.

Now, banished from the home she loved and the life she cherished and the man she required, Philippa felt as though her father's silent dissatisfaction and her mother's plaintive whining were chasing her still. Philippa dreaded failure for a multitude of reasons, one being the satisfaction it would bring her parents. Her abject defeat would vindicate them. Finally, once and for all, their hyperintelligent daughter with her bizarre lifestyle would learn her place in life. She could just hear them crow.

So Philippa worked until exhaustion shut her down, struggling to shut out the cries of her past. She took her meals in her room, leaving only for an occasional surf and sunset strolls. All day and most of the night, tinny strains of poolside music and the sound of practiced laughter mocked her efforts. And with each passing hour, the walls closed in a little more.

As she worked, she ached for the company of Alexis and the magic of Hale. The two best men in her life, both torn from her by the one thing which still held meaning. She missed her two men so much the blood in her veins congealed with sorrow. It slowed her pulse to a pace in time with the Mexican desert.

Even so, progress was being made. She could no longer deny what was taking shape. Ahead of her rose a phoenix of terrifying promise.

By late afternoon Friday she was fairly certain what was required. The answer was not sealed and delivered, but it was almost within her grasp. She needed to feel her way forward with experimentation now, watch the concept take on physical form.

She went into the bathroom and carefully applied her make-up, then practiced her smile in the mirror. Finally satisfied, she went to her case and pulled out the portable digital imager. The camera was imbedded in a little square box about the size of her fist, and easily fitted to the top corner of her laptop screen.

She plugged in the earpiece and mike, and dialed herself into the Finnish electronic haven. Checking for Alexis' message which was not there took all of two seconds, hastened by a need to avoid any more sorrow just then. She settled back, practiced her smile once more, then dialed another number from memory.

The image coalesced with a slight hesitation, caused by satellite facsimile bouncing up from Baja to Finland and back to Silicon Valley. Video-capture imaging meant the picture was sent line by electronic line, while the voice went instantly, resulting in sound arriving a fraction ahead of the picture, "Berkeley Products ... Hey, Filly, what's up, gal?"

"Hello, Senna, how are things?"

"Better than with you." She was a heavyset escapee from some small Arkansas town, and Philippa's contact with labs supplying northern UC campuses. "What's the matter with this picture?"

"Sorry. I'm calling from Maui. But don't tell anyone."

"Yeah, looks like you're off someplace. Got maybe a three-second bounce here." Labs doing everything from grinding specialty glass for spook satellites to producing micro amounts of non-natural substances sourced through traders like this woman. Gossip and such information was another reason for contacting her; scientists imprisoned in research labs hungered for news of their own kind. "Maui, hunh. Must be nice."

"Not really. It's the rainy season, and the surf is flat."

"There's all sorts of talk going 'round. Some low-life student claimed on TV you been 'sperimenting with worm holes or something like that, trying to drill your way to the center of the universe."

"Utter nonsense. I'm working on superconductors, same as always."

"Well, you sure did shake things up. Word is, they got to rebuild the whole front of your lab building. Everybody who calls been asking if I know what you been up to." Senna lied like she talked, with a Cheshire cat grin and no conscience whatsoever. "So what'd you do, anyway?"

Philippa hesitated, reluctant now. "Can you keep a secret?"

"Who you talking to here? You know I can."

"I've been mixing the compounds with naturally radioactive elements."

Senna tried for surprise, would have succeeded had Philippa not be watching closely. "You know how crazy that sounds?"

"Nonsense. There was a great deal of theoretical discussion earlier, but they abandoned that direction when more stable compounds began showing promise. But we're not getting nearly as high a superconducting temperature as we need for practical applications." Making for the weary professor, knowing she had just confirmed what the woman had already heard. "But I've got this feeling that combining the compounds with naturally radioactive elements could induce a stationary current at normal atmospheric conditions."

"Well, you lost me there." Senna gave a satisfied grin. "But it sounds to me like you in a hurry to meet your doom."

"Don't be absurd. I simply made a mistake in polar charges, nothing more."

"You gonna try that 'speriment again." Senna showed genuine delight. "There's a passel of folks up here, they'd love a ringside seat for that show." She leaned in, her tone conspiratorial. "Been getting some strange calls. Coupla visitors too. Everybody asking if I knew where you were, what you been up to."

"Probably grants-related." Philippa forced the words over dry lips. "Want to know the status of my work-in-progress."

"These people, they kept asking did I know if you was needing this compound for your work on propulsion. I said, the lady is into superconductors, is all I know." Then she waited.

"My so-called propulsion work is limited strictly to checking the computations of other teams." But knowing the search was this close cut to the bone. "It comes from my largest corporate sponsor, otherwise I wouldn't bother with it at all."

"You want me to say that, they come back?"

"I really am not fussed one way or the other. You're sure they didn't say who they represented?"

"All I know is, they were suits with an attitude. You know what I think about suits."

"Well, whoever they are, they can contact me at the school when I return." Philippa took small comfort in keeping her smile steady, her tone light. "Now to the matter at hand. I want to try my calculations with some of the more stable compounds. Didn't you tell me your contact labs had some of the latest boridium-based aggregates?"

"I believe I remember something like that. How much you want?"

"All they have. Three grams at least. But I must have it delivered immediately."

Senna made notes off screen. "Where to?"

"Why, the lab, of course. And be sure to have them pack it in a long-hold canister. Can you get it to me on Monday?"

"If they still have it laying around. Which they should." She tore off the order sheet, tried for casual. "So you plan on –"

A strident voice cut in as a red ambulance light appeared at the top left of Philippa's screen. "Warning, warning, your call is being traced. Searcher has isolated this location. Do you wish to counterattack?"

Senna's broad features showed terror. "What the hell was that?"

The strident voice would not be denied. "Do you wish to counterattack?"

Philippa cast the calm mask aside, showed the feral snarl she had been holding back ever since hearing the searchers were asking about her experiments. "Send me that material, Senna."

"Girl, what have you got –"

"*Send me that material.*" Philippa slapped the keys and cut the connection. She waited for the emergency trace sensor's coded beep, then demanded, "Feed me back down to the tracing source."

"Request confirmation for additional surcharge of five hundred – ."

"Effect a back-trace to the source," she snapped. "Give me the source location and hook me in."

"Seeking trace source connection. Five seconds to hookup. Four, three, two, one ..."

A young male voice spoke through the grey mist covering her screen, "We traced her call to Helsinki. But she said she was on Maui. Something about the rainy season."

An increasingly furious Philippa cut in with, "Which even a shit-for-brains spook should know is typical weather for Hawaii in June."

There was a very satisfying silence on the other end, so Philippa went on, "Do you think you might have the *common decency* of informing me just who in the *bloody hell* you are?"

A click from somewhere down the line, and a deeper and oilier male voice, older than the first said, "Dr. Laremy, we have been looking for you everywhere."

"And what if I don't wish to be found?" Politician, she decided. The older one was someone comfortable with power – statesman, senior diplomat, chairman of a blue-chip company. Amazing how half her brain could stay so objective while the other boiled like a volcano spewing lava with the words, "Do I not have *any* say in this matter?"

"Dr. Laremy, we have reason to believe that there are some very dangerous specialists out to destroy –"

"I asked you a simple question." Had she ever heard that voice before? Frantically she searched her brain as she screeched, "I *demand* an answer before this charade goes on any further. *Who the bloody hell are you and why are you harassing me?*"

"Dr. Laremy, harassment is the furthest thing from –"

"She's effecting a trace!" The younger man's voice shrilled like a broken pipe. "I don't know who's doing it but it's through our secondary perimeter! What –"

"Cut the connection! *Do it now!*"

She sat in front of her flickering grey screen, chest heaving, fists knotted with desire to reach through the ether and strangle whichever neck came into reach first. The electronic Finn announced, "Connection was terminated before source barriers could be breached. Trace source was initially San Diego, California, with secondary coupling to Washington, DC."

In a voice hoarse from exertion she asked the screen, "Who was that man?"

"We have no voice record of that speech," the computerized Finn responded.

"Thank you." She forced her shaky hands to code out and power down.

Philippa turned from the blank screen, only to see the papers on her walls for what they were – tattered shreds taped like adolescent posters, dreams to hold the fears of reality at bay. But she could not lie to herself any longer. She had to prepare. They were already so close she could feel them breathing on the hairs at the back of her neck.

12

The maitre d' had obviously been alerted to Hale's impending arrival, for he bowed Hale into the restaurant and led him to a corner booth with a coastline view. Hale ordered a beer and enjoyed the view. The Top O' The Cove was a smallish restaurant tucked within its own courtyard entry and perched on a hill overlooking the La Jolla Cove. The interior was softened by candles, and cushioned by layers of linen and plush carpets and hushed respectful tones. Beyond the tall windows a muffled ocean reflected the day's final rose-tinted hues.

When Natalie appeared, Hale joined every other male in the room to watch her progress. The butter-yellow leather miniskirt and cream tights and four-inch heels made her legs look like they started just below her neckline. Or, rather, just below her breasts. She used her walk and her smile and her body like weapons of choice, defeating all competition.

"Hale, sorry I'm late. Buzz caught me just as I was leaving the building."

"I don't blame him."

"Oh, you." She ignored the waiter holding her chair, moved in close, pressed her breasts onto his arm, kissed his cheek. Marking her prey. "Did you get lonely here without me?"

He could feel the eyes – the maitre d', waiter, customers, everybody. Knew she was playing good theater. Felt like a prop. Wondered why all of a sudden he found it so tough to play along. "Absolutely."

She pointed to the chair next to his. "I'll sit there."

"Certainly, Madame." The maitre d' jumped around. "Would you care for an aperitif?"

"Just some wine with the meal." A look of melting obsidian for Hale. "I need to keep my wits about me tonight."

Hale seated himself beside her, watched her inspect the leather-bound menu, found himself searching for a flaw. Old habit from former pressure times, as it gave him a lever for maintaining a distance. Fighting back desires that threatened to engulf him.

But tonight his mind fooled him. As though it had been waiting for the chance, looking for a weak point – not in another woman, but in himself. He found his mind captured by a crystal-sharp image, one from the last time he had found the weakness in a woman. Only that time it had been Philippa.

It was a shocking transition, from candlelit perfection to a gritty morning at Trestles. The image which held him came from the end of their surf, when they had made the long walk back to the carpark. Neither had spoken as they went through the routine of strapping on boards and stripping off wetsuits. Hale was leaving and not coming back. Nothing would change with more words.

As he had toweled his hair, Hale had glanced over, found himself held by a penetrating image; a single tear had escaped to traverse the red sand on Philippa's cheek.

Philippa had continued to hold to her grim silence and clenched features. She had a lifetime's experience at hiding her emotions. Only that morning, however, her facade had been mortally pierced by one tear. All the tormenting fragments of angry pain were drawn from beneath the mask she maintained for the world. A lifetime of secret sorrow tracked its way through the sand on her cheek. Leaving a trail of truth, a silent verdict Hale would carry forever.

Natalie slapped her menu closed and announced, "I'll have the medallions of veal with artichoke hearts, and the truffle mousse with a coulis of raspberry to start."

Hale handed his own back unread. "Sounds okay."

The waiter offered his leather-bound book. "Some wine, perhaps?"

"I'll take that." Natalie snatched it away. "After all, if I'm paying I should have the right to choose, doesn't that sound fair?"

"You're paying?"

"Well, SRC is. Same thing." To the waiter, "A bottle of the 'seventy-six Chateau de la Tour."

When they were alone, Hale watched her raise both arms, sweep back the glossy mane. The action pressed her breasts up against the blouse's creamy fabric. Natalie spotted him watching, held the moment with another unnecessary sweep of her fingers. Then dropped one hand from her hair to his arm. "Having French wine in California is so wonderfully decadent, don't you think?"

What he thought was, he felt torn in two. Half ignited by hormonal hunger, ready to burn his way into Natalie. The other half, though, the one affixed at heart-level, keened a cry of loss over one shed tear.

The two women could not have been any more different. Natalie with her carefully polished looks, Philippa without a care for her appearance at all. Skin reddened and chapped by sun and sea, hair usually a soft frizz. But the light in those eyes was sharp and intelligent and more real than anything he had in his life this evening.

Natalie cocked her head to one side, hair spilling over her shoulder. "What's the matter?"

"Not a thing."

"You look so serious."

There was a light to Natalie's dark gaze as well, liquid and enticing. But Hale could only guess what fueled the inner fire. "I was just wondering what is going on here."

"What's going on?" Her laugh was low, throaty. Almost a purr. "You look in the mirror every morning. It can't be all that strange to have a girl be interested in you."

"That's not what I meant." In the candlelight her red fingernails looked almost black. Long dark talons scraped tantalizing trails down the back of his hand. "You don't know how important this deal with SRC is for Keebler Plastics. And for me."

"I guess that puts you totally under my control, then, doesn't it."

"I guess so." Hale had a sudden urge to withdraw his arm, but found he couldn't. The slow scrape of her fingernails held him as secure as titanium chains. "If I don't land this contract I'm dead meat."

"Don't be scared. I'll take good care of you. And the contract is as good as yours."

But he was scared. Too worried and confused to give in to the moment and the girl and the night.

She grew impatient with his reserve. "Look, you represent an up and coming plastics firm. We're willing to do business with you. We tied the contract to your finding Dr. Laremy. What's so hard to understand about that?"

"Nothing." And that was the truth. But his worries were not silenced by agreeing.

"What's the matter?" She sparked an eye-level smile. "You don't like aggressiveness in a girl?"

"It's not that."

"I can give you weak and submissive." Big cat eyes taunting him. "I'm good at games."

He searched hard for something to say, something right for a change. "Maybe things are just moving a little too fast for me."

"Sure. I can understand that." Her lips were full and enticing and painted dark as her nails. "I come on too strong sometimes. It's just the way I am."

She backed off a fraction further as the waiter set down their starters. When the wine was poured, she insisted Hale taste it, smiled when he nodded approval as though he had accomplished the impossible. She raised her glass. "Here's to lots of exciting times."

"Cheers."

She hummed her approval of her wine, set down the glass, said, "Isn't it amazing how the strangest things bring people together? I mean, here we are, having dinner because of a scientist I've never met who's just disappeared."

"You don't know Philippa?"

"Why should I? She's handled by our research staff." She carved a forkful of her starter. "The report we had said you knew her better than anyone."

"Who was the report from?"

"I don't know, someone from Northstar probably. Mmm, isn't this delicious?"

Hale tried the mousse. It tasted like solidified cream of mushroom soup. "Natalie, I don't know a soul at Northstar. The first time I set foot in that place was the day before yesterday."

"You know how these things are. Somebody hits the panic button, we get drowned in reports and orders and paperwork." She made a quick smile. "I guess it was just your lucky day."

"Must have been."

"So how did you and Philippa meet?"

"Ryan introduced us." When that met with a blank stare, he went on, "Ryan Reeves. She's a NASA administrator down at Kennedy."

"Oh, sure. Ms. Reeves. Buzz has contact with her boss. Fuller Glenn, isn't that right?"

"I think so."

"Sure, that's how it all came together. Must have been." She scraped the plate clean. "I wonder if I could ask for seconds."

"Here, finish mine."

"You don't like it?"

"It's just a little rich for my taste. But great."

She switched plates. "So you've known her long, then."

"Who, Philippa? Almost two years." Nineteen months, to be exact. Thirteen of the best months he'd ever had, followed by six of the most confusing. "Ryan got interested in her work on superconductors through one of the Kennedy engineers. They became friends. When Philippa was in Washington for a conference, Ryan introduced us."

Natalie smiled as the waiter removed their plates. "You two have a lot in common, I suppose."

He had to laugh. Drew it out when she looked uncertain. Nice to have her control shaken, at least for a moment. "Philippa is the smartest person I've ever met. Physicist, mathematician, dreamer. I'm one step above a door-to-door salesman." Which is probably what he'd find himself stuck with if he bungled this opportunity.

"Oh, come on. I know a sharp guy when I see one."

He let the compliment pass him by with a shake of his head. "The only thing we have in common is surfing."

"I've never tried it. The ocean scares me."

Hale was not the least bit surprised. He had never met a control freak who was comfortable with the sea. "It scares me too, sometimes. When it's really big, the power is so amazing." He searched for the right word. "So *careless*. But when things go right, especially with a big swell, the experience is just awesome."

"Sounds great."

He noted the dulled glaze, knew the reason. Any topic where this lovely lady was not the center of attention was dreary in the extreme. "So tell me about yourself."

"I'm an experience junkie." The words came with the ease of having been often said. "I love life and living. I'm a glutton for experiences. Life's there to try everything, do it all. A fabulous day could be spent parasailing and waterskiing, getting drunk on pina coladas, going to sleep, then getting up at two in the morning and hitting the clubs."

"It makes me tired just listening."

"Oh, I hope not." The practiced look was interrupted by the arrival of their second courses. She looked down at her plate, said, "I want to see everything. Go everywhere. I just don't see how I'm possibly going to fit it all in."

Hale sat and listened through the entire second course. Responded on cue. Showed as much interest as he could bring to bear. In truth the conversation flowed in and out of focus like waves on a rising tide.

"I'm a very competent engineer," Natalie went on. "But I never could get the guys to take me seriously because of my looks. I hated their frozen attitudes, the time warp of the macho club. So I moved into sales. Nobody could compete with the sales I ratcheted up. Then when SRC bought our company eight months ago, they offered me this job. I jumped at it."

She waited, his cue to offer something. "Never regretted it?"

"I've never been any good at regret."

Hale nodded through her description of her contacts and her power meetings in DC and her plans and her ambitions. Inwardly he felt as though Natalie was taking her place in a long line of women, most of whom he could not name. Beautiful women who from birth had been told that the universe revolved around them, who gave pitches so practiced and repetitious they could have been recordings. Urgent talks, forced out by a furious determination to give power to unfocused lives. The only kind of women he deserved.

The restaurant was brought back into focus by a stockinged toe caressing his ankle. "How about if we go back to my place and plan some strategy?"

His smile was forced. But at least it was a smile. "That sounds incredible. But I can't." Watched the surprise come and go across those lovely features, wondered at how little he felt. Numbed from the heart down. "I've got to fly down to Cabo. There are a thousand things to try and arrange before I hit the sack."

"Ooh, I love impromptu trips to far-off lands." Something flickered deep within her gaze, there and gone. "You're going down to look for Philippa?"

"It's just one place I need to check." When this was not enough, he added, "And it's something that needs to be done carefully, at least until we know why she's gone."

She leaned close. "Let me come with you."

"Natalie, I –"

"Never mind, it was a silly thought." She leaned back, for some reason satisfied with her work. "Just don't say no, all right?"

She offered her platinum credit card before the waiter could set down the check. "I'll just have to learn to bide my time."

* * *

Hale stood and watched Natalie's BMW zoom away, did not bother to return the cheery wave. He shivered, despite the fact that the wind had died and the night was blood-warm. He walked down the sloping lot and climbed into his rental car. There was something which could only be done after midnight, and alone.

He could not help himself. He wound his way back up into the hills, did a slow sweep by the place where Philippa's house had once stood. Now it was nothing but a dark mass of cinders and shadows. A few charred posts jutted into the night sky, the streetlights turning them into accusing fingers aimed directly at his heart.

He drove by the charred remains, turned at the road's far end, did a second deliberate sweep. Philippa had loved that house. It had been far more than just a home to her. She had seen this as her haven in a foreign land, a place set apart for her and her alone. As he continued past the black-stained earth he recalled the first time she had brought him home, the shy way she had shown him around, the words unspoken but very clear. Look carefully. This is who I am. Even more, this is who I want to remain.

Hale wheeled the car around and drove down to the La Jolla Shores' miniscule shopping street. He parked in front of the North Shore Café and cut the motor. A group of doctors and nurses from the university hospital were gathered around one noisy outdoor table, still dressed in hospital blues. Hale knew a few of them from Philippa's casual introductions – they were almost as frequent visitors to the coffee shop as his old girlfriend. They cast hellos laced with knowing glances his way, especially the women. Philippa had friends everywhere.

The café was long and high-ceilinged and chic in a rough-hewn way. Tables and chairs battered by long use. Broad-beamed floors scuffed raw. The marble-and-mahogany bar, wooden-bladed fans and age-distorted mirror were all relics of California's earlier days, cut up and carted here when a goldmine hotel went bust up in the desert mountains. All this he had heard from Ben.

The aging relic himself stood behind the bar, wiping down an already gleaming coffee maker and studiously ignoring Hale's approach. The café was empty save for George Benson's crooning jazz. Ben waited until Hale had propped one foot on the bar-rail to declare, "I ain't got a thing to say to you. Not a single solitary word."

Hale looked at his shadow-reflection in the bar's dark-veined marble. It was all he had expected to hear. "I just want to find her, see if I can help –"

"Only way you can help the lady is stay over on the other coast." He was big enough to put some weight behind his gaze. "Where all the fools and losers belong."

"When did you last see her?"

Ben bunched the rag in a quick motion he'd probably prefer to use on Hale's neck. "You got some nerve, bringing your questions in here."

Hale recalled the way Ben had played it whenever he had entered with Philippa, the lingering glances for her, the double helpings of smiles and gab, never a single look in Hale's direction. He pressed, "She was in here sometime before she took off. She had to have been. She never let a day –"

"You never deserved her. I coulda told her that the minute I laid my eyes on you." Ben ground his words out like his throat was full of gravel. "We were talking about heading out, just the two of us. What do you think of that?"

Hale let it stop him. He turned to look out over the café, leaned against the bar, shook his head. The past few days stared back at him, one closed and mysterious door after another. Defeated by the enormity of all the questions he could not answer. "I don't know what to think," he said to the empty air.

Ben remained silent. Which was bad. The emptiness in front of him and inside of him beckoned and plucked at his chest, urging out the words he had scarcely thought, much less spoken to another. "I used to think I had the answers. That I knew where to go, how to live life like it mattered. But now ..."

The door creaked open, and one of the nurses came in bearing a tray piled with empty cups. She gave them both a smile and asked Hale, "You had any word from Philippa?"

"No, I haven't." Allowing his own masks to slip down another notch. "And I'm worried sick."

"Why, you think something happened?"

Hale met the nurse's concerned gaze, but directed the words at the man standing behind him. "I'm almost certain of it. You know Philippa. She wouldn't just run off like this. Not unless something forced her."

"You mean, like kidnapping?"

"I don't think so. I've been by her house. Or where her house used to be. You heard it burned down?"

The nurse's shock was mirrored by a murmur behind him, quickly stifled. The nurse said, "Philippa's lovely bungalow?"

"Not any more. It burned to the ground." Hale did not need to push out his anxiety. In his stripped-down mode it was there for all to see. And hear. "The police don't know what happened. But something has pushed Philippa to run away, I know that much. Something that terrified her. And something that's still after her."

The nurse studied Hale's face, her brow furrowed with worry. She glanced over his shoulder toward where Ben lurked. "Can we do anything?"

"I don't see how, but thanks for asking."

She cast another glance at the unseen Ben, then smiled as best she could and headed for the door. When it had closed and shut them into the silence, Hale stood there, still held by the room's empty reflection.

Finally Ben growled, "You were saying something about having all the answers."

"I used to think I did." The pressure to speak punched him, a giant's fist striking straight for the heart. "You know how it is when things hit you hard as a kid, everything is so scary? You feel like the only way out of this hellhole is to make it so nothing and nobody ever makes you feel that vulnerable, that weak and defenseless ever again."

To his surprise, there was a soft voice behind him, one without the anger or the growl. "I know."

Hale did not turn around. He could not direct these words to another man, especially a stranger who had been after his girl. *His girl.* What a joke those words were. What a lie. "Philippa scared me to death. Every time I left here to go back east, I felt like I was waking up. From a dream or a nightmare, I wasn't sure. Things would be fine here, then I'd go back to a world where I knew the only way to survive was to keep the armor intact. I *knew* this. So I'd leave for Richmond and feel like everything that made sense here was a myth. Someday soon I'd be waking up and hurting like ... I'd be hurting. Crushed. Defeated and shattered and never able to get the pieces together again. So I did the only thing I could do. I broke it off."

A moment's pause, then, "And now?"

"Now. Yeah." The power was there in his chest and his throat and his brain and behind his eyes, so strong a force he could put no strength to his words beyond a sigh. "Now I'm lost. Nothing works like it's supposed to. Nothing. Not work and not my life and not ..."

He wished for Ben to say something, to free him from this scalding honesty. He felt like every word he spoke was tearing him apart. But he could not stop. He did not understand why he was speaking at all, but he was powerless to end it without help from outside.

Yet Ben remained silent, and the pressure kept squeezing his chest until he had to open his mouth and release more of the blistering truth. "Until this morning, I haven't been in the water since we broke up. I haven't been able to go near the sea. I knew soon as I got close enough to hear it, I'd be thinking about her. Until tonight, I haven't dated once. I go into a bar, I sit there and I watch the players go through the motions and the emptiness feels like it's going to choke me with the smoke. My work has gone to hell. Everything I do seems tainted. I'm out here looking for her and fighting for my job at the same time, and not even that makes any sense. I've got people talking words I don't understand, like all of a sudden the whole world has turned against me and I don't even know the language any more."

And there he stopped. Finally he had enough strength to close off the rush, to stand there and stare at the empty room, and know a mirror could not hold any more truth than what he saw reflected in front of him.

"Philippa was really spooked when she came in here that night." Ben's own voice was roughened even further, whether by what he had heard or by the struggle it took to speak, Hale neither knew nor cared. "I mean, she's been dancing on a wire for months now. Concentrating on not falling off. But that last night was the worst I've ever seen her. Standing right there where you are now, leaning on the counter, drinking that quadruple espresso of hers, eyes darting all over the place. But I knew, she wasn't here at all. Something was pressing down on her. She wouldn't say what it was. All she talked about was winning the Nobel. But I knew. She was spooked."

Hale nodded acceptance of the gift, unable to turn and meet whatever was there in the man's eyes. Not wanting to see any trace of what he had just confessed in another person. Not ever.

Ben asked, "You got anywhere to start looking?"

"Cabo." The effort of forming even a sigh of a word was almost beyond him. "I guess I'll just go down and –"

"Funny. We talked about Cabo that last night here. How she'd been someplace for a conference."

"I remember." And he did. It had been two weeks after they had met, so soon that she did not feel right having him come along. Even though both of them knew what was coming, already the sparks and the gentle hunger-ache pulling their bodies together. And their hearts. Even then.

"She told me where she stayed. Hang on, it'll come to me. It's that big blockhouse of a hotel close to Zippers, you know the one?"

He shook his head. He had never been to Cabo. Another promise unfulfilled.

"Valencia. Yeah, that's the name. Hotel Valencia." There was the sound of a page being torn off. "Here, take this. It's my number here and at home. I've got a place down in Baja. Not more than a half-dozen people in the whole world know about it. You find her, you need a place to hang, this is safe. Call me here, I'll set things up."

"Thanks." Hale could not look around, not now. He was stripped to the bone, more naked than he had ever been in his entire life. Nude and ashamed. He swept up the paper and started for the door.

"Hale."

He stopped, his head bowed and staring at his fist wrapped around the doorhandle. Not looking back. Not a glance.

"Man, what I said earlier, it was just wishful thinking." The growl was hollowed by the power that still echoed through the emptiness. "She never got over you enough to look anywhere but inside."

"Thanks." He meant it for everything, for the offer of the house and the information and being willing to help. And for listening. But just then all his strength had to go into opening the door and forcing his legs to carry him out into the night.

13

Saturday morning Hale deposited his rental car at the San Diego airport, then used his cell-phone to call Jerry. "Sorry for bothering you over the weekend."

"No problem. What else am I supposed to do but sit around and wait for the ax to drop?"

"You don't know that. I'm still working on a really big deal over here."

"Great." The guy sounded beyond resigned. "That what you called about?"

"No. Well, in a way. I've got to travel down to Cabo San Lucas. It's at the very bottom of the Baja Peninsula."

"Sounds exotic."

"Not really. Mostly cheap hotels and tequila and scrub and garbage." Playing down the rest, the sea and the sun and the desert's stark beauty. "I'm still working on the Northstar deal. Only now it's being handled by SRC."

"Right." In his mind, Jerry was already fired and desperate. "What's her name?"

"No, listen, this is important. I'm pretty sure my mobile phone won't receive that far down. If you need anything, call me at the Hotel Valencia, that's where I'm booked." He read off the number. "You got that?"

"What would I want to call you for?"

"This is important, Jerry. I don't know how long this is

going to take, but I'm going to try and get back Monday. If you need me and can't get through, call Ryan Reeves in Florida. Her name's in my address book."

"Sure. If they set up the firing line in the meantime, I'll send you a postcard from hell."

* * *

The only last-minute seat Hale had been able to grab was on a small Mexican operator. The ancient propeller-driven craft had smoke-streaked sides and pilots straight from the comic books. There was no door between the cockpit and the cabin; each boarding passenger was welcomed by glimpses of two bearded men in leather racing gloves, mirror shades, and beat-up flight jackets. As Hale settled into his seat, the pilot turned from his controls and gave the travelers a thumbs-up and a pirate's grin. The single stewardess, a pretty Chicana in jeans and T-shirt bearing the plane's logo, was utterly bored with it all.

Once the take-off was complete and cruising altitude reached, the cabin's atmosphere declined to a half-step from utter bedlam. Aging tourists huddled and peered up frightfully as tattooed Pacific Beach surfers rambled up and down the aisle, shouting words only their buddies could understand. At the back of the plane, younger couples clustered and groped. Hale stared out the grimy window to where red-clad hills fell into the deep blue sea, and endured the torment of just another flight.

Evidence of El Nino-bred hurricanes still littered the road into Cabo. Houses and hotels that had not survived the tempest were left in battered heaps, the rubble shoved back far enough to clear the street. Hale stared out the taxi's window and wondered how to break the news about Philippa's home. If he found her at all. Philippa had treated her house as a trademark. It had defined much of what was good about her California life. He did not know how she would take news of losing something so precious. Especially here. Especially now.

Traffic was slow and bizarre. Everything from Porsches to donkey carts fought for space along the bumpy road. Older houses were ringed by fences of sage and wheel-rims. Newer structures were hidden behind tall concrete walls rimmed with broken glass and barbed wire. The ground was brown and hard and dry.

Closer to the ocean, highrise hotels jutted into the unblemished sky. Carefully tended lawns and palms made for refreshing stamps upon the desert's hostile face. Between the structures the sea sparkled and beckoned.

The Hotel Valencia's interior was attractively tiled and incredibly loud. Hard ceramic surfaces made a perfect trap for every laugh, every call, every cry by every kid. A mariachi band played in the distant corner. People trying to talk to the staff had to lean over the reception counter and shout to be heard. Hale marveled at how the check-in staff held on to their smiles.

Using the phone at the front desk, he asked the hotel operator to connect him with Philippa's room. There was no reply. His own room was not ready. Hale stowed his gear with the bellhop. He changed into trunks in the poolhouse, stripped off his board cover, and carried his board around the pool and crowded bar. The sight of a surfer headed for the shore was common enough to draw few stares.

Zippers was the name of the most popular break at Cabo, a rolling right-hander. The wave's direction was named by how it broke from the peak. Hale was a regular footer, which meant he rode with his left foot forward. A right-hand break permitted him to ride facing the wave, granting greater ease and flexibility on turns. Hale paddled out, but held back from approaching the peak. A crowd of locals clustered in a tight group at the primo take-off point, shouting at each other in Spanish and giving the killer eye to any outsider who came too close. Hale had never been one for the aggro of a locals-only break. He headed off to one side, positioning himself on the shoulder about fifty yards south of the peak, and waited for the waves which slipped by the jostling surly crowd.

He was returning seawards from his third wave, enjoying the beautiful day and easy waves and relatively warm water, when a familiar figure started paddling towards him. Hale turned and started towards her, pulling hard. He watched the longboarder stroke through the water, intent on meeting him halfway. Her lazy rhythmic paddling closed the distance with surprising speed. That was Philippa's trademark, this easy loping stroke she could keep up for hours.

Philippa pushed herself upright, the board's thickness causing her to sit almost spread-eagled. She wore her usual warm-water garb, a tight shoulder-harness top and men's boardshorts. The jade-green eyes held a tightly unfocused look, as though she carried a world of worried anger inside, too much to allow her to look clearly at anything beyond her own mind.

Her voice was as taut and enraged as her gaze. "Who sent you?"

14

Saturday morning Ryan made the dawn run with Jeff to Sebastian Inlet. The drive was punctuated by Jeff drumming time to the radio's music on the door, the dash, his seat. Sunrise was a little early in the day for rock and roll, but her son looked so excited and so happy she let him turn up the volume and perform his best air guitar for the gulls and the deep blue sky.

The impact of her Washington trip remained wrapped around Ryan like an invisible barrier. It filtered everything. Not even walking over the dunes at Spanish House and finding relatively uncrowded perfection could push away the confusion.

The surfing was good, but better for Jeff than for her. She cared little for the aggressive action at such a famous spot, or for the cliques which formed on the shoreline. When they moved down to the Sebastian jetty, Jeff knew enough of the locals to be granted a spot in the First Peak lineup. Ryan surfed as long as she wanted by the less crowded borderlands, then sat on the shore and watched her son. Jeff's surfing was definitely coming along. He was adapting well to the slash-and-burn tactics of current competitive surfing. He easily flipped his board about, without the fatal flaw of arm waving which made most young surfers resemble wounded gulls.

Jeff's talent had recently won him sponsorship from the Quiet Flight Surfshop, a true jewel in the Florida surfing crown, and now that she watched her son flail she could understand why. Jeff even managed one little aerial hop over a close-out section, drawing hoots from neighboring surfers. When he paddled out after that last maneuver he cast a swift glance shorewards. Ryan responded with a hoot of her own and double thumbs-up, not minding in the least when her son jerked his attention back seawards. It was certainly not cool to look toward one's parent for approval.

They made do with a burger at the local country store for lunch, sharing the shady porch with a score of other salt-encrusted water dancers. Ryan felt her chest swell with pride at the way even surfers twice Jeff's age called hello, gave him the casual greeting of one counted as an equal.

Back to the shore for a second surf, then homeward bound.

It was only when they were in the car and pointed northwards that the world threatened to crowd in. She knew the instant it happened, could feel the old familiar worries reach down from a cloudless sky to grip her gut once again. She watched Jeff's brow knot up and his lips compress, and knew it was happening to him as well. They kept the radio off, but did not speak. Both preferred to refrain from asking all the swarming questions for which Ryan had no answers. Such as, was their family still a family, and if so for how long.

They tried to hold their focus on the quiet satisfaction, the tired contentedness, the gulls which flew alongside their car. Ryan searched the afternoon's shimmering light and waving palms, and tried to make that be enough. At least for one day.

As soon as she crossed into south Melbourne, however, her cell-phone rang from the glove box. Jeff groaned, slid down in his seat and pulled the obligatory Billabong cap over his eyes when she reached in and keyed the switch. "Ryan Reeves."

But it was not Hale. Instead, Florence Avery demanded

querulously, "Where the hell have you been? I thought you were going to keep this thing on."

"I have. My son and I have been down south of here in a nature reserve. I guess I must have been out of range for my satellite phone."

A pause, then, "Is he there with you now?"

"As a matter of fact, he is."

"When will you be home?"

"Half an hour. But can't this wait until Monday and the office?"

"No, it cannot. I'll call you back in thirty minutes." Florence hung up.

After Ryan clicked off the phone and stowed it away, they drove in silence until Jeff finally whined, "Why did you have to bring that thing anyway?"

Concern over Florence's call added fresh fuel to all the other worries crowding in, leaving her no room for anything except honesty. "Because Hale is in Cabo San Lucas looking for Philippa and I'm worried about them. Do you know where Cabo is?"

"Sure." The facts and the plain speaking pushed him upright. "Uncle Hale is looking for Philippa?"

"He has been ever since I had to come home for the launch they just scrubbed."

"Why, Mom?"

"Why is she missing, why is he looking, or why am I worried?"

He was not accustomed to such simple directness. "I don't know."

She glanced over, saw not a child, not a boy, but the man who he was swiftly becoming. The realization left her aching inside. "A good answer. And the truth is, I don't know either. I've got a billion questions and no answers. Not one."

"Like what?"

"Like, well," she took a long breath. "How would you

feel about moving back to Washington?" Surprising both of them. "I've been offered an incredible job."

"Are you going to take it?"

"Nothing's definite yet. But even if it was, I couldn't do it against the wishes of my family." Pushing hard against the desires clenching her gut, feeling good despite the almost desperate hunger pulling her north. Feeling *right*. "I couldn't do that."

They passed the Melbourne causeway before Jeff finally said, "I wouldn't mind so much."

"What?" She slowed to stare at her son.

"I guess it'd be okay."

"Jeff ..." Not wanting to have him take it back. But needing to understand. "Honey, what about your friends? What about your surfing?"

"I had friends in Washington before." He kept his face pointed forward, but could not disguise the pinched quality to his voice. "You and Dad were happy in Washington. That's what I remember most."

It felt like her chest was breaking open, her heart forming a molten puddle in her lap. "Oh, son."

"I want us to be happy again. I want us to stay a family. If that means we have to go to Washington ..." He shrugged his tanned sandy shoulders. "When do we leave?"

* * *

But traffic slowed along Florida's coastal A1A to a typical Saturday crawl, and the remaining drive took closer to an hour. Ryan's cell-phone pinged twice more, but she left it in the glove box unanswered. Jeff remained silent and withdrawn, not even glancing over when Ryan told him not to pull out the phone again.

It began ringing a third time just as she halted in front of their Merritt Island house. Ryan pulled out the phone, punched the receive key, but did not raise the apparatus. Let the woman wait. As Jeff slid his board from the back she asked, "What do you want for dinner, honey?"

His young face still bore an expression hollowed from their discussion. "I don't care."

"How about pizza?" Which was his all-time favorite food. Given a choice between pizza and world peace, Jeff would have hesitated about one nanosecond. "Pepperoni, mushrooms, green peppers, double sausage, extra cheese, the works. You interested?"

"Sure."

"Go ask Kitty and your dad if they'd like that and a movie. Family treat." Watching her son's retreating back only stoked the flames. She waited until he was inside the house before finally lifting the phone. "What."

"Ryan, this call is not intended to jerk you around."

"You sure as hell could have fooled me." Letting the breath go ragged from releasing her frustration. "I've got enough troubles holding to shreds of a family life without spending time on my *only* free Saturday this *month* talking about NASA."

"This isn't official business. But never mind that. Do you know Kennedy's secure phone?"

"I know it," she said, the question calming her down. The secure phone room was located down the hall from the director's office, and probably had been designed as a broom closet. Ryan thought it looked like a cross between a phone booth and a padded cell. The walls were covered with layers of foam with egg-box bulges. There was a prison slit of wire-reinforced glass and a double lock on the door. "I've never used it."

"If the time ever comes when you've got something critical to report, do it over the secure phone. You call me over an open line, and ask about the weather up here in Washington. That's the signal. Wait a half hour, then go to the booth and call me. I'll do the same."

"You're about to get me very worried."

"Good. You'll have a better chance of staying healthy. Have you heard anything more about the position the Senator offered you?"

"Why should I? Washington has shut down for the weekend." The afternoon's anxiety raised another notch. "What are you getting me involved with here?"

"Ryan, you're already so involved you'd be safer playing Russian roulette with five bullets in the chamber. What about Dr. Laremy, anything new on her?"

"My friend is still looking. What's the connection here?"

"I wish I knew. You said the scientist was doing research into superconductors?"

"That's what brought her to NASA's attention."

"Semiconductors may be the research rage, but there's nothing here worth vanishing over. Most likely your Dr. Laremy stumbled onto something major. Something big enough to scare the bad guys." Florence chewed that over a moment before demanding, "When did you and Dr. Laremy meet?"

"Just over two years ago. Fuller Glenn was supposed to attend a scientific conference in Washington, but he got tied down and asked me to go for him. Said to make a point of meeting a woman whose work was grabbing some attention. See if we could string her along. You know the ploy."

"Of course." It was standard NASA fare. Offer entry to the nation's most exclusive scientific club, see if that would be enough to draw upon her expertise and her work, while offering a minimum of money. NASA was always short of research funding. "And she agreed?"

"She liked the idea of tapping into our research archives. A lot of superconducting work is classified." Ryan smiled at the memory. "She was your typical scientist when it came to bureaucracy. Never been fingerprinted in her life, had a horror of meeting with the Fibbies for her vetting." A FBI top-secret vetting was required for all scientists before they were granted access to NASA research documentation. "It was while I walked her through the vetting that we became friends. Good friends."

Florence was silent for a moment, then asked quietly, "How long after that did you receive the first of those big promotions?"

She felt her hackles rise. "You're saying they raised me from the ranks of thousands because of her?"

"Just asking," Florence replied.

Ryan tried to think, said reluctantly, "I suppose it was about that time. But that doesn't mean –"

"Just one question more. Did anything else happen at that conference where you met Dr. Laremy? Anything out of the ordinary?"

"For Pete's sake, Florence, that was two years ..." Then the sudden memory stopped her.

"Yes?"

"Clay East."

"Senator Townsend's chief aide? He was there?"

"He came over and introduced himself. Made a big deal of me, that's why I remember it. Not only did he know me, but he knew about my career." Said he would be keeping an eye on her. She remembered that too. Amazed and thrilled by the attention. "He might have introduced me to Philippa, I can't remember. Is he tied to this?"

"I have nothing to indicate that," she replied carefully. "One further question. How much does Harry tell you of his company's current operations?"

"These days Harry has trouble telling me the kids had dinner. I can't remember the last time we talked about work without arguing." Ryan stared at the pair of twisted Florida oaks flanking her drive. "What about this latest job offer they've made me? Is that tied in as well?"

Florence paused a moment, and when she came back on the line her voice had entered a battle-hardened mode. "A little history is called for if you're going to understand what we're up against. A few years back, Lockheed merged with

Martin-Marietta, and then Lockheed-Martin acquired General Dynamics. Competing with them on the super-grando scale is the conglomerate formed by Boeing, Rockwell, and a handful of other players. These players have been vicious competitors and enemies for years. Even so, when it came time to bid on the contract for supplying the space shuttle, what happens?"

"They formed a fifty-fifty merger and put in one bid." Ryan knew all about the resulting United Space Alliance. The USA Corporation was chief of the primes currently operating at Kennedy. "It was either that or face being shut out of Kennedy entirely. The risk was too great, so they buried the hatchet and formed the joint venture."

"Exactly. The issue now raging up here in Washington is, how long will they stay at the top of the heap. Their position is being challenged by SRC and the success they've had with the new shuttle concept. You know about SRC?"

"Some, not a lot. They're new kids on the block here." And they were Philippa Laremy's top research funder.

"Not long ago, Northstar and a couple of other major suppliers saw the writing on the wall and started the Space Research Corporation. There was a lot of resistance within Northstar to the move, believe it or not. Many of their senior directors felt they would be better off staying solo and working with whichever of the two biggies won the next initial contract. But the consolidators won out, arguing it would be better to join with other players and try to become the third giant prime. Most of the contractors coming into SRC have a Defense background. A couple of months ago, I contacted a friend over in Defense appropriations, and started running some detailed background checks. That's where I ran into Congressman Lassard."

Ryan walked impatiently along the perimeter of her lawn. Suddenly the air above her back yard seemed clogged with years of tense secrets. "Lizard Lassard supplied you with their corporate accounts?"

"Stop calling him that. No, their books are all on public record, stored with the SEC. Congressman Lassard happened to be involved in some checking of his own. He heard about what I was doing and got in touch."

Ryan knew she should be concentrating, but she remained trapped by the fact that Florence had truly become involved with Lester Lassard. For years he had been the nemesis opposed to every cent spent at Kennedy. He was a red-headed Florida cracker with the voice of a rusty foghorn. He wore his belly like a badge of honor. Loved to have his picture taken with his hunting buddies, guns in hand and grins in place, poised over a bunch of small dead furry animals. Ryan thought the hunting dogs with their lolling tongues looked far more intelligent than the men. "So he's done nothing but feed off your work."

"He's okay, I tell you. He happens to be as passionate about fighting government waste as I am. He is also running this particular show. These SRC companies, they really make a team. They're the kind who until recently would low-ball their bids, then tack on so many add-ons and research costs the final bill would choke an elephant."

Ryan tried to hear beyond her sense of revulsion for Lassard, but it was tough.

Along the Space Coast, where one job in four derived from Kennedy, Lassard was universally loathed. A bumper sticker had circulated for years that simply read, 'Skin The Lizard'. Ryan's had washed off during the last major storm. "They were cheating."

"Until not long ago their practices were standard ops for a lot of Defense work. Not that it hasn't happened at NASA as well. And now they're using their collective political clout and Washington expertise to win as much of our new business as they can. The new shuttle contract is a case in point."

"But are they cheating?"

Florence hesitated. "Ledgers can tell a lot of tales, if you know the language of numbers. When you're dealing with hundreds of millions of dollars, a lot can be swept under the carpet. Before, projects given to these companies made interesting reading, long as you didn't mind a bilious stomach and high blood pressure. But once they entered the SRC fold, things *appeared* to get straightened out."

"You're not giving me anything I can use, Florence."

"We're seeing a lot of smoke on the horizon. Nothing hot enough to set off our alarms, but danger signs are appearing all over the place." A pause, then, "We need your help."

"I can't believe you're disturbing my weekend for this garbage. You know how Lassard treated me. Far as I'm concerned, the Lizard's hide belongs on the wall of an alligator farm. The rogue beast too dangerous to wrestle. Had to be put down." Ryan stomped back through the lengthening shadows towards her home. "I wouldn't shake the Lizard's hand if I wore fire-retardant gloves!"

"That attitude is *precisely* what stymies me," Florence whipped back. "If you could only see how far this spreads. Every stone we turn over has more of the bugs running from the light. This is bigger than you think. I need allies out there, Ryan, and so do you."

"There is no way I'm going to meet with Lassard. The man is certifiable."

"He's a friend."

"You can't imagine how much it worries me to hear you say that."

Another sigh. "Just be careful out there. We're in the big league here. These guys are fighting for their lives."

* * *

Ryan came back downstairs from showering and changing clothes, pushed through the back door, called for the kids. The air smelled as fresh as it ever became during Florida's semitropical June. Harry was around, she could sense her husband's presence, but he was making himself scarce. Which she decided was fine with her.

Jeff skipped down the stairs backwards, shouted up at his younger sister, "*Flubber* is for sissies with a pinprick IQ."

"It is not!" Kitty was going through an awkward ten-year-old stage, growing into all knobs and clumsy movements. Her knees looked big as cantaloupes on her too-skinny frame. She tumbled down the steps and cried, "Mama, make him take it back!"

"Robin Williams is one giant freckle," Jeff shouted exultantly. It wasn't often he took the trouble of getting under his sister's normally placid skin. "He grins like he's got a permanent case of constipation."

"Enough," Ryan called, slipping the phone into her back pocket. "Who taught you to talk like that?"

"Daddy."

"He did not! He loved *Flubber*! He told me!"

"Of course he did, honey," Ryan soothed. "So did I. And so did Jeff." But not thirty-seven times, which was their best estimate of how often Kitty had seen the video. Her daughter's current goal in life was to become a scientist like Philippa and discover intelligent Jello with an oversized rear, an attitude, and a taste for tango. "Where's Daddy?"

"He's not coming," Jeff said, backing away and making faces at his sister's angry approach. "He says he has to work."

Which went a long way to explaining why her normally peace-making son was picking on his sister. "Jeff, stop taunting Kitty. And apologize."

"No way."

"Fine. Kitty and I will just go have pizza by ourselves. You can stay home and have some yogurt."

That stopped him dead in his tracks. He gave his mother a doubtful glance, took in the severe expression, and mumbled, "Apologize."

"Louder."

A fractional increase in volume. "I apologize."

Ryan watched Kitty's anger fade. She never had stayed mad for long, not even as a toddler. Ryan said to her son, "Fine. Now kiss your sister and make up."

Jeff stiffened. "I'd rather kiss the blowhole of a dead whale!"

Ryan tried for stern, but her grin could not be held down. "What?"

Jeff caught sight of the grin and leapt for the car. "Double sausage and Italian pepperoni! Come on, Mom, the movie starts in an hour!"

Ryan hugged her daughter, steered her to the car, released the chuckle. One big happy family.

15

"No one sent me, Filly." Hale sat there on his board, the water icy to his waist and the sun baking his shoulders and his chest. The exact same paradox he felt at seeing her again. Warmed by the sight of her, chilled by her look of quiet fury. "Ryan got worried when you disappeared. She asked me to help find you."

"That's all?" Philippa turned her incensed gaze shorewards. "Nobody followed you down?"

"The plane down was your typical Cabo riot. But I'm pretty certain I wasn't followed." Hale watched the breeze touch the water, framing the pair of them with a billion flickering prisms, all the shades of the rainbow, all of them blue. "What's going on, Filly?"

She pushed up onto her knees and began paddling. "I need to go in now. I'm growing cold."

Hale followed her to the beach, keeping a half-stroke back and to one side. Wishing he knew what to say. Wanting to sort through the sudden tumult of emotions and thought. Instead he found only the burdensome silence of storms beyond the horizon. He knew a sudden dread at the thought he would have to tell her that her beloved home was no more.

They climbed the steps to the hotel. After the hard-scrabble beach the stretch of lawn looked impossibly green. The sparkling pool and veranda of hand-painted tiles held the artificiality of a stage set. The desert was real. The crashing ocean and the sun and the heat, these were genuine. The people sprawled on lawn chairs, drinking from tall glasses decorated with umbrellas and plastic giraffes, their red skin plastered with sweet-smelling oils, their laughter brassy and their talk overloud, who were they? Where did they belong? Certainly not here, where desert wed with sky and sea.

Hale continued to follow Philippa's silent lead. He set his board down with hers so that they leaned against the sea wall. He pulled over a chair and sat with his back to the people and the noise. Like her, he looked out over the ocean, knowing his features held the same pinched cast as Philippa's. He had no idea what to say.

When Philippa spoke, her voice still held its frigid cast. "A successful experiment is based upon applying the proper stimuli in an isolated situation."

He thought her voice sounded rusty with disuse. "What?"

"You asked me what is happening here. I'm trying to explain."

The words freed him to turn and stare. Her naturally curly hair was matted with salt, pulled back to reveal a strong neck and aggressively pointed jaw. Her face was all lines and angles, even more than Hale recalled. And the eyes were far more suspicious. They inspected him carefully, utterly uncertain who he was. And clearly angry he was there at all. "I'm listening."

"Any experiment begins by isolating your environment." Her tone held the calculating penetration of someone distanced by ancient rage. She was pushing at him, shoving him back and down. Using her intelligence as a last and final shield. "The scientist must be able to dictate precisely which stimuli are applied, and to what degree."

Hale nodded. Not because he understood. Because he recalled this peculiar pattern of discourse.

"If this disconnection is not complete," she went on, "a stray catalyst could very well wreck your findings. The experiment would be destroyed."

Minus her anger, this talk could have led up to their last argument. Philippa tended to treat every problem as something which needed to be examined inside a lab, and the habit infuriated him. Hale found himself spanning the six months since their last meeting as though it was another crack in the pavement beneath his chair. He was drowning in the overwhelming force of returning to rhythms and habits he loathed. False cadences he had no chance of correcting. "But life isn't an experiment, Filly."

Her gaze was cold. "I beg your pardon?"

"Life wasn't designed for you to stand at a distance and peer at everything through a microscope." But now, in terms of their emotions, the roles were reversed from their last fight. This time it was Hale who felt the quiet yearning, wishing he could reverse the flow. "You can't control life, Filly. You can't reduce your world down until it fits on a Petri dish. You can't hold everyone and everything at arm's length and pick it apart with a mental scalpel."

Her gaze was oblique. "That's quite the little speech, coming from you."

"It doesn't work that way," he finished lamely.

"Shall I close up shop now, or will you permit me to continue?"

He waved a hand in defeat. The sun was a golden mallet poised overhead, pounding upon his head and shoulders. Every beat of his heart thudded in time to the desert and the waves and the vibrating heat. He was pinned by forces far beyond his control.

"A catalyst takes an activity away from randomness and moves it towards a specific end point." She swept a hand out in a gesture probably honed in one of her undergraduate classes. A grand closure to any wish he might have to come closer. "Simplicity is the key, in an experimental environment or in a formula. Einstein had the ability to boil theories down to that level. Planck's constant is another beautiful example. The ideal theory would explain everything and fit on a T-shirt."

Hale felt split by sun-fed lightening and sea-borne thunder. He knew a growing temptation to stand up and walk away. Wrap the shreds of his pride about him and accept defeat by leaving. But some deeper part of him moaned a tune as sorrowful and soft as the wind.

"My fleeing to Cabo was only partly to hide. This was also a test. I needed to see who would follow." Philippa's face took on a bitter cast. "And look what happens. I suppose I should have expected this. That they would use you to hunt me down. What lure did they use to hook you in?"

"I told you." The internal lament chanted he was helpless to do anything about this pattern. They were doomed to follow their pre-arranged course, dancing their desert melody into isolation and lonely abandon. "Ryan asked me to help track you down. She was worried, Filly. We all were."

"I'll just bet you were." Stabbing him with icy daggers. "How did you find me, Hale?"

"I asked around. Spoke to your lab assistant. It doesn't matter. Can you come back?"

"Not just yet. I still need to confirm or deny all these horrid fears that have been plaguing me."

"Not just fears," he murmured, hating to be the one to tell her. Knowing there was no choice but to share the news. "Not any more."

"I beg your pardon?"

"Filly, I'm really sorry." A moment searching for an easier breath, which was not found. No choice but to spill it out. "Your house has burned down."

"What?"

"I'm so sorry."

Naked pain shattered her gaze. "The bastards have destroyed my home?"

"The police still aren't sure if it was arson or accident. But it went up so fast, I'd say it had to be planned."

"How do you know that?"

"I was there. I saw it."

"What did you do?"

"There wasn't anything anyone could do. Filly, the place didn't burn so much as explode. All the windows –"

She showed the instant motion of an enraged cat, one moment seated beside him and the next standing with her rage bristling and claws bared. "You stood there and let it burn?"

"No ... I was on the phone with Ryan when it happened." The words sounded feeble even before they were spoken. "She told me to get out of there as quick as I could. She said I couldn't search for you if I was locked –"

"They set out to destroy the one thing left to me in the world that I cherish, and you *ran away*?"

"Filly, listen to what I'm saying. Ryan was berserk. She said –"

"What the bloody hell do I care how she was feeling!" Her voice raised to the point it turned heads all about the poolside. "You didn't try to save *anything*?"

Hale struggled to peel himself from the chair's plastic straps and rise to his feet. "Filly, slow down. Please. The thing went up like a bomb had been set off. Maybe it had. Two minutes earlier and I would –"

"Do you find it absolutely necessary to utterly destroy everything in your path?" When he did not respond, she shouted, "Did you set that fire yourself?"

"That's silly and you know it."

"I know nothing of the sort! It's *precisely* the kind of insane act I would expect from a man who is happy only when he is demolishing someone else's life!"

She was no longer talking just about her home. Hale knew that, knew also a sense of utter helplessness. He stood in front of her, battered by the flames from all her past hurts. "Filly, please."

"You utter *shit*!" She bent over, hefted her board, and swung it with a vicious force that would have felled him had he not backed away. "You *revolting* little man!"

"Wait, don't –"

"I have nothing whatsoever to say to you," she said over her shoulder. "Not now, not ever."

He stepped around the beach chair and followed her, trying to ignore all the stares that framed this horrible scene. "Listen, I came all the way down here –"

"Yes, your latest and biggest mistake." The words were brittle with rage. "Lead them down here so they can continue the process they've started with my *home*."

"That's not true. I wanted to help."

"Oh, *please*." She jerked to a halt. "Do you really think I care the slightest bit what you wanted? This isn't about you, Hale. My biggest mistake was in thinking it ever was."

Hale stood and watched Philippa storm away. The heat and the light and the stares all coalesced into a single thought grinding through his brain. That this was exactly what he deserved. The reason for the entire trip. Finally granting her a chance to do to him as he had done before.

16

Hale's afternoon was spent pacing the narrow beach with twin companions, frustrated anger and tight-chested remorse. He kept his back to the pool and the veranda and the tinkling laughter, shamed not by the attention which had long since been turned elsewhere, but rather by his own shattered absence. A better man would have known what to say to Philippa. A better man would have kept her from using rage to slice through whatever strands of their relationship were left. A better man would never have run away at all.

The late afternoon sun still had the force of a hammer striking steel. The desert accepted none of the heat, and reflected it all. Hale walked along the shoreline and felt every last trace of moisture sucked from his skin. Transforming him into a moving pillar of salt. Condemned as the man who had dared turn back.

It was not altogether a bad thing, this rage. He needed to set a distance between him and all that might have been. Every pace was a determined stride away from his futile hopes, and toward a different future. Perhaps now he could finally put Philippa behind him. Perhaps now he could move ahead. To what did not matter as much as the myth of motion.

He trod back up the hotel's back stairs and sank into the beach chair's plastic straps. Some meager shred of his heart still beat to the painful tune of maybe. Maybe if he went up to her room and threw himself on her mercy, she might forgive. Maybe once she had cooled down she would listen. But the rest of him simmered with defeated fury. She had made her choice. It was done. All he needed now was something to draw him away from what was finished, and focus him on what was to come. The mind's tune rang louder than the heart's sad refrain, perhaps because it was so familiar. Tonight he would hit the bars, find his patter and his steps again. Locate a willing one-night friend to remind him what was important.

He glanced at his watch, wondered if his room was ready. He scanned the crowded beach, hunting for a likely prey, wondered what her name would be.

"Hale! *There* you are!"

The lovely voice jolted him out of his seat long before he consciously realized whose it was.

Natalie rushed around the pool, ignoring the stares of guests and staff alike. "What a beautiful hotel! And this day, isn't it to die for?" She stopped two paces away and beamed in triumph. "Remember, you didn't tell me not to come."

He found his throat was sandpaper-dry. "Tell me you're a mirage."

"I've been called a lot of things before, but that's a new one." Natalie Durrant moved closer, enveloped in her own cloud of smiles and animation and perfume. She dropped her shoulderbag and beamed at Hale. "Well, it was such an impulsive thing to do, but I forgot to get your signature on some papers, and I thought, why wait until next week? So I had my travel agent check some of the hotels around here, and guess what, the second one she called had a reservation for you!"

Hale recalled Philippa's words, knew this could well be the follower she suspected. Was devastated to find he no longer cared. "Natalie, this is incredible, I can't believe ..."

"Oh, pooh, hasn't anybody ever told you too much loneliness is bad for your complexion?" She gave him a gay smile, waited for his reaction. When he said nothing more, impatience showed with the words, "Anybody else would be delighted to have me show up as a little surprise package."

"I am. Totally surprised and totally delighted," he agreed, and stared out to sea. Wishing he knew what to do with this gift. Wishing he knew whom to ask. Was it an answer to basic need, or just one more step along a blind and dangerous road? But the ocean's glittering blue held no answers, and the waves seemed to crash with a mocking roar.

There was a soft touch on his arm. He turned back to where Natalie stood plucking at the front of her sweat-dampened blouse. She gave him a slight pout and said, "Is there anyplace where a hot little girl can get herself a drink?"

* * *

Though her legs remained weak from the encounter with Hale, Philippa rushed through the remaining preparations. Her haste was fueled by the conviction that whoever was searching could not be far behind. As she was packing her last remaining documents she halted and stepped out the balcony door, suddenly out of breath. She gripped the railing with both hands and waited for the trembling to pass. The rough concrete platform jutted from the hotel's southern corner and was open to the afternoon sun and the sea-sounds. She kept her gaze down to ensure she did not look out and spot Hale. She could not have endured another sight of him sitting there in Cabo. It would have shattered her completely. As soon as she was certain her legs would support her, she went on with her work.

It was not like her to feel such weakness. But nothing of this entire experience fit the norm. Perhaps she should have expected them to dupe Hale and use him. The wandering errant knight sent on the impossible quest, it made for a tragic tale. And the news he had brought fit perfectly. Philippa padded back and forth across her room, hurrying and at the same time wishing she had more that needed doing. Anything, even the tedium of packing yet again, was better than stopping and giving in to the tumult of impossible thoughts. She showered and dried herself with a rough towel, rubbing so hard it felt like she was taking off a layer of skin. She then returned to her room and leaned against the wall, finally releasing the sigh she had been holding since Hale had paddled over, slicing through the field of blue on his waterborne steed. Her mind's eye replayed the scene, only now her gallant knight was wrapped in a cloak of doom.

She dressed and then carefully checked the room once more, ensuring all her preparations were complete. She hurried through the planned routine, her mind captured by a tragic litany. It wasn't her fault that Hale was blinded by his fatal flaw. She had neither made him so beautiful nor trapped him within a past which left him unable to love. She was not even partially to blame.

Philippa stopped because all was done. All but closing the little safe in her closet, stowing away her computer, and transferring the smallest case elsewhere. But still she felt trapped. Where was she going from here? Whom could she trust? Just seeing Hale again had brought out all the old aching yearning lusting hopes. She needed him in so many ways, and so desperately. But to have him return just to report the last remaining segment of the life she loved had gone up in flames ... Philippa kicked the safe door closed with her sandal. Life was so bloody unfair.

She walked over to her desk, sat down, and raised the computer screen. Her files were already organized for the ordeal to come, but it wouldn't hurt to check once more. Then she decided to see if the compound ordered from the Berkeley supply house had been delivered. If so, she'd need to arrange with the physics lab to have it forwarded ... where?

But when she logged into the Finnish safe-house, the telephone on the desk in her computer-generated room was blinking on and off. Her heartrate surged. Only one person knew the code for direct message access. Only one.

She keyed in for message delivery. When the face came into focus, Philippa cried out loud.

17

Hale stood at the thatch-roofed outside bar, surrounded as much by his own silence as the crowded shadows and brittle laughter. He gave the sweating bartender his order and stared across the pool to where Natalie did her swaying dance to the poolhouse. She paused by the door, gave him a little wave of invitation to join her. He hesitated an instant, pulled by what should have happened this day.

The familiar urgent flames filling the barren point at the middle of his chest tasted like dust carried by desert heat, but at least he knew them well. Hale set down money and gripped the two frosted glasses, the chill shocking against the rising heat of his own skin. He crossed the little bridge spanning the pool, felt droplets splash on his calves, could almost feel the steam rising as they instantly dried. Nothing that cool and clear could exist on him. Not then.

He pushed through the poolhouse door, had to stop to adjust to the relative shadow. "Natalie?"

"Back here. Hurry."

The interior was a single white-washed room partitioned into simple cubicles. Each was fronted by a pair of slatted swinging doors which began at knee-height and stopped at shoulder-level. More a suggestion of privacy than reality.

He walked down the central aisle, the rough concrete floor prickling his bare feet. A pool attendant walked by carrying a double-armful of clean towels. His knowing smile flashed white and broad in a brown face. Hale felt the push of light and air behind him as the outer door opened, and somehow knew they were now alone.

So did Natalie. She pushed open the cubicle's swinging door and cooed, "Oh, goody, you don't know how much I've been looking forward to this." Natalie wore her silk blouse. And nothing else. Tanned legs were bare to where they disappeared beneath the hem. She looked smaller without her heels, not merely shorter. Smaller and more vulnerable. And immensely desirable.

And available. She accepted the glass, hummed a low moan as she took the first swallow. Closed her eyes and rubbed the sweating glass over her forehead. The movement was enough to raise the hem of her blouse impossibly high. Hale did not know where to look.

She lifted dark eyelashes and caught his roving gaze. Reading him perfectly. Rewarding him with liquid eyes and another tiny pout. She raised her glass and clinked it against his. A musky breath made sweet from the drink as she said, "Here's to the good times."

Before he could recover she was gone, the door swinging back and forth in tantalizing glimpses. A moment's absence, then the blouse was flipped over the door.

One bare arm reached over. "Would you hold my glass for a minute?"

"Sure." Watching the hint of flesh rise and fall behind the slatted doors. Knowing she was utterly in control. Knowing he had no choice. She flashed him a look. "You're peeking."

"No kidding."

Natalie pushed through the door and reached for the glasses. "Here, let me take those." She turned her back to him, doing a little head-shake so her hair spilled forward. "Do me up, please. See the one tiny little button?"

"Yes." The fabric of her swimsuit was flesh-toned and sheer as a negligee. It was more a one-piece body stocking than a swimsuit, cut high over the swelling line of her hips, exposing more of each buttock than it covered. No shoulder straps. Arms bare. Cut so the swell of her breasts was visible from each side. A long gap like the back of a strapless evening gown, closing with a flimsy collar buttoned at the nape. Almost nothing covered. No support whatsoever.

And none needed. Natalie turned around, gave him his glass, used her free hand to sweep her hair back and reveal her breasts. More revealed than if they were utterly bare.

Natalie returned to the cubicle, came out again stuffing her clothes in the shoulder bag. She swung it over the arm carrying her glass. Her other arm slid in and around his own. Drawing him so close she pressed her flesh up his entire length. "Could we sit out for just a little while?"

"Sure."

"I'd love to go straight to my room." Breathless as he felt. Walking as though she desperately needed his support. If it was an act, it was perfect. "But I've come all this way, I'd love just a little sun."

Hale was so wrapped in her scent and her touch and all that was to come he could totally ignore the stares that followed them back to the seawall. Gazes as insubstantial as faces on a movie screen. The reality held by the day and the heat and the sun, and the blank space at the center of his being. And the inner lament he could almost block out entirely.

* * *

The face of Alexis reached across distance and turmoil and time. The slightly canted smile was all his own, a knowing look with more gentleness than should ever belong on such a masculine face. His image moved upon the screen, then halted, then moved again. Philippa told herself it was the result of Alexis using an earlier generation of continuous motion analogue imager and a computer with pre-MMX technology. Her mind stated that this prehistoric Russian technology caused the stopgap output, the images sticking in place for a second or so, then jerking forward. But her heart paid no attention to her analytical thoughts. Her dissection did not protect her. What she felt was that time froze and flowed there on the screen, as though Alexis sought to hold back what already was. And with each image, his smile challenged her not to weep.

"So, Philippa Laremy. We are a team, yes? Such a team the world cannot even imagine. We deal with impossibles. First your theory, and now this." The smile canted even more slightly. "We have learned how to communicate even from beyond the grave."

She forced herself to hold the tears in. Not one instant of this did she want to miss. She dug her fingernails into the bare flesh above her knees, each breath a quiet hiss through tightly clenched teeth.

"We must accept this, you and I. Of course, it is easy for me now, since I have no choice but to be dead. But you, yes, you are the fighter. You want to change all the world. But this not even you can change. You hear this because I am now beyond space and time. I make this delayed message in case they catch me before I can reach you.

"I wish I could tell you what I have found here, where life and death have now brought me. Such worlds, can you imagine? Yes, perhaps you can. Perhaps I could as well, but I am trapped in this universe of three dimensions by love. The only unbreakable chains, that is what life was proving to me, yes? Love *imprisoned* me, holding me with joy to our tiny space-time continuum. Ah, if only it could protect me as well."

The smile had dissolved. Vanished between one flickering image and another. The face was naked in its appeal. "I have written out all the formulae I could think of and scanned all my notes. They will download when I finish with the talking. Some are nonsense. Things from journals. Things important only because they are held in my hand this moment, and I see in them all the discoveries I will not make. And the most important of these discoveries, can you guess what that is?"

She nodded to the screen. The motion was enough to free a single tear. She wiped it away, determined to see this with utter clarity. Nodded again. She knew.

"It is not seeing my daughter grow up. It is not having another dawn to awaken beside my wife. It is not having another meal, the three of us in our little home, smiling and laughing and talking as only people in this three-dimensional existence can do, those of us lucky enough to know the power of love. Loves and fears and hopes. Dreams I share with you. All the distances, all the history and the mistrust, can we build a bridge from fragile sharing, you and I? I hope so. For my daughter's sake, I hope so.

"What I want to speak with you about here, it is not the formulae. It is to beg. My family, Philippa. My beloved wife and daughter. I am sending them to the refugee camp outside Vienna. They will be processed, photographed, and then within a few weeks they will be sent back. As soon as they arrive back in Russia, my dear Philippa, they are dead. If I am speaking to you here, it is because the theory is now fact. A return to Russia is a return to death."

He leaned forward, his voice remaining calm because there was no room in the screen for any more emotions. "Save my family, dear Philippa Laremy. Take my formulae and make them resound through the reality of our three-dimensional universe. Give them shape and form. And give my family a future. Do what I have been unable to do. Succeed where I failed. Will you do that? Can I trust you with the only part of my life that holds real meaning?"

"Yes." She whispered the word. Shouted inwardly, wrenchingly, seeking to catapult the message beyond the bounds of space and time. "Yes."

"As for this work, I think you know what it means now. We were on the verge, you and I, even that first meeting when it was lost in the shadows of the unseen future, we sensed the knowing. So now you must prepare. This is strong input. Strong force. Very strong. And dangerous. Prepare for the danger."

He hesitated then, caught by uncertainty. He forced himself to continue, "You will accept the advice of a colleague? Do not prepare alone. Accept strength from others. Gravity is stronger than you alone." A trace of the old smile, tilting his face back to one side. "Newton had no idea with what he played. But we know, you and I. This force, it has baffled the world and ruined every unified theory. There is only one force stronger, yes? One force more baffling. More *commanding*."

His features held the eternal sadness of one who had been felled by his own wisdom. "Will you help?"

* * *

Natalie was the first woman Hale had ever met who could actually writhe in a beach chair. She did it with mere fractional shifts, making her tiniest movement an erotic dance.

They were seated at the back wall so close to the beach that the crashing waves almost drowned out the poolside crowd. Hale could almost believe they were isolated from the throngs and the noise and everything that had happened earlier that day. He could almost push it all away, and give in to the simple vivid pleasure of dancing to a tune he knew so well. Almost.

Natalie rose from her chair and set down her drink. When he started to rise she motioned for him to stay where he was. She turned her back to him and made a process of pulling her chair a fraction of an inch closer to his – all that was possible with her standing between the two. Which was intentional, of course, for she then leaned over to smooth the towel over the seat, arching her back. The action caused her flimsy suit to hike further and further over her buttocks. She reached down a second time for her drink and stood there beside him, her bare bottom inches from his face, a single finger touching his shoulder as she pretended to stare out to sea and sip from her glass. Wanting him not just to look. Inviting him to *inspect* her.

Hale glanced seawards. No help there. The lowering sun flowed into an ocean turned molten by its arrival. Hot and wet and shimmering.

Natalie managed to graze his arm with her bare flesh as she lowered into her chair. "Isn't it lovely?"

"Fantastic." Hale watched her settle and felt a freak ball of lightening spin in his gut. Sparks flew in every direction. They shot from his eyes as he traced his way along Natalie's frame. She shivered as his gaze traveled slowly up her impossibly long legs, lingering at their point of joining, the almost transparent fabric hinting at folds and curls. Up further he went, shooting fiery stars at the indentation of her navel, the curves of her belly, the rising-falling swell of her breasts, the spilling hair, the enticing lips, the nose, the eyes. The smoky eyes. She shivered again. He felt reassured, knowing he was not alone in the fire.

And yet the cursed clarity would not let him go. Thoughts flashed strong as the fire in his gut, pulling him away and back to what he knew was impossible. Did she feel his hint of rage? The fury, the sorrow, the keening aching loneliness for all the emptiness that would engulf him afterwards?

The bitter wrath over all life's might-have-beens pushed Hale away from the moment's escape. He felt drawn toward the void awaiting upon lust's other shore. Though he wished for nothing but blind release, still he drew closer, until he saw vividly all the lies and all the absences he was normally able to mask, at least for the night.

Hale stared at Natalie, but saw more clearly the reason why he disliked waking next to some pretty panting head. Touching that desolate shoreline in the light of a new day threatened to drain every remaining vestige of light from his heart. He knew it would happen with Natalie, knew it was inevitable, knew it was justice being served. Knew also he would not have the strength to leave. Not this day. Not this woman. Because he knew as well that now there was nothing more to protect.

Natalie sensed him withdrawing into the regret to come. She fought for focus through her own smoke; he saw the flicker of clarity come and go. Then the heat returned, so strong it melted her obsidian gaze and turned her voice liquid. "Would you rub some oil on me?"

He felt the ball of lightening spin faster once again, wishing the sparks could somehow feed on the void and fill it. Willing himself to become lost in the spinning moment. Wanting to weave out of control, out of time, out of the lost contingencies. "If you like."

"I'd like very much." She lifted the bottle from her bag without taking her eyes from him. She handed it over, and shifted in her chair. She raised one hip and moved the other knee towards him, opening her legs as in an embrace. A tiny pink tongue touched her lower lip, wetting it like a rich red jewel. Then she whispered, "Start here."

Yet before he could move, his internal tableau changed. Somehow Natalie seemed to sense it as well, for the hand with the bottle retreated.

He knew he could not lose himself in another lie. Much as he wanted to. Much as he wished he were able. Even here he was defeated. "Natalie, I think ..."

Her face seemed poised to bite off the words he probably deserved to hear, about lost chances and guys who faded in the clinch. But before she could speak, she glanced behind him. And everything changed.

All at once Natalie brought her legs together and shoved herself upright. Across her features there flashed a look of solid triumph.

18

Hale rose from his seat before he knew the reason. He turned and saw her, and knew instantly that everything Philippa had said about him was true.

He glanced back down, one fleeting farewell glimpse. Natalie had fashioned a mask of regret and concern and pointed it out to sea. It did not matter. Hale turned back to Philippa and the tattered rags of his heart propelled him forward. He felt stabbed by sudden revulsion for all he was, all the wrongness in what he had done. The look in her shattered gaze said it all.

Philippa came stumbling around the pool. How she saw to walk Hale could not tell. Nor did those she passed, for they rose only to stand hesitantly, fearful of coming too close to whatever awful tragedy she carried. Blindly she struck the corner of a table and sent a rainbow shower of drinks tumbling. She did not stop, did not even hesitate. The people seated around the table let her go without a word, her face struck all dumb. Even the waiters on the pool's opposite side halted to observe this stricken woman, blinded by tears and wrenched so that she could not walk upright.

Hale reached her in three strides. She fell into his arms and sobbed, "Alexis is dead."

A sigh escaped from all those who heard, all hit by the invasion of unwelcome reality. Hale crushed her close, feeling nothing but empty aching guilt, drawn into the same embrace which gripped a sobbing Philippa. His heart had vanished. He held the only person who could ever have given it life, and felt her cry tears for his own eternal loss.

His sorrow hollowed his voice until it cracked under the strain of saying, "Oh, Philippa, I'm so sorry."

"He's dead. I was afraid of it before. Now I know. He told me. I have no choice but to accept it. He's dead."

Hale let the words pass, not questioning the impossibility of hearing from a dead man that he had expired. "Come on. Let's go upstairs."

Turning her around afforded Hale an instant's glance back behind him. Natalie had not moved. Hers was the only face not watching. She remained grimly intent, staring out to sea, lost in a void all her own.

* * *

Hale held Philippa for hours. He listened with the desperation of the lost to her words. Even the sobbing broken discord was better than facing his own guilty vacuum.

The snatches of words and half-formed thoughts taught him much, most especially how little he had actually listened to Philippa earlier. He learned how Alexis had confirmed her theories and helped fill in the gaps. How in the process Alexis had grown constantly more worried and frightened. How he had described their work as preparing to tilt the world's scientific axis.

She told him how Alexis had predicted that all who profited from the status quo would declare them dangerous. They would be identified as high-category risks. Enemies of the state. She wept as she had described how Alexis had dredged up all the old Communist words and gave them new life with his fear. And she had ignored everything he had said.

She blamed herself, Hale learned. She recounted the reasons in gasps, the words stabbing and wounding her and making whole sentences impossible. Hale listened and nodded, hearing his own conviction most clearly. He should have been there with her, through it all.

Alexis had urged her to hide everything. Not to allow anyone to know she had even *thought* of this new tangent. But she was infected by her own poison, permanently scalded by her burning need to succeed. A careless word over drinks at the end of an exhausting conference. A swift brag to people controlling the flow of grant funds. Another word breathed in the ear of an editor of a prestigious scholarly journal. A visitor from Washington. A four-star general who paid her more than polite attention at some formal dinner. A whisper here, a wink there. Never breaking Alexis' plea for secrecy outright. Or so she claimed to herself. Merely turning the barrier translucent, the truth to be guessed at by those who watched.

Until it killed Alexis as surely as if by her own hand.

Even when her sobbing and her words had diminished to rasping shaky breaths and the occasional moan, Hale remained silent. He held her body close, letting her draw herself around him there on the bed, caressing her hair, waiting. He knew she was listening, hoping he would tell her it was not her fault. But he could not say the words, could not risk letting yet another lie crowd into their space. Not then. He knew all about lies, especially the ones he told himself.

Finally she sighed acceptance of his silence, and lifted up her tear-streaked face. A glimpse into her eyes, and he knew what she asked. Here and now he did not hesitate, though he felt as empty of anything to give as a corpse. Softly, as gently as he knew how, he kissed her.

The movements were practiced, which was good. He felt her motions guide and beg, so he slipped her clothes away. He traced the taut suppleness of her body, feeling his hands gain strength merely from holding her. He sensed her moving communication again, and shifted so his own clothes could be pulled free. He held her with his entire body now.

Touching her with all of him, willing her to be drawn into his own central void. At least he could wish for that.

Love with Philippa had always baffled him. The scientist's mind had desperately fought for control, even when he was inside of her. He had felt it often, the veil of intelligence so strong she struggled constantly to keep him at an observable distance even when she was open and yielding and panting with desire. He had seen how it had made her love movements fumbling and clumsy. He had observed for almost a year how even the tiniest suggestion of novelty was enough to push her farther from passion, force her another mental step away, grant her mind the urgently sought lever to regain control. The control which she managed to lose only for the briefest instant, the flash of climax, there and gone and hidden behind the mind once more. As though losing control was an embarrassment. Something to be ashamed about. A flaw to hide in the dark.

Yet this was not what had baffled Hale. No. What had astonished him so much it had terrified him every time the thought arose, even amidst their quarrels over sex, was how little it had truly mattered. Even his arguments had been more form than content. Whatever Philippa had managed to give had in deepest truth been enough. More rampant sex had gradually faded from memory, as though he had finally awoken from a life-long dream. Or nightmare. Those thoughts had left him utterly dumfounded. And terribly threatened.

Yet this time, the sense of familiar newness reached far deeper than the mere unclothing of their bodies. This time her mind was stilled. This time she came to him as a supplicant, begging for alms, grateful for anything.

It could not have been more agonizing if she had stood and accused him of every miserable mistake. For he was broken by having nothing to give.

Broken enough to lie there as a servant. He gave from his emptiness. He gave from his sorrow, his guilt, his knowledge that he did not deserve her. He stared into the shadows and watched them congeal about the bed, there to transport him to the shore of eternal emptiness. The place to which he had been headed all his life. He squeezed his eyes shut and tried to concentrate upon her movements. But he could not hold back the vision or the rain. They were a part of him, now and forever. Their bodies convulsed together, his from the tragic weight of hollow humanity.

When she sighed and stirred, Hale tried to roll away. But the touch of her soft hand on his shoulder trapped him there. Philippa kissed the fragment of his face not concealed by his arm and whispered, "Why are you crying?"

19

The Lawton Building was at the bottom of Washington's bureaucratic office ladder – a mediocre sixties design which had been poorly maintained. Enormous glass windows absorbed every ounce of heat and did not open. Feeble air conditioning fumed its way through the summer, sullen and puffing hard. In Lawton's fetid halls the heat clawed at the back of throats. Staffers' hackles remained permanently raised. Snarls and snide tirades replaced normal conversations. Turnover was the highest in the federal bureaucracy, and assignments were treated like a prison sentence. Which meant only the most mundane tasks were performed there, such as record-keeping for the Securities and Exchange Commission. Which was where Florence Avery had spent her entire weekend.

But it was not the lousy air conditioning which had her running from the building that Sunday afternoon. She had survived more cloying Washington summers, and endured worse archives than the Lawton basement. Irate staffers were just another part of her normal scenery. Florence Avery also took great pride in her reputation for holding to a glacial calm. She did not lose it easily.

But it was gone now. A secret-service shredder could not have done a better job of destroying her poise. She stopped at the street, searched both directions, and realized she had no idea where she had left her own car. Her arrival that morning could just as easily been before the last ice age.

She forced herself to take a full breath, another, then said out loud, "Pull yourself together, dammit!"

It worked for a fraction of a second, long enough to recall where she had parked. She started east along M Street, only to be hit anew by what she had discovered there in the SEC archives. The realization of what she carried, and the impact it would have, left her reeling. She felt as though a giant hand had reached down from the sky, gripped the sidewalk, and shaken it violently. Her walk was as meandering as a drunk's.

But there was no getting around the need to make the contact, and do so now. Florence fumbled in her purse, gripped her cell-phone, coded in Ryan's number. She forced her legs to carry her forward as she endured three rings. Four.

On the fifth ring she answered. "Ryan Reeves." Ryan's tone stated precisely what she thought of a Sunday afternoon call on her business mobile.

"It's Florence."

"Oh, no. Not today. This is just too –"

"Wait a minute. Wait just one damn *minute*!"

"Call me tomorrow."

"This can't wait."

"I'm at Kennedy all day Monday."

"No! I'm calling you about the *weather*!"

"No way, Florence. Not today. You're talking about an hour's drive there and back. Which would totally destroy my day."

"It's hot as hell up here!"

"I don't care if it's raining conch fritters!" Matching Florence's shrill tone with one of her own. "I have a *life* here! I have a *family*!"

"Ryan, I've spent all weekend checking up on a rumor. I've discovered news of absolutely critical importance. We have *got* to talk."

"Fine. So talk away."

"No. I can't. You don't know." Grabbing her chest, gripping that instead of her cool. Which was *way* out of reach. "We have got to talk *now*."

"I'm hanging up. For real."

"Ryan –"

"Tomorrow. I'm down there from the crack of dawn. We can play all the games you like then. Have a nice Sunday."

Florence dropped her arm, stared at the street, said to the tourist traffic, "She hung up on me. I don't believe this is happening."

Her shoulders slumped. She had no choice. She had to fly to Orlando immediately. No matter that she had not been down since the astronaut major had dumped her. Just her luck the bastard would be pulling PR duty at Kennedy.

Florence coded in the number from information, said, "Give me the number for flight info at National Airport." And stepped off the curb.

She did not hear the car gun its motor, did not see it at all until it filled her entire world.

And shut her down for good.

* * *

Hale's departure from Cabo was delayed four hours – not altogether a bad thing, despite waiting in a concrete oven with broken air-conditioning. By the time the plane finally took off, the serious partyers were all comatose. The ride home was quiet as a tomb. He dozed on the plane, taking in what rest he could and storing it away for the trial to come.

The San Diego freeway was a suicidal rush though rough-hewn hills. The roads leading into La Jolla and the beaches moved at a glutinous crawl. Minimum wagers from the interior townships rubbed rusted fenders with the Jags and Rolls of beach dwellers.

This was the same desert as Baja, only the La Jolla lawns sparkled with water and gardeners' sweat – both imported. Incredible wealth bunched ever more tightly the closer Hale came to the sea. Behind him sprawled inescapable and grinding poverty; overhead, the sky stretched in open and endless blue. Such raw contrasts begged for furious conflict.

By the time Hale completed the check-in process and entered his motel room, the afternoon was gradually giving way to dusk. He dropped his bags by the bed and dialed the number for Ryan's cell-phone.

He waited through a half-ring, had his ear stunned by the shouted, "I have had all I am going to take of this crap!"

"Hey, no problem. Should I hang up now?"

"Hale?"

"Let me guess. You were expecting Harry?'

"Harry, no, he's upstairs taking his Sunday afternoon siesta." Breathing hard down the line, struggling to push aside the fury. "I thought it was Florence. A friend."

"Lucky friend."

"Somebody in Washington."

"That explains everything."

"Anyway, sorry." The breathing slowed. "Where are you?"

"Back in San Diego." His own turn to pause. "I found her."

"Who?"

"The tooth fairy. Who do you think?"

"You found Philippa?" Ryan's voice retightened. "Where is she?"

Speaking carefully now. Saying what Philippa had instructed. "She's still down in Cabo."

"What! You left her there? Why?"

"I was followed, Ryan. Somebody from SRC tracked me down there. Natalie Durrant. The name mean anything to you?"

"No. And you're not making sense. You found her and somebody followed you and you left her down there alone?"

"For the moment she feels safer down there." Holding to the prepared script. "SRC has offered her a major contract."

"Forget about SRC for a minute, okay? I want to know –"

"We met with Ms. Durrant this morning. SRC has promised Philippa round-the-clock security and her own lab. A place far safer than the university."

There was a long pause. "What are you not telling me?"

Almost everything, he was tempted to say. Almost as much as he did not know himself. "Nothing."

"Don't give me that. Why did she run?"

"She didn't say."

"I can't believe you left her down there alone!"

"I had no choice. I've got my job on the line here."

"That was stupid. Beyond moronic. When is she coming up, did she tell you that?"

"Soon."

"A great answer, Hale. So precise. I can't tell you how reassured that leaves me." When he did not respond, she continued, "Can I at least have her number?"

"She's at the Hotel Valencia." Hale did not mention Philippa's carefully planned departure. "Don't worry if you can't get through. The connections are terrible."

"Don't worry? Did I really hear you say that?"

"I have to go now, Ryan."

"Don't you dare –"

"I'll talk to you later this coming week."

"Hale!"

He hung up the phone, stretched out on the bed, took a long breath. That had gone pretty much as expected.

Now there was nothing for him to do but wait.

* * *

Ryan cut off the phone, stood staring out over the patio railing. Wondering.

"Mom?"

It was more than what Hale had said. More than what he had *not* said. There was something she was missing here.

"Hey, Mom?"

Something important. Something –

"*Mom*!"

"Just a minute."

The fading light glowered hot and humid, turning her back yard into grass-scented tropics. Ryan raised the phone to eye level, said quietly, "Just exactly who were you talking to there?"

20

The phone's ring woke him. Hale swung his feet to the floor and fumbled for the receiver. Even before he heard her voice, he knew. Before Philippa spoke, he knew. She had been proven right again.

"Hale, it's Philippa."

"What time is it?"

"Late. Did I wake you?" The phone's static chopped each word into staccato beats. "Something has happened. Something bad."

"Tell me."

"I've been robbed."

"Oh, no, Filly, that's terrible."

"I went down for a late dinner and when I got back the room was ransacked and everything was gone. They took it all, Hale. My notes, my computer, my clothes, my watch, money, everything."

"I'm so sorry." Hoping he sounded half as genuine as she did. "What can –"

"Why would they take my notes? The other things I can understand. My passport, my computer, they're all worth something. But my notes. Why, Hale?"

"I'll try to get back down as soon as I can. Maybe tomorrow night."

"All my work." Her voice sounded close to breaking.

"I have to go, the police are here again. Please come. Hurry."

He replaced the receiver and rubbed his ear to relieve the crawling sense of having shared the listening with invisible others. Hoped the ruse had worked. Hoped all else Philippa had planned was proven correct as well.

Hale reached for his briefcase, searched for the slip of paper with the other numbers. His instructions for now were precise, urgent. Vital.

* * *

"North Shore Café."

"Ben."

"Yeah?"

"How's it going."

"Who is this?"

"The last time we talked, you gave me this number. And another."

A pause, then, "Right. Right. Where –"

"You said I should call if things got in a certain way. Not for me. For a friend."

"Sure. Yeah."

"You know the big ramp below where she always used to park?"

Another hesitation. "Sure, the one down to where she liked to surf."

"That's the one."

"Twenty minutes. I've got to get rid of a couple of people and close this place down."

"Thanks, Ben. And watch your back."

* * *

Hale arrived early, found a place lost in night shadows, and hunkered down to wait. A soft wind blew off the ocean, chilled and salt-laden. The sky was desert clear and freckled with silver. Below and in front of his corner a concrete ramp ran from the road to the beach. To one side rose the Oceanographic Institute buildings fronting the Scripps pier. On the other side was a concrete blockhouse used for storing the Institute's inflatable craft and diving equipment. Farther out the waves were washed yellow by light from the pier. Their crashing sound was familiar, beckoning.

Hale cast back to the day's beginning, waking up in Philippa's hotel room to the sound of the phone ringing. For a moment he had been utterly uncertain over what the night before had held. He had opened his eyes to find Philippa already showered and clothed and listening hard to someone talking. She had said little, but somehow he had known it was Natalie speaking. He had laid there and watched until she set down the phone, then picked it up again and called room service. She had not even acknowledged his presence as he had padded for the bathroom, his swimsuit bundled in one hand. As he had stood beneath the shower spray, Hale had known something major had taken place. Not between them. No. Within himself.

The sensation remained through breakfast on the balcony of Philippa's hotel room. He had sat protected by a tattered awning from the sunlight, accepting her silence, feeling that a tiny kernel of honesty had been forged in the center of his being. A new sensation was taking root as well, that of seeing inside himself. Perhaps the first time he had ever done so with honesty in his entire life.

It was such a fragile thing, this new honesty. Hale felt as if he even blinked too hard he would lose it all. Or vanquish it by saying the wrong word. It would be so easy to talk his way out of this. So he decided then and there to say little and listen much, both outwards and to himself. A new commitment. A contract sealed and settled there beside this new seed. Search out the signs and portents. And act only when he knew what to do, or was shown by someone he trusted.

Like Philippa.

She folded her napkin into a precisely cornered square, settled it on the table, and began, "It is important we establish proper parameters for both seeing and understanding what might be happening over the coming days."

As though she had been reading his mind. Talking about something else entirely, yet giving form to his thoughts just the same. "Right."

Philippa jerked a glance his way, trying to see if he was making fun. After careful inspection she accepted he was striving to understand her remarks, and went on, "Think of it as our own little version of matter and anti-matter colliding."

He nodded as though he understood.

"In a lab we would generate this huge amount of energy, focus it through a series of carefully aligned electromagnets, and draw these two particle beams along diametrically opposite paths. Around and around they spin within an oval pipe almost twenty miles in circumference, flying through a near-vacuum until they attain ninety percent of the speed of light. Then, *wham*, we send them shooting into one another. And we watch the sparks fly."

On the outside it sounded like the same old, same old. Philippa reconstructing life in her mind, using the language of physics to set everything at a comfortable distance. Only now they were seated six floors above Cabo's yellow-baked sprawl. And the shadows beneath Philippa's eyes and the hollow point at the center of her gaze suggested things were neither removed nor controlled. And for the first time he could remember, Hale was listening with all the strength he could muster.

"Mind you, we never see any of these sparks. They dissolve in the blink of a subatomic eye. But we can study their traces. These are trapped on special photographic plates. We analyze their patterns. And by doing so, we unlock the invisible keys to the universe. Or we try to."

She stopped then, watching him with her hollowed gaze. Hale understood; in the past he had given her many reasons to wonder if he had been listening at all. So he said, "You want to see if you can analyze the patterns of what is happening to us, and see if you can discover what is actually behind it all."

Surprise that he was actually listening, for a change, pushed her back in her chair. "My prediction is that we will not see them directly. Not until it is far too late."

He said it then because he had to. "That girl I was with. Natalie Durrant, she works for SRC. You were right. She followed me down. Was that her calling this morning?"

"Indeed it was, with an offer they clearly think I could never in my right mind refuse." There was a shift to her gaze, and she opened her mouth to say something more. Then she checked herself, and instead simply said, "In my opinion, Ms. Durrant and her arrival are little more than traces. The real catalyst lies hidden beneath quantum layers of mystery."

Hale felt slapped in the face with the realization of what she had been about to ask. *Were he and Natalie an item? Did he sleep with her?* All the questions she had started to ask of all the girls who had come and flirted and disturbed their harmony in the past, all were there as well, crowding their way into the balcony, the unspoken doubts all pointing accusing fingers at him. No matter what his deeds had been. Not now. The worst crime he had indeed committed, he knew; he was convicted of never granting Philippa the ability to trust him fully. The condemnation hung between them, acrid as the diesel fumes drifting in the hot air.

The realization saddened him. But he had lived with sorrow all his life. Only now, after six months of lonely preparation, was he able to admit it to himself. He knew all about the sorrow of unhealed wounds. And unfocused rage. What granted such a strange feeling to this young desert morning was how the night had robbed him of a lifetime's blindness. He saw with a newborn's gaze, unfocused and roaming. But he *saw*.

"Hale?"

He swiveled his attention outwards again. "Yes."

"I lost you there for a moment."

There was nothing to offer her now, nothing except total honesty. "They offered me a hundred thousand dollars to find you and get you to sign their contract." Swiftly he sketched out the meetings with Natalie and Buzz Cobb.

Philippa accepted the news with a fractional nod. "I need to go downstairs and meet with Ms. Durrant in a few minutes. Will you come with me?"

"If you want me to."

"I would prefer not to face her alone. I don't know which side she or SRC are on, but right now it doesn't matter."

As far as he could recall, it was as close as Philippa had ever come to admitting weakness. "Sure."

"Thanks very much." A big breath. "Are you going back to San Diego?"

"I should. For my job."

"Could you go back this afternoon?"

"If that's what you want."

"Please. I need you to do something for me. Several things, actually."

"Anything."

The immediacy of his responses finally sunk home. "Just like that?"

"I owe you a lifetime of apologies, Filly. I'll start by helping you any way I can."

She blinked. "Thank you, Hale."

He nodded. The words he had spoken felt real, even after they had been said. "Tell me what I need to do."

* * *

Somehow the sea scents were stronger in the night. Hale waited by the ramp leading down to the Scripps Pier and listened to the waves crashing down below. Their phosphorescent glow was a gentle painting that swept in and out with ghostly strokes. He stepped further into the shadows as he heard the scrape of footsteps descending the cliffside road. He watched the bulky shadow pass him, and waited until Ben had walked the entire length of the ramp and stepped into the sand.

Hale then moved from his shadows and called down, "I'm up here."

"Damn, man, you coulda said something before I got my shoes wet. Tide's totally high."

He stepped fully into the pierside illumination. "I needed to make sure you were alone."

Ben squished through freshly deposited seaweed. "Shit."

"Thanks for coming."

Today's T-shirt was from a recent contest on Reunion, an island east of Madagascar. Ben walked back up to where Hale waited and stomped sand from his shoes. "Tell me this is for real."

"As real as it gets. They robbed Philippa's room at the Valencia, stole all her work."

"When?"

"A couple of hours ago."

"She sent you?"

"She knows I'm here." He caught Ben's moonlit look. "She trusts me, Ben. That's all I can tell you."

"Okay." Thwarted hopes lowered his voice to a resigned growl. "So she needs a hidey-hole?"

"If the offer is still open."

"You joining her?"

"Tomorrow afternoon."

He nodded. Not liking it, but expecting nothing less. "Figured this was why you called. I drew a map. Place is hard to find. Come on back up here." Ben stepped closer to light over the divehouse door. "Take a look."

Hale squinted over the crudely drawn map, read the lettering, "Angel's Camp."

"She'll be coming up from the south?"

"Yes."

"Okay. Soon as she passes Ensenada, tell her to start looking. All she'll see is a dirt path skirting off beside the roadsign that reads what I've written there. Get to the bridge overpass and she's gone too far. Same thing in reverse for you."

Hale folded the paper. "Thanks, Ben."

"How is she travelling?"

Hale hesitated, gave the answer as a symbol of trust. "Taxi. Several of them."

Ben grunted approval. "Think maybe I'll take a few days off, head on down tonight. Get things ready. You two can have the place to yourselves. I got a buddy I can stay with along the cove. You want to come down with me?"

"I can't. She wants me to check on some things."

"Guess I'll see you down there." Ben started to turn away, checked himself, offered a hand. "When does she plan on travelling?"

It felt like he was gripping a flesh-warm statue, Ben's hand was that hard. "She leaves at dawn."

21

Monday morning Philippa took the hotel's shuttle to the Cabo airport. The dawn bus was full of pained expressions and super-dark shades. The majority of other passengers were suffering severe tequila withdrawals and watching the sun rise from the wrong end. Not a single word was spoken the entire journey.

The airport was a throwback to fifties vintage, one huge hall whose concrete walls and cracked linoleum floor acted like an amplifier for the tiniest sound. She checked in at the Aeromexico counter, accepted her boarding pass, went in search of a coffee. Not that she needed any. Her nerves were already stretched tight as optic filaments. But airport coffee shops were open and policed and safe.

She found a corner table where she could sit and observe and pretend to sip from her cup. She saw nothing out of the ordinary. Then again, she had no idea what she was looking for. She tasted the bitter-black coffee, far too strong now that she had grown accustomed to weaker American blends, and felt immensely foolish. Not for her present actions. For the previous morning. Pretending to Hale that she knew what she was doing. Playing the eternal professor.

Natalie Durrant had arrived for their meeting with bags packed and set at her feet. Making it perfectly clear to both of them that she was departing immediately. Natalie had played it cool, laying it all out like a consummate saleswoman. When Philippa had made a point of asking if she had been followed, Natalie had showed the poise of a film star, making round eyes and demanding to know if Philippa was in danger. Wanting desperately to help. Offering to send down security, a private plane, whatever she wanted. Backing that up with SRC's offer – full-time directorship, her own lab, budget, staff, the works. Full control over her own research agenda, so long as she remained willing to check up on other groups' activities. Making the pitch so breathlessly urgent Philippa found herself wondering if she had not read it all wrong, if perhaps here was indeed the haven she desired.

Now, as she waited for them to call her flight, she was still not sure. And Hale had been no help whatsoever. He had sat and watched the two of them, silent and barren of all but a readiness to act. Like an arrow notched and tensely waiting for her fingers to release him, pointed to whatever target she chose. She was not certain how she felt about that either.

Finally they called her flight. Two hours late – barely noticeable for Aeromexico. Philippa resisted the urge to search around her as she walked through the terminal and joined the press of passengers. As she had noticed on the way in, security was rudimentary. The US carriers supplied their own; the rest was mere theatrics. Both baggage x-ray machines were turned off. Bored guards gave attention only to the pretty ladies.

Philippa handed her boarding card to the attendant, pushed through the door, and entered blazing sunlight. The glare was so fierce most passengers bowed their heads in abject submission. They walked across broken asphalt and around two older planes destined for interior cities. It was almost too easy to use the stark shadows to step away.

By the first pair of landing wheels Philippa stepped back, stood there and sucked hard for air. She felt eyes everywhere. She waited for the shout and the grab for her arm. Yet she heard nothing but the grinding roar of revving turbines.

Only when the last passenger was up and in and the stairs pulled back did she dare walk away. Briefcase in one hand and purse in her other, head back and step as sure as she could possibly manage, Philippa left the shadows behind.

She marched the length of the terminal and passed through unguarded outer gates. She did not manage a decent breath until she was in the parking lot.

The line of taxis stretched endlessly. She made a show of selecting one, shaking her head when several impossibly scruffy men pressed her for business. To the others she simply asked, "Airea condicionado?"

Finally she found the desired combination, a relatively new cab driven by a decidedly scrawny older gentleman. When she had settled in the back he started the engine and proudly blasted her with refreshing coolness. Without her saying anything he left the airport and turned towards Cabo. Only when they were rolling south down the highway did she lean forward and say, "How much to Ensenada?"

That drew him to a halt by the roadside. "Ensenada? Norte?"

"Si. How much?"

"Dollars? You pay?"

"Fine. How much?"

"Tre cincuinta kilometros." He thought a moment, then, "Dos cientos. Two hundred dollars."

"Great." Too relieved to dicker. She leaned back and waved him on. "Vamos."

He displayed a vast array of gold in his grin, then swung the taxi around and headed north. "Ensenada."

"Right." As they passed the airport she glanced behind them, saw nothing but blinding sunlight and empty highway. She turned back, rubbed where the briefcase's shoulder strap had bitten deep. The leather satchel contained her satellite transponder, critical diskettes, single change of clothes, and back-up computer. Everything she had moved down to the safe in Hale's room the night before his departure. Everything she had left in the world.

Philippa closed her eyes, tried to recall how it felt to take an untroubled night's sleep for granted. She found herself fervently hoping they would find a way to make them all pay. Whoever they were.

She was exhausted by the previous day. Drained and spent. The night with Hale had been both good and bad – good at the time, hard on her now that it was over. She found herself missing Hale in the most physical of ways. Reliving the night with him, and the sensations. Feeling the wrench deep in her heart at the sight of him weeping. She had never before even seen Hale shed a tear. The memory left her lusting for him and feeling wounded anew. The agony of their breakup seemed closer at that moment than since he had first left her behind.

Yet what had taxed her the most had been the robbery. The fact that she had been expecting it or something similar had helped prepare her far less than she had anticipated. She had gone down for a late dinner, and returned to find chaos. She would never forget that sight as long as she lived. The room had not just been searched. It had been destroyed. Remnants of the robbers' fury was everywhere. The mattress ruptured by a dozen jagged rips, the chair's cushions slashed open, the desk overturned, the curtains yanked so hard their rods were torn from the ceiling.

Two hotel attendants had already arrived, which meant she had been forced to give her best performance without any preparation whatsoever. The savage destruction had helped. Philippa had walked around the room in numb silence, then raced for the closet. Every room had a little safe bolted to the floor, an alternative to safety deposit boxes in a land where everything had to be locked away. She had taken one look at the safe's open door, and let loose with her number-one shriek.

After the police had come and gone they had moved her to another room. But she had not slept, only drifted through fitful dozes, jerking awake time and again, frightened anew by the possibility of having been in the room and having all that fury directed at her.

She had slipped down to Hale's room while the hotel was still held by pre-dawn silence. At her insistence Hale had paid for three nights and departed without telling the hotel. Philippa had pulled the briefcase from the desk's bottom drawer, and breathed a sigh of relief to find her second computer and zip-file still there, the disks all present. The papers still in the folder. The ruse in place.

Now, as she sat in the back of a taxi rattling north along the Baja highway, she felt chased by all the questions and fears of the course she was trying to chart. Added to that, multiplying her sense of life running beyond her control, were doubts of renewing her relationship with Hale. And fears. Philippa released a sigh of pure dismay. She felt so weak. So helpless. So afraid. All the confidence she had known while planning with Hale was drained from her. The future seemed an impossible tangle, her foes immensely powerful.

Why was it so much bloody easier to be strong whenever he was around?

* * *

Hale pulled his rental car into the sluggish Monday morning traffic. Philippa's final words accompanied him on the drive south toward San Diego. The smoke of his smoldering remorse was lessening, bringing her instructions into clearer focus. Now he was intent upon the tasks at hand. Ready to hunt the prey of truth.

His first appointment that morning was the most difficult, the only point over which he had questioned Philippa's strategy. But she had been adamant, going so far as to mention it in their meeting with Natalie. Telling her point blank that Hale would be coming by Monday. Nine o'clock sharp. There to clarify things further and pick up a clean document for Philippa to sign. Not asking Natalie. Telling her. Natalie had played the professional, though it had cost her. She had managed to sit at the table across from them for over an hour without looking at Hale once. Not even acknowledging his presence when Philippa had said he would be acting on her behalf. Simply nodding and making notes, saying that unfortunately she would not be present as she had urgent business in Sacramento. Which was why she was leaving right after their meeting. Hale had made it as easy for her as he could, not speaking a single word the entire time.

As they had returned from the meeting, Philippa had told him, "Observe and report. Analysis is only as good as your observation and your record keeping. Sloppy reporting has destroyed many a good career."

"I understand." Not exactly a romantic farewell, but more of a second chance than he had deserved. She had tasted a smile then, the first and last of their time together. "And studiously avoid all exploding objects."

He pulled into the SRC parking lot and lifted his cellphone from the briefcase beside him. He punched in the number for his office, then sat staring out the sun-drenched windshield.

"This is Jerry."

"Hey, Jer. It's me."

"Hale, oh man. Where are you?"

"San Diego. Got back last night."

"I called and called yesterday afternoon. Never could get through. Mack's on the warpath. Didn't even wait until Monday. Basically told me to pack my bags."

"Did he fire you?"

"Pretty much. He might as well have."

"Either he did or he didn't, Jerry. And since you're still sitting at your desk I assume he didn't actually pull the trigger."

"What are you saying?"

"I'm just wondering why he'd go to the trouble to call

and harass you over the weekend." Hale pondered hard. "Unless ..."

"What?"

"Did he ask about me?"

"Yeah, that was Saturday afternoon. He got a kick outta hearing you had taken off for a long weekend."

Hale tried to fit the pieces together. "When did he call you back?"

"Sunday afternoon. Man, it was like being torpedoed out of a bright blue sea."

"Look, do something for me. Try to find out where Don worked before coming to Keebler."

"How am I supposed to do that?"

"You're chummy with Keebler's secretary. Try to sit with her at lunch or something."

"What for?"

"Just a hunch. See if you can do it without drawing fire."

"Don't worry. I've been shot at all I want for one week, and it's only Monday morning." A pause. "I've got to pass you upstairs. Mack wants to personally deliver the word."

Hale felt his anger build. Just the prospect of talking to the guy was enough to raise the morning's heat by ten degrees. "Everything's okay, Jerry."

"I wish. Hang on."

Hale waited through the series of clicks. The company's cheery muzak only added fuel to the fire. By the time Don MacRuthers came on, Hale was too hot to be worried.

"Andrews, where on earth have you been?"

"Long story."

"Cabo San Lucas, did Jerry actually get that one right?" Don snorted his derision. "Tell me you did this on the company's nickel. Make this easier for everybody concerned."

"I did this for Northstar Avionics. As in possibly the biggest new account Keebler has seen in years."

"Promising to pull a rabbit out of the hat isn't going to do it this time, I'm afraid." Relishing his position. Pressing the point. "Frankly, I can't believe you'd take off in the middle of a crisis like this. It shows remarkably poor judgment in my view."

"Is that so."

"I don't have to tell you how hard times are just now. The ax is falling right and left around here." A delicate pause. "This belt-tightening is going to affect every department."

Hale decided he had heard enough. "Don, I think you're mistaking me for somebody who gives a shit."

"Eh, what's that you said?"

"Northstar Avionics, Don. They paid my way down. We're talking government contracting." It was Hale's turn to pause. "If I leave Keebler, I take this contract with me."

MacRuthers snapped, "And just exactly what contract is that?"

"The one I'm going to bring back and ram down your throat." Hale cut the connection, sat breathing hard. Had to smile. It may have been the stupidest move of his career, but it had gone down mighty fine.

When his breath had steadied he continued with the plan. The second call went much faster, which was good, as the clock showed it was fast approaching the hour. When the Northstar operator came on, he said, "Zack Conway, please."

"Mr. Conway's office."

"This is Hale Andrews. Is Mr. Conway in?"

"Oh yes, Mr. Andrews. How nice to hear from you. Just one moment, please."

He scarcely had time to take in the secretary's response before, "Conway."

"Mr. Conway, this is Hale Andrews. We met last week."

"Sure, I remember. What can I do for you?"

"I was wondering if we could meet this morning. I realize it's short notice, but I have to leave this afternoon and –"

"What about?"

The million-dollar question. "I, ah, have some questions about SRC."

"You do, huh." A pause. "How does eleven o'clock sound."

"Great. Thanks very much."

"I may be around the plant somewhere. Have them page me downstairs. Don't come up to my office."

Hale cut the connection, rose from the car, and headed for the SRC entrance. In the strong morning sun the marble stairs shimmered like a mirage. He passed through the mirror-glass doors and gave his name to the receptionist. As he waited while she filled out his visitor's badge, he found he could not shake the impression that Conway had been expecting his call.

22

Monday morning at six-thirty sharp, a very sleepy Chuck Evans appeared in Ryan's doorway at the Kennedy Space Center and asked, "You ready for me?"

"Sure, come on in." She saw what he was carrying. "Coffee and doughnuts, perfect."

"I haven't been in headquarters this early in years."

"Shut the door. It may be a tomb now, but things will crank up fast, especially with the launch rescheduled for Thursday night. Sit down." She waited as the sleepy man dragged over a chair, knew she was going to have to draw him into better focus before the work could start. "Walk me through this project of yours again, okay?"

She could actually see the light go on. It was like a new mom being asked to describe her baby. "Right. Okay. As you know, we have to maintain absolute clean-room conditions within the shuttle's payload area. The satellites are designed to operate in vacuum. Conditions are critical. They're built in clean labs, transported here in hermetically sealed units, lifted up to the shuttle payload bay inside a sterile elevator."

"And that's where the problem comes in." Ryan selected her first doughnut with care. "The connection between the gantry and the payload bay has always been the weak link."

"Exactly right. The current seal between the retractable unit and the orbiter is proving impossible to operate. We're needing to rebuild it after almost every launch." Chuck in his lecturing mode, reviewing the basics, long accustomed to explaining things to the money men. "We can't hold this seal perfectly tight launch after launch. The question has always been why."

"You've found the reason?"

"We think so."

"This is good news, Chuck. Constantly having to replace those seals is eating holes in my discretionary budget."

"Good and not so good." He pushed the glasses back up his nose. "You've got to remember what kind of conditions we're facing here. Salt, high winds, sea-borne storms, they eat away at the sealing system. The slide we've been using was based on the system that connects a plane to an airport terminal jetway. But the connecting point is relatively thin, and has to be in absolutely perfect condition. Are you with me so far?"

"Yes."

"Each time you open the connection and salt touches the edge, the rubber seal is rendered useless. Not on an airplane, of course, you don't need sterile conditions here. But here on the payload gantry, the thing is just not working out."

"It's been in use for years."

"And for years we just replaced the seal and hid the cost. Another line-item charge. And the thing works fine for a while, that's how it's escaped notice. Two or three launches, especially in winter, no problem. Then we get a storm off the sea or this crazy heat and humidity, and the seals on both pads are blown."

Ryan stared at him, enjoying the exchange, liking the man and his crazy combination of years of experience and juvenile energy. Chuck had to be in his fifties, but he still talked like a teenager when it came to his work. Rapid-fire bursts with his mind moving far ahead of his tongue. "So you want to redesign the system."

"It's the only way. And I think I've found a new method, something that will clear up this problem once and for all."

"How much time do you need?"

"Just another day or so. I'm supposed to receive a sample of new material later today."

"Fine. I'll walk you through the preliminary request now, you can fill in the blanks when you have the final schematics. I'll see you tomorrow afternoon, that all right?"

She took him step-by-step through the administrative red-tape required for a new requisition order, then helped him structure the Work Authorization form. By the time the last doughnut had been devoured, they were done.

Chuck gathered his pages, brushed off the crumbs and sugar frosting, stowed them in his folder. "I can't thank you enough for your help, Ryan."

"What are you talking about, we're on the same team."

"Some of the NASA admin types around here, you could have fooled me."

A worried expression flitted into view, and Ryan knew Chuck feared he had gone too far. So she covered by changing the subject, turning to the thoughts that had accompanied her in that morning. "You been following progress on the XLS-1?"

Chuck relaxed into his chair. "Now and then. I'm not afraid of the competition."

She was surprised by his confidence. The Experimental Launch System was being designed and produced by Northstar and the Space Research Consortium. Chuck was an employee of the United Space Alliance, their direct competitor. His entire career was tied to the current shuttle. "Why is that?"

"You mark my words, Ryan. Our orbiter is going to be the DC-3 of the aerospace industry."

She studied him. "Excuse me?"

"You know the DC-3's history, right? Designed in the thirties, still flying today. Just repair the landing frames and watch out for metal fatigue. Those planes will outlast us all. Same with our current shuttle."

She set down her pen. She felt as though a little chime had gone off in her head. The one which said, this was important.

But Chuck was too caught up in his thoughts to notice. "X-33, X-34, XLS-1, all this is just crap."

"We need cheaper ways to get stuff into orbit," she pointed out, wondering to herself, what am I listening for here?

He dismissed it with a casual wave. "To fly people, the very first concern is to man-rate the vehicles. Know just exactly what the risk is. Space test for safety, design the backup systems to delete as much risk as possible."

"Okay, so?"

"Think about it. The shuttle is the safest product ever made by man since the post-Challenger redesign. What do we want, start all over again, face losing astronauts to an untested design?"

Ryan leaned back in her chair. Searching. Hunting for what it was she felt she should be catching. "You've been around a while, haven't you."

"Got here just in time for the last Apollo flight." Chuck smiled at memories only he could see. "We should never have decommissioned those Saturn 5 rockets. Big mistake. That baby would send two locomotives into orbit. Took twenty seconds to clear the launchpad – a lifetime and a half when your own work was riding on that flame. Shuttle does it in three seconds. First time I watched the orbiter take off, I thought, that's it? All that work, whoosh and it's gone. My first Saturn launch, one of the old hands pulled me out of the firing room, we snuck up the back stairs to the VAB and stood there. We could feel the bass drum pressure from those huge engines just beat at our chests. The engines burned for eight seconds before it even started lifting. Monster engines. Biggest babies ever made by man. First stage burned kerosene and liquid oxygen."

Big and hugely expensive, Ryan thought, but said nothing. The Saturn had cost twenty thousand dollars in sixties-era money per kilo of load. The shuttle had been brought in on the promise of lowering this to under ten. But the powers-that-be had scuttled the Saturn program, and almost overnight the shuttle bureaucracy had bloated to incredible proportions. Within two years the per-kilo cost had doubled. Only in the past eighteen months, with Congress insisting on a strict belt-tightening regime and the XLS-1 threatening to take the shuttle's place, were costs finally dropping. Per-kilo load costs were now under fifteen thousand and fast approaching twelve – and in nineties dollars. But Ryan did not tell him this. Chuck was well aware of the realities.

And there was something else she was not hearing.

"What we were after was dispelling mass," Chuck went on, his tone almost dreamy. "The more mass dispelled, the more power. So we armed the Saturn 5 with engines the size of *houses*. They took impellers larger than a 747's entire turbines to pump those engines to maximum velocity. Eight seconds we held it trapped to the launch pad, building up mass-burn and power. Finally the mix was right, the thrust was solid from all engines, and the hold-downs were released."

Ryan sat and watched and waited until she was sure he was done. Then she grabbed for the single thread she could identify as a possibility. "What would happen if they designed something which made the shuttle program redundant?"

Chuck focused on the here and now with great reluctance. "Never happen."

"Technology is changing all the time. It could happen to the shuttle." She thought of Philippa's latest line of work. "Say there was a change to propulsion."

"No chance. You know why? Technological advances come in areas where there are consumer applications. Propulsion hasn't changed in decades. Even the X-33 Venture Star and Northstar's XLS-1, they're using linear strike engines, right? Those suckers were designed in the fifties. Only back then they didn't have the composite materials required to take the intense heat. Now they do.

Propulsion is the slowest item to change because there's only one client."

"Governments."

"And you know how fast governments are at accepting new ideas." Chuck shook his head, certain about this. "The XLS-1 has another ten years of testing before they're ready to go online. Nobody is going to replace the shuttle."

"But if they did," Ryan pressed.

He gave her a sharp look. Focused now. "Then in ten years Kennedy would be a ghost town."

"You really believe that?"

"Think about it, Ryan. The VentureStar people are already flight-testing over at Edwards. They and the XLS-1 aren't using stages to make orbit. Single stage, fully reusable launch vehicles. No need to keep the ocean as a safety net for falling debris. Not to mention how people like Sea Launch are coming up with innovative ways to send up payloads with no pads at all."

She nodded slowly. The Johnson Space Center remained viciously jealous of all the public attention showered on the launch site. It sought revenge through making Kennedy's task as tight and small as possible. In the past two years Johnson had restricted them to launches only, preparing the shuttles, throwing them up, nothing more. "A ghost town."

"We're like IBM, the Big Blue of launch systems. Billions and billions of dollars sunk in one particular infrastructure for one specific purpose. Sending rockets safely into space." He laughed without humor. "You think competition is vicious now, imagine what it'd be like if somebody came up with a propulsion unit that made us obsolete."

Before Ryan could respond, there was a knock on her door. It was not yet eight-thirty, nobody was expected, and her secretary knew better than to enter without calling through first. But the door opened anyway, and her second visitor of the day stepped inside.

Ryan resisted the urge to stand. "Fuller, good morning."

"Ryan." Her boss wore a new expression, one she had not seen before. Equal mixture of grave distress and wary concern. "We need to talk."

"You know Chuck Evans."

"Sure." The slouching engineer was already on his feet. "Morning Mr. Glenn."

"Alone, Ryan." His only notice of the engineer was to step out of the doorway. "Now."

"I'll get those documents to you by tomorrow," Chuck said, moving for the door.

"Thanks." She tried to still the sudden nerves. Her job. It had to be about her new job. "What's up, Fuller?"

He shut the door, stood there, unwilling to come any closer. "Prepare yourself, Ryan. I have some terrible news."

She was glad she had not risen. "Okay."

A breath. Another. "Florence Avery is dead."

23

Buzz Cobb was out of his chair before Hale crossed the threshold. "On time. Good. I like that."

"Hello, Mr. Cobb."

"Call me Buzz. We're all pals here, right?" His grip was iron hard, the grin pugnacious. "Lot to cover today. Shame Natalie couldn't join us."

"Yes."

Cobb carried his grin back around the desk. "Told her to put off that Sacramento bullshit. Those yo-yo's will still be up there making laws nobody cares about when hell freezes over. This work with you won't wait. But she wouldn't listen." He found humor in that as he jammed his bulk into the leather seat. "Take a load off."

"Thanks."

"Everything go well down in Cabo?"

"Fine. I located Dr. Laremy."

"So I heard. Things are looking good, sport. Which is strange, on account of something down there didn't suit my assistant. Natalie really had a bug up her backside when we talked." The image pleased him. "But what the hell. These control freaks, they gotta do everything exactly by the numbers, right?"

Hale hid in silence.

"You're okay, Andrews. I like a man who doesn't need to

blow his own horn. That's good. Okay, enough of that." Buzz clapped his hands together, gave them a vigorous rub. "Way to go, finding the scientist lady."

"Laremy. Her name is Dr. Philippa Laremy."

"Right. Whatever. Good work, kid. I like results. What we pay for in the big league. Results." He slid his chair forward. "So now's the time for the payoff."

"Dr. Laremy hasn't signed with you yet," Hale pointed out.

Buzz Cobb waved it away. "I got the contract right here. You handle this like you handled the first part, we got no problems." The gaze sharpened. "You tell her about the hundred grand signing bonus?"

"Yes."

"Honest, too. What are you, a knight in shining armor?" He gave an explosive bark. "Never mind. Listen, I'm thinking we need to do more than mess around, setting you guys up as just another supplier. We've done some checking. We're good at that. Keebler's under a lot of pressure, am I right?"

"Keebler Plastics is a well-established company. We're over forty years old and have a long record –"

"Cut the crap. I told you, we checked things out. Junior's running the show now and he doesn't have what it takes. One more contract is not gonna pull Junior's fat outta the fire. What you need is a buy-out. You got any problems with that?"

"I'm not in a position –"

"Because your guys ought to go absolutely over the moon when they hear we're interested." He planted stubby forearms on his desk. "SRC's found it makes good sense to own our most important suppliers. We search out hi-tech companies with room to expand and solid enough management to leave pretty much alone. We're not into micro management. Junior don't impress us, but you do."

Cobb reached into his pocket, pulled out a stogie, began the process of unwrapping and lighting. Drawing out the moment. When it was burning strong he continued, "If we go ahead, we'll deal only with you. You'll be on point for the whole process. You know that that means?"

"The chance of a lifetime," Hale replied quietly.

Cobb eyed him through the smoke. "You don't sound all that fired up."

Hale shook his head. Just last Friday, three days and two ice ages ago, it would have been the dream deal. Now, "Like I said, Dr. Laremy hasn't signed up with SRC yet."

"She will." The fierce grin reappeared. "I'm betting your career I'm right."

Cobb reached for the ashtray, rolled the cigar to form a burning cone. "Look. We're a research consortium working with two dozen of the world's top high-tech companies. The job I've got, I spend my nights worrying about loose technology floating around, getting to the wrong people. We haven't been sitting on our hands here since Laremy split. I happen to think she's right. There *are* people after her. Bad people. People who want to take her research and put her away."

Hale kept his face calm. "What was she working on that was so vital?"

"Hey, you're the one talking to the lady. Me, I'm just an old fighter-pilot. Somebody tells me this gal's work is hot, that's all I need to know."

Cobb bounced from his chair, scooped up a file as he came around the desk. "You get back down to Mexico and tell the lady she's in mortal danger. We're ready to supply round-the-clock protection. All she's gotta do is sign on the dotted line."

Hale stood and allowed the man to snare his arm in a vise-like grip. As they moved to the door he said, "I'll get to work on this right away."

"Sure you will. And I'll have Natalie fly straight on to Richmond, get the ball rolling at Keebler." Cobb flung open the door. "Let's play ball, sport. You need yourself a buy-out, I'm ready for a buy-in. Like they say, it's a match made in heaven."

* * *

The Northstar receptionist informed Hale that Mr. Conway was in the plant's engine-testing division, and pointed him out the side door. A silent worker in hard hat and blue jumpsuit sat behind the controls of a battered golf cart. As soon as Hale was seated he scooted down a narrow concrete path. As though everything had been laid out, waiting for him to arrive.

The factories looked like giant corrugated tin cans split in half lengthwise. The lots were broken concrete and weeds. They passed building after building until the driver entered a pair of great hangar doors and halted. He pointed down a noisy central aisle, waited for Hale to rise, then drove away. He had not spoken a single word.

The testing hall was enormous, busy, and very loud. From where Hale stood, he could look down three halls connected like dividing lines to a triangle. The ceilings were fifty feet high, and each hall was at least a thousand feet long. All were filled with union workers in their blue jumpsuits and company hard hats.

He walked slowly down the central hall, battered by the continuous roar. Giant engines with intake manifolds taller than Hale were repeatedly cranked up to full bore. There was nothing neat or high-tech about the place. Big men were intent on building big machines. Oil spills on the floor vibrated to the engines' grind. Huge wall posters shouted safety tips.

"Mr. Andrews! Good to see you again!" There was no smile to Zack Conway's greeting. The executive kept hold of Hale's arm and led him back towards the hangar doors.

Just inside the entrance, Conway pulled off his hat and safety glasses and hung them on the wall. "What can I do for you?"

It felt strange to choose his words carefully, then have to shout them over the din. "I'm confused about my meetings with SRC. And worried."

Pale blue eyes scanned out through the great doors and over the weed-strewn lot. "You realize Northstar is no longer directly connected to whatever arrangements you work out with SRC."

"But Northstar is a major shareholder."

"Doesn't change a thing. They're separate. Totally different entities."

Hale decided he had to risk it. Just as Philippa had predicted. "When we met in your office, I had the impression you weren't happy with the situation. I need to know who I can trust over there."

Conway backed from the doors, moving behind tall metal shelving holding rack after rack of tools and parts. The shadows were so deep Hale saw more of a silhouette than the man. And his eyes. "You struck me as a good sort, Mr. Andrews. And a man who's getting in way over his head. That's why I agreed to meet you here." From his position Conway could scout both out the doors and down all three halls without being seen. "This is a huge company. Thirty-two divisions, eighty-six thousand employees, operations in thirty-one states and twenty-seven countries. My one division is allied to one hundred and fifty-three subcontractors."

"A maze."

"Exactly. Now multiply that by a factor of twenty, as we link up with all those other SRC partners. You can hide a lot in a maze that complex."

Conway waited as an engine revved in the distance. The roar built until the tools around them vibrated in noisy unison. Hale flinched and jammed fingers in his ears. It only seemed to make the din in his chest worse. Conway stood calmly until the noise died and Hale unplugged his ears, then continued, "Some suppliers in our industry have a reputation for cost overruns and overbilling. They consider it a normal part of business with the government. Not us, of course. Others."

"Of course."

"Some prime contractors, are you familiar with that term? A prime is any supplier who is actually a line-item within the government budget. They negotiate directly with NASA,

Defense, whoever. With all the cost-cutting that's going on these days, a prime might decide to hide their excesses by lowering them down one level. So that when they are audited, their books are perfect. But one level down, the subcontractors and secondary suppliers, they're charging the prime a premium."

"Which is then charged on to the government."

"Exactly. This premium is kept under the table, then carefully funneled back up to the guys at the top. The subcontractors insist it's this or lose the business."

He waited through another engine rev. Hale forced himself not to flinch. Conway went on, "These guys at the top, they could be in the company or they could be important sources. Not of parts. Of new business. Do you understand what I'm saying?"

"Politicians," Hale said. "Senior officials who decide which contractor gets the business."

Conway might have given a small nod. It was hard to tell in the shadows. "These top guys have a lot to lose. They can be pretty vicious when it comes to protecting their turf."

Another engine began the run up to max. Hale shouted, "SRC has decided to make an offer to buy out my company."

Frosty blue eyes studied him until the noise abated. "Then you must have something they want very badly, Mr. Andrews."

"I was told this morning that there are other companies out to get it for themselves."

"Sounds like you better learn to sleep with one eye open." Another scan in all directions, then the gaze returned to him, floating in the half-light. "Something they want that bad, chances are they'll either own it or destroy it. One or the other."

* * *

Hale covered the distance back to the university at record time, driven by Conway's words and a desire to get on the road to Baja. Hale parked the car, entered the scaffolded lab building and followed Philippa's instructions to the second floor. Midway down a dust-carpeted hallway was the departmental secretary's office. He knocked on the open door.

A middle-aged blonde woman turned extremely tired eyes his way. Hale started, "My name –"

A drill bit into the floor directly overhead. She showed him a weary open palm. Waited for the grinding clamor to stop, then said, "Yes?"

"My name is Hale Andrews. I'm here for –"

The drill whined into action again. The woman did not even blink.

The silence rang louder when it returned. "My name –"

"Andrews, yeah, I got that already. You gotta learn to –" When her words were chopped off by the drill, she mouthed, *Talk fast.*

When it stopped, Hale raced on, "Dr. Laremy sent me. She was supposed to receive –"

The secretary's features said she was too tired to be angry. She mouthed, *Box?* Hale nodded. She held up a UPS parcel. Hale nodded again.

The drill stopped. "Three days they've been going straight for my brain. Before, I'd ask you all the details. Now, I'd just like to –"

He couldn't tell if her next word was shoot or scream. He found himself extremely grateful for the drill. Hale accepted the box, smiled both in thanks and sympathy, and turned away.

The next silence caught him in the doorway. "She coming back?"

Reluctantly he turned back. "She hopes to."

"Tell her, not too soon. You've met Dr. Digby?"

"The head of the department."

"We're talking serious rage here. He's mentioned frontal lobotomy several times. Tell Philippa to give me –"

The noise resumed. She gave the thumb and little-finger sign for a telephone. Hale nodded his understanding and left.

The noise followed him down the hall, diminishing gradually until he turned the corner.

There he met the guys coming towards him. Two of them. Matching grey suits and bland ties. Sunglasses indoors.

The shorter one asked, "You Andrews?"

"Hey, this is smart." Hale slipped into the fool's mode without even thinking. "Standing back here away from the noise. You should hear what it's like down at the other end."

"I asked if you're Hale Andrews."

"Yeah, sure, that's me." He moved a step closer.

"Mr. Andrews, we believe you have information –"

"Wait just a sec here." The moves came amazingly easy, as though all the intervening years did not exist. Teach 'em young, teach 'em well: that was the motto of scarred Sergeant Dubolchik. The one who had taught him how to fight. *Really* fight. What to do, what to say, how to move when two larger men came looking for trouble. Which was to grin, slouch, look like no threat at all. No big movements. But close to within easy reach, one tiny half-step at a time. Give the grand smile and say whatever came to mind. "You know me. Can I ask who you are?"

The blond guy had a slight lisp. Almost a whisper. "Security."

"Right. San Diego? University? I'm just asking, you know, 'cause people say I should."

"We're looking for Dr. Philippa Laremy. We understand you know her."

"Sure, she's a great gal."

"Where can we find her?"

A lab technician pushed through the hall doors. Pretty, dark-haired, pristine white coat. Brisk smile. Winced as the drill started again, but kept on moving. Both men's gazes flickered as she passed.

Which was just the distraction Hale had been waiting for.

"I don't want any –"

Then Hale dropped the package and struck. Eight, ten years since the last time. And all the speed was still there.

Two fingers stabbed hard at the taller man's eyeballs. He whipped around, the hand hard-edged now and aimed for the shorter man's throat.

The guy moved, ducking his chin. But Hale's force and surprise was enough to wedge in there, chopping at the larynx. Not as hard as he would have liked, but hard enough.

The taller guy was screaming and clawing at his eyes. The lab technician joined in with some noise of her own from farther down the hall. The second man threw a punch weakened by his gasping for breath. Hale slipped under the fist and landed a solid left into the guy's diaphragm. A satisfying punch with some shoulder behind it. Even though he hit a solid wall of muscle, it slowed the guy down.

Hale caught movement at the corner of his eye and spun and ducked, missing contact with a cosh swung so close he felt the breeze. He grabbed the taller man's hand as it went on around, swinging with it, spinning the half-blind guy back against the wall while keeping his grip tight on the cosh. The guy slammed hard into the wall, Hale's shoulder and other elbow tight on his chest. The guy's breath expelled in a quick whoosh. Hale clawed and gripped and came away with the cosh in his hand.

Hale spun back, swinging the cosh hard. He spotted movement and aimed slightly lower, aiming for the shorter guy's arm, the one reaching inside his coat. The guy gave a satisfying yell when Hale connected, and dropped the gun he was drawing. Hale kicked it clattering down the hall.

He yelled to the shrieking lab technician, "Call the police!"

He had no more time for her. Turning toward the taller man he saw a similar movement. He lashed out but the guy was seeing well enough now to dodge the blow, and pulled the gun free. Hale stepped in, starting a swing with his free hand from somewhere near the floor. He brought his right up with all the force in his body, clobbering the guy's chin.

The guy bounced off the side wall and went down hard. Hale slammed the cosh into his fist, knocking the gun free, then kicking it away. He turned back to where the blond man was crawling towards the screaming girl. And the gun.

Hale took one step forward and brought the cosh down hard. The guy slumped without a sound.

The girl made words out of her screams. "What are you *doing*?"

He did not look up from his search of the guy's pockets. "I told you to call the police!"

"This is *crazy*! You're in a lab, for –"

The weary-looking secretary stepped up and grabbed the teckie's arm. Shook her hard. "Will you kindly shut the hell up?"

The sound cut off. She stared at the older woman. "But he's got a *gun*."

"Hey, welcome to California. Besides, it was them crawling, not him standing." She turned to Hale and said, "I called the cops. Are you okay?"

"Yes. Here." He slid the second gun down the hall. It made a scrabbling sound as it scooted over the dusty flooring. "Give that to the police."

"Who are they?"

"Somebody asking after Philippa."

She scouted the two men with tired eyes. "Is this why she ran?"

"Maybe. You'll have to ask her." Hale finished his equally futile search of the other man's pockets and picked up the package. "I've got to go." He saw their doubt, drew out the only card he had left to play. "I've got to warn her."

The secretary picked up the gun, held it like she knew what she was doing. "Tell Philippa to take good care."

24

Fuller Glenn drove Ryan to Orlando and flew up to Washington with her. Fuller said something about the memorial service taking place in lieu of a swift funeral, as the police were holding on to the body while they tried to track down the car. Otherwise he remained largely silent, which was good. Ryan was in no state for small talk.

A Washington staffer met them at National Airport and drove them to the service. The memorial service took place in a stone chapel near the city's largest cemetery. Ryan ignored the greetings and the stares and the murmur of voices as she made her way down the aisle. Towards the end of the service she finally managed to draw the world into focus. Not because she wanted to remember. Because it was fitting. She needed to be there in more than body to say goodbye to this dear friend.

The service proved a powerful leveling tool for all the fragmented parts of Florence's life, save one. Ryan searched the faces gathered but could not locate the astronaut. She found herself concentrating hard, using his absence as the focal point. No. Major Jack Stone was nowhere to be found.

Someone had shown the foresight to do away entirely with the front row for family. That way there could be no threat of people who had refused to reconcile in life rejecting her in death. Still, Florence's kids and former husband were there, the same kids who had hardly spoken with their mom since the divorce years ago. Ryan inspected their faces, found herself recalling the only time she had ever seen Florence Avery weep.

It had been late one evening, months after the astronaut had dumped her. The divorce had recently come through. Ryan had entered Florence's office on one errand or another, and found the woman sobbing so hard she could scarcely draw breath. Kids, Florence had finally managed to say. They're so damn self-righteous, they can't imagine ever making a terrible mistake. One that hurts others, one they'd give anything to take back. Florence had struggled to find control, and asked her younger friend, "Why the hell does forgiveness have to be such a tough lesson for kids to learn?"

The question had hit her at a bad time. The seams of her relationship with Harry were just beginning to shred, and their increasingly frequent arguments had taken on a biting edge. The one that morning had been about Ryan's desire to take a Kennedy assignment.

Ryan had replied to Florence, "It's not hard just for kids." For some reason, Ryan's words had helped Florence regain control. No, the older woman had agreed, I suppose I shouldn't get so mad at them for something I can't seem to do myself.

Now the service ended, and slowly they filed out into the sweltering summer heat. They all stood there, like actors in a scene which had ended far too abruptly. No one certain how to restart the theater of life. Gather up the tattered fragments, mold the masks back into place, hide all the regrets and the mistakes down where they couldn't be seen.

The gathering dispersed reluctantly, invisible forces pulling people away from the chapel. Ryan moved because all the people around her did, enduring the hugs and handshakes and pats from people who knew how close they had been. She was in the process of turning back, wanting a final moment there alone, though she knew she would find only a reflection of her own inner void. Her own lack of answers.

But she never made the turning. It was almost as though Florence had put him there, then directed her gaze so that Ryan could not turn back to the empty chapel. The tall stooped posture was as immediately identifiable as the freckled face and the hair going from cracker red to aging transparent. The eyes measured her across the green lawn and the distance. Waiting.

Ryan walked over, her step fueled by bitterness and loss. "I remember you." So very glad there was a reason to take aim. "Weren't you the one who said every feminist should serve a life sentence chained to her kitchen sink?"

Congressman Lester Lassard waved back the aide who started to intercept her. "Long time ago, Mrs. Reeves."

"That's *Ms* to you." She cocked her body by raising fists to her hips. "I recall a similar attitude shown to me personally."

"Lots of water under that dam."

"Not enough for me."

"Lots of hard lessons learned."

"I'll just bet." Surprised at her own coolness. A singular pleasure in a terrible day. "You're a freak of nature. A throwback to cave dwellers. And you probably got my best friend killed."

"I resent that greatly."

"Which part?" she snapped back. Wishing she had something she could throw in his face. Settling for words. "Tell me so I can elaborate further."

Surprisingly, he neither backed away or gave in to the rage flushing his features. "I counted Miss Avery a friend."

"Then your math is as bad as your attitude."

"My *attitude*, Ms. Reeves, reflects my heritage. My *attitude* has gained me election seven times. Despite that, I am learning to change *my* attitude. I happen to be a product of a legacy very different from your own. I have struggled to overcome my heritage and my upbringing. I have learned to unbend, to accept the world's turning, and change." He stopped, breathed hard. Despite the rage in his eyes, he held to a calm voice. "But you wouldn't know a thing about that, would you, *Ms.* Reeves? Certainly not. Why should you, since you were born perfect and knowing everything."

"I don't even know why I'm standing here having this conversation," she snapped, but a fraction less certain.

"What if you *are* wrong, Ms. Reeves. What if Florence and I *were* on the brink of uncovering a very daring connivance between some extremely powerful players. A collusion, I might add, which has left me wondering if it has not snared you as well."

"That's insane."

"This whole mess is insane. Florence's tragic demise is insane. But I for one refuse to allow them to win, Ms. Reeves. That would result in something far worse than insanity."

"And that, Congressman, sounds like an election speech."

To her surprise, he smiled. The action released a bit of the sorrow which had been hiding within his gaze. "A useless gesture, I am sure. I would never expect you to vote for me. All I can hope is that you might be willing to work together with me."

"I doubt that in the extreme."

Still he did not turn away. "A peace offering, then. Something for you to carry away and think over. But first a question. Florence's mobile phone records showed she called you just before her death."

Remorse burned a hole straight through her. A raw summer wind, uncaring as it was heavy with heat, poured through the emptiness that was her center. Tears of physical pain sprang to her eyes and she could not help but whisper, "Guilty as charged."

"I beg your pardon?"

Ryan used both hands to wipe shaky tracks down her face. "Florence called me Sunday afternoon. She said she had something important. I put her off."

"She was simply following instructions, I assure you, when she insisted that you discuss these issues only by secure phone." He showed her another sadness-tinted smile. "I must say, Ms. Reeves, I admire your spunk. Nothing I hate worse than time-wasters. Especially on my weekends."

"My spunk, as you call it, probably caused all this."

"Don't you think that for a moment. If you had agreed to run out to headquarters and talk again, you might still be there waiting for her call, did you ever think about that? Florence's fate was sealed long before she called you."

The news permitted Ryan a single steady breath. "You said you had something for me."

"Indeed I do. A missing piece of the puzzle. One of many, I'm sorry to say." Lassard leaned closer. "Florence spent the entire weekend inspecting records at the Securities and Exchange Commission. She called you as she was leaving the building, we have a note of when she checked out. Which meant she had found something there. Something to do with a recent merger or buy-out. But she has covered her tracks well, Ms. Reeves. I cannot for the life of me identify what she had discovered."

Ryan found it impossible to think that hard. "I can't help you."

A flicker of regret, and Lassard straightened. "I am hoping you will retract those words, Ms. Reeves, and come to help us a great deal. We need you and your intelligence and your skills."

She tasted a hint of ancient bitterness. "That's not what you said the last time we met."

He had the decency to wince. "I regret that still, Ms. Reeves. Both what I said and what I did. I hope you will find it in you to forgive a foolishness I have tried to leave behind."

Lassard could not have surprised her more if he had reached across and slapped her. As though he had delved within her memories there in the service, and thrown them back in her face. She had no choice but accept his outstretched hand and say, "I'll think about it."

Ryan started for the remaining line of cars. She had not seen Fuller Glenn since the service and had no idea how she was to return to the airport. Then she veered away, heading for the distant cemetery gates and the road beyond. If she couldn't flag a passing cab she would walk until she found a phone. She had endured a lifetime's worth of sympathetic faces and people attending a funeral for all the wrong reasons.

"Ms. Reeves!"

Reluctantly she slowed. Recognizing the voice. Knowing it was someone she could not just walk away from and leave standing there.

Clay East, Senator Townsend's aide, came hustling across the lawn. "Can I give you a lift?"

"I'm not going into town. I just flew up for the service."

His bulk made a shadow from the sun. "I had thought we were supposed to meet and discuss matters."

She stared at his chest, it being safer than looking up and showing him the remnants of bitter anger. "Plans changed."

"Well, let me drop you off at the airport. National's not that far out of my way."

"I don't want to talk about the position. I'm not ready, and I'm not in the mood."

Her bluntness kept him off balance. "All right. Certainly. I understand."

Ryan could think of no other reason not to accept. She nodded, followed him back to the cars, slid into a blistering hot Lincoln. East granted her silent space until they were almost to the river, then said, "She was a good friend of yours?"

"Very."

"Florence had a rather abrasive manner. It rubbed some people on the Hill the wrong way. But personally I always had the highest –"

"I'd rather not talk about her right now."

"Certainly. I do understand." He joined the traffic crossing the Fourteenth Street Bridge. "I, ah, couldn't help but notice you talking with Congressman Lassard. Is he a friend?"

"No. Definitely not."

"You seemed to know one another quite well."

"I've only met the man once before in my life. And that was years ago."

"Really." He took the airport exit, halted at a light, squinted at the signal overhead. "He seemed very interested in what you had to say."

"He should. I basically called him a slimeball."

East glanced her way, saw she was not joking. "I'm not certain that was a solid career move."

"He had no business being there. And *especially* no right to corral me at a funeral."

"But what –"

"I don't want to talk about it any more, all right?"

"Yes. Certainly. Fine." East held to his silence until he coasted up the Departures ramp and halted in front of the terminal. "We really do need to sit down and discuss things with you in detail."

"Wednesday," Ryan conceded, reaching for her door. "I'll come back up the day after tomorrow."

"Could you at least tell me whether Dr. Laremy –"

"Wednesday," Ryan said, and slammed the door on his voice.

25

"Hale?"

He was slow in coming up from the depths. "Yes?"

"You left your phone in the living room. There's a call for you. Someone named Jerry."

He opened his eyes, saw Philippa standing in the doorway of an unfamiliar room. Then it came back to him. The drive south from San Diego. The chaotic Tijuana border crossing. Getting lost trying to find the Baja highway. Trying not to panic as he raced the setting sun. Finding the overpass and the Ensenada signpost in the day's final light, understanding Ben's warning to arrive before dark. There had been no exit for Angel's Camp, not even a glimpse of the sea or the cove. He had found nothing to denote the turn-off but a small cairn of rocks and a two-rut track leading off the highway and into the desert.

Philippa asked, "Should he call back later?"

"No, I better take this one." Hale swiveled his feet to the cold tile floor. Their voices bounced loudly off the hard surfaces – brick walls, high wooden ceiling. Ben's Baja bungalow was full of echoes and mid-morning light. He accepted the phone, said, "Hello?"

"Hale! Can you hear me?"

"Stop shouting, Jerry."

"This connection is awful. Where are you?"

"Back in Baja. Working on the deal."

"Man, why stop there?" Jerry's tone was jubilant. "Might as well go someplace really nice. Fiji, maybe. Do it all first class."

He smiled his thanks as Philippa handed him a steaming mug. He sipped the bitter Mexican brew, said, "I take it things have changed."

"You are not going to believe this. What am I saying, *I* don't believe it."

"Something happened?"

"Not something, my man. Everything. We're rocking and rolling now."

"Jerry, calm down a sec. Did you check on what I asked?"

"What, oh, how MacRuthers got the contract to work here. Sure. But what the hell, why worry about him now?"

"Tell me what you know."

"Keebler himself is waiting to talk with you."

"Then make it fast. This could be important."

"If you say so." Going along against his desire to celebrate. "I talked with Keebler's secretary. Did over lunch, kept it casual just like you said."

"Good."

"Turns out there's been some mystery about how MacRuthers was hired among the staff upstairs. You know Clarence Allenby?"

"Not personally." Allenby was Keebler's newest board member, elected the previous year in a special session. "He bought something like nine percent of Keebler stock, right?"

"Turns out he actually controls a lot more. Or votes it. According to scuttlebutt upstairs, anyway."

"So?"

"So Allenby personally insisted on the firm hiring Mack the Knife. Rode over a lot of objections. Keebler's secretary knows because she typed the minutes of that meeting."

Hale pushed off the bed, began pacing the room's narrow confines. "That doesn't make sense."

"Hey, how much does around here these days?" Jerry was not letting the mystery bother him. Not now. "But who cares? Lights around here have all gone green. Thanks to you."

Where is MacRuthers now?"

"Haven't seen him this morning." Jerry actually laughed. "Talk about a perfect cap to the day."

"Jerry, I need you to check on something else. Find out all you can about Allenby. Do it fast and quiet."

"Sure, sure. No problem."

"Jerry, this is *important*."

"Okay, Hale. I heard you the first time. Wait, Keebler's secretary is standing in my doorway. Time to pass you on."

"Jerry –"

"I said I'll do it. Hang on."

There was a series of clicks, then the voice of his chairman saying, "Hello? Hale, my lad, are you there?"

"I'm here, Mr. Keebler." Hearing the chairman's tentative voice was enough to explain how Allenby had railroaded the board. "How are you today?"

"Couldn't be better, my boy. Couldn't be better. And I'm sure you know why."

"Yes." Six years previously, Keebler Senior had been felled by a stroke. At fifty-one, Keebler Junior had a lifetime's experience of following the orders of a dictatorial father and none whatsoever in showing leadership on his own. He tended to search out the most powerful voice and glue himself alongside. In calmer times he would probably have made a decent director. But these were not calm times, and Keebler Junior had responded to the unfolding crisis by dithering. Hale could well imagine Allenby selling MacRuthers as the answer to their crisis, leaving Keebler in the comfortable position of following a stronger man's lead.

"I have just gotten off the phone with Mr. Buzz Cobb of the Space Research Consortium. Of course you know whom I mean."

"Yes."

"This follows conference calls yesterday evening with SRC's finance and legal teams. Their interest is most certainly genuine."

Hale stopped his circling at the back by the window, and stared at the yellow desert sand baking under the morning sun. Distant ochre mountains floated in the heat-stroked air. "It sounds good, doesn't it."

"Good! My boy, this is absolutely fantastic. The entire board is over the moon. Mr. Cobb indicated his assistant, a Ms., wait, I have her name written here somewhere."

"Durrant."

"Precisely. Ms. Natalie Durrant should be arriving here this afternoon. But he made it clear that you will be the one to guide the acquisition process. Absolutely crystal clear."

The room suddenly felt constrictive, so Hale walked down the hallway and into the bungalow's main room. Brick side walls upheld a front facade of raw timber and glass. The bungalow sat in a terraced row with perhaps a dozen identical houses, all lining the top of a steep-sided cove. Older structures dotted the southern peninsula. Down below the ocean beat upon an empty shore. The sound was much louder at this end of the house.

Keebler's tone turned nervous under the weight of Hale's silence. "I'm sure you understand this changes everything. I have already spoken with the board. As of this afternoon, you are Keebler's newest vice president." When Hale still did not reply, he continued, "Naturally, we are ready to discuss a hearty remuneration package. And I hope you agree with me that our earlier woes and the pressures everybody suffered under are absolutely behind us. They are totally forgotten, my boy. Never happened."

"It's not enough."

"I beg your pardon?"

Hale sipped from his cup. "I want Don MacRuthers fired."

Keebler gave a nervous cough. "I'm afraid that's not possible."

"Sure it is. You call him into your office and you fire him."

"Hale, my boy –"

"I'd prefer to see him taken out and shot at dawn. Or better still, drawn and quartered. It's what he deserves for the shambles he made. But I'll settle for having him fired."

"I'll have to go to the board on this. You'll be calling in basically all your chips. If I were you –"

"Go wherever you want." Hale watched the sea crash and rage beneath him, battling the implacable shore. Desert on one side, ocean on the other. Impossible opponents in constant connection. "But the longer it takes the harder it will be to make this deal. They want speed. And I'm not moving on anything until Mack the Knife is fired."

"My boy –"

"Take it or leave it. Don't call me until he's gone." Hale clicked off. He stood in the sudden stillness listening to his heart and the crunching surf. Saying to the empty room, "My last great act as a company man."

"Not your last."

Hale turned to find Philippa watching him from the kitchen doorway. They had spoken little since his arrival, letting Ben fill the air over dinner, then retiring to separate bedrooms soon after. Hale said, "There is so much I need to tell you."

"From your time in San Diego?"

"Yes." And suddenly felt the urge to add more. To speak about all that tumbled through his inner space, the unseen longings, formerly hidden behind carefully erected barriers. Yet now his shields were down, his life exposed.

Philippa caught the meaning of what went unsaid. Her eyes darted to the sea, seeking escape. "It will have to wait," Philippa said, her tone brisk. "Did you bring your board?"

"It's in the car."

"You'd best go suit up, then. Ben has come by a half-dozen times already. He's calling it a world-class day."

26

In surfing, fear came and went like the tides, dependant on forces as solidly certain as the moon's pull upon the sea. Courage in surfing required channeling this fear, utilizing it. The goal was a union of muscular strength with all the internal forces – aggression and anger and lust and breath and intelligence and vision – matching the power of sea with everything the surfer had to offer. And sometimes more than that. Much more.

To declare a day of big waves was not merely a study in size. A big swell was one which tested the surfer's limits, and thus measures varied from one person to the next. Some searched for big waves with the famished hunger of adrenaline junkies. Limits were barriers to be shattered. Size was measured not only in terms of height, but thickness and speed and current and temperature and frequency, and the best waves were hunted with the intensity of warriors after big game. Others avoided huge surf like the plague, sticking to places and sizes that kept limits safe and protected.

That Tuesday morning, Hale stood on the crest of the ridge, and saw his own limits stretched out before him.

He did not need to go any closer, did not need to feel the water's chill, nor see the wave-height from sea level. He hefted his board, measured the inner resources he had to call upon, and knew he was to be tested.

To his left, a rock point jutted two hundred yards into the sea, rudely ignoring the waves that pounded it with the force of an artillery barrage. Hale stood captivated by the sight. Waves peaked and hung for impossible seconds before falling forward in slow-motion grace. They struck the surface with such force that great spumes sprayed up and back in rainbow-clad clouds.

Hale drew back from his fear, and began tracking a way out. It was a form of mental preparation, and had served him well in the past. Even so, he felt his heart and breathing accelerate in time to the coming trial. He watched the water swirl around the rock point's inner face. This formed a churning whirlpool-pocket, and his best chance of paddling out would be to hug the inside of the rocks as closely as possible, using the current's outward rush to speed him through the impact zone.

"Entry should be quite tricky," Philippa said, coming up alongside.

Hale nodded silent agreement. The paddle would have to be timed perfectly. Otherwise they would risk being pushed back by the next incoming swell just as they rounded the point. Which would mean being shoved from the open water onto the rocks, and hammered to a pulp.

He turned from his water-borne fear to inspect her. Philippa looked seawards with the ocean dweller's thousand-mile stare. Her hair was a soft red froth, her features flecked with gold by the sun. She seemed to him a mighty Valkyrie, a queen of sun and sea, strong beyond physical might and time and any measure he might bring to bear upon himself. "I haven't been out all that much lately."

"Ah. That might make for an interesting day." She offered him an excited, mocking smile, and started down the slope. "Coming?"

For a swift instant he found himself caught in the crystal blue amber of a sun-clad desert day. He stood upon the crest watching her lope down the sandy cliff with angular grace.

When she arrived at the base she turned back and shouted something caught and echoed by the wave's roar. Hale forced himself to move, to descend, to approach the testing field.

At the water's edge they did not speak at all. They held it in, moving through the stretching routine with an intensity that fed upon the thunder ahead. Philippa was the first to rise to her feet, attach her ankle leash, and start for the water. Hale dithered a moment longer, twisting a body taut with adrenaline flush, before following.

The water was cold enough to force a hiss between clenched teeth. Three steps and his feet were burning so bad that numbness would be a welcome change. Hale braced as the first inner wave rose to slap him in the chest. The waves' din was continuous.

Philippa hooted as she rose from diving through the shorebreak. She slid onto her board and paddled out. Hale followed because he had no choice. A third wave rose in front of him, this inside reform already shoulder high. Hale pushed his board down and kneed into a duck-dive, shouting into the water as it engulfed him. The shock was electric, incandescent.

By the time they neared the rocky point, the exertion had warmed him to where the water no longer burned. Hale halted within the frothy protection of the sheltered waters, pushing up and straddling his board beside Philippa, breathing hard. The salty water-chill felt like champagne to his lungs, filling his veins with radiant excitement.

From this close, the point was a rubble-strewn battlefield. Wave after wave reared up to the height of a two-story building, then pitched over, smashing down, raging onto the rocks. Each wave blasted them with foamy spray. They did not try to speak. The noise was deafening, the view awesome.

A part of Hale's mind continued to function in logical little steps. He traced his way out beyond the point to where the south swell swept in, rising with the underwater ridgeline, held in place by the offshore wind. The waves wrapped up the coast in long streaming lines a hundred, a hundred and fifty yards long. It was a perfect natural left. Hale saw all this, told it to himself in quietly practical terms, while the other side of his brain was frozen solid. The part connected directly to his gut felt trapped like a tiny animal in an oncoming pair of headlights. He watched helplessly as the last wave of the set reared up, higher than the others, and bellowed with a force he felt in his chest as it ground upon the rocks.

Hale shouted a word not even he himself understood as the ocean reduced to sullen shifting calm. Beside him, Philippa slid prone and pushed as hard as he did, paddling like mad for the open sea.

Every alteration in the surface sent another gallon of adrenaline through him, but he was committed now. They had to get out beyond the point, beyond the impact zone, and into safety before the next set arrived.

On small days, *inside* was the path through which a surfer paddled to reach the take-off point. It was an obstacle course of froth and duck-dives and work. On a big day, however, inside was the danger zone. The pit. The point of impact, where the waves peaked and crested and fell.

A dark stain pushed into view on the horizon. Hale shouted a warning and pushed harder. He felt his shoulder joints stretch until the tendons popped with each paddle. They had to make it out. There was no other way.

Four guys were already out, Ben one of them. They sat slightly farther south, almost directly in front of the rocky point. Hale kept glancing over, pushing to move out in line with them, using their position as his own point of safety. When they proned and started paddling for the horizon, he groaned. It was all the breath he could afford to expend on anything other than the push for outside.

Another pair of strokes, and a slight bump in the surface lifted him high enough to catch sight of what was coming. Only when he was a good ten strokes beyond where the four had stopped did he finally accept he was safe. Even so, he watched the set's approach with one hand gripping close to the nose, ready to paddle for all his life was worth. The waves were that big.

Philippa paddled up beside him, smiled and gulped for air. When she could manage she said, "Chicken."

He was too busy sucking breath and watching the wall rise to respond. The wave was so big its approach seemed slowly casual. He tensed as it began lifting him, higher and higher. Philippa whooped beside him, pointed to where one of the four had taken off and started flying towards them. Hale did not watch. He found himself caught by the sight of the shore and the ridgeline. When they reached the wave's peak, it seemed as though he was looking down on the houses. He turned his face seawards, saw he remained in safe position for the next wave, tried to hide from Philippa how the entry had rattled him.

The next wave was a solid face, one without a ledge. On a big day such waves were liquid nightmares, especially in strange territory. A wave like this, with a face drawn level, meant that it risked breaking straight across the cove. Such a wave was called a close-out, meaning there was no shoulder upon which a surfer could ride. Taking off on a close-out wave meant taking the weight of the sea on his head. Hale watched the remaining three surfers farther out sit tight, not trying. They were farther down the peak and thus had calling rights on any wave they wanted. Hale sat beside Philippa and let the second wave carry him higher than the first, then break in a solid single-impact explosion that filled the cove from edge to edge with whitewater and foam. Spray peeled off the top as it fell, dousing them with stinging needles. Hoots from the three guys floated across to him. He fought down tremors with a death's grip on the rails of his board. The impact zone.

The wind was too mild for the waves to hold to clean tubes. They fell in layered steps and formed a ragged foamy core. It also caused the waves to section; Hale saw that with the third wave. He watched as another of the guys with Ben raced with all his might to beat the wave as a segment perhaps thirty yards long started to fall all at once. He found himself hooting with the others when the guy made it. Hoping he would do as well. Or at least as well as he could.

Then it was there in front of him, a towering behemoth whose peak appeared to be aimed straight for him. In the distance Ben shouted something. Hale's heart was racing so hard, blood pounding so fast he had time to measure the windblown words in his mind and replay them clearly. *Go for it.*

"Go! Go!" Philippa's shout was a cry of joy, one so strong it unlocked his muscles. "You've got it!"

He wasn't ready. His lungs still ached from the paddle and the morning's internal struggle. He would have preferred to wait out the entire first set. Even so Hale spun about, paddled, and felt the affirming surge of power. As though the ocean chose to help him out, fill him with all that he did not have alone.

He twisted to check his position, and felt a pumping spike of adrenaline. The wave was a dark wall that filled his world. Higher still it rose, carrying him to the peak of a salt water mountain.

He used the grip of his chest on the board's waxy surface to angle the board slightly. The wave was a left, which meant he would ride it backside. Not the easiest way to tackle something this big. But there was no longer time for thought. Just commitment.

Philippa leaned over the peak to scream something he could not hear, only feel, her excitement joined to everything else as he started the push down the face. His paddle was a frantic constant. Great surging heaves of both arms, powering him both forward and down.

The face angled away from him, the board surging just ahead of the crest. He felt the wave's power take over. A final deep-shouldered heave, then he gripped the sides of his board and did a quick push to his feet.

He slid down the bumpy face. All was noise and speed and flight. He kept his eyes angled for the next move, saw the breaking crest speed ahead of him. He angled the board tighter into the face and leaned forward slightly, moving up the side of the wave, defying gravity.

The board angled sideways, his body held in place by the forward-sideways thrust. He rocked the board with his feet, a subtle back-and-forth motion which added to his speed – the magic art of accelerating on three-fin boards called thrusters.

Then there was that ringing moment, the unspeakable high found only on limit-testing waves, when he knew he was going to make this wave.

He shouted the news, a wordless cry of exaltation. The wave's power was his and his alone. He lifted himself and his board, climbing up this personal Everest, until the crest was there and feathering just above. He jammed all his weight onto his back foot and pointed his hands down, grabbing into the shadow-dark pit, no longer afraid. He was beyond vertical now, the marriage of wave and board and body so complete he could hang there, his speed suspending him beyond gravity, beyond even time.

The wave pushed and sped, and he swept his front foot around as hard and fast as he could manage, a move as much for the people behind as for himself, knowing the act would fan a rooster-tail of water high overhead. The board was angled straight down now, the wave rising to vertical and pushing him with a speed that left him no choice but to scream. And scream and scream again as he backed and reached behind him, planting his left hand into the wave face, drawing a water-trail, pushing for more speed, and even more.

Another cut off the top, then back down, leaning so deep on his scoring of the pit that he lifted two of his three fins clear of the water. Then back up the face, the angle more exaggerated, testing each new limit as soon as it was formed.

Another bottom turn, and the wave lessened, a quietening more felt than seen.

Hale spun over the top and stood still as the board slid to a halt. He jammed his fists over his head, shouting out the remnants of an impossible thrill.

He proned and paddled straight for the horizon, making it through the set's two remaining waves with relative ease. When he started back toward where Philippa still sat, she showed merry teeth and shouted something lost to the wind and the waves. But the words weren't that important. Having a friend there to see him make the wave was enough.

Philippa made a motion with her hands like a wounded gull, the act made famous by the wide-arm stance of a former world champion. Only this time she was mocking Hale, suggesting he had gone for windmill effects on his turns. Hale laughed and shouted his denial, then halted in his paddling long enough to point towards the horizon. A wave was peaking in perfect position for Philippa.

She turned and whooped. She slid down, paddled a few strokes further out to meet the incoming wave, then sat back up in preparation for the take off.

Then she stopped.

Philippa did not even try for the wave. Did not move when Hale called over the lessening distance, demanding to know what that was all about. Did not turn when Ben shouted frustration over a wasted chance. Just sat and stared at nothing.

Hale was puffing hard when he sidled up to her board. Still she had not moved. Philippa sat there, clenching the board with her right hand, her left just lying limp in her lap. Hale asked, "What's with you? That was ..."

Hale's voice trailed off at the sight of two tragic eyes turning towards him. Eyes filled with the anguish of the ages. And mortal fear.

"What's the matter?"

A wavelet nudged Philippa's board, pushing her closer and around. And Hale noticed the hole in her board.

It was a gap the size of a saucer, jagged edged, chewed out just above the water-line. Hale's first thought was, *shark*. He had seen photos of attacks where sharks mistook the board for prey and gouged huge chunks from the fiberglass. But nothing this clean. Nothing where the board was pierced clear through.

Then he saw Philippa's arm.

The wetsuit was ripped just below the shoulder, a grazing cut that had blown the stretchy fabric into a hundred unraveled knots. Blood seeped from the wound.

Philippa started to speak. Then her eyes rolled back, and she slipped from the board.

27

Hale moved before his thoughts had caught up. He flipped off his board and dove for Philippa, catching her before her head went under. He struggled to pull her back onto the board, but it was impossible. She was out cold, and there was no way to balance her.

Thankfully the wave she had missed had been a single. But the next set was already staining the horizon.

Hale searched, felt a flood of relief when he saw that Ben was watching him. He screamed with panic strength, "*Help me!*"

The two guys outside started over with Ben, throwing nervous glances towards the horizon. They paddled hard until they drew close enough to spot the hole and the spreading dark stain. One of the guys made huge eyes and shrieked, "*Shark!*"

"No, wait, it's not –"

"*Shark!*" The kid was already hightailing for shore, his paddles so frenzied they threw rooster-tails. His buddy was not far behind him. The guy paddling out saw their panic-paddle and turned shorewards instantly.

But Ben was made of stronger stuff. Hale gulped with relief at the sight of him approaching. Ben spilled off his board, felt for his leash, and pushed his stick away. He swam over and helped Hale balance Philippa. "Lose your board, man."

"It's not a shark," Hale gasped. "She's been shot."

"Hey, that's great to know, but there's a set coming. *Lose your board.*"

Certain now Ben would not let Philippa's head go under, Hale ducked below the surface, grabbed his leash, and tugged the Velcro-grip free. He surfaced in time to see Ben swimming one-arm as hard as he could manage, heading away from shore. The set was huge and closing. Hale swam over, grabbed Philippa's suit with one arm and her board with the other. "Wake up, Filly. Come on, help us here."

"She's out of it. Must be shock. Help me balance." With Hale holding the board steady, Ben slid onto Philippa's longboard. He grabbed for the back of her suit, grunted with the effort of hauling her up. Hale struggled to hold them upright. When she was partially out of the water, her head and wounded shoulder on the board, Ben settled on top. "Okay, help me keep her there and *kick.*"

Ben sprawled over Philippa's upper torso, paddling as hard as he could for outside and safety. Hale worked to keep her in place, kicking in time to Ben's strokes. His breath came in gasps.

The first wave was a monster. They scrambled up the face, Hale giving a solid 'uh-uh-uh' with each kick, fanning his legs harder and faster than he would have thought possible, doing an overhand paddle with his free hand. He watched the crest begin to feather up above them, the wave starting to slide over and take them with it. Then they were pushing through, their combined weight keeping them from toppling backwards and down and into oblivion.

The second wave was even bigger.

Hale groaned a protest, Ben gasped a curse. Ben's stroke was frantic, digging around Philippa's body, rocking the board so much her face went under from time to time. Hale did not protest. If they didn't make it over, she was finished.

The wave was a solid moving mountain. Ben shouted with the final effort, his face and neck clenched into taut corded lines. Even so, it did not look like they were going to make it. The crest was feathering and they were not even halfway up the face.

Hale gripped the rear of the board as Ben clawed his way upwards, took hold with both hands and *pushed*. The effort shoved himself back and under, throwing him into the full force of the wave.

He was tossed like a leaf in a hurricane. The wave surged him up and forward, carrying him all the way over the top. The ride launched him with the force of a skydiver. He landed so hard the water felt solid. The impact zone.

The wave landed on top of him, shoving him down, and down further still. His lungs were empty from the explosive effort of having pushed the board forward. The burning reached from his lungs to his throat to his eyes, and he clawed up, ignoring the violent wash, knowing he had to have air *now*.

Hale pushed up through the foam and heaved a painful gasp. Another. Then he wiped the foam away. Terrified he would see another wave, or even worse, an empty sea. He shouted with what strength he had left upon seeing Ben. He was sitting outside, still holding Philippa's head clear of the sea, his shoulder slumped in exhaustion. The set was past.

Hale paddled over, so tired he could scarcely lift his arms clear of the water. Ben watched him approach without moving. When Hale gripped the board's rail Ben croaked, "You get worked?"

Hale nodded, took hold of Philippa's head, saw the bluish tint. He slapped her face, got a flinch in response, and felt tremendous relief. "She's still with us."

"That was something, man, pushing us up and over like that. I thought we were done for."

"Come on, Filly," he pleaded, his voice creaking from the salt and the wave. "You've got to wake up."

"Seen this happen before. It's shock. You say she got shot?"

"I think so. I didn't hear anything. But one minute she was fine, the next and she's bleeding and there's a hole in her and the board."

"Sounds like somebody's tracked her down."

"We've got to get her in."

"Hang on, there's another set coming." Ben squinted at the horizon. "We'll wait 'til it passes."

"I don't think I can go through that again."

"No sweat. That last one was a freak. Biggest I've seen here in weeks. Maybe we should move over towards the center of the cove, though, get ready for the paddle in."

"Right." Hale shook Philippa's shoulder, but the head flopped limply. "Think she'll be okay?"

"Long as she hasn't taken in too much water. Which I doubt, since we've kept her face pretty much in the clear." Ben proned, started paddling, and added, "Long as we don't get worked on the way in."

Ben was right, the next set passed them safely. They were far enough out to ride over the crests with weary calm. And aware enough to hear the sound when it came. Off to their right. A musical *plunk*. A second. And in the distance a quick low crack.

"Gunshot for sure!" Ben slid off the board, his eyes registering new fear. "Who the hell is after her?"

"I don't know."

"Well, she's done something to somebody." Ben waited for the last wave to rumble onto the shore. When all was relatively quiet he pushed off the board, rising up as high as possible, and yelled a guy's name. *Carl*. Another quick rise, another shout, and one of the guys on shore waved at him. Ben rose up again, and this time pointed at the top of the ridge, doing a broad arc with his arm and shouting, "Somebody's shooting at us!"

It took a second shout before the guy understood. This time he did not flee. Instead, all three of the surfers and two girls who had been standing and watching from the shore raced up the cliffside. Hale pointed as a figure rose from behind the hilltop greenery and fled.

Ben flopped back with a relieved sigh. "That oughtta scare him off."

"We'd be crab bait for sure if you hadn't been there."

Ben shrugged off the thanks. "Or safe, if I hadn't brought you down here."

"I doubt it. They would just have tracked us somewhere else."

"Yeah, maybe so." Ben gave him as much of a grin as he could manage. "Guess that physics stuff of hers is more exciting than I figured."

Philippa chose that moment to moan. Hale stroked the hair from her face, said, "Come on, Filly, wake up." Another moan, the eyelids flickered, but stayed shut.

In the lull between waves Ben asked, "Think maybe you could ride the board, paddle her in? My arms are gone."

Two more waves brought little groans from Philippa, but she did not regain consciousness. Together they maneuvered her around so that Hale could stretch out half on and half beside her, bringing Philippa further out of the frigid water while Ben rode alongside, kicking and holding them stable. Then they started in, pushing hard, finding new energy from the horror of getting caught midway by another set.

But the water remained clear. When they were within fifty yards of shore one of the guys swam out to greet them, his eyes great moons of panic. "What the hell happened?"

Hale could only spare breath for one word. "Shot." Ben simply paddled and huffed.

The guy gripped the board's other side and pushed along with Hale, speeding their progress. When his feet touched bottom, Hale could only groan with relief. Ben slid away from the board and stayed there, inert. Another guy and both girls sped down the shore and helped carry Philippa out to safety.

Hale dragged himself out of the water, his limbs so weak each step was a strain. He felt the cold now, and the chills ran through him in tight waves. Ben stumbled up beside him. They stood with chests heaving as the two girls stripped off Philippa's wetsuit, rolled her onto her back, and pushed on her chest. Then Hale's legs just gave way. No notice, no warning, just no strength left. He tumbled to his knees in time to hear Philippa cough.

He sat there, trapped by fatigue inside his wetsuit. One of the girls handed him a sandy towel and he rubbed his face and hair until the blood started flowing. With the help of many hands Philippa rolled over and sat up. She coughed, groaned, coughed more water, and finally opened her eyes.

"All right," Ben said weakly. "She's back."

Philippa coughed again, turned and searched until she was staring at Hale. And showed him the cloud of fear.

28

Late Tuesday morning Ryan awoke to the smell of fresh-brewed coffee and the sound of a stranger saying, "Honey?"

She had arrived back home late the previous night, and for the longest time had sat there in the car, unable to find the energy to carry herself inside. Jeff and Kitty both had greeted her with hugs and sympathy, bringing fresh tears. Upstairs she had found Harry standing in her dressing room, looking extremely worried. Ryan had silently moved past him, picking up her robe and gown from their hooks, too exhausted to even care what he was doing in her private domain. She had simply informed her husband that she was moving into the guestroom. For good. The time for pretenses was over.

"Sweetheart?"

She had no choice but to open her eyes and allow in all the world's anguish. And the sight of Harry standing over the bed. He wore golf shirt and shorts, his normal Saturday outfit. But it wasn't Saturday, it was Tuesday. Or had she slept through an entire week? Her brain felt so mired in sorrow she had difficulty identifying what he was holding.

A breakfast tray creased his bulging belly. On it steamed a coffee cup from their best china. A single pink rose stood in a tiny vase.

"It's almost eleven," Harry said. "I thought you might like some breakfast."

She scooted up until her back rested on the headboard. "Why aren't you at the office?"

"I took the morning off." Nervously he settled the tray down in her lap. "Is it okay?"

"It's beautiful." A cloth napkin was rolled into an engraved silver ring she had forgotten they even owned. A crystal glass of fresh orange juice. Toasted bagel. Dollop of cream cheese. Strawberry jam on the side. And the rose. The sight and what was behind it invited more tears. "Thank you, Harry."

"I'm really sorry about Florence, Ryan."

The rose swam in its own liquid frame. She said the words she had repeated all night long, her silent litany of guilt. "I should have been there for her."

"She was hit by a car, Ryan. Isn't that what your office said? You couldn't have done a thing."

She sipped from her cup, looked up. Harry appeared much more than nervous. He was scared. Genuinely frightened.

Apparently her moving into the guestroom had rocked him. Hard. Ryan patted the covers. "Sit here beside me."

Ryan inspected her husband without anger or remorse for the first time in what felt like years. She decided to move straight in. This was no time for roundabout maneuvers. "Harry, I don't know if there's anything for us to salvage."

His nerves grew more apparent now that he had nothing to hold. "Hey, sure there is. What kind of talk is that?"

"I feel like the past five months have scalded my heart. Ever since the promotion I've lived in a battle zone." She lifted the tray and set it aside. Drew up her knees. She had not eaten since hearing about Florence, and felt no appetite now. "I am what I am, Harry. A mom and a career woman. Ambitious, focused, driven. Nothing is going to change that."

"Look, I've had all the battles I ever need." He forced his hands still by clasping them across his spreading belly. "Where has it gotten us? Nowhere. I say, let's put it all behind us and work this out like adults."

Ryan could scarcely believe she was hearing this. From Harry. But the sweat on his forehead and his eyes' constant dance declared this was no act. Ryan knew an instant of searching for some ulterior motive, but the strain was too great. She said, "I need you to start helping more with the kids. And not using every night you're here alone with them as a reason for another argument."

"Sure, sure, no problem. Hey, maybe we could take them out for the launch this week. Like the old days. Remind them of all the good work their mom is doing."

"That may not be possible, Harry. I may have to go back up to Washington." A big breath. "They've offered me a new position back there. A big career move."

Harry blinked. "Yeah? When was this?"

"Last week. I was going to tell you." Ryan waved it aside. "No, maybe I wasn't. Maybe that's where I've been headed all along, moving up there without you, and didn't want to admit it to myself."

"Don't talk like that." Harry's hands escaped and renewed their nervous crawl, touching his cheek, his hair, the covers, his pudgy knees. "They've been talking about wanting me back up at our Washington headquarters again."

This was news. "Since when?"

"Oh, I dunno. Coupla weeks."

Ryan started to ask when he had planned on telling her, decided it didn't matter. "Do you want to know what my job offer is?"

"Sure, sure. Of course I do."

"Chief Advisor to the Senate oversight committees. Both of them. And SES status thrown in."

"Hey, that's great."

Something was missing from Harry's reaction. Surprise, maybe. Or perhaps his nerves simply left no room for anything else. She did not want to stop and inspect. Not when it was time to finally let a major long-term peeve out into the open. "Harry, there's something else I have to tell you."

His movements stilled.

He thinks I have a lover. Ryan bit her lip. Then she said, "If we're going to try this, and I'm not saying it'll work, but if we're trying at all, you have *got* to go on a diet."

"What?"

She reached over, touched him for the first time in what seemed like years. Patted his belly where it rested on his bare pasty thighs. Making it bounce. "A major diet. A permanent one."

He focused on where she had touched him. "Sure, babe. Whatever you say."

"And exercise. Every day. Enough of this doughboy look. We can do it together if you like. Before work."

"No way I'm gonna try and keep up with Superwoman here."

It took her a moment to realize he had tried for a joke. She tasted a smile in reply. "For you, for now, I'll walk."

* * *

Ryan went to the office that afternoon partly because she had promised Chuck Evans, the engineer, she would meet him. But mostly she made the journey because she needed to give some shape, some normalcy, to the day. Help shore up the internal defenses with the work at hand. She was approaching the security checkpoint closest to Kennedy HQ when her cell-phone rang. "Ryan Reeves."

"Ryan, finally. It's Hale. Where have you been?"

"Long story." Ryan held the phone with her shoulder, the steering wheel with one hand, and stuck her pass out the window at the guard. When she was waved through she dropped the pass and hurriedly rolled up her window. The afternoon air slapped at her like a hot wet bathcloth. "What's up?"

"I tried to call you this morning. Your cell-phone wasn't on. Your office wouldn't tell me a thing. I called the house, and Harry said you were sick and wouldn't put me through."

She glanced at the console clock. Just past five. Two in the afternoon, California time. "Harry didn't mention that you'd called, otherwise I would have gotten back sooner."

"Ryan," Hale hesitated. "Ryan, Philippa's been shot."

"*What?*" She slewed the wheel and slammed on the brakes, halting by the side of the NASA Causeway. "Where?"

"Baja. I came down again yesterday evening. It happened this morning while we were surfing."

A vulture swooped down on the canal beside her car, captured a fieldmouse and flapped away, its wingspan topping four feet. They swarmed over the Kennedy swampland, so populous they had been adopted as an unofficial mascot and renamed Florida condors. "How is she?"

"She seems okay. She went into shock in the water and really scared us. But she's okay. Weak. Frightened." A pause. "We're all pretty shook up."

"Can she move?"

"Yes. The bullet grazed her arm below the shoulder. We've had a doctor in, he says there's no permanent damage."

The phone hissed, and Hale's voice faded into the ether. "Hale!"

"I'm still here. Ryan, the reason I talked with you like that on Sunday, Philippa is worried that somebody's been listening in."

She thought of Florence's warning, knew she carried enough regret to burden her for all the ages to come. "That's notoriously difficult to do with cell-phones, Hale. You have to triangulate with two trackers just to get a location fix."

"Anyway, they found us. And there's no time left for games." Swiftly he recounted the attack on him at the university lab building, then told of the robbery in Baja.

Ryan struggled to fit all the pieces together. "Philippa knew they were going to rob her?"

"She suspected it. So she set them up."

"The records on the computer and the notes they stole, all fake?"

"Bogus as cold fusion. Months of dead ends. The real stuff is with her."

Anger was a welcome coldness, freezing her heart, sealing the wounds with icy fury. "Those bastards."

"Tell me about it."

"Where are you?"

"Just north of Ensenada."

"Is she safe?"

"For tonight. The place is surrounded with friends."

"I need to get to my office and try to work out a couple of things. I'll get back to you as soon as I can." Ryan thought swiftly, came up with what she thought would be a workable plan. "We don't want to take her back across the border. That would be an ideal spot for them to make another try."

"Ryan, Philippa doesn't have a passport." Letting more of his worry show through. "They stole that. She felt like she had to leave it in the hotel room safe, you know, to make it all look authentic. All she has is the lab teckie's driver's license."

"Stay calm, Studley. Crisis control is what I'm best at. Can I speak with her?"

"Hang on, I'll see if she's awake."

Ryan spent the moments making swift notes in her head. Then there was the sound of a familiar but weak voice saying, "Hello, my dear. How are you?"

"I should be asking you that."

"Oh, it's nothing. Really. The bullet just grazed me. More fear than anything, I should think. And Hale is taking marvelous care of me."

"We're going to get you out of there and someplace safe."

"Ryan, I can't tell you how much it means to hear your voice again."

"Likewise." She found herself tempted to open up, tell

about Florence. But she held back. No need risking a total loss of control. "Listen, I have a lot to tell you."

"Not now. Not like this."

"No. First we get you to safety." She hesitated, then asked, "How are things with Hale?"

"Fine." The voice suddenly flat.

Ryan gave a mental shrug. No time to worry about that now. "I have to go work some things out. I'll get back to Hale as soon as I can. Don't worry. We'll soon have everything under control."

* * *

"Johnson Space Center, Astronaut Deck."

"Major Jack Stone, please."

"You mean Colonel Stone?"

So now he wore the eagles on his lapels. "All right. Yes."

"Who is calling, please."

"This is Ryan Reeves, Deputy Administrator at Kennedy. Authorization seven zero alpha emma."

"Stand by one." A pause, then, "Colonel Stone is probably at the Officers' Club, ma'am. I'll put you through."

Another series of requests, these ones done under noisier surroundings, then a voice she vaguely recalled. Deeper than she remembered. "Stone here."

"This is Ryan Reeves, Colonel. You probably don't remember me. We only met twice and that was years –"

"I remember, Ms. Reeves. Florence used to talk about you. A lot, as a matter of fact."

"Oh." The connection was suddenly stronger than expected. But the news made it more difficult to speak. Ryan swallowed hard, said, "I see you decided not to attend the memorial service."

"No." A long sigh. "I thought it would be better for everyone concerned if I made my farewells in private." He hesitated, then asked, "How was it?"

"Horrible. Awful. I wish I could have missed it too."

"No, you don't."

She heard it distinctly. Felt his regret echo in time to her own sorrow. "No, I guess not." Pushed hard to make room for what needed to be said. "Colonel, there's something else you could do. For Florence, I mean. Well, for me, actually. But indirectly for her. She thought it was very important. I do too."

Ryan grimaced. That was the lousiest sell she had ever made. But it was all she had in her just then.

She waited through a long silence. When Stone spoke again, it was with a stronger tone. "I'm listening."

"There's a lot I can't tell you," she warned. "The questions I'm bound to raise I simply can't answer. All I can say is that it's a matter of life and death, and I mean that literally."

"Is this related to Florence's death?"

"I don't know. Truly. They say it was probably just a hit and run ... I don't know, Colonel."

"Call me Jack." A longer pause, then, "Tell me what you want done."

29

Organizing Philippa and Hale's routing took until after six. The work drained her utterly. A few people stopped on their way home to express their condolences, people who knew she and Florence had been close. Each visit sapped a bit more of her strength; holding in the sorrow took most of what she had left.

She went over her calendar with her secretary, shifting everything except the meeting with Chuck Evans until after her Washington day-trip. Wishing she could put that off as well, but knowing it had to be done. Senator Townsend's office had phoned twice that afternoon, and both times she had refused to take the call. She had to go.

She left headquarters and drove out to the OSB, the Orbiter Support Building. The OSB was the center for all orbiter staff – orbiter was how the shuttle was referred to among the engineers. The nondescript building nestled up close to both the huge Vehicle Assembly Building and the slightly smaller Orbiter Processing Facility. Its first five floors housed the United Space Alliance engineers responsible for servicing the shuttles; the upper three floors held the NASA support staff. Ryan entered and moved against the flow of departing workers. All of Kennedy worked to round-the-clock shifts, but the majority of engineers and admin types held as close to standard days as possible.

There were eighteen thousand people employed at Kennedy, but the number was cut by two-thirds within the restricted zone containing the processing units and the launch pads. The Orbiter Support Building was a nuts-and-bolts kind of place, with employees pushed to extreme limits by deadlines and a universal drive for excellence. Ryan loved the place, which was why she agreed to meet Chuck here rather than at her office. She felt a desperate need for a reality fix.

"Ryan, great, you made it." Chuck was like most of the top engineers, a hyper-intelligent guy who had grown from a starry-eyed nerd into an overweight scientist who lived and breathed his work. He steered her around to a work-station shared by himself and three other teckies. Only one of the other desks was occupied and that one by Chuck's principal assistant, a teckie Ryan knew vaguely. Chuck waved her towards a chair. "I can't tell you how sorry I was –"

"Thanks, Chuck." She remained standing. "What have you got to show me?"

"Right." Accepting the change of subject with swift comprehension. "Review of the problem. We have to maintain sterile conditions within the payload bay to protect the satellites and experimentation equipment. The weak link is the seal connecting the gantry arm to the payload bay doors. It was a faulty design. You with me?"

She forced herself to concentrate, and recalled, "The form we're using was based on airport concourses."

"Right. And that's fine so long as you don't mind a little dust. Which we do." He cupped his hands, forming an oval. "The problem, Ryan, is the width of the seal. One tiny bit of sand, one microscopic corrosion, it's enough to ruin a seal. Why? Because the thing is built wrong. It's a hard rubber surface about an inch thick. Totally wrong for what we need."

Chuck turned to a lab table and hefted what looked like slabs of tire rubber. "Now I want you to imagine something. Think of a seal that *inflates*. Just blows up and presses in around the payload bay."

Ryan crossed her arms, forced herself to concentrate. "Like a giant inner tube."

The teckie looked up at that. He stared at Ryan and allowed, "That's a good way to describe it."

Excitement over the concept and nerves over dealing with a money person drove Chuck's voice up a half-octave. "A slightly oblong inner tube, thirty-six feet high and twenty feet wide. And here's the best part. The tube itself would be four and a half feet thick."

Ryan accepted the slab of rubber from Chuck. It was about a quarter-inch thick and surprisingly heavy. Yet it was as supple as silk. It almost flowed from her grasp. She turned it over. The outer skin was cross-hatched with a diamond pattern about a millimeter in depth. "I suppose these little holes would act like suction pads, adhering to the orbiter."

The two engineers exchanged glances. "That's it."

"Four feet thick would mean that even the worst storm couldn't penetrate and wreck your cleanroom status." Ryan held up the material. The movement made it shimmer like a black waterfall. "Now I suppose you're going to tell me this stuff is expensive as spun gold."

"Actually, it's a little more than that." Chuck's pace accelerated. "Dupont developed it for seals on deep-sea drones. We can inflate this a thousand times, slide out the retractable flooring, filter the air, load the orbiter, deflate it and pull it back. No risk of cracking. Guaranteed for twenty years. We can even swab it down with industrial cleaners. It's impervious to almost anything."

"And the damage?"

"Turnaround time would be dropped to a matter of two or three hours, if necessary."

"How much is this going to cost us, Chuck."

"This stuff is highly experimental. Our order would be four times the total amount Dupont has produced up to now."

"I'm still waiting."

The older man jammed his spectacles up tight on his nose. "For the material, one point two mil."

Ryan stared at the engineers, waiting for the laugh. "You have got to be kidding."

"Plus fitting costs and high-compression pneumatic pumps." Chuck rushed for the finale. "And we'll need back-up generators in case the power fails. Got to keep the pressure constant."

Ryan stepped over to lean against the wall. "Ball park figure?"

"Two mil plus change to get it up and running on both pads."

"He argued them down almost forty per cent," the teckie added.

Ryan turned to stare out the window. The idea was sound. Better than that. It had the simple correctness of genius, and over the long run it would actually save both time and money. Currently the seals they used cost upwards of eighty thousand dollars, plus five days to replace and test. For this particular launch they had gone through four seals before cleanroom status had been achieved and maintained.

Their window looked out towards the Vehicle Assembly Building, the single structure with the largest interior space in the world. But she was not looking at the building. She was thinking about her job.

Despite everything else pressing in on her, she loved this part of her work. Loved making a difference. Loved helping to solve problems that actually brought the impossible one step closer – designing a space program that would guarantee a launch turnaround of two weeks. That was the goal. Shuttles coming in and going out twice a month. Supporting a viable and expanding space station. Bringing costs down to where the Kennedy operation actually showed a profit. Expanding the list of workable space-programs. Satellite television, microwave telephone transmission, these were just the start. Gravity-free spacelabs and spacebound science parks were literally just around the corner.

She turned back to the two engineers. "I'll try and finagle the money."

The two engineers looked stunned. Chuck recovered first. "No kidding?"

"This is a good idea." And she was genuinely grateful for being brought out of her worries and her woes, and reminded of what she was actually here for. That meant more than she could ever say. "Actually, it's a great idea. It deserves to be done. How fast can you get it up and running?"

An unsteady hand raised to adjust his glasses. "Two months from order, maybe a week less."

"I'll talk to the money people as soon as I've got your paperwork. When can you get the forms and diagrams completed?"

"Tonight if I have to. They're almost ready."

"No need to overtime it. I'm in Washington all day tomorrow anyway. Have it on my desk first thing Thursday." She gave them both a genuine smile, the first of the day. "Good work. Really."

Chuck hustled to catch up with her. "Ryan, I really appreciate this."

"It's okay, Chuck. It's my job."

"No, it's more than that. You've always been a friend." Then he surprised her by pressing his arm down on her shoulder, turning her away from the elevators, guiding her into an empty office. Closing the door. Lowering his voice. "I heard a rumor this morning. About how you're being appointed to Washington to help steer through more job cuts down at Kennedy."

The good feeling vanished. "Who told you that?"

"You know I can't say. Some of the shop guys, down on the VAB floor and over at the processing facility. Is it true?"

"Of course it's not true. You should know that as well as I do. I fought like hell the last time they started with cuts."

"I remember."

"Talking about going out on a limb, I risked my job over that." The previous year, six hundred Alliance jobs had been axed. Ryan had fought against it, warning that safety could suffer as a result, and suggested all future orbiter refittings should be done at Kennedy. Going directly against the grain of Johnson's planned phase-down of all KSC activities. "The Johnson people wanted my head."

"That was months ago. You know how fast people forget the good stuff. Still, you're moving into a position of power, don't they have that right?"

"Maybe. Nothing's been settled."

"That's not what I heard." He jammed his glasses up so tight they creased his forehead. "If I were you, I wouldn't walk around the operations areas by myself. Especially not at down times."

"What, somebody is going to threaten me?"

"No, I doubt they'll waste time on that. These guys were hot."

"This is crazy." Despite herself, Ryan felt fear knot her gut. "If anything, I'd be their strongest ally. I want Kennedy to expand, not shrink. You tell them that."

"They wouldn't listen. Just be careful, okay? These are desperate times."

"I can't believe they'd try anything on NASA grounds."

"You get somebody heavy into gambling debts, couple of divorces, behind on house payments, any number of things. Then let him hear there's some Washington hotshot out to ax his paycheck." Chuck waited, then, "You see where I'm headed?"

* * *

After dinner Hale settled Philippa back down into her bed and walked through the house, turning on lights as he went. Night had fallen without his noticing. He passed through the front room and walked out to the small terraced landing which fronted the ocean. Down below, waves crashed and receded, the one constant in his life that night.

Caring for Philippa in this state was harder than he had ever expected. There was no room for distance here, no room for the games of old. She needed all he had to give her, all the strength, all the confidence, all the caring. All the love.

That the giving came so easily made it harder still. Each act, each movement, spoke of the past lies he had erected to keep from caring. How he had pretended that he needed time to know himself, when in truth all he had wanted was space to keep his ancient lies intact.

He felt himself lifted free from himself, from the beach, the waves, the earth. Nothing held him to this place or this life. He had no commitments, no burning passion, no love, nothing larger than himself. He took in air, he let it out – the sole sum of his existence. When he stopped breathing, there would be nothing left. He would vanish, leaving not even a void in the heart of another.

"Hale? That you?"

He turned, grateful for the company. "Yeah."

Shadows coalesced and formed into Ben. "How's our girl?"

"Better. She's been talking on the phone."

"Okay if I check in on her?"

It was a friend's kind of question. They were staying in Ben's house, Hale had nothing to say about Philippa's actions, but Ben had asked just the same. In that moment, it was a gift of merit. "Sure. She'd love to see you."

But Ben was in no hurry. "Just made the rounds. Everything's quiet."

"It's great that people would pitch in like this and keep an eye on us."

"Down here, you help each other out. Nobody to rely on but each other. It's the only way to survive the bad times."

Hale nodded to the sea and the sky. This was something

he could well understand. "The doctor seemed like a good guy."

"Yeah, known him a lot of years. He'll keep this quiet. Far as he's concerned, the lady was never here."

"You sure we don't need to inform the local police?"

"No cops. Not in Baja. Down here, guns and gringos mean just one thing."

"Drugs," Hale guessed.

"If they don't find anything, they'll just look harder. And use tougher methods of asking all their questions. Believe me, you don't want to mess with the Baja federales." Ben started to move away, then said, "You did good out there today."

"So did you. Thanks, Ben. For everything."

The big man moved away, leaving Hale alone with the night. He watched the waves roll in steady cadence, the break lit by stars and phosphorescence. The wind blew salt mist over him, and such was the cavity in his heart that the breeze continued straight through his center. As though he had already vanished.

30

Hale and Philippa left the cove in a cloud of morning dust. They shared the pickup's front seat with a driver whose arms were as large as Hale's thighs, and a wide-bodied pregnant woman. The driver was wedged into place, his enormous belly creased by the wheel. The pregnant woman was as stolidly silent as the driver.

According to Ben, such trucks made regular runs down Baja, transporting day-workers who endured the journey rather than live in Tijuana squalor. Ben and some buddies had helped buy this local driver a new truck, and earned the sort of gratitude that guaranteed a safe and secret departure. Though the truck-bed was crammed even fuller than the seat, still they stopped at each village, and still more people quietly found room in back. Hale could see nothing out the rear window except a jumble of dusty shirts.

Hale spent the entire journey talking quietly. Philippa spoke only a few times, terse questions softly spoken. Her good arm held the other, cushioning her injury against the jouncing ride. Her left shoulder was padded and bandaged, her arm slung under her shirt. Much of the time she rode with eyes shut, features taut, pallor grey. But she listened.

Her questions walked Hale through the problems at work, his meetings with SRC and Northstar. She showed no reaction, not to Cobb's warning nor the attack at the lab, nor

Conway's information. She listened and Hale talked, creating their own tiny island there in the heat and desert and dust.

The only time the driver and the woman showed any interest in them was when Hale's cell-phone pinged. He pulled it from his pocket and said, "Andrews."

"It's Ryan. Where are you?"

"Somewhere south of Tijuana." Hale was distracted by the moon-faced woman watching him, dark eyes wide as her grin. She turned and shared a laugh with the driver, who was leaning forward and watching Hale more than the road.

"You're heading for the airport?"

"Just like you told us," he confirmed. Ryan had called back twice the previous evening, filling in details as she worked them through.

"How is Philippa holding up?"

Hale pressed the phone to his chest, ignoring the eyes following his every move. "Ryan wants to know how you are doing."

"Gathering data." She did not open her eyes. "Letting my mind roam on automatic sort mode."

Hale said to the phone, "She seems okay. Tired."

"I can imagine. Okay, a Gulfstream is scheduled to pick you up in about forty-five minutes at the satellite terminal. It's the older building, what used to be the main airport. The plane will take you to Albuquerque. Check into a hotel there, let her sleep for a while. Use the lab teckie's driver's license to register and pay cash, in case they're watching your credit card usage."

"I don't have enough money."

"I figured that. The guy who's coming to collect you will have some for the hotel and for your flights onwards. His name's Stone, by the way. Jack Stone. I've had a little trouble with your connections, all seats are booked solid. You're priority listed on a couple of waiting lists. There shouldn't be any problem, since we're using a little NASA muscle."

"Quietly, I hope."

"Extremely. I'm leaving here in about an hour for Washington, I should get in just after lunch. Call my mobile from a pay phone. I'll go somewhere and call you back."

"Using pay phones, is all that necessary at this stage?"

"I don't know. Florence thought so."

"Who?"

"A friend." The words sent Ryan's voice down a tragic octave. "Never mind. Call when you get her settled."

Hale clicked off, said to Philippa, "Sounds like something's wrong at her end too."

"She's caught up in all this, just like us." Philippa grimaced as the truck bounced from the gravel track onto the main highway. "Tell me exactly what the man at Northstar related to you. What was his name?"

"Zack Conway. I already have."

"Do it again, please. For me. Try to remember any details you might have missed."

* * *

At the Tijuana airfield Hale helped Philippa from the truck, then turned to wave his thanks. One brown arm rose and fell as the truck departed in a dusty plume.

A windsock hung limp in the gathering heat. The field and the parking lot were locked in yellow dust and silence. Together they sought the relative cool of the older terminal, a concrete bunker with paint falling in plate-size chunks and no glass in the windows. A panting dog shared the front veranda with one scrawny chicken.

As they entered the building, a man and a woman behind the counters looked up, gave them a brief inspection, then resumed their conversation. The airfield schedule was a single bulletin board, announcing in fly-blown letters that the next scheduled flight left for Juarez at mid-afternoon.

Philippa walked in the carefully upright manner of one carrying serious pain. Their footsteps echoed loudly in the empty air as she led them to seats in the far corner. Hale carried his bags and her own meager luggage. He dumped it by the bench she selected, helped her to sit, then asked, "Do you want something to drink?"

"Don't leave me. Can you see the airfield from here?"

"Sure."

"Then just sit beside me and tell me again about Buzz Cobb."

Hale started to object that he had already been through all that and she needed to rest. Her skin was stretched taut across her features, like invisible hands were pulling it thin as gauze. But Philippa chose that moment to open her eyes, and show him the naked appeal.

Hale dropped into the bench beside her. He did not understand her reasons, but her need was clear. "Buzz Cobb has all the charm of a two-hundred-pound scorpion."

She slid over to rest her head on his shoulder and closed her eyes once more. "Tell me."

* * *

"You Andrews?"

"Yes." Hale scrambled to his feet, facing a compact man with shadows for eyes. "Sorry, we were talking and I must have –"

"Jack Stone. I've been sent to collect you and a female passenger."

"We're ready." He reached down, eased Philippa to her feet.

"This way." Stone led them through the empty hall and up to the glassed-in customs booth. "Understand there's a problem with her passport."

"It was stolen."

"Right." He pulled five crisp new hundred-dollar bills from his pocket, made sure the customs officer watched as he flipped open an empty passport folder, slid them inside.

Pushed the folder through the opening in the window. "Price goes up when you're leaving on a private jet."

Hale watched the official accept the folder, slide out the bills, push the folder back. He followed Stone past the control booth and into the empty hall. When they were alone, Stone offered him a thick envelope. "Ryan Reeves said you'll need this for your tickets onwards. Tell her not to worry about paying me back. Tell her it's all part of my atonement."

"Excuse me?"

"Take the money." When Hale had accepted the envelope and stuffed it in his pocket, Stone asked, "You need a hand with the lady?"

"I can handle her, thanks."

"Okay, this way." He led them out into the blazing sunlight, and through a gate in the field's chain-link fence manned by two hot and sullen guards. He gave them a single nod. When Hale slowed, looking for some form of permission to pass, Stone said, "Already taken care of these gents. Just show them your bags."

Hale released Philippa long enough to open each case in turn. Their attention was thorough. Stone said, "Only way we're able to do this is by not having much in the way of luggage. These days, bodies carry a lot less heat than other stuff."

Stone led them across the tarmac, and demanded, "What happened to your friend?"

"She was shot."

"Bad?"

"No. Just grazed her arm." Even so, Philippa was leaning heavy on him, drawing strength and support. "Are you a friend of Ryan's?"

There was the slightest hesitation to the military stride. Then the pace and tone turned brisker. "In a sense. Did she tell you I can only take you as far as Albuquerque?"

"Yes."

The plane was a small Gulfstream jet. Stone twisted the handle and pulled out the door and extended the stairs. "I don't even want to list the regs I'm breaking here. But I've got buddies who'll cover, long as I make this an in-and-out and as fast as possible."

"Fine." Hale helped Philippa up the stairs, felt the wash of air-conditioning spill over them. He eased her into the first padded seat. "It's just fine."

31

Early afternoon found Hale standing curbside in Albuquerque. A trio of Hispanic women were walking by when the pay phone rang. One of them shouted as he reached for the receiver, "What are you selling, honey?"

"Who cares?" the second said, while the third made kissy sounds. "Just you leave enough for me."

Ryan demanded over the phone, "Who's your cheering squad?"

"Just some ladies looking for a party. Where are you?"

"Dulles Airport. You ready to write?"

"Shoot."

"Okay. You've both got seats on the Delta flight to Orlando. It leaves in about an hour and a half. I used the lab teckie's name. You are flying as her husband. First class. Pay cash. Did Stone give you the money?"

"Yes. He said something about atonement. What was all that about?"

A pause, then, "Tell you later. I'm scheduled back in Orlando earlier than you, so I'll be there at the gate to meet you. If not, take a taxi to my house. Everything clear?"

"Yes."

"How is Philippa?"

"She had lunch and went to bed. She looks pretty tired. But she says she's fine."

"She can travel, then."

"She says yes."

"Okay, by tonight we should have her somewhere safe. I have to go now, Hale. Take care."

"Hang on, there's one thing Philippa says can't wait." As swiftly as he could, he sketched out Philippa's request. Command was more like it. She had insisted he write it all down, say it all precisely as she had laid it out.

When he was finished, Ryan was silent a long moment. Then, "You can't be serious."

"She says it has to happen, Ryan. And now. Immediately."

"In case you two haven't noticed, Hale, I don't have all that many contacts in Vienna. Especially with refugee camps."

"She isn't bending on this. Philippa said to tell you, whatever it takes."

"I don't believe this." Ryan's tone was hoarser than normal. Bitter. "As if I didn't have enough to worry about already."

"Something is wrong," Hale declared. "I knew it when we talked this morning."

"It'll wait until I see you. It has to."

"Okay. Can you help her with Alexis' wife and child?"

"I'll try." An explosive breath that might have contained a yes. "I've got to go, Hale. See you in Orlando."

* * *

Ryan slammed down the receiver and stomped away from the bank of pay phones. The problem was, she knew exactly how to handle Philippa's request. Yet the pressure of having to declare herself squeezed like a vise.

She walked through the airport doors and entered the hot humid Washington day. The stench of car exhaust and jet fumes was numbing. Ryan cursed as she realized she was upstairs, and the taxi ranks were all downstairs at Departures. It was illegal for a taxi to take a fare from the

Arrivals level. She swung back around and started for the doors.

Her anger almost carried her past the first watcher.

The man wore a grey suit and ultra-dark shades. Walking alone, about ten paces behind her. Ryan would not have noticed him at all except for the fact that the man was talking to his wrist, and as soon as she turned back, he turned away.

But the man was an instant too slow, probably because his attention was on his wrist and the communicator. Ryan had seen enough officials and their bodyguards to recognize the habit, the wrist limp and hand akimbo, the head tilted to bring the wrist-mike as close to the lips as possible.

Ryan pushed back through the doors and increased her pace, but not nearly as much as her heartrate.

She flew across the marble hall and took the escalator at a skipping gait. As she hit the bottom ramp Ryan pretended to wrestle with her shoulder bag, and risked a glance up. She could not see the man.

There. The guy was hanging back, the sunglasses still on, staring out and over the crowds. But she knew where his eyes searched.

She raced through the lower level and up the ramp to the street, her hand raised and calling for a taxi before crossing to the middle island. She pressed past slower-moving customers, ignoring their angry words, and dove for the door opened to someone else. All the hated habits of high-stress 'crats. She didn't care. She simply screamed, "Emergency!"

"Sure, honey, sure." Typical Washington cabby. Shutting her door, pointing the arm-waving passenger back to the next cab in line. Making a slow parade of his walk around to the driver's side, sliding in, asking in a bored tone, "Where to?"

"Russell Senate Office Building on Independence."

He grunted, unimpressed by another pushy 'crat out to pretend they ruled the world.

Ryan swung in her seat, searched for the man. When she couldn't spot him, she knew an instant's doubt. After all, Dulles was full of high-powered ...

There. The spotter came racing out to street level. Had she not been watching carefully she would have missed him entirely, the pick-up was so smooth. He was in sight only an instant. A nondescript station wagon, the bumper splashed with enough mud to mask the front plate, slid up and slowed. The door opened and he jumped in without the car halting. The wagon slipped behind a hotel van and disappeared.

* * *

Philippa was awake and waiting when Hale returned to the hotel room. "Well?"

"I told her."

"And?"

Hale went over and sat on the bed. "She hung up on me."

Philippa shut her eyes on the world. "Ryan will do it. She'll find a way. She has to."

32

From the instant of her arrival in Senator Townsend's office, Ryan knew what it meant to be a star on the rise. Nothing drew respect from a Washington insider like new power. Ryan accepted the staffers' congratulations as best she could, and gratefully allowed Clay East to steer her directly into the Senator's office.

The Senator was up and moving before she passed the doorway. "Here she is. The lady of the hour."

"Thanks for seeing me, Senator."

"Don't mention it. This time next week we'll be begging for a minute of your time. Right, Clay?"

"Afraid so."

His smile faded, the chin lowered, the jowls creased. "I understand Florence Avery was a friend of yours."

Ryan gripped one hand with the other. Hard. "Yes, sir. She was."

"Tragic thing. Tragic. Still haven't caught the driver of that vehicle, I understand. I was so sorry not to have made the funeral personally, but I was back home visiting the constituents. I believe Clay saw you there."

"Yes."

The Senator accepted her tenseness with a nod, and showed a pro's ease at changing gears. "Right. On to your future, Ms. Reeves, and it's a bright one if I do say so myself.

Now just when exactly are you aiming on making the move back to Washington?"

"I haven't heard that the appointment was finalized."

The Senator and his chief aide exchanged glances. Clay East said, "Fuller Glenn was supposed to have informed you of that Monday."

"We came up for the funeral. I haven't seen him since. I assumed he stayed up here. The budget talks are still under way."

"He should have called you about this." Senator Townsend patted his silver hair. "Sounds to me like old Fuller's tugging on the reins, trying to hold back progress. Problem is, those reins are about be cut off and leave him standing there with nothing. You let me handle Fuller."

Clay asked, "Any word on that missing scientist?"

"Dr. Laremy's been located," Ryan said cautiously.

"Excellent!" The Senator beamed. "The committee will be delighted to hear."

"There have been some problems." Ryan searched the faces. Wishing she knew whom to trust. What to do. "Her hotel room was ransacked and her work stolen."

"What?" If East already knew, he masked it well. "When?"

"Sunday. But I only learned about it last night." She started to mention the shooting, but something held her back. Concern about where it might lead, hating to tell them where Philippa was headed. "And I'm almost positive I was followed in from the airport."

Another glance between the two men. Then Clay said, "Looks like you were right, sir."

"Not me. That fellow Cobb. And I wish he wasn't." The Senator turned to her. "We've been hearing rumors of some major forces at work here. People out to harm your scientist friend."

"Who?"

"That's the problem, Ms. Reeves, we don't know anything for certain." He said to his assistant. "Have Doris see if she can locate Cobb."

Clay was already moving for the door. "Right."

Back to Ryan with, "There's a man I'd like you to meet, Ms. Reeves. Somebody who's a lot more familiar with the industrial espionage game than I am."

"That's what this is?"

"It's our best guess. For the moment, that is." The Senator looked up. "Well?"

"Found him first try," East announced.

"Good. Put him through here." To Ryan, "Can't hurt to speak with the gentleman. That's my advice."

Ryan rose and moved to where East stood holding the Senator's phone. "Hello?"

"Ms. Reeves, this is Buzz Cobb over at the Space Research Consortium."

Ryan reduced her voice to a deadpan. "I know your company, of course."

"I'd hoped your buddy Andrews might've mentioned my name. Would've made things easier for me."

"Not that I recall," she lied.

"Never mind. East tells me you and your pals have run into some heavy flak. I think we need to talk, and so do the people up there in the Senator's office."

"I'm not so sure –"

"I am. You don't know what's at work here. I do. Go to the Air and Space Museum. Walk under the Apollo 4 command module, past the lunar roving vehicle. I'll meet you by the Saturn engine display."

"Do you mind telling me what all this is about?"

"Let's just say you'd be doing everybody a favor, Ms. Reeves. Especially yourself."

* * *

Situated on the Washington Mall opposite the National Museum of Art, the Air and Space Museum was the most heavily visited tourist attraction in all of Washington. Ryan paid off the taxi, scouted in both directions, saw nothing she could call suspicious. But the place was crammed with summer tourists, busses, vendors, cabs, cars, people sunning on the steps and kids throwing frisbees on the green. An army in camouflage fatigues could have escaped notice.

Ryan climbed the stairs, pushed through the tour groups clustered around their guides, and passed beneath the Wright Brothers' plane. She slipped around the throngs waiting to enter the IMAX theaters and took the stairs to the second floor. She paused and looked back over the balcony railing, though she knew the act was futile. There was no way she could spot a tracker in this mob.

Then her eye was caught, her forward motion halted. Directly ahead of her, a model of the space shuttle hung suspended from the ceiling.

But it was not the model which held her. It was a memory so packed with emotions she sighed with the effort of remembering. The sound was enough to draw stares from people milling nearby. Ryan paid them no mind. This particular memory had been lost to her for far too long.

She clutched the railing with fierce strength, wanting to recall not just the moment, but all that it had signified. All that she had allowed herself to lose.

She recalled her first journey down to the Kennedy Space Center. NASA Tiger Teams had been a new concept at the time. The teams had been designed to bring together specialists from many different NASA departments, then sent somewhere to solve a specific problem. Her second year with NASA, there had been a serious defect with the orbiter's new onboard computers, an expensive issue that had justified having Florence Avery head up the team. Being Florence's protégée at the time, Ryan had been permitted to tag along.

After four grueling days of meetings and engineering and costing, the Tiger Team had completed their mission. It had been a poster-perfect Florida spring day. Ryan still remembered how huge and endlessly blue the sky had seemed.

Around mid-afternoon, the team had decided to stretch their legs and walk from the support facility to the Vehicle Assembly Building.

The entrance doors were a full five hundred feet high, as huge as everything else about the VAB. The building's interior space was so vast that on very humid days clouds would sometimes form up near the ceiling, and it would rain indoors.

The VAB had originally been built for the Apollo-Saturn moon projects, then adapted to suit the shuttle program. Everything about the VAB was larger than life. It had taken eleven hundred gallons of paint for the building's flag, one so large each stripe was broader than a highway. Yet when compared to the wall on which it rested, the flag looked miniscule.

That day, Ryan had entered the VAB with the rest of the Tiger Team. The others had seen it all many times before, and had walked around discussing the spectacle in cool engineering tones. But the sight had stopped Ryan dead in her tracks.

The shuttle Endeavor hung suspended in the largest portion of the VAB, the sector known as the high-bay. Multiple gantry cranes were hooked to the nose, tail and wings. Brilliant halogen lights blazed upon the orbiter, so bright the suspension cables were lost to the shadows. To Ryan the shuttle looked like a giant and glorious bird, frozen in mid-flight within its own island of light.

Slowly, slowly the shuttle was being raised to a vertical position. Once at the proper height, assembly with the booster structure would begin. It hung there between heaven and earth, impossibly beautiful. Ryan stood underneath and felt as though her heart was suspended there alongside this shimmering man-made phoenix.

Conversation among the Tiger Team grew hushed and respectful. Even so, Ryan moved further away. No one could be permitted to disturb this moment. She stood and watched the coupling process, an operation completed with painstaking precision. And she knew that she had found something worth the cost of all the days she had to give, all the work and worry to come. Just to see this impossible dream be made real.

Ryan watched the shuttle complete its rebalancing and felt herself transported, lifted far beyond earthly realms. She became a part of what she was witnessing. Her eyes blurred until the lights mingled together, and it seemed to Ryan that far overhead the ceiling opened. Slowly the stars drifted down, descending to hover there around her, almost close enough for her to reach up and touch.

* * *

A pair of shaky breaths were enough to bring the world back into present focus. The worries and the fears and the pressures pounded her with the noise of the crowd. Ryan stared up and saw nothing but a painted plywood shuttle mock-up, hung from the ceiling of an overcrowded tourist attraction. People pressed and shoved as they passed, making quick empty memories with their cameras and videos, turning away, looking for the next momento to freeze and cart away.

Ryan sighed a third and final time, then turned away. As far as she was concerned, the blues were sung for moments just like this.

As she rounded the next corner, a stocky man in a raincoat and unkempt suit walked over. His military razor-cut hair was as grey as his skin, his eyes as cold as his smile. "Ms. Reeves? I'm Buzz Cobb. You're late."

Ryan ignored the stubby-fingered hand. "What is this all about?"

Buzz seemed to approve of her reaction. He dropped his hand, revealed teeth ground to small white pebbles. "Spirit. I like that. Shows somebody who can survive in a clinch."

"I asked you a question."

"Take a look here, Ms. Reeves." He pointed to a huge display there beside them. "Saturn 5 propulsion unit. One of five on each Apollo rocket. F-1 engines, they were called. Developed eight million pounds of thrust."

Ryan broke in impatiently. "They burned five hundred thousand gallons of liquid propellants in their two and one-half minutes of life. By first-stage jettison the rocket traveled at six thousand miles per hour. I know the stats, Mr. Cobb. I asked you what all this was about."

Another flash of approval. "Good to hear I'm dealing with a lady who knows her stuff. Come on, got one more thing to show you. It'll soon be five-by-five."

He led her along the balcony, past the Douglas rocket, the Skylab mock-up, the Spirit of Saint Louis. He stopped and pointed out over the railing at the next display. "Take a look here, Ms. Reeves. The F-15. First winged aircraft to reach Mach 4, four times the speed of sound. Then five, then six. Bridged the gap between aircraft flight and space exploration. Reached an altitude of one hundred and eight kilometers."

"I don't have time for –"

"Now look here. See that?" He pointed to the sign at the base of the display. "Manufactured by North American Aircraft. Ever heard of them? Course not. They're dead as the dodo."

He leaned against the railing, crossed his arms, went on, "The defense and aerospace industries are littered with carcasses, Ms. Reeves. Happens all the time. Only one buyer, see. The government. Most fickle customer on earth. Why? Because the rules are always changing. One day it's quality, the next day it's price, the next and ten years of research and a billion dollars of development money are turned to garbage."

"What are you telling me?"

But Cobb would not be rushed. "This fosters an air of desperation and fear. Tremendous fear, Ms. Reeves. Fear so strong they'll do anything to protect their turf."

She crossed her arms. "Who is behind all this?"

"Whoever is threatened by what your scientist pal has discovered."

"Do you know what that is?"

"I know she was checking superconductor materials on her own time and overseeing our research on propulsion. Two areas that apparently weren't worth a fighter pilot's time, back when I was in training." Cobb's granite jaw jutted forward. "But I know enough to watch the horizon, Ms. Reeves. Anything that's stirred up as much smoke as Laremy's work, that's bound to be lighting a fire. A big one."

Ryan searched the inner tumult, wished she knew whom to trust. SRC had backed Philippa, sponsored the research, paid the money. "So who do you think it is?"

"Who the hell cares? Look, over the past couple of years the field has shrunk and the number of teams with it. Those that are left are so big they write their own rulebook. Being the fastest and the best isn't enough any more. Nowadays it comes down to power. Who's got it, who controls the most players."

"That's all Laremy is to you, a player?"

"Sure. One about ready to get squashed if she isn't careful." Cobb grew impatient, and stabbed the air between them. "You tell that scientist if she doesn't come in where we can protect her, she's gonna get fried. So you need to help us bring her in, and now."

Ryan was so wracked by doubts all she could manage was, "I'll pass on your message."

Cobb gave a disgusted grunt, dug in his pocket and passed over a card. "You do that, Ms. Reeves. Call me day or night. We'll move into action. If it's not already too late."

33

Ryan's appointment with Congressman Lassard was set for the lobby of the Mayflower Hotel. It was a wedding-cake sort of place, full of towering cupolas and plush carpets and servants and flowers and pillars and marble and gilt. Washington's power structure felt very much at home at the Mayflower.

Ryan joined the flow of uniforms and dark suits headed up to the ballroom. Heads turned her way, but nothing out of the ordinary. Certain segments of Defense and the aerospace industry remained a restricted white males' club. Something she was determined to change.

She entered the ballroom foyer and instantly spotted Lassard. He was standing with another woman, one beautiful enough to slow traffic to a crawl. Lassard waved her over, said, "Good of you to join us, Ms. Reeves. I don't suppose you know Ms. Durrant."

"Ms. Reeves, this is a genuine pleasure, I can't tell you. Please call me Natalie. Hale has told me so much about you."

"You know Hale." Of course.

"We met just last week."

"Ms. Durrant is with the Space Research Consortium," Lassard said, his voice even, his inspection of her microscopic.

"I'm over in Richmond working on acquisition discussions with Keebler Plastics," Natalie added

Ryan tried to recall what Hale had said about his company. "SRC is buying them out?"

"Yes, didn't you know? Oh, I suppose he wanted to keep it quiet until it's all confirmed. We're in the process of preparing a bid, and Hale is operating as our front man. I'm taking a break just to come over and deliver this talk." Natalie glanced at her watch, flashed Lassard a brilliant smile. "Well, since I'm the next speaker I suppose I'd better go in. It's been such an honor meeting you, Congressman. And you, Ms. Reeves. We really do need to meet up again sometime soon."

Ryan waited until Natalie had disappeared into the hall before saying to Lassard, "I'm listening."

Lassard fiddled with one wing of his bow-tie before saying, "This whole thing did not start out with NASA at all, Ms. Reeves. We were picking up rocks over in the military-industrial complex, watching the bugs scurry." A hard glance at the door to the ballroom, then back to Ryan. "I first got involved with this latest battle when they put me on the board of the Florida Space Authority."

Ryan felt rocked by the news. The Florida Space Authority was patterned after successful airport authorities. It was intended to bring in new business and jobs through selling commercial launches at the space center. The fact that Lassard had been involved in anything related to space came as a total surprise.

A little known fact about the Florida space center was that it actually contained two entirely separate entities. Kennedy was operated by NASA, Canaveral by the military. The military also had two older pads they were no longer using. After a great deal of political arm-twisting, one of these sites was turned over to the Florida Space Authority. Their first launch had been the rocket carrying the Lunar Prospector, a probe intended to search out water at the moon's poles. It had been a huge success.

Ryan admitted, "I didn't know you had anything to do with that."

"No reason you should, Ms. Reeves. No reason at all." Lassard was clearly pleased at having caught her out. "Launch Complex LC-46 finally got up and running despite some serious foot-dragging from the Defense staffers. We designed the new commercial venture as a quick-response launch capability, aimed at competing with the private sector. Book the sucker in, set it up, send it up."

"Aimed to be ready for launch within six hours of receiving a phone call, if necessary," Ryan supplied. "Working with both Lockheed and Boeing EELV rockets. I read your brochures."

Lassard nodded sharp approval. "After the Lunar Prospector was launched and things went from paper to reality, things got even hotter inside Defense. A few people offered support, but most were bitterly against us. Same kind of split, or so it seemed to some of us, that we faced when trying to get you NASA folks to downsize. Only over on the Defense side the folks were a lot scareder."

"Not scareder. There's no such word. Try more frightened. Makes you sound almost intelligent."

"Missy, we all know what you think of me. Now just sit on that overlong tongue of yours and let me get on with the tale." He huffed his way into his pocket, came up with a handkerchief, wiped his forehead. "Inside NASA we found a solid group who were rooting for us to succeed. Over at Defense there were only a few friends to be found. Most folks acted like the enemy had moved in right down the hall. They were vicious, plain and simple. Did everything they could to slow us down, other than blow up our rocket on the pad." He shook his head. "Shrinking budgets are sure bringing out the snakes and the gators."

"You're saying they're into illegal operations over at Defense?"

"Not just at Defense. Our enemies in the military were dancing their greedy jig to somebody else's tune." He stuffed his handkerchief back in his pocket. "The military-industrial complex is a two-headed snake, you see where I'm headed? There's people in the commercial sector who're telling themselves, whatever it takes to survive, that's all right. Rulebook don't apply no more. They do whatever they need, right down to murder and mayhem, long as they get the contract."

"Then Florence comes up and shows you the same thing is happening inside NASA," Ryan surmised. "Which I suppose shouldn't come as much of a surprise. All the major aerospace companies work in defense as well. They've had a long time to pick up bad habits."

"Miss Avery was right," Lassard allowed. "You got yourself a sharp eye and a better aim."

"Who did it to Florence?" she demanded tightly. "You know, don't you."

"I might." Eyes hard as agate stared back. "But what I want to know first is, are you with us or against us?"

Ryan had to drop her eyes. Her mouth felt filled with grit, the residue of too many impossibles in her life. She shook her head. To trust this man went against everything she felt was right.

When she did not answer, Lassard suggested, "Why don't we mosey on inside, have a listen to what the lady has to say. Give you time to think things over."

* * *

Ryan followed him into the darkened chamber. The gloom only seemed to strengthen her host of internal foes. She stood against the back wall, as angry at Philippa as she had ever been. She knew it was ridiculous to be incensed with her friend because she had asked Ryan for help. But logic played no role here. Ryan was furious she was being forced to make a decision without all the necessary data.

Ryan inched her way down the back corridor, hoping the shadows would mask her movement away from Lassard.

If he noticed her shying away he made no sign. She leaned against the back wall and looked up to the podium where Natalie Durrant stood in a pool of light.

The all-too familiar shape of the XLS-1 launch vehicle appeared on the giant projection screen behind her. Durrant intoned, "Cost reduction and first-level scientific advancement motivated all our thinking at the Space Research Consortium. Every concept, every study on the XLS-1 was dominated by three factors. First, how to make it run more efficiently; second, how to use the newest and the best technology to ensure it would remain within operating parameters for years to come." Her voice rose with polished pride. "And third, how to develop a single stage-to-orbit vehicle."

As Natalie continued, the pictures behind her shifted. Computer-generated images appeared showing the orbiter floating in high apogee orbit. Computer-generated because the drone's trial lift-off had only raised it to a height of sixty miles. "First of all, we determined it would be necessary to move away from solid fuel boosters. SRC wanted a single-stage fly-back." She paused for effect. "And because we were also moving away from hypergaulic orbital boosters, we could reduce the refueling time from two weeks to two days."

Those in the audience who understood moved forward in anticipation. Ryan found herself caught up by the concept. Refueling was a principal cause of time-lag in readying the shuttles for relaunch. The current orbiter's solid fuel boosters were literally packed with solid explosive, a time-consuming process which often required shipping the boosters back to Utah. And hypergaulic fuels, used to pilot the shuttle once in orbit, were incredibly toxic. Whenever the orbiters were being processed by the hypergaulic fuel teams, the cafeterias all filled up. Nobody could work anywhere in the buildings when hyperloading. It literally shut down that entire segment of Kennedy.

Behind Natalie Durrant the orbiter became transparent, revealing the long mouth of the single booster engine. "Our XLS-1 is to be powered by the utterly new linear spike engine. While the concept has been around for forty years, it is only recent materials advancement led by Northstar engineers that has permitted us to move from the design to the implementation stage.

"New metallurgy processes have permitted us to build a turbopump system with no engine valve. This means no moving parts in the flamed areas. Which means no repair time must be built into the turnaround calendar.

"SRC and Northstar now have an operational system whereby exhaust gases are redirected to form a constantly readjustable nozzle." She paused, flashed a glorious smile to the rapt audience. "You engineers in the audience, please excuse my ignorance here. I am simply repeating what I have been told by the experts. But all former rocket designs, if I have understood our people correctly, are powered by *hard nozzles*. And the problem with hard nozzles is that they are *compromise systems*."

Ryan caught heads nodding around the room. She felt eyes on her, turned to find Lassard watching her intently.

Natalie continued, "If the hard nozzle is tuned to maximum efficiency at sea-level, this means it is far from peak efficiency at zero atmospheric pressure. A hard nozzle cannot change its geometry. But as many of you have already heard, our linear spike system can do precisely that. By constantly adjusting the exhaust flow, and thus altering the geometric design of the power system, our new craft will maintain peak efficiency at *every* altitude."

The image shifted once more, revealing a translucent skin set over huge internal tanks. "And because our fuels are the relatively stable liquid oxygen and hydrogen, our tanks may be included within the bird itself. This means that we can do away with the airframe entirely. And as you know," again the flashed smile, "the airframe is the heaviest single component of the current shuttle – far more than the payload. Our orbiter's skin is attached to the tanks, and the tanks are shaped to form the internal frame."

Ryan felt a touch on her arm. Lassard whispered, "Heard enough?"

"Yes."

He motioned with his head to the outer doors. "Why don't we head on back outside."

In the lobby's relative calm Lassard went on, "Ms. Durrant gives a mighty impressive performance, doesn't she."

"Very." More confused now than she had ever been.

"They got themselves a good spokeswoman. Somebody who puts a touch of polish on the two billion dollars they've made and spent on this so far."

A pair of older men in suits came over, smiles in place, hands outstretched. The Congressman met and left them with the slickness of long practice. When they were alone again he said to Ryan, "Where was I?"

"Two billion dollars."

"A whole lot of time and money invested in this thing. Lot to be proud of. Lot to protect. Not to mention the seven billion more to whoever builds the next three." Lassard showed her a keen eye. "I bet you a dime to a fresh-laid egg I know what you're thinking. You're wondering who's standing on the right side of the creek."

Ryan tried to show more clarity than she felt. "I suspect you're only about half as hick as you make up to be."

"Less than that, sometimes." He motioned her into a corner seat, a pillar and a potted plant protecting them from the lobby traffic. "You know, they made the same cost predictions between the Apollo-Saturn rockets and the space shuttles. How they were gonna drop from twenty thousand to four thousand a payload kilo. What happened was, the shuttle came along and the Apollo-Saturn was shelved. That was wrong. *Real* wrong. Ain't nothing a bureaucracy loves more than a monopoly. Costs just *exploded*. Now, though, just having the *threat* of competition has dropped the shuttle's per kilo costs by half."

Ryan watched him carefully, this reedy man in his seersucker suit, a throwback to some hazy era of porch rockers and coon dogs and wood-burning stoves. "I thought you hated the space program."

"I know you do, Missy, and that's exactly where you start going wrong." Lassard showed her a freckled finger curved by age and hard use until it seemed perpetually ready to curl around a trigger. It pointed straight at her head. "Listen up, now, you might learn something. I hate big government and I hate *waste*. I hate how bringing Kennedy to Florida ate up every tax dollar sent to the eastern half of our state for nigh on twenty years. I hate how the three counties I represent were left mired in poverty like you can't imagine. I hate how you can drive just thirty miles southeast from my constituency and see a land fat from political spending."

Ryan tried hard to see past the political posture, the practiced tone, the stance polished by a hundred thousand times at the podium. She was so busy wondering who she could trust she had no time for his anger. "There's a lot of truth in what you say."

Her reaction pushed his hand down to his knee. Lassard stared at her. "Do you know, Ms. Reeves, that is the very first time we have agreed on anything."

"I suppose that's so."

"How much do you know about superconductors, Ms. Reeves?"

"Not a lot."

"Myself, I've been studying up of late. And I've made some interesting discoveries." He fingered a gold chain attached to his vest, pulled out a miniature pearl-handled penknife. Lassard opened it and began paring his nails. "What the experts can't seem to explain is how electrons in superconducting compounds *act as one particle*. They do, you know. It's one thing all the whiz-kids agree on. Shoot a current through a superconducting material and the electrons act as one big unit. They show collective qualities. All the particles join into one, at least as far as anybody observing them can tell. How does that happen? Nobody knows. And the problem is, acting this way violates the law of conservation of energy. Don't ask me how 'cause I don't know. But it does."

"I'm impressed."

He showed a quick flash of even white teeth. "Beneath this redneck exterior dwells a mighty curious nature, Ms. Reeves." Lassard returned his attention to his nails. "One other thing I came across, caught my eye. There's this Frenchie by the name of Chardin, he declares the only way to understand this collective quality is by the study of tiny little particles called mesons and their relation to anti-matter. We're getting pretty far out beyond my reach here, but lemme see if I can tell you what I've learned. His study of black holes suggest that anti-matter shows opposite qualities to matter in a gravitational field. I'm told his theory makes excellent sense."

Ryan shrugged. "Sorry, you've lost me there."

"Me too, Ms. Reeves. Me too. But like I say, I find the thought mighty interesting."

"Why are you telling me this?"

"It's a lure, Ms. Reeves, plain and simple." He snapped the pen-knife closed. "I'm trying to lure you into working with me and using the only bait I've got. Honesty."

She took a breath, knew it was time. "How about giving me something I can use as evidence of your good will?"

"Name it." Not hesitating an instant.

"Just like that?"

"You're looking at a man who always runs on dead ready, Ms. Reeves."

"This is going to seem a little out of left field." She hesitated, then added, "Actually, more than a little."

"Ain't it all." He showed even teeth, a politician's smile and something more besides. "I've made a profession out of playing it loose, ready to grab whichever rung comes into view. Now tell me what test I've got to pass before we can hunker down and get to work."

Ryan took a breath. "Dr. Laremy is concerned with the wellbeing of two Russian refugees."

Lassard blinked. "Pass that one by me one more time."

"These refugees are hiding under assumed names in a camp not far from Vienna."

"Vienna." Very slow. "The town over there in Austria."

"Philippa wants them safe. And here."

This time his smile was genuine. "Down where I live, folks've made an art form outta tall tales. But I swear I don't recall ever hearing a beginning as fetching as that one." He leaned back in his chair. "Why don't you just untangle that a little ways further for me?"

34

The flight from Albuquerque to Orlando was long and silent. Even when awake, Philippa remained quietly private. She kept her attention on the clouds outside, turning back only when Hale asked how she was. Collating, was her reply, assimilating and analyzing. Hale let her be.

He sat and felt the plane vibrate around him. Gentle and constant, the motion appeared intent on shaking loose the fragmented lies which had formerly defined his life. Here and now, for reasons he could not understand, the ability to fool himself was lost. Perhaps forever.

* * *

When they exited the terminal gate Ryan was there to greet them. Hale stood back and watched the two women move together with the smoothness of silent need. Philippa bent over the shorter woman until the russet curls hid her face and gripped Ryan with her one good arm. Holding fast. Holding hard.

Philippa released and took a half-step back, knowing how Ryan hated looking up at anyone. Ryan asked, "How are you?"

"Not too terribly bad, all things considered." Philippa glanced at Hale. Under the airport's fluorescent lighting her face looked waxy, with plum-colored crescents under her eyes. "Hale has been taking good care of me."

Ryan followed her gaze. "Hello, Studley." She reached out one hand, inviting an embrace. Hale made do with catching the hand in one of his and giving what smile he could. Ryan seemed to both understand and accept.

She slung Philippa's bag, held the taller woman tight to her other side, and said, "Let's get out of here."

They walked to the monorail linking the terminal and the main building. There were no seats, so Philippa settled down on the padded rear shelf. Ryan stood beside her, stroking the healthy shoulder, talking so quiet Hale could catch only the comforting tone. Ryan appeared waiflike from exhaustion, her features whetted to an overfine edge, her eyes feverish bright.

When Ryan's gaze turned back his way, Hale ventured, "You look exhausted."

"I haven't been sleeping so good. Or eating. Or exercising much."

"I never thought I'd see the day when Ryan Reeves stopped eating."

Ryan's face contracted, searching for her last memory of a smile. "Never thought I'd see days like this, period."

The doors closed and the monorail pulled smoothly away. A brilliant cascade of summer evening colors greeted them, flowing from faint pastels in the east to a brilliant crown of clouds and fire on the world's western rim. To Hale's eye the sky was almost too small for the sunset.

Hale's cell-phone pinged. He pulled it from his pocket without taking his gaze from the sky. "Andrews."

"Hale, man oh man." It was Jerry. "You're not going to believe what's happening around here."

"Don't you believe it either."

But Jerry was too high to hear. "The lady from SRC showed up here yesterday."

"Natalie Durrant?"

"Talk about hot. Is she the reason you went to Cabo?"

Hale swiveled to hide his shame from the two pairs of watchful eyes. The phone felt alive in his hand, crawling with vermin. "Not really."

"Your stock has gone through the roof. I mean, we always knew you were the office stud."

"Jerry –"

"But when this Natalie comes strutting in and tells Keebler you're the prime mover and shaker on this acquisition deal, hey, we're talking Olympic gold."

"Jerry, calm down a second. Is MacRuthers gone?"

"Yeah, old Don. He was in and outta here before I arrived this morning." Jerry's voice oozed pure bliss. "Ain't it a crying shame?"

"That's done. Good. Now what about Allenby?"

"What?"

"You were going to check on the new board director for me."

"Oh. Sure. I talked to Keebler's secretary again. You were right on the money, pal."

"About what?"

"Turns out Allenby is director of another company in this same group."

The news shot through him. "Allenby works for SRC?"

"Nah. Somebody else. But SRC owns them. How'd you know? Oh, never mind." Once more Jerry was off and running. "Hey, they've already got your name on Mack's door. And you're not the only one being moved upstairs. Guess what, old son. They're making me senior manager of the design team. Corner office, my own secretary, the works."

"Jerry, listen to me. Try and find yourself another job."

"What for? They've fired Mack the Knife, things are great around here."

"Do it now, Jerry. Believe me, all this is a mirage. Tomorrow, the next day, it's all crashing down."

A pause. "You're kidding."

"I wish I was." The monorail pulled into the main building. Hale grabbed his satchel and followed the pair. "Did you get any other job offers?"

"Yeah, I was shortlisted for a couple of things. Had one of them call me this morning, as a matter of fact. But –"

"Jump on it. Today." The central concourse was a tribute to America on vacation. Ferns and waterfalls and huge Disney mementoes abounded. "Use the promotion as a lever to cut yourself a better deal somewhere else. Tell them Keebler is blowing hot and cold. You need someone you can trust, someone who values long-term dedication. They always like that."

"What the hell's going on, Hale?"

Ryan mouthed the word, luggage? Hale pointed at his carry-ons, which mostly contained Philippa's remaining computer and data. Philippa just shook her head. Ryan led them towards the outer doors. Hale said to the phone, "Believe me, you do not want to know."

"You're sure I can't just hold out here? This acquisition –"

"Is a mirage. I'm telling you, it's going to disappear in a flash of smoke and fire. If you don't want to get burned, move fast."

"Okay." Resigned once more. "Can't shoot a guy for trying. You okay?"

"No. But I'm getting there."

"You always played it straight with me, Hale. I appreciate that."

They passed through the outer doors, and Hale felt as though he was slapped in the face with a hot mildewed rag. "Take care, Jerry. And get out now."

He cut the connection and turned off the phone. Hale hustled to catch up as Ryan helped Philippa across the street. "They're all connected!"

Ryan pointed with her chin to the multi-story car park. "Who?"

"Allenby. SRC. Keebler Plastics. Natalie. Mack the Knife." His thoughts spun and tumbled. "I don't believe it."

Ryan unlocked the Jeep, settled Philippa into the front seat, said, "Can this wait?"

"No." It was Philippa who responded. Eyes closed but voice firm. "No, it bloody well can't."

Ryan shot Hale a questioning look. He replied, "She's been like this all day."

When they had both climbed in and Ryan had started the car, Philippa commanded, "Now tell me everything."

"Allenby is my company's new board member. A mystery man. He pushed Keebler to hire a consultant called Don MacRuthers. The guy has spent the past five months boxing me into a corner. Putting me under impossible pressures."

"Five months," Philippa said bitterly. "About the point when I opened my bloody mouth about my new experiments. It all comes back to that. All of it." She sighed. "Go on, then. What happened?"

"Now it turns out Allenby holds some senior position in another SRC subsidiary. Who have now made a bid to buy Keebler out."

"Come on, Hale." Ryan wheeled onto the Bee Line Expressway and pointed the Jeep towards Cocoa Beach. "You're telling me they started hunting you down five months ago?"

"No," Philippa said. "Not Hale. Me."

"Sorry. I'm not following."

"Of course you're not. You're still living in a world where rules matter. But these days there exists a whole new dimension to the realm of wealth and power. One which is certain that rules were made simply to keep people like us in our place." Philippa's words emerged with the steady pace of a metronome. "We are moved about, set into place and then shifted at will. The power players are so big and so powerful that such things as individual achievement, personal growth, ambition, all are merely items to be bought and sold at market value. Or quashed entirely if the little person proves too troublesome."

Ryan tossed a glance at Hale in the rearview mirror. One to which he had no response. Philippa swivelled her head toward Ryan and said, "Now tell me what has happened to you."

"You should rest."

"There's no time for that. I need to know what has transpired on your end."

Ryan shook her head, her features tense in the dimming twilight. "Things are such a jumble I don't even know where to start. Washington does that to me."

"Never mind about that, dear." A slender hand emerged atop Philippa's shoulder, a finger rising in supplication. Hale reached over, gripped it, felt warmth to his toes as she pulled his hand close to her chin. She went on, "Sometimes raw data is best. Just give me all you can. We'll work out the order later."

Ryan talked as she drove, the words taut and fast despite her fatigue. The only moment when she revealed just how close she was to the edge was when she related Florence's death. Philippa released him then, so as to reach her good arm over and rest it upon Ryan's shoulder. Hale kept his hand there against Philippa's neck. The three connected, drawing strength and comfort from each other, hoping it was enough.

They crossed the Intracoastal Waterway, passed the Merritt Island turnoff, and continued down to Cape Canaveral Beach. The sunset had dimmed to rose-tinted hues on the horizon as Ryan pulled into a narrow side street. She pointed to the neighboring strip-shops, said, "Health food store and groceries. The shop on the end makes a great cup of coffee."

The road roughened from tarmac to seashells, and the headlights illuminated an overhead canopy of twisted Florida oaks. Hale asked, "Where are we?"

"A slice of old Florida. When my dad passed on, we used the inheritance to buy a place back here. The kids weren't adjusting well to our home becoming a guesthouse when the weather turned bad up north." Ryan slowed and rolled the Jeep over uneven grassy terrain, halting when her bumper nudged a tree. "It's old, but it's clean and we own it outright."

Hale stepped from the Jeep, tasted air laden with salt and humidity and a nighttime shadow of heat. Already his clothes felt too heavy. From between a pair of neighboring buildings glinted dark bayside waters.

Ryan helped Philippa rise from the Jeep and walk the few steps to the building's entrance. It was one of an inland row of identical structures, all two stories and silent. Hale carried their meager luggage up to the second floor, and entered a compact unit with fresh paint, new carpet, and the feel of a fifties condo.

"Three bedrooms, but only one bathroom. Kitchen should be in a museum, but everything works fine. Look there, a Frostpoint fridge, bet that takes you back."

"It's fine," Hale said.

"It's better than that," Philippa responded tiredly. "It's ideal."

* * *

Hale checked in after Ryan had left, could see nothing except Philippa's form in the bed, yet knew somehow that she was awake. "Is there someone you'd like me to call?"

There was weariness to her tone, but no sleep. Only the lack. "Of whom were you thinking?"

"I don't know, Filly. Maybe your parents. Just to let them know you're okay."

"Haven't I ever told you of my family? Surely it must have come up at some point."

He stepped into the room, freeing the doorway so that light from the hall could spill inside. His eyes had adjusted so that the room seemed almost bright. "Maybe you have." A slow nod to the bed. Slower words. "I think there were too many times when I wasn't listening at all."

She stared at him, her reddish curls spilling over her pillow like the tumbled wealth of autumns past and yet to come. "Does it bother you, being my eyes and ears?"

"No."

"It surprises me, I must say, this willingness of yours to take orders and follow them through. It surprises me very much."

"I like it, Filly. I feel like I'm listening better because of it. Not to you, to me."

"Listening to what?"

"I don't know." He opened his mouth, struggled to shape the words. "Like I can trust you to point me in the right directions. Inside directions. I guess that doesn't make any sense."

Philippa released him by turning to stare at the ceiling. "My parents." She raised her good arm and pressed the hair away from her face. "Dear daddy is an insurance executive in Exeter. That's a rather large town on the Devon coast. Quite nice, actually. Boring as mud and extremely provincial, but very pretty in a quaint sort of way."

She turned back and observed Hale as he drew over a chair and sat down. "There's something new to your gaze. Something I haven't ever seen before. Deep and unreadable, my lad, that's the way you look at me these days. Watchful." She examined him. "What are you seeing, Hale?"

Hale told her because it was there. The truth easier just then than trying to make up something safer. "I feel like the better I listen to you the more I'm hearing myself. I've never given that much time before. Listening to what's going on inside."

She lay there, caught in the same quiet intensity he was feeling. Then, "Where was I?"

"Exeter."

"Yes. Exeter and Daddy are very much alike." She turned back to the ceiling. "Stolid and stodgy and utterly set in their ways. I can tell you precisely what his reaction would be to learning his elder daughter had been shot in Baja."

She dropped her voice an octave. "'Really, my dear, this is all too bloody much. It's high time you put this gallivanting behind you and settle down, dammit. You're not so young any more. Biological clock and all that. Pretty soon you'll wake up and discover you've squandered your chance for children. And where will you be then? High and dry, I can tell you. High and bloody dry. Why on earth you can't show some sense like your sister, is what I'd like to know. Find a decent man and settle down. Stop living it up in San Diego or wherever the hell it is you're fiddling about these days. Thirty years old is high bloody time to straighten up what's left of your life. Act like a lady for a change."

"Sounds like you've heard this before."

"Every time I go home. Every time I call. Every letter, every message, it drips with scorn over my chosen path." But the words did not wound her. Instead, she looked back at him, tasted a tentative smile.

"What?"

"I was just thinking, Daddy would find you quite suitable," she said, her smile growing. "And my sister would positively drool."

He sat with her a while longer, not speaking, just being there and letting her know it, inviting her to draw from him enough comfort and solace to sleep. Then he left, and took with him all that remained unsaid.

* * *

Ryan arrived home to find the kids up waiting for her. She absorbed the stable sanity of their nighttime routine, following them upstairs and watching them prepare for bed. When Kitty had her nightdress on and was under the covers Ryan gathered her daughter into her arms, drinking in the soft fresh scent of her skin. Loving her anew.

She walked down the hall to Jeff's room, and entered a chamber adorned with surf paraphernalia. She stood by the bed, wondering if she should risk hugging him. Her son had become very touchy about huggy-kissy moments with his parents. She knew it was all a part of growing up, but it was hard just the same. Especially now, when she was the one in need of comforting.

Jeff looked up at her and said, "Tell me something."

Ryan had to smile. Those were words from an almost forgotten era. "Like what?"

"I don't know." He snuggled lower into his bed, suddenly a child once again, the teenager lost and forgotten save for the long blond hair spilling over his pillow. "Something about when I was little."

Her smile broadened and gentled both. When he had been younger, Jeff had never cared much for the normal run of nighttime stories. Such moments had been spent relating reality in childsize chunks. Telling him what it had been like before his memories had taken shape. Of Kitty's birth. Of his own early days.

Ryan settled on the edge of his bed, flattened the cover with one hand. "Let's see. I knew you were going to be a surfer back when you were still in diapers."

Jeff watched her face as much as listened to her words. The story he had heard a hundred times before. "Awesome."

"That's right." Strange how she could feel so full in that moment that she would want to laugh and cry both. "It was your first word. You would crawl around the house, pointing to everything, then looking for me and calling over and over. Awe Some. Like that, two words. Almost breathing in between. Putting everything you had into getting it right. Awe Some."

She looked down at her son, her most favorite being in the world, and saw the child in his eyes. The fragile little boy who could make her laugh just by opening his eyes in the morning. She swallowed down sorrow over what was lost and continued, "Especially sunlight. You would crawl over the rug, going from room to room until you found the place where the sun was brightest. Then you would sit there and try to pat away the shadows from trees and the window panes and the curtains. Push them all away, give the light more room. Saying over and over your one big word."

"Awesome," he murmured.

Ryan took a breath, working to press her heart back to normal size with an extra load of air. "Then you started walking, and you shut up for two months. Your daddy was getting so worried. But I knew. You were the most focused little kid I had ever seen. You were just concentrating on getting this next task right. Then when you started talking again, you went straight from one word to whole sentences. It astonished everybody but me."

The sadness took her then. She sat there, the dark room so crowded there was scarcely space to find breath.

It was her son who saved her. The son grown from childhood, never to be the baby ever again. "Mom."

"Yes?"

"Philippa's in trouble, isn't she?"

She looked down, and saw it was so. But there was comfort in the clear light of his eyes, a calm strength that not even these shadows could overcome. "How did you learn about that?"

"I heard you talking on the phone. A couple of times."

She brushed at the stray blond hair streaked across Jeff's tanned forehead. "We're trying to make everything all right."

"Where is she?"

She hesitated, but could find no reason not to tell him. "Over in the guest condo. For a while, anyway."

"Can I see her?"

"Maybe." Another breath, this one trying to keep the worries at bay. "Philippa needs a place to work. Someplace safe. I'm not sure we'll be able to see her much until the work is over and things have settled down again."

Jeff looked up at her, said, "I've got an idea."

"About what?"

"Where she can work. And live." He grinned. "A good one."

* * *

"The kids asleep?"

"Yes." Ryan was still caught by her discussion with Jeff, and was halfway across the kitchen before she noticed the steaming mug and the sandwich. "What's all this?"

"You haven't been eating much of anything lately," Harry said, nervous and flickering even when standing still. "Thought you could use a snack. You gotta eat, hon."

"Philippa said the same thing. Or maybe it was Hale." She rubbed her face. "I'm so tired."

"Want me to rub your shoulders?"

"Thanks, Harry. That's sweet." And also a first. He had never offered that before. Not ever. "Can I take a rain check?"

"Sure. Sure." A nervous tap on the plate pushed it across the counter separating them. "So everybody is safe and sound?"

Ryan picked up half the sandwich, took a bite, tasted nothing. "Sometimes I wonder if they'll ever be safe again."

"C'mon, hon. You're doing all you can." He crossed to the fridge, ducked his head inside. "Where are they now?"

"Here." She sipped from the mug. "Good cocoa, Harry."

"Glad you approve." He emerged with a beer. "Want one?"

"The cocoa is fine. Philippa got shot, did I tell you that?"

"You're kidding. When?"

"Day before yesterday. It's not too serious, though. Anyway, that's why they're here." Another bite. She wasn't hungry. Not really. But the hot chocolate wanted for something to cut the sweet. "I met them at the airport this evening and brought them back."

"She with Hale again?"

"Yes."

A long pull from his beer. "I thought that was all over."

"So did I. It may still be." Look at them. Standing around the kitchen, the kids upstairs in bed, the house all theirs, talking like a regular family. "It's all so confusing."

Another pull. A glance out the window at the night. "You put them over at the guest condo?"

"Yes." Watching him. Knowing something else was at work here, uncertain what it was. No longer sure who she had married. "I'm sorry, Harry. I should have asked."

"Hey, that's what it's there for, right?" He inspected the half-empty bottle, set it down on the counter. "Better not finish this. I haven't done my twenty minutes yet."

He turned for the basement, where a brand-new NordicTrack had been set up. "Guess I'll go do it now before I lose what interest I've got left."

"Harry." She waited for him to turn back. "Thank you."
"For what?"
"This." Ryan held up the mug. "Everything. Especially for trying."

For some reason her words shot him where he stood, blowing holes where his eyes had been. Harry looked so wounded his nerves were finally stilled. He gave her a smile with all but those wounded eyes. He turned and started down the stairs to the basement, leaving her trapped in all the sadness her thanks had exposed.

35

Sometime after midnight Hale stepped out onto the balcony, and instantly felt the heat envelope him and seep into his bones. He walked over to the screen and stared out at the night. The surrounding apartment buildings were mere shadows in the dark. A Florida summer night was unique, each its own impossible chorus of a billion voices: screaming, singing, croaking, pulsing with the heat, at odds and somehow in unison. Overhead the silent silver audience hung in rapt attendance, while thunderous percussion rumbled yellow and distant beyond the horizon. The air dripped thick and rich with smells and humidity. A tropical night with a civilized edge.

He stood staring up at the sky, naked as the day he was born. Feeling the heat and the night and his needs pulse through his loins. The internal fire had woken him, driven him from his bed. It was either walk out here or walk down the hall and into Philippa's bedroom. And he could not do that. His heart remained scalded by the last time they had lain together.

Yet what his body called vital was enough to tear at his mind, separate him into the man who stood there empty and lusting, and the man who stood empty and remembering and watching and seeking desperately to learn. He strove to listen beyond the throb of his body, and heard glimmers of past times. How sex had always been an issue between them – him wanting, Philippa wanting but holding back. She feared the loss of control, he saw that now. Fighting herself and the constant need to monitor. Finally giving in with stiff awkwardness. Wanting him too much to do otherwise, almost despite herself. Turning him angry and frustrated with his inability to do what had come so naturally with so many others.

Just beyond the balcony rose a pair of twisted Florida oaks, gnarled with age. He stood watching them, feeling the weight of the sky they carried. Wishing he was wise enough to know what to do, even with his own life.

"Hale?"

He turned his upper body only, saw Philippa standing silhouetted in the doorway, shadow upon shadow. Her long cotton nightgown showed a faint white glow, which to him seemed natural. She had been drawn from sleep and out to the balcony by the power of the night, pulled by forces as deep and fundamental as the sea. Her gown was woven from bits of clouds and melodies of long ago. Of course it glowed.

She stepped forward, floating gently. "I couldn't sleep."

Hale remained as he was, his feet planted forward and his shoulders turned to watch her approach. Shielding his passion and his desire as best he could. Feeling the same magnetic draw in his loins, building like an approaching storm. That and something more. A new awakening stirred within his chest, a silent lesson all its own.

She came to stand beside him. No mention of his nakedness or his silence, just standing and looking out through the screen. Until at last he felt the gentle brush of her fingers, sliding across his bare buttock. Framing his flesh with a molten touch.

Beyond their porch the wind shifted branches of the old oaks. That, or a breath of the same rising passion that turned her breath to quick sighs. Hale kept his gaze half turned to the night, until he saw her hands illuminated by starlight and the shimmer of skin. Hands which rose and released the straps of her gown, a gown which fell in cloudlike folds to the floor.

He raised one hand, touched her shoulders up where the soft curls of her hair bunched and gathered. She closed her eyes and arched her head back. For an instant he thought she was nestling his hand in her hair. Then he realized she was trying to press it downwards. To guide him.

The night spoke to him then, as though all the events and all the struggle had been leading to this point. When finally, finally he would be ready to ask the right question. His hand stilled, his movements frozen by the night's challenge to accept direction in his blind and vacant quest.

Philippa turned eyes made luminous with hunger towards him. She let him feel the soft panting breath, the unspoken entreaty. Hale leaned forward, kissed lips as warm as the night. And tried to still the sudden terror of being invited to give without bounds.

* * *

Thunder pealed across the heavens, or perhaps it was just his heart. As Hale disengaged and rose to his feet he heard a cry behind him, a pleading, plaintive note. But he went just the same, padding down the hall and moving to each bedroom in turn. She smiled a welcome to his return and watched him shape his bundle of pillows and bedcovers into a pallet. Before, the night had been hot and close. Now, with the sweat drying on their skin, the air formed a proper coverlet. All they needed. Philippa slid down in liquid motions and held out her lonely arms. Hale lowered himself, the moment demanding that they breathe in unison.

And then he waited.

After a moment's nestling into his arms, Philippa rolled onto her back and said to the invisible ceiling, "I have something I need for you to do for me tomorrow."

Hale nodded in recognition of Philippa's habit. Intimacy brought to a grinding halt with discussions of science. Or work and the lab. Anything except the moment, the closeness, the calm. This need for reserve had always infuriated him. Her inability to admit any need, any weakness, any hunger for human intimacy.

Yet now as Hale lay holding her, he felt nothing save the night's constant challenge. Here and now he realized he had been angered mostly because her withdrawal had mirrored his own frantic need. The insight brought no comfort. None at all. He could no longer hide from the fact that he had spent their entire relationship preparing for his departure. Pumping himself up. Looking for all the things that were wrong, all the slights which would justify him not caring any more. Holding it all in, letting none of the bad go, forgiving nothing down deep where it mattered most, until his love was overcome. Waiting for it to finally reach the point where he was *right* to turn away.

All he said was, "You should get some sleep, Filly."

"I'm so tired, if I slept a thousand years it wouldn't make any difference." Gradually her voice drew to a more focused line. "I feel like I'm drawing sustenance from you just lying here. More than if I went away by myself into dreams. And this simply cannot wait."

He saw then how he had repeated this same pattern with every girl. Only with Philippa it had taken more than a year, instead of weeks. Because this time the love had been real. But in the end he had won. Oh yes, he had won.

Philippa said, "I need to set up a lab here. I *have* to. And do so swiftly. I must recreate the experiment and see if my calculations are correct. That the force can be controlled." She raised her head to look at his face. "I don't need much in the way of equipment, nothing you can't find at any lab supply house. There must be several of those around here, working with NASA and the local universities. Will you help?"

He kept his eyes averted as he nodded. All the fragments of a life he wished he had never lived. All the impossible chains. The past he was determined to leave behind had become the ghost which haunted his every step. He had spent a lifetime recreating the same tragic mistake, running not from this woman, but from himself. He said quietly, "Anything you want."

"Thank you, Hale." She resumed her place beside him, was silent for a time. Then, "For years and years, decades and longer, science rolls along. Moving in a state of natural progression. But gradual change does not bring about world-transforming discoveries. Rather, the majority have resulted from intuitive leaps."

He spoke because he wanted her to know that he was listening. "Like what you've done here."

"Well, yes, that's what I am hoping. One moment we're plodding along at this level, the next and we have sprung to an entirely new plane." Her eyes glowed with soft intensity. "But the giant corporations and the political establishment loathe sudden change. They view such discoveries as earthquakes which fatally alter the economic landscape. Work such as mine destroys calm and threatens their hold on power and profit."

Philippa rose to sit there beside him, the movement altering her silhouette. A halo of curly hair, a face of angles and edges and sharp intelligence. Looking at the dark like this, Hale could see how easy it would be to stay frightened of this woman forever.

"This isn't about my discovery", she quietly told him. "It's about money and it's about power. A basic law of human nature is, power protects power. It is as true in a faculty setting as a boardroom. It's always been true. What has changed is the rules. Nowadays, there are no rules except the ones they have to get around. Absolutes no longer exist, you see, beyond the demand to protect what is already theirs and add to their loot. This isn't science at all in their eyes. Either it is theirs, and then it is profit, or it is someone else's, and then it is a threat. And all threats must be eliminated. The rules be damned, and the threats with them."

She looked down at him, searching through the surrounding darkness. "We are the little people. The expendables. If we cannot be controlled, we must be eliminated and our threat of change with us. I'm threatening to topple the giants, Hale. It's inevitable. And they hate me for it."

He wished he understood more than he did. "So you want to give me a shopping list."

"Yes. And for starters I'm going to need," she did a swift mental calculation. "About thirty feet of solid gold wire."

He nodded. Accepting this with all else. "What do you plan on doing?"

"We, Hale. What we are doing." She gripped the night with two tight fists. "We are going to wrest back control."

36

Philippa drifted in bright-edged slumber. Awake enough to think, to feel Hale's arms and the gentle rise and fall of his chest. Awake and knowing she was safe for the moment, both from the threats without and the fear within.

The wound to her shoulder pulsed with dull regularity, the pain timed to her heart. Not too strong, not even after the exertion of love. Yet enough to hold her drifting in between wakefulness and sleep, utterly aware, yet at rest.

In the safety of love's languor she could ask herself questions. Wrapped in a satiated cocoon, where fear held no barb and tomorrow was as distant as dreams from another life, she could ask herself, Why don't you run? Flee now, before you are trapped in love again.

She knew there was every reason to leave, and none to stay. None that her mind could accept. No matter that her heart beat comfortably again, feeling as though it fit her chest for the first time in months. No matter that she drew from his strength with each easy breath. She should run from him. Why on earth should she give him another chance to wreck her world?

She was terrified of Hale. Of giving too much, opening too much. Of being hurt by him again. Hale's greatest problem was, he was an easy man to love. And here in the comfort of a moment created only with him, she was both able to see the fears and be protected by him. And ask herself the impossible question, Why don't you run?

Almost in reply, she felt herself drifting further away. Moving from half-slumber into deeper sleep, carrying the inquiry with her. One moment she was in Hale's arms, breathing in time to him. The next and she was seated by the sea.

She knew it was an eastern sea because the sun was rising over the water. Only it was not just the sun giving light. A shimmering golden orb hung directly overhead, one of her own making. She was pleased with that, but there was little space just now for more than mild satisfaction. Her mind and heart were too caught up with the peace she felt. Hale was not here. But he was close. Close enough to sense his strength and continue to draw comfort from that.

Then she discerned movement behind her. She turned and saw who it was, and knew that she was indeed dreaming.

Alexis wore his cantilevered smile. Gulls circled around him, and somehow even their raucous cry rang a sweet refrain. She sat there smiling back, pleased with herself and pleased to see him again.

He approached, but not too close. He stood looking at her, ignoring the globe floating overhead. Which was as it should be.

She stared back, and knew the answer she had been looking for. Searching and not knowing even which question to ask, finding it all there for her now. She said, "I am working on my photograph."

"That and more," Alexis said, his smile pleased. "But now you must wake up. Wake up, Philippa. Wake up."

She did not want to go, did not want to leave either her friend or this place. But she had to. She felt it in the pulse of his words, and whatever sounds were there on the outskirts of this fading dream.

Philippa awoke to the feel of Hale's arm lying across her, and the sight of his eyes staring at her. As though he had been drawn awake by Alexis and his quiet alarm. He lay there looking at her, waiting.

Then she heard the quiet rustling yet again.

She whispered, "Someone is coming."

37

Ryan did a four-wheel skid into the lane leading to the bayside condos. She gunned the motor and scattered seashells and gravel to the winds. The oaks whipped by as she raced down to where the water sparkled beyond the bulkhead. She had no time for the morning, however. The old apartment building was ringed by police cars and curious onlookers.

An officer approached before she had climbed down. "Mrs. Reeves?"

"Yes."

"Thought I recognized you." He had to hustle to keep up with her headlong rush for the entrance. "My boy is on the Quiet Flight junior team with Jeff. You were called on account –"

"Excuse me." Ryan pushed passed him and ran up the steps. She found two more uniformed officers and a plainclothes detective in her living room. Their hulking presence and the squawk of their communicators made the space feel very cramped. The officer huffed up the stairs behind her, called in, "This is the owner."

"Mrs. Reeves, I'm Detective Lou Fernandez. Can you tell me what was going on here?"

She forced herself to turn from the wreckage. "You're asking me?"

"The reason is, we received a nine-one-one call. Male voice. Said a burglary was in progress. But we asked the neighbors and nobody claims to have seen a thing. You have any idea who phoned us?"

The steel cable tensing her body snapped cleanly. Ryan took the first easy breath since the police had interrupted her second cup of coffee. "I can't help you. Sorry."

He was a stout hard-eyed man who wore his skepticism with practiced ease. "The first car arrived in time to catch the perps in the act. The burglars, there were two of them, overcame my officers. Dislocated the shoulder of one and broke the other's jaw. Some kind of kick, coulda just as easy been my man's neck."

Ryan covered her mouth with one hand, forced down the rising sick. The thought of how close Hale and Philippa had been left her nauseous. She shook her head.

"Who was using your place here, Mrs. Reeves?"

She swallowed, said weakly, "Family friends. From Richmond."

"Names?"

"Hale Andrews. His girlfriend. I don't know her name."

"His girlfriend." The gaze was hard, probing. "I find that interesting, see, because two of the bedrooms have been used. Not one, like you'd expect. Not to mention a pile of stuff out on the porch."

"They've been having a hard time." The understatement of the decade, not caring how it sounded. Then Ryan stopped, hit by another realization. Dropped her head in shame.

"What is it?"

"Nothing." Ryan just realized she had left her cell-phone in the glove compartment all night. Forgot to take it in and charge the batteries. A sign of the grainy fatigue she was carrying. "They came down to try and work things out."

Fernandez let his doubts hang with the silence. Then, "Is there a Mr. Reeves?"

"He left very early for the office this morning." Another curiosity. Harry hated mornings with a passion, but today was up and out with the dawn. A note saying he might have to travel, would call. "Which is where I should be too."

"Mind taking a look around before you leave?"

"No. Sure." Forcing herself to move slowly. Feeling as though she had been physically molested, seeing the rooms tossed by a savage storm. "This place is a wreck."

"It's a professional job, Mrs. Reeves. A pair of pros came in here looking for something specific." He was following close enough for her to smell the stale coffee on his breath. "Any idea what that might be?"

"Look around, Detective. This is old Florida here. Other than an antique stove, there isn't much of value."

"What about drugs?"

Ryan spun about. "Excuse me?"

"I'm just wondering, see. On account of how the occupants were definitely not here when my officers arrived, and haven't showed up since."

"Hale Andrews doesn't touch drugs, Officer. He is Vice President of Keebler Plastics. A very responsible man."

"Right." A quick note in his book. "Where did you say you worked?"

"NASA."

"Got a contact number?"

Ryan recited it as she completed the circuit and returned to the living room. "Everything is still here, far as I can tell. You say there's no sign of my friends?"

"No. Any idea where they could be at seven o'clock in the morning?"

"Surfing, maybe." Heading for the door. "That's why they're here."

"Surfing." Another doubt-laden pause. "I need them to come in for statements."

"No problem. But right now I really have to be going."

"Here." He pressed a card into her hand. "If you think of anything or find something missing, give me a call."

"Of course."

Hard eyes followed her. "The Cocoa Beach police force is pretty small, Mrs. Reeves. Sort of an extended family. Somebody hurts one of our boys, we tend to take it personal."

* * *

Ryan was almost back to the highway when Hale stepped from behind a neighboring oak. He walked up and climbed in, the Jeep never coming to a complete halt. His face was grimly intent as he demanded, "What the hell were you doing turning off your phone?"

"I'm sorry. I wasn't thinking at all." Feeling weak with relief. "Are you all right?"

"When your mobile didn't answer I called the house. First time nothing, then the second time it was busy."

"We unplug the bedroom phone at night. The cost of having a teenager in the house. You must have called back when I was talking to the police."

Hale pointed across the highway at the all-night Perkins Restaurant. "Filly's in there. Only place that was open."

Ryan looked both ways, gunned the motor. "How did you know? That someone was coming, I mean."

"Now that's a curious thing. I guess it must have been a sound that woke us both up. Philippa insists Alexis told her."

She pulled the Jeep in behind the restaurant where hopefully the police would not spot it. "Alexis, the dead Russian scientist?"

"That's the one." Hale stepped from the Jeep, waited for Ryan to shut and lock the doors. "Anyway, that's what she said."

A trace of the old Philippa greeted Ryan as she slid into the booth, despite features still smudged with fatigue and the shoulder-bandage puffing up her blouse. Her battered and dusty briefcase rested on the booth seat. Ryan asked, "Are you okay?"

"Fine. Some coffee?"

She watched Philippa pour her a mug, all poise and control. Philippa asked, "Did they catch the assailants?"

"No."

"Pity."

"It doesn't matter," Hale said. "They'd just send more."

"Who are 'they'?" Ryan pressed.

"That is precisely the issue." Philippa replied crisply. "The time for theories is behind us. We are after proof now. Cold hard facts. Which means I must find a place where I can complete my research."

Ryan glanced at Hale, looking for the punchline. Found only a new sense of watchful silence. His eyes steady on Philippa. Ready. Ryan said, "You're kidding, right?"

Hale responded, "She's not kidding."

"Here." Philippa slid a sheet of paper across the table. "I've made a list of what I need. Hale will watch me until Ben arrives."

"Ben?"

"A friend from La Jolla. I phoned him as soon as we arrived here. He's already on his way over, managed to catch a pre-dawn flight with very good connections. Should arrive early this afternoon."

Ryan swallowed her questions, scanned the page, was halted by an item halfway down the sheet. "Twelve meters of twenty-four carat gold filament?"

"Keep your voice down," Hale said.

"I assure you," Philippa said. "It is absolutely essential."

"And a vacuum pump? Hundred kilowatt direct-current transformer?" She looked up. "Just exactly where am I supposed to find these things?"

"Lab supply house in Orlando." Hale again. "I've already called. Address is on the back."

Ryan kept her gaze on Philippa. "Excuse me. Aren't you

the lady who's just been shot?"

"There's no time for rest now, my dear."

Hale added, "She's been at a dead run since they rousted us."

Philippa leaned across the table. "We have to *know*. Is this real? Does this function correctly? Can it be controlled? Knowledge is the only possible way for us to wrest back control. The *only* way."

"We need to find her a place to do her experiments," Hale added.

"I'm working on that," Ryan replied, racing to catch up.

"Someplace safe." Hale's face was stone hard. "Someplace nobody knows about but us."

Ryan nodded, accepting Jeff's idea as the best she could offer. "I need to know what it is. What you're working on here."

"What *we* are developing. This is a team effort." Philippa stared at her, the intelligent gaze catching glints of light which were not truly there. Sharp flickers of green lightening in the quiet restaurant. "You must promise you'll not breathe a word of this to anyone. I need to confirm my reasoning and I need to monitor the experiment. I *have* to."

"I promise." As somber as her. As tightly held by the moment now as Hale.

"All right, then." A big breath, pushing herself more upright still. "The original idea came from research carried out by a Russian. I really should have seen it then. Perhaps I did, but didn't want to acknowledge it."

"Seen what?"

"The danger." Philippa raised her gaze to where sunlight filtered through the restaurant's side windows. "It started with an article in *Science* magazine. Some preliminary data suggesting that certain superconducting compounds induced a stationary field which repelled all external magnetic forces. And perhaps even more than that. But in the next issue they issued a retraction, stating that the entire thing was a hoax. I tried to contact him then."

"Who, Alexis?"

"No, I didn't know Alexis at that point. Well, of course, I had heard of him by reputation."

"Then who –"

"Sergei Petrovich, the scientist mentioned in the article. But he had disappeared. Vanished without a trace." Philippa's stare was hollow, not from the memory, but by the thought of it happening to her. "I put out an all-points on ScienceNet, requesting any information about him or his work. Such a bloody idiotic thing to do, I see that now. But at the time I was like a hound following a scent. The strangest thing was, it was like his study had never taken place. Any and all vestiges of his research had vanished with him.

"I called the *Science* journal offices in England. I talked to friends right around the globe. They all preferred to treat it like a crank, an embarrassment best forgotten because it had made it onto those auspicious pages." She stopped for a long moment, then finished with, "But I knew. I didn't know why I knew, but I knew. And so did Alexis. That was why he contacted me. He had read my work on superconductors. He was coming to America for a conference, and he had some calculations he wanted to share with me. That was all he would say over the phone, even though I had set up a secure line. Or at least I think it is secure."

"Philippa, help me out here. What exactly did Alexis know?"

"Quite remarkable, that." Lost in remembering. "We sat down at the conference and instantly realized we had derived the *exact* same calculations. Two minds nine thousand miles apart, coming up with precisely the same results. Long before I began my experiments, I knew we were onto something major. Something genuinely *new*."

"Which was?"

"That certain superconducting materials could be made to generate stable fields which repelled magnetism." She focused on Ryan then, grave and solemn and scared. "I knew this was big. That this was *real*."

Philippa's tone was infectious. "This was important, setting up an anti-magnetic field?"

"Think about it. Magnetism is an elemental component of energy fields. What other fields could be included here?" Watching with such force she *compelled* Ryan to search for herself. "Do you see?"

38

"I don't get this." Natalie Durrant tried for angry, but all she could manage was exasperated. The call from Buzz Cobb had woken her at four in the morning and she had been moving ever since. "You fly me to Richmond to start work on the Keebler acquisition. Then you pull me over to Washington to give a speech you were slated to deliver."

"I was busy. Damage control." Cobb shifted in the leather seat, looked angrily about. "Whose idea was this, banning smoking on these flights? What're we flying first class for anyway, these jokers still tell us what we can and can't do?"

"Then you send me back to Richmond, I still don't know what I'm doing there, with Andrews off on the other side of the nation and he's supposed to be in charge."

"Not any more. Anyway, I told you we needed to show the flag." Stubby fingers marked time on the armrest as the plane pulled away from the terminal. "Let them put a face to the SRC bid."

"*Then* you call me in the middle of the night –"

"Dawn. Almost, anyway."

"– And tell me I've got to drop everything, race up and meet you at Dulles for a flight to Orlando. What is going on here?"

"All hell is breaking loose, that's what. They've pulled a fast one on us."

"They who, Hale and Laremy?"

"Them and that Reeves witch." Cobb's teeth gripped the words, bit them out. "Snuck the scientist outta Mexico, carted her across the nation. I sent some guys down to get the pair under wraps. But they slipped through the net. This is gonna take my personal supervision. And I need you in Florida as back-up."

Natalie stared at him. "You're kidnapping them?"

"Whatever it takes." He stared out the window at the long line of planes waiting to take off. "Think maybe they'll get us in the air sometime today?"

"Not me." Natalie shook her head. "I'm finished with this."

Slowly Cobb turned towards her. "You trying to back out on me?"

"Not trying, doing. Burglary, bribes for key players, some corporate pressure tactics, that's one thing. But kidnapping, who knows what else – no thank you, not this girl." Meeting his stare, determined not to flinch. "It never stops with you, does it?"

"Like I said, whatever it takes."

"Well, you can count me out." Crossing her arms. "I'm finished."

"Is that so." His voice growled in time to the engines outside their window. "Listen, legs. There's just one reason I gave you a chance in the big league. One."

She *hated* this guy. Hated everything about him. Hated his awful cigar-tainted breath and his permanent stubble and his lousy cheap suits and his stumpy body and his beady eyes and his dominating attitude. The macho *shit*. "What's that?"

"I thought maybe, just maybe, a control freak like you would also be *hungry*. Hungry enough to do whatever it takes to get the job done. No holding back, no thumbing through the little golden rule book." Pausing for an asthmatic breath. "It's a new world out there, legs. If you want to hold the winning ticket, you got to burn the rules. Every last one."

Natalie found her own breath coming hard. As though she was being infected with the Buzz Cobb virus. "As soon as this plane lands, I'm leaving."

"Is that so." Cobb measured her with a predator's gaze. "Well, before you make up your mind, let me tell you a story."

"It won't make any difference."

"We're stuck here for a while. It'll help pass the time." He grinned without humor. "When I went up for this job, I got to meet a couple of the top men. I don't mean top SRC guys. I mean top of the top. They told me, they had to know was I committed, and would I stay committed. No matter what. They asked how I could convince them of my staying power. I told them the same little tale I'm gonna tell you."

He looked at her with eyes grey and hard as a winter storm. "Back in the dark ages, I was a squadron leader flying sorties out of Laos. All hush-hush. We were bombing supply lines used by the Viet Cong. Strafing their camps over the borders. That sort of stuff. Only Laos was neutral territory, far as the politicos and the press were concerned. We were there, the Cong were there. But nothing officially happened."

"This has nothing –"

"Wait, it gets better. See, working like this breeds a special esprit. We didn't have anybody to count on but each other. If we went down, it was curtains. The pressure was severe. This one guy, a pilot I thought I knew pretty well, one day he just cracks. Can't take it, ejects under the psycho clause and gets sent down on permanent R&R to Thailand."

Cobb turned his face to the seat in front of him, his voice a metallic drone. "Next leave we had, some buddies and me, we hunt this guy down. Find him in this little village, their staple crop was magic mushrooms. Turns out this guy was doing pretty good for himself. Had this little hippie chippie he was living with, stayed high pretty much all the time. The two of them eating mushrooms like popcorn."

He waited through another rev, the plane turning a big circle onto the runway. "Wanna know what we did?"

"No. No, I –"

"Next day, we waited until they had eaten their daily dose. Then we got us some rope and tied the two of them together at the waist. They were tripping so hard they had no idea what was going on. Just laughing and babbling about colors and shit."

"Stop." It was all Natalie could manage.

"We led them out of the village a ways. Then we started letting off our sidearms. Right in the guy's face." He turned his gaze back then. But he did not see her. Not at all. "We kept screaming all sorts of shit about incoming, and hits, and strafing, anything that came to mind. This guy, he starts totally freaking out. The girl too, but this guy is beyond scared. We chase them all over the jungle. Spend hours firing rounds and screaming and sending them farther over the deep end.

"Next day, they find the girl sitting by this tree, still roped to the guy. Only he was dead. Not a mark on him, except for scratches he got running through the jungle. Nothing severe enough to do him in. The locals figured it was just another round-eye who took a ride on the OD express."

The plane's engines revved for take-off, drawing Cobb's eyes into focus. Horror pushed Natalie back in her seat, as far as she could manage to crawl from him. Cobb gave her a pirate's smile, all teeth and empty eyes. "Believe me, legs. You do not want to quit on me. It ain't a healthy choice to make."

39

Ryan took coastal highway A1A into what passed for downtown Cocoa Beach. There the highway split and broadened, the north and south lanes separated by an island three blocks wide filled with houses, offices, restaurants, and semi-tropical undergrowth. Most of the low-slung relics dated from 'I Dream Of Jeannie' days and the Apollo boomtime. Ryan passed a mock Tudor restaurant that had started life as an English pub and now housed a Chinese restaurant. She circled the block, watching her rearview mirror, and pulled into the police station parking lot. Got out, went inside, pretended to wait to speak to the desk sergeant. Exited and did another careful check. Sat in her car and watched some more. All according to plan.

When the southbound lanes emptied, she drove across the road and entered a graveled track running alongside the Quiet Flight surf shop. Ryan passed the shop's factory, surfboard planks stacked like white lumber alongside. The only sound was birdsong and the more piercing whine of industrial planers. The fragrance of fiberglass varnish sharpened the hot air. She did not see a soul.

Beyond the factory, the gravel became almost lost beneath a carpet of weeds. She pulled up next to an ancient barn, a relic of a bygone era when this land held four orange groves and a vast pumpkin farm. When Philippa appeared at the open door, Ryan said, "I found everything you had on your list."

"Excellent. Let's move it inside." She leaned the broom she had been wielding against the door. "Any trouble?"

"Not a bit. You'd think they had requests for a half a pound of gold every day of the week."

"They just might, actually. It's a remarkable conducting material, especially under low atmospheric pressure."

"I'll take your word for that." Ryan hefted the heaviest box, the one containing the vacuum pump, and asked, "Where is Hale?"

"I sent him down to the hardware store. I needed a pair of mixing bowls and a joystick. He was going to stop for lunch on his way back."

Ryan lifted the box containing a miniature refrigeration unit, carried it inside. "Mixing bowls?"

"It could be anything, really. I need to form a rough globe, one which will permit the transfer of pressure. The two halves mustn't form a solid closure, of course, since I will suspend it within the vacuum chamber. Otherwise the imbalance of pressure when I bleed out the air would cause the globe to explode."

"Of course." Ryan went out for another load. "Where do you want this vacuum pump?"

"Under the lab table."

At the center of the utterly bare room stood a pair of sawhorses supporting an old door. "You sure this will be okay?"

"What, this barn? It's ideal, actually. Roomy and quiet and relatively clean. And private."

"It was Jeff's idea. You stay here and save that arm, I'll bring in the rest." With her next load, Ryan continued, "Jeff surfs for Quiet Flight. They're the best shop on the beach if you listen to him, and he counts being on their team as a great honor. The surfshop bought the apartments next door so nobody would complain about the noise from their board factory. They rent them out to visiting surfers, which is all they know about you, by the way. Since it was Jeff doing the asking, they didn't mind throwing in use of the barn for a few days. Jeff said you'd be holding a meeting here tomorrow."

"Which we shall, if all goes well." Philippa stopped for breath, eyed her friend. "The intention here is not just to effect a proper experimental study. We are designing a lure, I hope you realize that."

"A lure for what?"

"Whoever has been chasing us. They are desperate to have what they fear I might have discovered. It is either possess it or destroy us. They see no alternative. Our only hope is to hunt the hunters."

Ryan watched her friend begin arranging her equipment, utterly at home. "Shouldn't we get more help?"

"Certainly, if we knew who to trust. That is the critical issue here. How to isolate the vermin from the allies." She surveyed the spread of boxes and equipment. "We'll need to arrange a proper power source for the lure, but I have an idea about that."

"I can't believe how calm you seem about everything."

"Activity is a great salve for a worried state of mind. Besides, this is niggling work that only requires half my attention." She lifted a battered Federal Express package Hale had retrieved from the San Diego lab. She pulled out an internal container and set it by the huge glass vacuum chamber, one the size of an aquarium. "Would you mind keeping me company until Hale returns?"

"Not at all."

"To be perfectly honest, I'd feel more comfortable not being alone just now. That's one of the reasons I asked Ben to come. So we both could have company."

"Must be nice, having a friend who'd drop everything and fly across the country just because you asked."

"Yes, Ben is very sweet in his own gruff way. But we must keep his action in perspective. Ben would do the same for a rising swell on Kauai. Which means I am perhaps as important to him as a good wave."

"How does Hale get on with him?"

"Hale?" Philippa's hands stilled. "Actually, Hale and Ben appear on the way to becoming friends."

Ryan asked delicately, "And how is Hale?"

A long hesitation. "Quiet."

"He was always the silent type."

"Quieter than ever. But when he speaks he can come up with the most astonishing things. And he listens. For the first time since we met, I have the feeling that he hears everything I tell him. And more besides."

Ryan tried to hold to her casual tone. "And how are you two?"

"Ah. That is a most difficult question. One I fear I can't answer just yet."

"Hale still loves you very much. That much is clear from the little I've seen of you together."

"He also broke my heart." Philippa's eyes and hands drifted over the items, touching everything, seeing nothing. "I don't know if I can truly ever leave that behind. Which I must, of course, if he is to have a proper second chance." She looked over to where Ryan stood by the door. "You can't expect me to live out your fantasies, my dear."

She managed to cut off the automatic denial before it was spoken. "Why not?"

"Because in the end you will resent me whatever happens. Blame me for the bad, curse me for the good." Lilting the words, turning the impossible into acceptable matter-of-factness. "And you are far too precious a friend to lose you over something so intensely personal."

When Ryan did not respond, Philippa resumed her work, the casual motions releasing them. "Please, Ryan. For me. For us both."

* * *

Ryan stayed long enough to pass over the Jeep's keys to Hale, then walked across A1A to the National Car Rental agency. From there she went straight to Kennedy. As usual on the day of a launch, the radio stations were all broadcasting last-minute mission details. Especially about how the launch window was extremely tight, under ten minutes, as the shuttle had to make a precise connection with the orbiting space station.

Hurricanes seemed to be on everyone's mind, which was a surprise, as the day was sweltering but windless. Even so, the radio announcer shouted the weather report as she drove. High temperatures, high humidity, a sultry pressure squeezing down the sky. Sunlight taunted her on all sides, licking at the car with hot shimmering streams. The concern was that if the shuttle did not lift off tonight, it might become trapped by incoming storms.

The cell-phone pinged as she was passing over the deepwater canal bridge, the one they had been rebuilding for almost four years. As she answered she noticed the battery power was down to fifteen percent. The result of not having recharged the battery the night before. "Ryan Reeves."

"Les Lassard here, Ms. Reeves. I've got what you want."

"Outstanding." Thrilled with the thought of telling Philippa. "This is great news."

Lassard did not share her enthusiasm. "Our exchange needs to be done in person."

"I couldn't agree more."

"Things have become a great deal more urgent since we spoke yesterday."

Ryan decided she had no desire to know what he was talking about. There was no room just then for urgency at his end. She had all she ever wanted right where she was. "We'll need to make it a public place, I can tell you that right now. Dr. Laremy is beyond scared."

"Where is she?"

"Right here."

"Very well. I will come down to Cocoa Beach this evening."

"Great. There's a night launch, it'll be a perfect setup for us to meet. Hang on a sec." Ryan slowed, lowered her window, showed her badge to the Kennedy guard, then sped on. "I'll inform PR that you'll be coming. We can meet at the VIP stands."

"VIP stands it is." There was a moment's hissing silence, then, "Ms. Reeves, I never asked. Who does your husband work for?"

"Harry? He's an accountant with OrionSat. Why?"

"No reason." The words were slow in coming. "I'll see you tonight."

Ryan cut off the phone, held it alongside the steering wheel, staring and wondering.

* * *

Instead of driving to NASA headquarters as planned, Ryan sped to the press site. The main press office was a cinder-block structure beyond the Vehicle Assembly Building. It was flanked on one side by the press viewing stands and conference hall, and on the other by tiers of television vans and aerials. The big networks – CNN, CBS, ABC, NBC – all had permanent structures and towers. Others, including numerous visiting contingents from as many as twenty foreign countries, erected their filming stands along the adjoining rise. Their cables spread out like a parade of snakes.

With less than twelve hours to the launch, the press site was a hive of activity. Ryan pulled into the press parking lot, climbed from the car and stopped to stare at the big stationary bird. Situated alongside a man-made lake, the press stands commanded a spectacular view of the two shuttle pads. That evening's launch was from 39B, the closer pad to the site. The Retractable Service Structure had been rolled back, leaving the orbiter exposed and poised for flight.

Ryan headed into the press center. Back in the bad old days, NASA was as much a white men's macho club as

Defense. Things had changed, but slowly. Equal Opportunities had fought a brilliant battle. Gradually, grudgingly, places had been made for women, minorities, even people with disabilities. Some positions were genuine, some advancements to higher ranks were won. Others were wall-hangings. Media support was an early favorite spot to park minorities and women, and pad the total numbers. Ryan had friends there, even a few who cheered her on rather than poisoning their looks with envy and their words with spite.

One such ally sat at the desk in front of her. "So how is it going up in the stratosphere?"

Evidently news of her coming promotion to Washington had made it this far. "You've heard?"

"Honey, I've got volunteer retirees who're deaf and blind both, and they know. News like that travels fast." She was big and settled, her early ambitions cushioned by a family and years in a job she happened to enjoy and did well. One which gave her the chance to dine with her children six nights out of seven. This granted her the ability to smile at Ryan without rancor, and mean what she said. "Way to go, girl."

"Thanks, I guess."

"Rocky climb?"

Ryan did not want to get into that. She leaned across the desk, said quietly, "I need two press passes for tonight's STS launch."

The request was not only incorrect, it was illegal as hell. Passes were assigned only to accredited journalists with credentials from established newsgroups.

To her credit, the woman did not bat an eyelid. She merely asked, "This is important?"

"Absolutely vital." A press pass was valid for the entire period of a launch, from initial countdown to the shuttle landing. No official record of press comings and goings were made, as they were for all holders of machine passes.

"No problem. Who are they with?"

Ryan took a breath. "Freelance."

"Freelance." The woman set down her pen. "You know that's a bad word around here."

"I have got to have these. I am facing a bind like you wouldn't believe."

The woman searched her face. "We have room here for eight hundred. Know how many we had for the last launch? Two thousand. Freelancers don't even make the bottom of the barrel."

"I have never asked you for anything before. Not once."

"Promise me they're not up to anything nasty."

Ryan told her, because she deserved it. "I have got to arrange a secret meeting here with a visiting congressman. And have them show up at the very last minute."

She sighed, picked up a sheet with a long list of names. "I don't suppose they could pass for Japanese."

"Not a hope."

"We've had a couple of last minute cancellations." She flipped a page. "How about Italian?"

"Long as they don't open their mouths."

She drew a line through two entries, said, "Names?"

Ryan leaned back, allowed herself half a breath. "You decide."

The woman set down her pen and studied Ryan. "There's only one way you can get people on the site without a passport control, and you know it."

Which was where Ryan had been headed all along. "I thought you had withdrawn all the gold badges."

"We've kept a few. For emergencies."

"Which this is. I swear to you."

She cocked her head. "Girl, you're truly desperate, aren't you."

Ryan had to smile. "I left desperate behind a long time ago."

"All right. Fine." She opened her bottom drawer, came up with an unsealed manila envelope. Handed it over, said, "I don't want to know anything more, do I?"

Ryan accepted the envelope, said, "Absolutely not."

40

When Ryan entered the outer office shared by all four Deputy Administrators, her secretary announced, "The whole world has been looking for you."

It was to be expected. "Start at the top and work down."

"Right. Fuller is tied up in Washington and won't make it back for the launch."

It was most unusual for her boss to miss a launch, but not necessarily a bad thing right then. "Fine."

"Senator Townsend's office called. His chief aide, Clay East, is desperate to talk with you. Says it's extremely urgent."

"Not a chance. Next."

"Congressman Lassard's office." Receiving calls from both Houses in one morning had clearly made her day. "Also urgent."

"That one is done. Next."

"Chuck Evans has come by three times. He left the Work Authorization forms."

"Let me have those."

She passed over the folder. "Looked like he was ready to jump out of his skin. Said for you not to contact him. He'll stop by again later."

Ryan had no time for the engineer's games. It was down to now or never. "Find where Chuck is working today."

The secretary reached for the phone. "There've been

about a thousand more calls. I lost count. The message slips are on your desk."

Ryan entered her office, dropped the briefcase with the press badges, and reached for the phone. She took mild pleasure from calling the finance offices and throwing around the weight of her supposed promotion, insisting on an immediate appointment with the director. When questioned about the purpose, she announced she was walking over a Work Authorization, and expected immediate approval, as she was meeting Senator Townsend and Congressman Lassard that evening. Before she went to Washington. Pressing the weight of those names, getting what she wanted. Which was instant action.

Her secretary popped in the office, said, "Chuck Evans is at the Orbiter Processing Facility. And Townsend's office has just called again. They're on line one."

Ryan was already up and moving. "I'm not here. You don't know when I'll be back. Definitely not until after the launch."

Eyes grew round. This was not standard protocol with the senators responsible for NASA funding. "Where are you, if anybody else wants to know?"

Ryan said as she left, "Off lighting a few fires."

* * *

After finishing her work with the finance people, Ryan drove through the Orbiter Processing Facility's external fence and showed her two passes – admin and op center – to the uniformed sentry. She parked the car, entered the OPF, and went through the second check-point. A big board by the internal sentry announced this shuttle had another twenty-seven days to its own scheduled lift-off.

Prior to launch, each orbiter went through a carefully monitored three-stage procedure. Upon landing from their last mission, the orbiter was transported directly to the

Orbiter Processing Facility. Shuttles remained in the OPF between sixty-five and seventy-five days, depending on how many faults required checking and what new outfittings were required by the next mission.

Once repaired and prepped, the shuttle was transported by crawler to the Vehicular Assembly Building. Shuttles generally remained in the VAB about seven days. Once the orbiter was hooked to the two solid booster rockets and the external fuel tank, the transporter was brought back and the entire structure was carried to the launch pad. This final land-based move took about a day, as the crawler's top speed was just under one mile per hour.

Ryan walked down the ultra clean hallway and halted by the steel fire-doors. She slid her entry-card through the magnetic lock and punched in the code for that particular orbiter. When the doors sighed open, she stepped up to the OPF Control Desk. This final check was cautious and military in precision, barring entry to all but those employees specifically related to work-in-progress. The intention was to keep traffic around the extremely sensitive orbiter to an absolute minimum. As Deputy Administrator, Ryan was one of only fourteen admin workers with constant on-site access to the OPF.

Sensitive was a strange word to describe a reusable rocket, but it was also the most accurate. The orbiter's structure was a mastery of balance between weight and strength. Every extra pound of the orbiter's composition-weight meant a pound less of payload. And yet, at atmospheric re-entry, the orbiter was subjected to temperatures so high they would melt tungsten carbide. The eleven thousand ceramic heat-plates forming the orbiter's nose and belly were the strongest shields man had ever created against fiery temperatures. Yet their weight was less than the same volume of goosedown. They were also so sensitive that a pencil-tap could crack one.

This same exactness was utilized throughout the entire orbiter. Which meant that careful attention and great caution was required in each stage of the shuttle's launch preparations.

The OPF Controller was a former Marine drill sergeant. His face was all blades and angles, his eyes hard as the business end of a carbine. "Afternoon, Ms. Reeves. Could I see your passes, ma'am?"

Ryan extended both for inspection. "I have some papers for Chuck Evans. Something that requires his instant attention."

"I believe Chuck is calibrating the nose wheels." He noted Ryan's entry on his record sheet and cocked a thumb towards the gimbaled thrusters. "They've just finished draining the excess fuel, so you'll want to steer clear of the rear portals."

"Right, thanks." Ryan stepped around the steel shield and headed straight for the nose.

The shuttle was barely visible, draped on all sides by sheeting and scaffolding. Workers in protective whites and surgical gloves moved about with quiet intensity. Draining the unused fuel was always a tricky maneuver, and Ryan was glad she had missed it. The orbiter used a hypergaulic mix, elements which instantly ignited when brought together with oxygen. The chemicals, especially liquid hydrazine, were highly toxic. A single escaped drop would trigger a red alert and force an evacuation of the entire building. A pair of drenching showers flanked the two fuel points; anyone coming into contact with even a microscopic amount was immediately stripped and subjected to a thirty-second dousing before being rushed to the base hospital's emergency room.

Ryan spotted a pair of legs rising into the bay which held the shuttle's front landing gear. The wheels had been removed, exposing four polished brake disks larger than those on a formula one racer. She called up, "Chuck, can I have a minute?"

"Ryan." The white-clad engineer slid down the scaffolding. "What the hell are you doing here?"

"You sure know how to make a girl feel welcome." She extended the file. "Here. We're ready to rock and roll on your gantry seals."

Chuck eyed the folder as he would a live snake. "I can't be seen talking to you."

"Too late. We're talking and this place is lit up like a stage. Take it."

He glanced behind him, made no move for the papers. "I've been warned off."

"What?"

"You remember the warning I gave you the other day?" He jammed his spectacles up tight. "Somebody saw us. Or heard I stopped by your office. Or something. I've gotten some warnings of my own."

Ryan closed the distance between them. "Tell me."

"That's it. I've been warned. Isn't that enough?"

"Who threatened you, Chuck?" Her rage finally had a direction. "They are already gone."

"I've got a wife and kids, Ryan." Worry turned to outright fear. "Besides, you can't get to these guys. They're not NASA."

"Is it a supplier?" Pressing him with everything but her fists. "A subcontractor?"

"I can't –"

"Are they connected to SRC?"

His gaze froze. His breath caught in his throat.

Ryan stepped back. Nodded slowly. Breathed for him. "We're doing important work here, Chuck. Vital. You shouldn't allow the scum of the universe to jeopardize that."

Her quiet fury calmed the engineer. And shamed him. He thought it over, pressed his glasses up tight, said to the floor, "Show me a way to keep my job and my family safe, and I'll shout it to the moon."

"I won't contact you again," Ryan agreed, "unless I can guarantee it."

"What about now?" Lightening glances were cast about the room.

Ryan thought swiftly, then asked, "Are you done here?"

"Pretty much."

She grabbed his arm. "Come on."

"What –"

"We need to lay down a smokescreen," she said, pulling him towards the main entrance. "Play along."

The controller looked up from his mission-work flow chart, interrupting the discussion of four engineers gathered around him. "Can I help you, Ms. Reeves?"

Her rage was real. Only the direction was false. "I am hereby ordering you not to permit this man back inside here until my secretary calls and authorizes it."

"But Mr. Evans is doing vital –"

"Mr. Evans' failure to complete authorization paperwork has threatened the timing of our next launch!" Ryan halted all work within hearing range. She wheeled about, snapped off, "I stepped out on a limb to help you, and this is how you repay me?"

Chuck could not have faked his surprise. Or his stammer. "Ryan, Ms. Reeves, it's all a mistake –"

She slapped his chest with the folder. "Get back to your office and get this paperwork done *now*." She was known as the lady who never raised her voice, never lost her cool. The shouting match became the focal point for the entire chamber. Heads popped out of the orbiter's main portal, craned from the ops control room. "After that, if you want anything from procurement right down to a paperclip, you take it up with somebody else. I only work with people I can *trust*."

Ryan spun on her heels and stomped away, barely granting the doors time to get out of her path, leaving utter silence in her wake. She ignored the guard's request for her name, the second shouted request for her to halt and check out. She carried her rage out into the sultry afternoon sun.

Somebody was going to pay.

41

The sunset wind tasted of a spicy melange, orange groves and tropical blooms and lush Florida undergrowth. Despite the cloying heat Hale found it a clean scent, a spritzer for the soul. He rode alongside Ryan with all the rental car's windows rolled down. The sun was a half-hour to the horizon and the clouds shone like towering crowns, with streamers of gold and purple spread across the sky.

The launch crowds gathering along the roadside canals transformed the spaceport highway into a long slender party. A long line of campers, vans, dogs, frisbees, folding chairs, and ice-coolers stretched out as far as he could see. Talk and music and laughter floated on the wind. Hale caught glimpses of thousands of faces raised in homage to the sky's casual power. The radio whispered softly about NASA's concern for a rising storm, and their hope it would not strike until after launch.

Ryan cut off the radio, stated flatly, "This is stupid."

"Ryan, when an engineer you trust gives you a second warning, it's not stupid."

"I can take care of myself."

Hale sat in the passenger seat. They had left the Jeep with Ben, carefully hidden in the grove behind the surf shop. Hale studied the compact figure behind the wheel, dark hair pulled taut from the face and lashed into a ponytail. So much power concentrated into her small form, so much raw determination.

Ryan glanced over. "Okay, buster. What's so funny?"

"Ryan, anybody who has spent one nanosecond around you will know without a doubt that you can take care of yourself."

Ryan slowed to allow the car in front of them to change lanes. It was still four hours to launch, but traffic was already building. She did not speak for a moment, and Hale had the impression that she was satisfied with his response. As though the objection had been partly for show, and she was secretly glad for his company. Finally she said, "I wish Philippa had come."

Hale shook his head decisively. "She's safer where she is. And I'd have to agree with her that every minute counts."

"You trust this Ben?"

"Absolutely." He felt her swift glance, said, "If he hadn't been in the water with us, Filly would have drowned."

"It must have been bad, her getting shot."

"Horrible." The chilling waters and the memories and the fear touched his gut, even there. He pushed them away, pointing through the windshield at the Vehicular Assembly Building up ahead. "I've never seen anything like that."

She released a tiny smile. "Never did get you down for a launch, did I?"

"No."

"Then you're in for a treat. A night launch is something else." At the NASA Causeway the tourist traffic was routed west towards the Visitor's Complex. Ryan turned east towards headquarters. "When the solids ignite, night becomes day."

"What –" He cut off at the ping of his cell-phone. They had left Ryan's with Ben. With the battery low he had been told to leave it off unless there was an emergency. Hale saw Ryan's features tighten as he hit the switch and said, "Andrews."

A shrill male voice shouted, "What in the hell are you doing?"

Hale shook his head at Ryan's anxious gaze. "Mr. Keebler. How are you this evening?"

"Don't you *dare* dither about with me! I've just gotten off the phone with Buzz Cobb of SRC. Do you know what he told me?"

"Mr. Keebler, if you'll just –"

"He said you were on the brink of destroying the acquisition!"

"We have discovered something vital about this group. Something which alters everything."

"Then it's true, isn't it?" Disbelief fought with outrage. "You have *deliberately* set about wrecking our negotiations!"

"The SRC group appears to be involved in illegal activities that –"

"I don't care if they're Russian mafia druglords and white slavers!" Keebler's shriek caused the phone to vibrate. "That deal is our only possible hope of salvaging this company! Am I getting through here?"

"Loud and clear."

"I don't know what it is they want you to do and I don't care." He paused for a hard breath, then shouted, "Just do it!"

"Mr. Keebler –"

"*Now*!"

Ryan watched him cut the connection. "Your company?"

Hale stowed the phone away. "Not any more."

* * *

Ryan pulled up to the headquarters gate and showed her pass and a plastic gold square. "This is for my guest."

The guard stepped closer. "Howdy, Ms. Reeves. Didn't know they were issuing these gold badges any more."

"Special case, Frank."

"Right." He nodded at Hale. "Down for the launch, sir?"
"Yes."
"Night launches are something special, all right." He stepped back. "Y'all have a good one."
"Thanks, Frank."

When she had pulled away, Hale asked, "Gold badge?"
"Old system for VIPs. We're phasing them out."

Ryan pulled into the Kennedy headquarters parking lot, led him through the lobby and into an elevator shared with a trio of white-coated engineers. They stood with heads almost touching, arguing over a schematic blueprint. The elevator stopped twice, both times adding more pressure with the passengers.

When they exited on the fifth floor, Hale remarked, "Place is pretty tense."

"L minus four hours, you better believe it."

"You're not affected?"

"Anybody who breathes this air is affected. But I'm not part of the launch team, so it's not so bad." An attempt at a smile. "With me it's more like a permanent state of mind."

Her secretary was up and moving before Ryan cleared the door. Breathless and fearful. "Senator Townsend's chief aide just called."

Ryan pulled up so sharply Hale jammed into her. "Clay East."

"Yes. He's at the Orlando airport. And he's *very* angry. He wants you to drive over and pick him up."

"I'm not here."

"Ryan –"

"You heard me. Call him back. Say there's been an emergency and I can't come."

The woman's mouth worked a moment before she managed, "There is."

"What?"

"An emergency. Chuck Evans' assistant has called about ten times in the past hour. Something about a problem on pad 39A."

"The payload bay door gantry seals?"

"Yes. How did you know?"

"Never mind. Call Chuck back, tell him I'm on my way."

"It wasn't Chuck, he's away somewhere. That was the problem."

Probably off licking his wounds after this afternoon's set-to in the OPF. Ryan turned for the door, said to Hale, "This is important."

"Let's go."

The phone rang as they were leaving. Ryan urged Hale down the hall until the secretary reappeared behind them. "Ryan, it's Harry."

She slowed. Stopped. "I better take this."

"Go ahead." He followed her back to the doorway, heard her say, "Yes?" A pause, then, "It's cut off. I forgot to recharge the batteries last –"

Another pause. "They're safe, Harry. I had a warning, and I thought it would be best to have them spend ... It's just for one night. Maybe two. They've stayed over dozens of times. The kids are fine."

Another pause. "No, I'm not overreacting. Harry, I've told you, they're fine, they stay with friends ... Harry, I've tried to call you at the office all day. How can I tell you anything if ..."

Her face flushed bright red. "No I'm not changing the subject ... Harry, Harry, please ... Would you just wait –"

She stopped, looked at the receiver briefly before settling it down in the cradle. She turned away from the secretary's gaze and walked back over to Hale. Grim now. Pinched up tight. "Let's go."

* * *

Hale granted Ryan all the space he could. He was content to sit and enjoy the drive. The sun had just touched the horizon, and the scrubland was tinged with fairy gold. Ryan drove past the operations buildings, then turned away from the shuttle, aiming for the second empty pad. "Sorry about dragging you out here like this."

"No need for apologies, Ryan." He stared at the pad and gantry up ahead. "This is a pretty awesome sight."

"I've been working with an engineer on a new project. One that we hope is going to solve a serious problem once and for ..." Ryan slowed at the first of two circular fences, the second an inner ring of chain link and barbed wire. "That's odd."

"What is?"

"There's nobody in the launchpad guard house. Must be walking the perimeter. Things get a little slack this close to launch and all attention is focused on the other pad."

She drove on through and past the empty parking lot. Hale leaned forward as they started up the rise. The slope was gentle, the structure at the hill's top incredibly tall. Hale stared through the windshield and quietly announced, "This is absolutely amazing."

"Launch Pad 39A. Discovery is over there to your right, on 39B." She pulled the car up next to the steel flame-cavern. When Hale had shut his door and come around to join her, she went on, "Pad 39A launched all of the Apollo flights. The rockets that took man to the moon started off right where you're standing."

Ryan stomped the hill beneath her feet. "This man-made hill contains sixty-eight thousand cubic yards of concrete and five thousand tons of reinforcing steel."

The entire structure seemed to glisten with the evening's residual heat. "The central gismo there is the Fixed Service Structure. In the Apollo days it was known as the Gantry. See how the outer segment is hinged on that big pole there? That's the Retractable Service Structure. It's built to swing away when they bring the orbiter in and position it for launch, then back for prepping and packing the payload, then out again before launch. Look over at Discovery, you can see how the RSS is rolled back now."

To Hale's eye it looked like an impossibly complex piece of modern art, built of grey-green piping and steel plate. "Where is everybody?"

"This close to launch, most of the staff will be busy over at the other pad. The others use this as down-time, finish outstanding paperwork, that sort of thing. There's an office complex built into the side of the hill. Admin staff call it the Troll House, for obvious reasons, but not to a teckie's face." She looked up, searching, then out over the empty expanse. "But I don't see Chuck's assistant anywhere. Come on, let's see if we can find the problem for ourselves."

Ryan led Hale to the central steel staircase and started climbing. "Up there, see that big tunnel leading across to where the shuttle sits? That's our problem. It's called the Payload Changeout Room. It's part of the retractable structure. What happens, the arm swings out, and the trawler brings the orbiter right up inside the flame cavern and parks it." She stopped and pointed back towards the distant Vehicular Assembly Building. "That's the trawler road you see there."

Hale stared down at a red-dust ribbon stretching back to the huge square VAB structure with an American flag painted on its side. In the gradually dimming light and heat, the flag appeared to shimmer and wave. "I can't believe I'm actually standing here."

"Come on, let's check this out and get back inside the car's air-conditioning before we bake." Ryan continued up stairs running alongside the central elevator shaft. "After the orbiter's in place, we bring the payload out here in a special clean structure. Sometimes it's loaded in the shuttle back in the Orbiter Processing Facility, but usually it's handled out here. The payload is set into place in the retractable structure, the arm swings back over and fits onto the shuttle's payload bay doors, and the transfer is made."

Sweat began to bead and trickle. Hale felt his breath loud in his own ears. Ryan seemed unfazed by the climb. "Sounds incredibly complex."

"It's worse than that. These instruments designed for outer space are unbelievably delicate. The transfer casing, the gantry's service structure, the payload bay itself – all of these have to maintain absolute clean-room conditions." She reached the seventh level and waited for Hale to catch up. She was not even breathing hard. "The trouble's been with the door seal. See that rubber frame surrounding the outer edge?"

He kept his mouth cocked wide, trying to hide the noise of his breath. "Yes."

"That's the seal." She frowned, walked closer. "What the hell?"

"Something the matter?"

"No. Nothing at all." She traced her hand around the black seal. "How could there be? I just got Finance to sign off on the authorization today."

"That doesn't make –" The sound of a racing motor turned them around. A blue van climbed the hill and stopped alongside the gantry. Hale said, "Maybe that's your guy."

"Maybe." Ryan leaned over the railing and called down, "You work for Chuck?"

Hale counted seven figures clambering from the van. All bulky men. Ryan shouted down, "What's going on here?"

Hale spotted a glint of sun on metal. "Ryan, that guy's carrying something in his hand. It looks like –"

But she was already spinning away. "Come *on*!"

42

Together they raced up the stairs to the next metal-clad level. Hale was hard on her heels.

"We're trapped!"

"The astronaut elevator," Ryan gasped as she ran. "Kept at the top. For emergencies."

Feet pounded below them. At the next landing Hale risked a look below, saw only steel and heat. Overhead there was the scraping sound of elevator doors closing. A whirring noise, and they watched with dismay as the elevator began to descend.

"They've called it down to ground level," Ryan groaned, "We're done for."

Hale leaned over, saw just two men scrambling up the stairs. He hissed, "Head on up top. Make as much noise as you can."

"But they're –"

"*Go.*"

Ryan stared at him an instant, then started up the next flight, scraping her feet and urging speed to a man who wasn't there. Hale crouched behind the elevator shaft and waited.

Nine steep flights taken at a dead run were enough to wind the fittest person. This pair were strong but not fit. The first man who wheezed into view carried two feet of steel pipe and forty extra pounds. Hale sprang from his crouch, propelling himself around the corner. He slammed his left straight at the guy's heart.

The man's eyes widened in shock and pain, his guard utterly down, the pipe forgotten. Hale crossed a right hook to the jaw-point just below the guy's ear, and felt the connection to his elbow. The man's legs turned to jelly. Hale grabbed the pipe as he fell.

The second guy was trying to aim his pistol around his buddy. Hale kicked the falling body down the stairs, causing the second guy to grab for the rail and clamber over his pal. Hale lashed down hard with the pipe, catching the guy's hand where it gripped the railing.

The man's shout of agony was cut short as Hale stepped in close and jammed the pipe so far into the guy's middle he could feel it grate on the spine. The guy folded and slid back down the stairs. The pistol rattled over metal stairs and disappeared far below.

"Hale!"

Ryan's scream jerked him around.

"The elevator!"

He glanced down in time to see the doors close and the elevator start its ascent. Two more men stepped back far enough to peer upwards, searching for him, aiming into the sun.

Ryan shrieked, "Come on!"

He gestured below. The odds were bad but not impossible. Unless they had guns. "You –"

She waved him frantically up. "This way!"

Hale clambered up the three final flights, chased by the winding elevator. He came around the gantry's central pillar, looked down, and halted in mid-stride. "Oh, no."

"Don't you *dare* freeze up on me!" Ryan raced over, gripped his arm and hauled him forward. "Come *on*!"

Hale forced his legs to move, though it felt like he was struggling to walk on air. The steel flooring had given way to metal mesh, an inch gap of open space between each little square. Millions of empty square gaps falling away below him, floor after floor, all the way to the launch pad. Twelve stories, five hundred and fifty feet below.

Try as he might, he could not drag his gaze away from the swooping openness below him as he shuffled along. Which was good, because he did not see where Ryan was headed until he arrived.

"Step in the slide-wire basket. Hurry, hurry."

Hale lifted his gaze to see he was being urged into a tiny open cage. One less than three feet long and two feet wide, held by a single gleaming metal arm to a long steel cable. A cable that swung down and away. A long, long way down. Almost a quarter mile away from the launch pad's base.

Hale froze, half in, half out. "Unh uh. No way."

Ryan did not bother with argument. A trio of pistol shots were fired from down below, little cap-gun sounds that might have been lost on the wind, except for the whanging cymbal clatter when one struck steel supports over their heads. Ryan shoved hard, tripping Hale on the cage's side, then tumbled in on top of him.

Hale struggled upright in time to see three men emerge from the elevator. They spotted Ryan rising to her feet in the cage, and aimed.

Ryan leaned over and whacked down hard on the catch. A rod snapped back, the cage dropped, the cable tightened.

They flew away. Singing down a wire at a speed so fast Hale was too scared to scream. Down and down, the cable zinging through the runners, the cage swinging crazily, the ground rushing up at an impossible surge.

The braking was totally unexpected, a catch of the drag chain that flipped the cage up almost vertical, then back over, tossing them out and grounding them in a rolling dust cloud.

Hale was still hacking and clawing at his eyes when Ryan grabbed his arm. "Let's go."

"Can't," Hale wheezed.

The pressure lifted him anyway. "Look behind."

Hale squinted through the grit on his face. The trio on top of the gantry were struggling into two more cages, and the pair on the launch pad were sprinting for the van.

"Not safe yet," Ryan wheezed. "Run."

Hale stumbled along, caught his foot on a root, righted himself, felt strength return in dribs and drabs. Behind him came the zinging chime of other cages releasing and flying towards them. He fought to keep up with Ryan as they sprinted over rough earth. His lungs worked like a rusty pump.

They rounded a looming hump in the earth, one with a tall yellow marker planted at its crown. Ryan did a sharp jink and disappeared. Hale followed, gasping, and discovered himself at the mouth of a man-made cave.

And inside the cave stood a tank.

Ryan was already scrambling up the side. She reached the top, wrenched at a two-handed catch.

It was not a tank, Hale decided in his fatigue-addled state. There was no gun-barrel. And huge shoulder-high tires instead of tracks. And it was white. But it was still ferocious.

Ryan wrenched open the second catch, flung back the metal cover with a clang. She looked down at him and gasped, "You coming?"

Hale clambered up the side, followed her down into the hole, helped her shut and seal the top.

"Emergency Egress Vehicle," she managed. "Modified M113 armored personnel carriers. Keep them permanently stationed here for pad evacuation."

"Right." It was all he could manage. His heart yammered to spring from his chest.

She slid into the control seat, then cried, "Oh, shit!"

"What now?"

Ryan slapped a red knob, and the motor caught with a thundering roar. "I'm too damn short!"

Hale stepped forward, started to grin, caught himself in time. Try as she might, Ryan's feet could not reach the pedals. She slid disgustedly from the seat and shouted, "Drive!"

When he took her place, he discovered, "There's no steering wheel."

Her hand pressed down on his shoulder. "Improvise."

Hale gripped the two tall metal rods rising from the floorboards in front of him, and jammed his foot down on what he hoped was the accelerator. The vehicle lumbered forward. Hale laughed aloud. The beast was not fast, but it ate anything in its path – scrub, stone, cactus, trees, anything.

"Head for the pad!"

Hale jammed the right lever forward and pulled the left back. The carrier responded by spinning sharply, taking a mature orange tree with it. Hale over-straightened, corrected, squinted through the narrow view-panel. Two men directly ahead raised guns and fired. He winced as shots struck their vehicle, loud as sticks hammered on tin cans. When the men realized the lumbering transport was bullet-proof and aimed directly for them, they turned on their heels and struck off for parts unknown. The third tried to limp after them, then sprawled heavily in the sand.

Ryan struck his shoulder, pointed through the inch-thick glass. "The van! They've gotten stuck in the sand!"

Dimming light and heat distorted his limited view, so it was a moment before he realized what she was talking about. Then he saw, and laughed again. The ones who had remained down below on the pad had tried to drive the van out to the bunker, and now were mired in the soft earth. Hale jammed the pedal to the floor. The metal beast snorted once, then roared ahead.

Ryan whooped and pounded his shoulder. Hale watched the two men fling open their doors and dive for cover. "Hang on!"

The carrier smashed headfirst into the van, pushed it back a solid ten paces before the earth snagged and held. Then it proceeded to nose up and over, the van mashing flat underneath. Metal shrieked and groaned, glass smashed, the noise bringing the two of them to the point of hysterics.

Hale spun the vehicle around, began a lumbering dance in pursuit of the men. One made the mistake of looking back long enough to wing off a shot, and Hale almost caught him. The others fanned out and headed into the surrounding groves. When nothing was visible through Hale's view-port except dusty green and rising heat, they turned back toward the tarmac. Ryan pointed up at the launchpad. "We need to dump this thing. Head for the car."

Hale stopped at the top of the pad and gunned the motor a couple of times, reluctant to give up his toy. Ryan popped the top, searched carefully, called down, "All clear."

Hale left it running because he had no idea how to turn it off. He scrambled up and out, vaulted onto the pavement, wanted to dance and weave to the sunset's cadence.

Ryan already had the car running. "Come on, Studley. We've got a launch to catch!"

43

The clock was held at nine minutes, and all the world seemed to catch its breath. Even the freshening breeze stilled as the announcer tersely said there was a glitch with one of the onboard computers. No attempt to claim it was minor. With such a tight launch window, any delay was critical.

Hale and Ryan had repaired their dusty state as best as possible in the confines of the VIP center's restrooms. Thankfully, this was a crowd brought together by an intensely shared interest. They drew a few stares, but not for long. All eyes remained fixed upon the stationary bird on the lagoon's opposite side.

A pair of Gulfstreams flew tight circles overhead, doing continuous touch-and-goes from the orbiter landing strip. Their purpose was to continually check visibility in case the shuttle suffered a post-launch emergency, and had to jettison the boosters and glide home. Ryan watched as the jet banked high, catching a final glint of daylight on its wings.

They sat in the VIP bleachers alongside the Saturn Building, a structure built to house the last remaining Apollo moon rocket. In front of them stretched a broad man-made lagoon. Other than the astronauts themselves, they were the closest humans to ground zero.

"Somebody's giving us the eye," Hale said, pointing with

his chin to the lawn before the stands. "Is that Congressman Lassard?"

Ryan looked down, gave a soft groan. "No. Clay East. Chief aide to Senator Townsend." She rose to her feet. "I guess I better go speak with him."

The tall man watched their approach with stern hostility. "You look terrible, Reeves."

Ryan motioned Hale to stay back. "We had a little glitch."

"Tell me about it." The man tried to hide his bureaucratic padding beneath a well-tailored suit. But nothing could be done about his eyes. He shifted his gaze to Hale. "Are you Andrews?"

"That's right."

Back to Ryan. "You certainly know how to pick your friends. Where's the professor?"

"Somewhere safe," Ryan said. "You mind telling me why she's so interesting to you?"

"You wouldn't understand. I thought you might be brought to reason, so did the Senator." He shook his head in disgust. "What a loser you turned out to be."

Hale sensed a shared anger, heard her ask, "What's your and the Senator's connection to SRC?"

East sneered. "Nothing you'll ever be able to prove. And that's all that matters. Of course you realize our offer of a position has been withdrawn."

Ryan stretched her features into a smile. "What offer would that be?"

His gaze narrowed. "Townsend ordered me down here to make sure they were correct in their assessment of you. I told him it was a wasted trip. I was right."

"Who are *they*, East?"

"You're finished. That's the only thing you need to know." He shot Hale another glance, spun, and turned away. "All of you."

Hale watched his departure, caught sight of a familiar face on the border of the shadows. "Stay here a second, will you?"

"Hale, wait."

"I'll be right back." He hurried over.

Natalie watched him coming, poised on the edge of flight. Her eyes looked haunted, her body so tense her voice shook. "You bastard."

"I never did a thing to you, and you know it." He halted, searched in all directions. "Where's Cobb?"

"You destroyed my life," Natalie hissed. "Don't you call that something?"

"Natalie, get serious. The only people who've done any damage around here are your crowd." If Cobb was there, he was well hidden. "Look, you've got to get away."

He stopped, expecting a laugh. Sarcastic derision. When she remained stiffly silent, he went on, "These people are bad. Dangerous."

"You don't know the half of it."

"Don't let them suck you in. Get out now while you still can."

She worked her mouth around acidic contempt. "Listen to this sudden concern. How touching."

"Natalie –"

"You're the one who better run, Hale. Or, should I say, you should have when you still had a chance."

* * *

As Hale rejoined Ryan, the speakers connected directly to the firing room announced, "The computer glitch has been repaired. We are go for launch. Repeat, go for launch."

A cheer rose from the bleachers as a second voice announced, "Launch Director, this is Weather. We have no constraints."

"Roger. Discovery, you are cleared for take-off. Start the clocks on my count – three, two, one, mark."

The large digital clock stationed by the lagoon resumed its count. Ryan craned and searched, then said, "Where the hell is Lassard?"

"I don't like those two being here." Hale looked back to where East and Natalie had last been seen, saw neither of them now. "Think we should go check on Filly?"

"We can't. I told Lassard I'd meet him here and I don't have any other way to establish contact." She checked her watch, the count-down clock, the night-draped lawn. "Damn."

"We'll wait until the launch is over," Hale said, deciding for her. "Then we'll head on back."

The announcer's voice, flat and impossibly calm, intoned over the loudspeakers, "T minus two minutes and counting."

Ryan stood with her back to the bird, scanning the crowd. Hale could not help but turn around and look out over the lagoon to where the shuttle stood silent and waiting. The pad was illuminated by a trio of giant spotlights, an island of potency amidst the sea of man's failings and thwarted hopes.

Over the loudspeakers a new voice stated, "All systems continue to be in good shape for a 9:05p.m. launch. *Discovery*, you are clear to go."

The announcer added, "Very quiet in the firing room. Always a good sign."

The lightest possible breeze ruffled the palms; the spotlights' reflection on the lagoon was transformed into silver prisms upon a field of black velvet.

Suddenly all lights surrounding the bleachers were cut. The only light came from the spots around the shuttle, and the moon. The spots formed a brilliant tent around the orbiter. The announcer intoned, "The auxiliary power systems are now configured for launch. Main engines are being gimbaled and positioned."

The bleachers grew increasingly quiet. Even the children were silent. All eyes remained glued on the bird poised in silent expectation.

"Main engines are now ready for launch. On-board computers now have control."

The firing room intoned, "T minus thirty seconds and counting. Auto sequence start."

All the world was dark. The night was utterly silent. Movement in the bleachers had ceased. All conversation ended. Even the crickets and nightjars stilled their cries.

A final klaxon, then nothing but the countdown drone. The announcer was obviously chosen for nerves of steel, because his voice changed not one whit.

At five seconds and counting, Ryan sighed her way around, and joined Hale for the viewing.

"Three, two, one ..."

The first light was dim only by comparison, a soft and glowing rumble as the shuttle's liquid-fuel engines ignited and built to full power. An electric tension gripped them all, a single unified breath caught and held.

Then at zero seconds came the explosion. And the light. In one single instant night vanished, replaced by a man-made dawn.

The solid-fuel boosters exploded with a force more felt than heard. Their sudden brilliance brought a gasp from all, a sharp intake instantly transformed to a single shout of joy and pride and delight. Hale found himself shouting with the others, too full of the moment's thrill to keep it all inside. A thousand people screaming words and cheers heard by none.

The rumble grew to a full-throated roar, and the shuttle lifted skywards.

The rainwall system released thirty thousand gallons of water in twenty seconds, a cold rushing geyser meant to buffer the delicate shuttle from its own sound and power. A millisecond after the water's release, the boosters turned it to steam. In the sudden dawn, clouds leaped out like two ecstatic wings, eager to rise up and fly with the shuttle. They split and curled and mounted like curving wings of gold.

The shuttle seemed to move both too slow and too fast, rising on a pillar of fire that grew in length and light until even the stars overhead vanished from sight.

All the world was gold. The water, the earth, the people,

the air itself, all illuminated by the torch rising on its golden smoking pillar. And the sound was as brilliant as the light.

The shuttle rose to where it reached the first cloud, and the man-made dawn began to dim. Each new cloud it touched became a glorious rainbow, a prism of accomplishment reaching across the sky.

Too soon it was over. Too soon. The shuttle rose to become a distant beacon, and dawn continued to fade. Hale drew his first real breath, and felt himself separate from what had been a moment beyond time, beyond boundaries. He kept his eyes turned heavenwards as the light dimmed in silent crescendo, and the stars reappeared to greet humanity.

* * *

As if on cue, a lanky redheaded gentleman stepped up beside them and said, "That was quite a little show you put on over there with Townsend's aide, Ms. Reeves." He nodded to Hale, offered his hand. "You must be Andrews. Les Lassard."

"Where have you been?"

"Watching and waiting, Missy. Watching and waiting. Where's the lady prof?"

"Dr. Laremy couldn't make it."

The eyes narrowed. "What's that supposed to mean?"

"If things go right, we might have a little demonstration lined up for you tomorrow morning."

"You're all crazy as loons, you know that?" Lassard's eyes flashed fire. "She doesn't have a day! She's lucky if she's got a couple more hours!"

Ryan seemed untouched by his ire. As if the day had moved her beyond the reach of such things. "I believe you have something for Philippa."

Lassard watched her intently. "You taking that job they offered up in DC?"

"What job?" The smile was as bitter as the light in her eyes. "It's not real, is it? Not any of it."

"Depends on whose tune you're dancing to, Ms. Reeves."

"That's a strange thing for you to be asking me here and now."

"I was expecting to trade what I have to offer for a heads-together meeting with Dr. Laremy."

"You will," Hale confirmed. "Tomorrow morning."

"No, there's something else," Ryan said, her eyes narrowing. "You've found out something. Or think you have."

"No thinking about it. Not any more." Lassard waited for a pair of roving Cape Crusaders, astronauts assigned to Kennedy PR work, to saunter by. Their space-blue uniforms became electric as the halogens were turned back on. "Your husband works for OrionSat, don't I have that right?"

"I told you that earlier. He's an accountant with their Kennedy operations. Why?"

"He told you what they've been up to lately?"

Ryan shot Hale a baffled glance. "Communications hardware."

"Communications. Right." Lassard shook his head. "Half my mind and most of my allies tell me I'm a fool for trusting you, Ms. Reeves. But my gut tells me you're the real thing. And I've made it a practice of following my gut." Lassard sighed, pulled his cell-phone from one pocket and a card from another. He slipped on a pair of reading glasses, held up the card, began punching numbers into the phone.

He waited a long moment, said, "This is Congressman Lassard calling from the United States. Put me through to the Consular Office." A pause. "Yes, I know what time it is. Somebody is there waiting for this call. Put me through."

Another wait, then, "Yes. This is Congressman Lassard. Is everything ready? All right, hold on there."

He offered Ryan the phone.

She shook her head, pointed to Hale. "He'll handle this."

* * *

Tentatively Hale accepted the cell-phone. "Yes?"

"This is John Dunforth with the United States Embassy in Vienna." The voice was crisply irritated. "I am instructed to inform you that two Russian nationals, a woman by the name of Alena Vilnieff and her daughter, have been retrieved from the Austrian detention camp for refugees. They are here with me now. They will be granted papers and flown to the US port of entry –"

"Put her on."

"I beg your pardon?"

"Give her the phone."

"Her English is very limited."

"If she's the woman we're looking for she speaks enough. Give her the phone."

A pause, then a voice in heavily accented English said, "This is the Professor Doctor Laremy?"

"No. This is a friend. A good friend. I am calling for her." Hale unfolded the paper from his pocket, the one containing the instructions dictated by Philippa. "Your husband, if you are Mrs. Vilnieff, has told Philippa that you have learned some English."

"Yes. But please to speak slowly."

"Right. Anyone could say they are Mrs. Vilnieff, just like anyone could claim to be Dr. Laremy's friend. Do you understand?"

"Yes." Despite the hiss of space and air and different worlds, Hale could clearly hear the woman's relief. "Yes. This I am understanding very well."

"Good. So we need to be sure who each other is. Correct?"

"Yes. Is true. Please, you are to be asking questions first."

"Thank you. Now." A breath, time to scan the next lines. "Alexis Vilnieff had many experiments. He would work on as many as a dozen at a time."

"More," the woman replied. "More than a dozen. At night, at day, all the time he was to his experiments."

"Yes." Hale found himself wondering why Philippa had looked so stricken as she had walked him through this, and why her voice had become so shaky. "But no matter what he worked on, there was one experiment which was his most important. One he said he wanted to be remembered for most of all. What was that?"

There was a long pause. Long enough for the slight keening on the phone's other end to come, to go, to come again. "His favorite experiment," the woman finally said, "was learning to be a man in love. His parameters, that is the right word, parameters?"

"Yes," Hale said, not caring if it was right or not. Knowing it was her.

"His parameters were his family. His key results were our daughter."

"It is good to speak with you, Mrs. Vilnieff," Hale said, dreading what might come next. "Do you want to ask me anything to identify Dr. Laremy?"

"That we speak like this, that I sit here with my daughter, that it is you with the telephone and not my husband," the woman had to stop. Finally she continued, "I am asking no more questions now. Not like this. You understand?"

"Yes." Hale felt shame at his own relief. "I understand."

"More questions can be waiting for when we meet, yes?" The voice trembled through the air. "Now I must be to telling my daughter, our daughter, that her Papa is ..."

The line went silent for a moment. Then the irritated male voice said, "Are we through here?"

"Yes," Hale said. "All through."

"Let me speak with the Congressman."

* * *

As Hale spoke on the cell-phone, Lassard quietly said to Ryan, "You've got to take me to Dr. Laremy tonight."

"I can't."

"That was not a request, Ms. Reeves."

"Philippa expressly forbid it." It was far easier watching Hale than Lassard. "She says she will meet with you tomorrow morning."

"Then there ain't no help for it." Lassard sighed heavily. "You know my colleague Fred Lawson?"

"I know of him, sure. He's the congressman from this district."

"Right." He's got an office on Fourth Street in Cocoa's old town. I want you to drive over and meet me there."

"What, now?" Cocoa was the sister-city over on the mainland, thirty miles round-trip from Ryan's home and a shower and bed. "In case you haven't noticed, we've had a pretty hard day."

"And it's about to get a damn sight tougher." His face was firmly settled into grim lines. "This is absolutely vital, Ms. Reeves. And it cannot wait."

Hale walked over, handed Lassard the phone. Nodded once. "It's her."

Lassard accepted the phone, and said, "That was fine work, sir. Now you just hold the lady and the daughter someplace safe until I get back to you. Yes. Yes. I'll make contact with your Ambassador tomorrow, tell her personally what a fine job you've done. Count on it."

He cut the connection and stowed away the phone, said, "Time to travel."

"But –"

"Now, Ms. Reeves. At once. The grim reaper's done started his dance."

44

Hale clenched his eyes against the grit being flung at his face. "How can a night wind be so strong and not cool things off?"

He and Ryan stood by the parked car, looking across a street empty of everything but dust and wind. The old-town Cocoa buildings were low-slung and refurbished, making for an art deco funnel. Gusts moaned around eaves and shutters and wrought-iron balustrades. Palm fronds chattered angrily at being disturbed by such a hot and humid night.

"I wish it'd go ahead and rain and get it over with." Hale swiped at his face with both hands. "I feel like the sweat is being sucked from my body."

"South winds are strange, especially this time of year." Ryan continued her careful search of the night and the street. "They come hurtling up from the Caribbean, and the old-timers hunker down and hold their breath. Nobody knows if its just another thunder and lightening spectacle or a full-blown hurricane in the making."

Hale leaned against the car. Above the shivering eaves, dancing treelimbs caused the yellow streetlights to flicker. Across the street, the building's facade of polarized glass gave nothing away. "This is a funny sort of meeting, the middle of the night and nobody around. You're sure you can trust Lassard?"

"He made good on his promise to find the refugees, didn't he? Besides, we're running out of options." Ryan checked the night one final time, then started across the street. "The first sign of anything, sound the horn."

Hale slid back into the car. "Don't hang around a second longer than you have to."

Ryan leapt up the four front steps, pushed inside the building, stopped and searched the silent foyer. Nothing. She decided against the elevator. Waiting through endless seconds in a metal-bound cage was out. She bounded up the back staircase, stopped at the second floor landing, checked again. Utter silence. The only office light came from the door at the hall's far end. She walked over, pushed it open.

"Howdy, Ms. Reeves." Lassard greeted her in seersucker trousers and a cotton poplin shirt. The collar was open, his tie cast aside, his suspenders loosened. Every inch a grim Florida cracker. "Care for a seat? Coffee?"

"I won't be here that long."

"Fair enough." He stood in an easy slouch. "Ms. Reeves, we've got ourselves a stack of memos tying SRC to Senator Townsend's office. Going back years."

"That's what you brought me here for?"

"No ma'am, it's not."

"Because I don't need to see memos. I've already got all the proof I need."

"Care to share that with me?"

"Another time, Congressman. It's late and I've had a very hard day."

"Right." Lassard turned to the room behind him and demanded, "You about ready?"

Ryan stiffened. "There's somebody with us?"

"Just my aide. Step this way, Ms. Reeves." Lassard moved back, freeing the doorway. "Please."

Drawn against her will, Ryan entered the inner office. She saw a young man in rolled-up shirtsleeves connecting a lap-top computer to a trio of other devices. A collapsible satellite dish pointed out the window. He tapped the terminal's keyboard, watched the screen, tapped again. "Ninety seconds."

"Ms. Reeves, I'm sorry to be the one to ask you this. But have you noticed a change in your husband over the past several days?"

Ryan glanced from the terminal to the dish to the young man to Lassard. "What are you talking about?"

"I'm talking about your husband's company." He motioned to the array of equipment. "This is OrionSat's latest development. Has your husband mentioned any of this to you?"

"I don't even know what it does."

"This is a top secret communications monitoring device. Implemented by Orion satellites, designed for our secret services and the Pentagon, recently launched by military rockets."

"We're aimed and primed," the aide confirmed.

Lassard asked, "Is your cell-phone turned on, Ms. Reeves?"

"I ... No. I left it with Philippa."

"With Dr. Laremy?" Lassard and his aide exchanged worried looks. "Is it on?"

"No. We needed to conserve the battery in case of an emergency. I forgot to charge it last night." She looked from one man to the other. "What is this?"

Lassard pulled his phone from his pocket, keyed the switch, said, "Use mine."

"Right." The young man plucked a phone unit from one box, keyed numbers into the pad. "We're rolling."

"Watch the screen there, Ms. Reeves."

The terminal offered a series of soft beeps, then chimed twice. The screen flickered, focused, flashed up a series of maps in blinding speed. The state of Florida appeared and vanished, to be replaced by the state's central portion. Then the coastal counties, then the town of Cocoa. Tighter still, and streets sped into formation. A light blinked in time to the chime, one centered midway down a street the computer named as Fourth.

"Pinpoint location system, fully operational for almost a month now."

Ryan whispered softly, "That son of a bitch."

Lassard said to his aide, "Hit the switch."

The young man touched a key. When Lassard spoke into his phone, the voice sprang from a side speaker. "Up to now tracing and monitoring cell-phones has been notoriously unreliable. OrionSat has made this a whole new ballgame."

The young man added, "They don't even need to make the connection. If they code in a phone talking to somebody else, they've got it programmed so they can locate both calls and hear every word that's spoken."

"The bastard." Her voice sounded choked to her own ears.

"It gets worse, I'm sorry to say." All the edges of Lassard's face folded down. "Ms. Reeves, last Monday OrionSat was acquired. The supposed buyers are a consortium of banks and companies all over the place."

Ryan looked at the older man, too stunned to speak.

"The day Florence Avery made her call to you, she had been at SEC archives. Since then we've been trying to piece together what she knew." Lassard's face showed real pain. "We've finally managed to fit it all into place. The banks, the companies, the individuals, every single one of these OrionSat investors, they are all part and parcel of one group. Some controlled more directly than others, but eventually one name popped up each time."

She managed, "Tell me."

"Ms. Reeves, the Space Research Consortium is behind them all."

* * *

Hale watched as Ryan opened the office building door, then had it torn from her grip by the aggressive wind. She scanned the street, staggered, did not seem to see him. He blinked the car's lights, then leaned over to open her door. The nightwind blasted him with the heat of a giant blow-dryer. Ryan shielded her face and ran for the car.

Hale had to shout to be heard. "A couple of times I thought I was going to play like Dorothy and fly off to see the wizard."

Ryan slammed the door on the grit and the night. The wind responded by giving their car an angry shake. "Drive, dammit!"

"Right." Hale started the car. "How did it go?"

"Let's get out of here!"

He looked over, and this time saw the wet streaks through the dust. "What did he do to you, Ryan?"

"Nothing." She pounded the seat. "That *bastard*."

"Ryan, tell me!"

"It's not Lassard." Her voice cracked over the words. "It's Harry. Now drive!"

"I can't see much for the dust." He drew his face up close to the windshield, squinted and drove as fast as he could. "Where are we headed?"

"Philippa's. She's in ..." Ryan joined him close to the glass. Impatiently wiped her eyes. "Is that a truck?"

A form converged within the swirling dust. It was not a truck, it was a van. Black as night, crawling up towards them without lights. A shadowy funnel around which the yellow-lit dust had to swirl.

Ryan whipped about. "There's another one behind us!"

Hale gunned the engine. He felt his nerves race with the motor as he jammed down the accelerator. The car headed straight for the dark van.

But dark no longer, for they were instantly met with lights blazing on bright beam. Hale swerved as much from the sudden light as from the van. The tires screamed as he swerved and struck the sidewalk with enough force to bounce Ryan's head off the ceiling.

Ryan jammed her arms on the door and dash for support, which was good, because an instant later the van climbed the curb and smashed into their side. Jumping the sidewalk slewed the van so that its aim was spoiled, and instead of shoving a metal wedge directly into Hale, it rammed the back door so hard the seat buckled and crumpled against the other side, bursting out the window.

Hale clenched the wheel and fought to keep the car moving forward. Ryan shrilled words he could not understand, not even really hear, because there was another roar, this one from behind them. In his rearview mirror he saw the second van bounce up and onto the sidewalk, the lights tracking through the back window in a leaping rush.

He had the split-second image of a giant metal cat pouncing. Then he was thrown forward as the van struck with enough force to blast their trunk lid up and over the car. It landed on the hood, slid off, and became caught between the car and the concrete building.

The roaring continued, one van trying to smash them into a pulp against the building, the other mashing them forward. Metal screeched in wrenching protest, their fender and bumper tore free, and they were launched like a pip squeezed from a grape. His foot was jammed so hard on the pedal he threatened to ram through the floorboard. Over the shrieking metal he could hear the whine of spinning tires.

Hale struck a wooden bench and turned it into matchwood, before catapulting over the sidewalk and firing down the street. The car was filled with the stench of hot oil and burning rubber. An almighty clatter rose from beneath what was left of their hood.

Ryan shouted, "We're slowing down!"

"We've lost our left tire," Hale said, wrestling the wheel to keep them headed straight. "And probably thrown the universal joint to the moon."

Through the demolished back window they heard the sound of rending metal. Ryan turned around, shouted, "They're coming!"

"They're going to catch us," Hale said grimly. "The pedal is right on the floor."

"We've got to run for it!"

Before the words were completely formed, Hale had already stomped on the brakes. Ryan slammed open her door, leapt out into the night, and rolled away. Hale tried his own door. It did not budge. He threw his shoulder against it. Nothing. A shouted curse and he slid across the car's central console, leapt out, and hit the pavement hard. A bright light smacked inside his eyes in time to the piercing pain in his knee.

The van roared closer, aiming straight for him. Hale kept rolling, used the sidewalk as a lever and scrambled to his feet. He dove behind a palm. The van roared over the sidewalk a second time and slammed into the palm with enough force to crack the tree and the bumper both. Hale spotted Ryan waving from the alley and raced over. His knee was throbbing.

He passed under a streetlight then back into dusty darkness. Ryan fell into step beside him. "We've got to make for the water."

Hale did not try for words. Together they raced down the alley. With each stride his right knee throbbed more painfully. He struggled not to limp or groan, then stumbled over some unseen trash and almost went down.

Ryan gripped him in a half-embrace and ran as hard as she could under the impossible load. The alley's entranceway seemed to dance enticingly just beyond their reach. Hale could not even risk a glance behind them, did not need to. He knew they were being tracked. Knew also he could not keep up this pace for much longer, with or without Ryan's help.

Beyond the alley's opening, the river beckoned. The water was a white-flecked ribbon sparkling under the bridge's lights. Hale understood Ryan's plan. If they could make it there, in this weather, they could wade out and disappear. On the water's far side beckoned the cheerful lights of Merritt Island and Cocoa Beach and safety. But there was no chance.

Not together. The water was two blocks and a million miles away.

A siren pierced the darkness, a ribbon of hopeful sound. But it was too distant. Overlaid above the siren was another noise, that of racing motors and squealing tires. And those sounds were much closer.

Three paces, two, and they launched through the alley entrance and into the yellow streetlight. Then it was over. Desperation, panic, defeat, all were there in his mind as the car raced around the corner, four tires screaming as it bit for purchase and careened up and over the sidewalk to stop in front of them. They were jammed up against the hood so tight Hale collapsed onto the hot metal, beaten. He barely had enough breath left to groan, "Go on, run."

Before Ryan could either reply or lift him back up, the door slapped open, and a familiar voice yelled, "Get him in here! Move!"

It was Lassard.

45

Hale sat behind the Congressman and alongside Ryan, and cradled his throbbing knee. The Congressman's aide drove expertly and silently and fast. They crossed the first of the Causeway bridges at such a pace that the sidebars melded into a yellow-grey blur. They sped off the first bridge and through a night-draped Merritt Island. The wind shook their car and the palms lining the Causeway. The sliver of land came and went, and they launched onto the second bridge. In the moonlight the Intracoastal Waterway frothed a milky silver.

Lassard seemed to pick up a thread he had been discussing internally, as he said towards the front windshield, "The military-industrial complex is in a panic. They've sat there and watched the government go through the most serious cutbacks in fifty years. Funding for new projects, which is where the real profit lies, has been stripped down to almost nothing. Either they win the one big project for their industry, or they're staring extinction in the face. Desperate times, desperate men."

Hale flicked glances at Ryan beside him. He was not sure how much she was taking in, but at least she had settled somewhat. Her breathing was still ragged and her face looked stricken, but her eyes had refocused. And she had finally stopped seeping those unnoticed tears. The ones he still did not understand.

"The crisis is hitting those in politics just as hard. These days a senatorial race costs between thirty and fifty million dollars. Even if they're not addicted to the lure of money, politicians know that money is the grease that keeps the election wheels cranking," Lassard went on. "The folks addicted to power games, nowadays they're in a pure-bred panic. They want to keep up their high lifestyles, their expensive habits, their power lunches. They're scared enough to take money from whoever does the offering. They dance to the tune of whoever pays."

Ryan spoke then, her voice a shadow of its former self. "You're talking about SRC."

"Yes ma'am, I am indeed. Up to now we've lacked any real proof, but far as I'm concerned, SRC is a consortium of the truly desperate. And it's run by folks who don't give a tinker's damn for scruples. I met a lot of such people in my walk down the halls of power. Always made me sick to my stomach. The way they figure things is, since they got the power, they *deserve* to rule. Their hold on power gives them the right to do whatever they damn well please." Lassard shook his head. "Far as they're concerned, a nation's laws are for the little people, not themselves."

The young man behind the wheel said, "The turn onto A1A is up ahead. North or south?"

"South," Hale replied.

The driver braked, but still took the turn with the speedometer over sixty. Hale braced, then grimaced as pain shot through his injured knee. They did a controlled slide through the empty intersection, tires screaming. The driver whipped the wheel about, seeking control. Soon as the car straightened, he gunned the motor and raced through the night.

Ryan asked, "How do we fit into all this?"

"An interesting question, Ms. Reeves. Back about five months ago, our sources began talking about movement on several new fronts. One whisper after another pointed towards your Dr. Laremy and her research. Just rumors, mind, but with enough force to start shaking the power tree right down to its roots. How the lady scientist was on the verge of changing the space industry's entire structure. How she was going to rewrite the whole rulebook. The power people, now, they heard this stuff and they grew plain terrified. That was the main reason we became interested. But we couldn't seem to find anything with real meat. Then you pop up in Florence's office and offer us what we thought might've been the key to SRC's secret hidey-hole."

Lassard waited as the driver slowed slightly, checked in both directions, then gunned his way through a red light. The late-night streets were empty of all but the wind. Lassard went on, "From everything we've been hearing, it appears that Dr. Laremy has come up with something that SRC either must have, or must destroy."

"Slow down," Hale said. "Your turn's just up ahead on the left."

Hale directed the car into the gravel drive by the shuttered surf shop. In the rising wind the surrounding shrubs and trees weaved a frantic dance of warning.

Before they opened the car doors, a shadow coalesced to one side and a deep voice growled, "Who the hell are you?"

"Friends," Hale said. "Ben, meet Congressman Lassard."

A flashlight scanned the strangers. Then backed up to take in his and Ryan's battered forms. "Who took a bite out of you?"

"Long story. How are things?"

"Everything's been real quiet." Ben turned and started for the barn. "I was just getting ready to give you people a call."

Ryan stepped forward. "Is she –"

"Philippa's fine." Ben opened the barn door, and the light from within illuminated his grin. "Matter of fact, she's about ready to rock and roll."

* * *

From within the barn, the wind growled low and menacing. Breezy whispers found their way through the cracks in the ancient planking. Naked bulbs strung high overhead swung a looping dance. The barn's corners and high ceiling were alive with flitting shape-changers.

If Philippa was surprised at the sight of strangers, she did not show it. "That was speedy."

"I never got a chance to call," Ben announced.

"Philippa Laremy, Congressman Lassard and his aide, sorry, I don't know your name." Ryan limped over to inspect the apparatus. "You're done?"

"All but the shouting." Her smile disappeared as she inspected Ryan, then Hale. "What on earth happened here?"

"Don't ask," Hale said. He sank onto the floor, massaged the throbbing kneecap.

Lassard stepped forward. "Dr. Laremy, it's a real pleasure, ma'am. But we've really got to get you to safety."

"And leave all this?" Philippa's clothes and face and hair were streaked with grime. The bandage on her shoulder was a filthy grey. Her eyes looked sunken in dark exhaustion. "Don't be absurd."

"Dr. Laremy –"

"Ben, go hook up the power." To the group she explained, "The power was always the question here. But it turns out Ben has gained valuable experience with the Hawaiian electric authority."

"Eight months triple time after the hurricane took out Kauai," Ben confirmed. He hefted a coil of heavy cable and began paying it out as he backed into the darkness. "Give me five minutes."

Lassard did a slow sweep of the barn, took in the sawhorses supporting the door with its load of computer and instruments and cables and equipment. Little wisps of dust filtered through cracks in the wall, blown by the rising storm. "A strange place to be making history, if you don't mind me saying."

"I could not agree more." Philippa's gaze ran down the array of knobs and switches. She then glanced over at Hale. "Did everything go well with Vienna?"

"Far as I can tell, everything is fine," Hale replied. "But that's not the issue right now."

"No, it certainly is not." Philippa watched cautiously as Lassard took another step towards her lab table. Her hands came to rest protectively upon the bell-shaped vacuum chamber. Suspended within was a globe fashioned from the pair of small mixing bowls Hale had purchased that morning. The globe was tightly wrapped with bands of solid gold wire. Within the globe itself was what appeared to be a three-dimensional spider's web of gold filament, suspending a central black object about the size of Hale's thumb.

"I know Ryan feels I should trust you," Philippa told the congressman. "And I am indeed grateful for your assistance with Alexis' family. But there is only one way you will ever rise from the ranks of spectators as far as I am concerned. And that is by giving your solemn oath that you will protect me from whatever pressures I may face to go public with my discovery."

"That's beside the point right now, ma'am. We have every reason to believe you are in the gravest danger here. I must insist –"

"How *dare* you speak to me about danger!" Her shriek rose to compete with the wind. "I have been chased from my lab, burned out of my house, shot, had my research partner murdered, and tracked across the country! I know everything there is to know about living with danger!"

"Yes ma'am, I do believe you." Lassard grimly held his ground. "And our sincerest hope is that you will continue living for a very long time to come."

"That's all well and bloody good, isn't it." Philippa's breath was so ragged it scratched over the rising storm. "But you have not addressed the issue. I will not be pressured, Congressman. If you want me to agree with whatever plan you may have been hatching, you will first promise me, *on your honor*, that you will not permit *anyone* to force me either to withhold my work or to publish my findings until I and I alone make that decision."

Lassard said quietly, "Ma'am, I can only promise to try."

"That's not bloody good enough." Philippa crossed her arms. The overbright gaze signaled she was running on nerves and adrenaline, ready to crack at any moment. "Your people are going to want to jump on this with everything they have. They're going to insist on secrecy and then stuff me inside some huge lab and chain me to a team the size of Manhattan. And I won't have it, do you hear me? This is *my* work. I will do with it as *I* see fit!"

"I don't even know what it is you're working on."

"Reshaping history," Philippa snapped back. "You just said so yourself." Her gaze flickered over Hale and Ryan, then she added, "That and fashioning ourselves a lure."

"You didn't need to do all this just to get me here."

"My dear Congressman, the world does not revolve around your august presence, much as you may think otherwise. No, I am after a much more elusive prey." She glanced out to the darkness beyond the open door. "I wonder what on earth is keeping Ben."

Lassard sighed his frustration. His aide spoke for the first time, "Perhaps you should use the phone now, Congressman, dial 911."

Lassard did not even turn around. "And just exactly where in the hell am I supposed to tell them to come?"

"The police station is one block up on the right," Hale offered.

"By all means," Philippa said, her eyes feverish. "Run along there, invite them over. The more the merrier."

"I'm on my way," the aide said, and slipped out.

Ryan ventured, "Philippa, maybe you should consider –"

"I have done all the considering I require." Her attention returned to the congressman. "If this gentleman does not yet know for certain what I have discovered, he at least suspects it. And he understands full well what I mean by governmental pressure. I simply won't stand for being pushed and prodded, either towards making this a state secret or coming forward before I am fully ready."

The barn became caught in the amber silence of premonition. Hale felt Ryan's eyes on him, turned to find her urging him with a thrust of that determined chin. He shook his head. He was no longer pushing Philippa to do anything she did not want to. This was her show, and hers alone.

Lassard started to speak, only to be halted by the dials on the array of instruments suddenly coming alive. "Excellent! Ben has come through once again." She slipped on a pair of heavy rubber gloves. "Now we'll just wait for him to join us and –"

"Afraid the big guy's gonna sleep through this one," a rough voice announced, and Buzz Cobb stepped from the shadows. "But you go right ahead."

46

Hale was up and moving across the floor before Cobb had fully entered the barn. Cobb raised his arm, waggled the gun so that it glinted in the light. "I don't think so."

A taller man stepped in behind Cobb, and Hale recognized the senator's aide from the launch. Ryan spit the words, "I should have known you didn't have any sense, East."

"You shut your mouth." Clay East stabbed her with his gaze. "It's your damn meddling that's brought us to this."

"Couldn't keep the boy away," Cobb said. "Had to come and see the show with his own eyes."

"Correction," East retorted angrily. "I had to make sure you didn't lose what little control you have. Who knows when you might start thinking with your balls instead of that peanut of a brain."

Cobb's gaze turned steely blank. His grin lessened, then pulled back into shape. "The boy here thinks he could have done a better job by himself."

"I know for certain if I had been in charge my men wouldn't have missed twice in one day!" East's remaining hair formed a bird's nest about his head. He towered over the stocky man. "What kind of cretins are you associating with?"

"Been asking myself the same question," Cobb replied, and casually backhanded East with his gun.

East's eyes snapped back into his head. He crumpled without a sound.

Cobb stared at the man, muttered, "Sack of no-account bureaucratic shit." He stood over East, his chest heaving. "As if this whole damn mess wasn't his fault to begin with. Him and those namby-pamby politicians he's always sucking up to. Not one of them could fight their way out of a wet paper bag."

Cobb turned back to the room, resumed his rictus grin. "That's been their problem since the beginning of time, damn politicians messing with the fight. Oughtta just aim the warriors and let us go. But hell no, they gotta meddle." His gaze swept through the barn. "This pandemonium is a perfect case in point. They order us to leave the Doc here alone, tell us how they'll just manipulate her from a distance, direct her into doing what they want. What a crock. Shoulda picked her up soon as we heard. Either she worked for us or she didn't work. Simple as that."

Lassard took a single step forward. "You're Cobb with SRC."

The agate eyes honed in. "And you're the bastard who's been causing me all kinds of grief."

"You're in a whole heap of trouble, Mr. Cobb. I'm –"

"You're one dead turkey if you don't shut the hell up." Cobb swept the gun around. "The rest of the world may call you Congressman, but far as I'm concerned you're nothing but a loose end. You get any ideas about playing for the cameras, keep in mind you're my number one choice here to get shot."

Cobb turned his gaze back to where Philippa stood by her apparatus. "Go on, Doc, crank the sucker up and show us what all the fuss has been about."

"Certainly. Now that you're here, we can most assuredly begin." Philippa moved in jerky precision, as though she had been waiting for her cue. "As all of you may know, my research has focused upon the essential qualities of superconducting compounds. I was working in conjunction with

Alexis Vilnieff, that is, until his recent and tragic demise." A feverish glance towards Cobb. "Which I assume I have you to thank for."

"Pals working the other side," Cobb said easily. "All part of the big power play."

Lassard demanded, "What about Florence Avery?"

"Florence, now, she was a pure personal pleasure. As big a meddling fool as you're turning out to be."

Hale saw Ryan lean forward, almost ready to pounce. She managed to check her motion when Cobb waggled the gun in warning. She whispered, "You sick bastard."

"Let's see, this is coming from the lady whose hubby has been supplying us with a steady flow of data, do I have that right?" The man was obviously enjoying himself. "The one who thought things were turning lovie-dovie back in the home arena?"

Hale demanded, "What about shooting Philippa?"

"Yeah, the stupid jerk was meant to hit the board, not the lady. Just another prod to sweep her into the corral." Cobb's flat gaze aimed at Hale. "You're the surprise of the bunch, sport. Never figured you for anything more than a pretty face. My biggest mistake was thinking you got lucky when you took out my boys at the university lab."

"You arranged to have me attacked there? Why? You already knew where Philippa was."

"I just told you. Pressure tactics. Get you moving in the right way."

Hale struggled to fit the pieces together. "That's why you moved on Keebler? To pressure me?"

"Come on, Hale, darling. *Think*." Philippa's words were as stiff and jerky as her movements. "He wasn't after you. He wanted you to maneuver *me*. Keep me in line. Make me jump through all the proper hoops."

Ryan demanded, "You're going to shoot us, aren't you?"

"Nah." The gun swiveled back toward Lassard. "The Congressman's hanging from a mighty thin line, but you two are more useful alive. The Doc's coming with me. Got a lot of stuff for her to work on. Years of it. You two are our insurance. She behaves nice, you live. She doesn't, we lower the ax. You ever open your mouths, the doc here dies. All neat and simple." The gun moved back towards Philippa. "A little less talk and a little more action, Doc."

"We are waiting for the vacuum chamber and the refrigeration units to attain proper levels." She bent over her equipment, adjusted a dial. "Which will be very soon indeed."

Cobb demanded, "What are the chances of you knocking another hole in the roof tonight?"

"None whatsoever." She turned a lever beneath the table and continued, "In my first experiments all the force was channeled in one direction. I assumed this was the obvious corollary. After all, our primary source of gravity is generated from *below*. From the *earth*. I presumed my field must be designed to repel itself from this primary source. I was wrong."

Lassard took a step towards the table. "Anti-gravity, I *knew* it. You're –"

"You take another step and you won't know shit," Cobb snarled. "Not ever again."

"I made the same vital mistake, Congressman," Philippa went on, not looking up from her work. "*Anti*-gravity. The results clearly showed my error, as I created a projectile. One which removed a significant proportion of the lab building. But the projectile's path was cone-shaped, which demonstrated beyond the slightest doubt that I had successfully created the intended field. One so stable it existed temporarily after disconnecting from the power source."

She examined several meters in turn, then raised her face and smiled to the gathering. Hale had the impression she saw nothing at all. "The materials I used initially were not intended to exist under earth-normal conditions at all. But the *field* existed. It *protected* the material, only gradually dissipating as it raced away from the power source. Propelled by its repulsion from the earth's field of gravity."

The vacuum pump beneath the table began humming loudly enough to be heard over the roar of the wind. Philippa glanced down, then continued, "As a matter of fact, it was Alexis who showed me the answer. In a dream, actually." The feverish gaze fastened on Cobb once again. "Not even your mighty bullets could stop that, now, could they?"

"Get on with it, Doc."

"Yes, of course." She pulled a pair of cheap sunglasses from her pocket and slipped them on. "So this time I have used more stable elements as the field's generating core. And I have designed a *globular* structure. One which will hold the field in place in *all* directions."

"Action, Doc. I'm not warning you again."

"There will be no need." Philippa checked a dial on the chamber's base, then glanced up and announced, "I would advise you all to cover your eyes."

She snapped a switch, and for the second time Hale saw night become day.

Glass shattered and fell like glittering dust as the vacuum chamber disintegrated. Hale took a step back and raised his hands in defense against the glare. But kept looking. Though it was as hard as trying to stare at the sun, he could not turn away.

There above the table hung a perfect, shimmering, brilliant globe.

Philippa's voice rang loud in the awed silence. "To be successful, I needed to stop seeing this as anti-*anything*. My globular field should remain both stable and constant until its power dissipates."

She picked up the computer joystick from the table. "A truly stable field is one which can be directed into motion through the tiniest of power-shifts. You see, I did not need to do battle against gravity. I needed to *nullify* it."

Philippa hugged the joystick to her chest with both hands. "It is through nullification that the enemy is truly defeated. Is that not so, Mr. Cobb?"

"Put that down!"

"Here, Mr. Cobb." Philippa rammed the joystick far over. "Catch."

With the sound of softly searing air the globe whooshed straight at Cobb. He swiveled the gun, managed to get off one shot before the fire was on him.

He screamed and flailed and fell. The air was suddenly filled with the stench of burning flesh.

The globe continued in a straight line, striking the back wall just above the door. The old structure groaned and splintered. Wall timbers crashed in a shower of sparks and rotting lumber. Overhead the roof creaked, groaned, showered them with dust. And held.

Cobb rose from the floor, one side of his face and shoulder a raw smoldering wound. He gripped his gun with his good arm. Before he could take aim, Hale leaped across the distance. Cobb tumbled down once more, roaring his fury. Hale struggled to roll the man over, searching for the outstretched hand, his nostrils filled with fumes from Cobb's smoking flesh. Cobb fired off a wild shot. Hale rolled with him, fighting for the weapon he could not see. A wild kick connected with Hale's damaged knee. Cobb elbow-punched him in the face and he saw stars. Blindly Hale kept a manic grip on the man. Even with his injuries Cobb was hard as granite.

Then Cobb slackened. Hale gripped the gun-hand, tore the pistol free and kept rolling, the gun now cradled to his chest. He rolled another time before realizing Cobb was no longer fighting him.

Hale staggered upright in time to see Ryan heft a board from the demolished wall, and swing it side-armed at Cobb's head.

Cobb crouched on his knees and raised his good shoulder. He tottered under the blow, shouting pure venom. Ryan cocked for another blow, and when he raised his arm higher to try and grasp the incoming board she lowered her aim and slammed it into his ribs. Cobb grunted and went for her.

Philippa raced over and planted a solid kick into the side of Cobb's head. The man groaned, crawled like a wounded crab. She backed up, aimed again, let fly, screaming, "You rotten *bastard*!"

As both Ryan and Philippa were preparing for another strike, a voice from beyond the demolished wall shouted, "Police! Nobody move!"

Slowly Ryan let the plank fall to the floor. Philippa lowered her foot, stood panting alongside the other woman, looking down on the supine form. Philippa said hoarsely, "Consider yourself nullified, Mr. Cobb."

47

Soon after they bedded down that night, the rains arrived. The downpour was savagely tropical, a force more suited to a distant primitive land. Hale stood by the window to Jeff's room, surrounded by all the paraphernalia of a surf-mad teen and imagined the gale blown far off course by this hot, angry wind, until finally it beached upon this supposedly civilized shore. Lightening flashed like maddened strobes. On Jeff's walls a dozen bronzed poster-gods flew across waves unfrozen by the storm.

The thunder and the hurtling rain finally pushed Hale back to bed. Strange that he would find such natural fury comforting. But at least it masked the sound of Ryan sobbing in the guestroom next door.

Rain was falling in steady grey sheets when he awoke the next morning. Hale padded through the house, drawn by the smell of coffee. He favored his knee, though both the swelling and pain were muted. Hale entered the kitchen to find the back door open and Ben seated beneath the rear awning, cradling a mug with both hands. The white bandage wrapped about Ben's head was at direct odds to the colorless day.

Hale poured himself a cup. Ben watched and waited in silent invitation as Hale brought his mug outside. He asked the burly man, "How's your head?"

"Hurts. Didn't sleep so good."

"Didn't the doctor give you pills for the pain?"

"Don't feel like I should take any until we're sure this thing has been put down."

Hale leaned against the door and studied the seated man. This morning, Ben's T-shirt came compliments of the Surf Masters contest in Biarritz, France. "It's over, Ben. I know because I couldn't take any more."

Ben sat and stared as water dripped in ragged sheets from the awning. He drained his mug, set it aside. When he spoke, the words were directed to the weather-beaten day. "Think maybe you'd like to come over, hang out with me down in Angel's Camp for a while?"

Hale cocked his head in surprise. "That means a lot, coming from you." He sought some way to show how much the invitation meant, and settled on just laying it out straight. "I think I'm going to have to take a while to try and sort out what's left of my life. To start with, this thing has cost me my job."

"Where is Philippa going to be?"

"Washington, if the Congressman has anything to say about it. Least that's what he said after the cops got through with us last night. Plus the Russian lady, Mrs. Vilnieff, she's scheduled to arrive there next week."

Ben nodded to the rain. Rocking back and forth, accepting it all. "Listen, Hale. You ever need anything, you give me a shout. Just let me know when and where. I'll be there."

"Thanks, but far as I'm concerned the fireworks are over. Time for my life to get back to the same old same old."

Ben looked over then. "Don't be too sure."

"What's that supposed to mean?"

"Just a hunch. I've seen it often enough to know it happens." Ben rose slowly to his feet, keeping his head as steady as possible. "Some guys just know how to find the big swell. They draw it like human magnets. When that happens, the thrill gets deep in their blood, pushes them into all sorts of situations they'd never have expected."

Hale did not know what to say.

Ben closed the distance between them, offered his hand. "That's what friends are for, helping out when the hurricane hits."

* * *

A fragment of sound unlocked Hale from his private thoughts. He stared out into the deluge, saw a form congeal and become a lanky boy scrambling down the drive on his bicycle. Hale stood under the awning's safety and watched Jeff step off the bike and let it fall on the sodden earth. More than just the weather had formed the kid's face into all downturned edges. "Hey, Jeff. What's up?"

"Hey, Uncle Hale. I've got to pick up my gear." Jeff stepped onto the porch, peeled off his sopping shirt. "The guys are coming by for me."

"Let me get you a towel." Hale walked through the kitchen to the downstairs bath, returned to find him stripped to his shorts. "Any waves?"

"I dunno. Maybe." Jeff wrapped the towel around his shoulders and clenched it tight, as though trying to deny his body room to shiver. "Is everybody still asleep?"

"Far as I know. Ben came downstairs for a while, but he's gone back up. Have you met him yet?"

"No."

"He's a friend of Philippa. And a friend of mine." It felt good adding that bit. Even here, even now. "You'll like him. He's surfed monster waves all over the world."

Jeff did not have room just then for interest. "Is Aunt Philippa okay?"

"Sure. She's upstairs asleep too." In his parent's bed, but there was no need to mention that. Nor how Ryan had refused point-blank even to enter her own bedroom the previous night. "I bunked down in your room. Hope that's all right. We got in real late and sorta took what we could find. Ben slept on Kitty's floor."

Jeff continued to stare out over his back yard. The lawn was as washed of color as the day. "Is Dad here?"

"No." Understanding now what Jeff was thinking, that they had gathered around Ryan because of Harry's departure. Uncertain how to correct it without offering false hope. "No, Jeff. He's not."

Jeff's tone was as bleak as the invisible sky. "My parents are gonna get a divorce." And then he was crying. Tight sobs he fought to keep down, but emerging just the same. "I told them not to. But it's gonna happen."

Hale started to reach for the boy, then let his hand drop. Jeff straddled the impossible divide, part child and part man. The man would not want to be held by one of his mother's friends. Hale stood and offered quiet company, and searched for something to say. He found a strangeness within, and it took a moment to recognize it as his own changing nature. He took a breath, willing the strangeness into a shape he could offer to another. "It's not your fault, Jeff. I know part of you thinks it is. But it's not."

Hale recognized that the words were as much for him as they were for the boy. The perception rocked him back a step. He fought to relocate his internal balance. When he could, he continued, "Sometimes it's not even their fault. Loving someone is about the hardest thing anybody ever tries to do. So hard a lot of people prefer not to try at all."

Jeff snuffled, fought for control. He wiped his face on the towel's edge, resumed his quiet inspection of the grey and weeping day.

Hale stopped there, at least the words he spoke aloud. But internally the dialogue continued. He told himself how people spend a lifetime lying to themselves, claiming they're looking for love. But they're not. Soon as they get anywhere close, they run. They fight. They argue. They dig for reasons to turn away. Sometimes the best thing anyone can do is just to try. Even if life wins in the end. At least they've struggled for something bigger than they ever would be alone.

Something worth the effort. Hale wanted to say those things, all that and more. But the thoughts were so new and devastating in their challenge it was hard enough to form them within, much less say them aloud.

The rain paused then, a brief lifting of the veil. Overhead a sky formed of scuttling clouds, driven by a wind which did not reach down to where they stood. A bird cheeped tentatively, a faint song of hope that the worst of the storm had passed.

Jeff turned for the door, keeping his face averted. "I better go get ready."

"Jeff." Hale hesitated, then said, "Your mom is a hero. I've known her since the year before you were born. And she's one of the strongest, finest women I've ever met. The love she had for your dad just didn't work out. That's all you can say, that they tried, and tried hard."

The boy pushed through the door and disappeared. Hale nodded his acceptance to the gray day. As though Jeff's response was the only correct one. He scarcely had enough wisdom to offer the boy anything of value. Especially about love.

He remained where he was, the mug cold and forgotten in his hand, and stared out to where the palms and oaks stood burdened by the day. In time, the rain descended to envelope his world once again.

* * *

Hale spent the afternoon with Ben, Ryan and Philippa in the Cocoa Beach police station. Congressman Lassard arrived shortly after they did, and showed no qualms over shoving his substantial weight around. He gave the detectives precisely four hours to complete their preliminary depositions, then backed up his words with an incoming squadron of FBI agents. Hale sat in a windowless chamber for much of the time facing a policeman, a court stenographer, two agents, and a video recorder. He answered what seemed like an endless series of repetitive questions.

His second sortie to the hall brought him face to face with Ryan. Her features were drawn, her eyes stained with sadness. "Got a minute?"

"Until they call me back. You okay?"

"Fine." She shook her head at further questions; Hale understood. She had no energy for anything not absolutely crucial. "Look, do you think maybe you could stay with me and the kids for a couple of days?"

Somehow the question did not surprise him. "Unless Philippa needs me up in Washington, sure, I'd be happy to."

She accepted her second-tier importance with a tiny nod. "They just told me that there's a warrant out for Harry's arrest. Illegal diversion of classified equipment, I think that's what they said. As long as it keeps him away from us, I don't really care. But I'd like you there, you know, just in case."

"I'm happy to help." Hale accepted another nod in response, and stood watching as Ryan shuffled back down the hall. She was a figure transformed from endless energetic drive to waiflike helplessness.

* * *

When Philippa emerged an hour later she looked wrung completely dry. The police and the local district attorney followed, trying feebly to order her to remain in town. But by this time the FBI recognized what they had, and responded with a hastily compiled federal court order authorizing them to take her into protective custody.

Hale insisted on travelling with them to the Orlando airport. The agents were unclear as to his exact status, but grudgingly made room when Philippa and Lassard both insisted. There was no chance to speak during the drive, however, not with two agents accompanying them and two more with Lassard and his aide in the car directly behind theirs.

The rain finally ceased as they pulled up to the terminal. The pavement was dotted with pools and the trees hung weary and wet. But the air had freshened, and the late afternoon sky showed patches of veiled blue. Hale found himself staring at the puddles, grateful that at least the sky had wept over the separations to come.

While the agents saw to the check-in procedure, Hale shook the Congressman's hand and promised to appear when asked to testify. Only then did Philippa announce that they needed a moment alone. She drew him as far apart as the agents would allow, down a side concourse to where a pillar offered a hint of privacy.

Philippa's tone showed the stiffness of knowing she was being watched. "You'll be staying with Ryan?"

Hale sighed, defeated by her question. He had spent the entire journey hoping against hope that she would have a last-minute change of heart and ask him to come along. That she would say something about needing him, wanting to have him along. "She's asked me to hang around for a few days. Just to make sure Harry doesn't try anything stupid."

Philippa sensed his mood and responded to that, not his words. "I feel myself to be the centerpoint of gathering forces. The focus of a giant swirling vortex. It leaves me feeling so weak. So helpless." Her lips took a tiny taste of a smile. "I need your strength."

"Then let me come with you." Not caring that it came out like he was begging. Desperately pleading. "Please, Filly."

The smile was more in her weary eyes than upon her lips. But intact. "I can't, Hale."

He had known it since the night before. Since she had given him a one-armed hug in the upstairs hallway and then shut the bedroom door in his face. Even so, hearing the words hurt so much he felt his chest being ripped apart. "Why not?"

"Because it would be too easy. If we stay together now, it would be because of your own strength, not mine. But there is no future along that course, not for us as a couple. Can you understand that?"

Hale wanted to shout, to argue, to scream denial. But his heart would only permit a whispered breath of truth. "Yes."

Philippa's gaze revealed her own sorely wounded heart. "You are an accomplice of my soul. A companion to all my memories. All those I want to hold dear."

He said it because he had to. "I don't deserve a second chance. But I would give anything if it could happen."

"Maybe," she said slowly, "maybe this time apart was a necessary portion of our time together. Does that make sense to you?"

"Too much."

"You see? So much has changed within you during these months apart. Before, you would have laughed me off. Or changed the subject. You never wanted to see what was below the surface, much less talk of it. You were too focused on retaining hold of that perfect outside appearance. Keeping the externals intact."

The impact of her truth shook him like the last leaf of autumn. He could only nod.

"But it is life unseen that delivers happiness or sadness. Not what we present to the world, not what we want them to see. Not our achievements or our failures, our deeds and our titles. Or lack of them. What matters is what we carry around inside, beneath the carefully constructed barriers and all the fancy lies we tell ourselves. It's not just men who tell them either. Women are mistresses of fable. We claim to be searching for the right man, when all our time is spent cursing the male race and keeping them away. We grasp with one hand and strike with the other. We search out the archetypes who prove that our twisted view of maleness is not only true, but universal."

"Maybe it is."

"Only because we want it so. A caring gentle male would force the finder to *change*. To release all the frail underpinnings and secret flaws and accept that perhaps the fault lies partly in her. Questions unasked, life unseen, all would be revealed. What a positively terrifying thought."

She examined him for a long moment, then forced out the question, "Why did you come back, why did you go to San Diego for me, why did you ...?" A breath big enough to push away the fear he felt for her. "Why are you here?"

"Because." Hale wondered if there were words enough in the whole world to explain what he himself did not fully understand. If so, they were words he did not know. He felt like a pauper even before he opened his mouth. "There's a greatness in you I will never have."

Philippa did not laugh, did not draw away, did not do any of the billion things which would tear away the fragile filament set in place between them. It hung there, a gossamer thread of silver light only he could see. No, perhaps she had the vision as well. For her voice held to a quiet delicacy, as though she shared with him the moment's magic. "For centuries there were men who measured their worth by how well they served the maiden of their dreams. Knights, they were called, glorious warriors who knew the worth of strength given to protect another."

He shivered again, touched by winds beyond time and space, and felt yet another filament spinning from his heart. And another. All the lessons he was learning too late.

"My homeland is filled with legends of knights blind in their quest for the impossible, blind in how they reshaped these maidens in their heads and hearts until the image held no connection with reality."

"I haven't done that." Quiet yet firm. Knowing it was finally true.

"No." And with the agreement came another thread, and another still when she touched his arm. Philippa's hand felt strong and yet fragile as it rested there, the touch another communication between them. An emphasis to her whispered concord. "No. You are finally moving beyond lies."

His heart's remaining filaments trembled with the force of her whisper. For the first time ever, despite the fact that he knew he would ever remain unworthy, he could see what remained of his internal tapestry. "For the first time in my entire life, I feel as though I may be."

Green light poured from the eyes staring at him, eyes so open her heart's luminescence shone upon the tapestry as it shimmered there within him. "My gallant knight. So wounded, so valiant."

"I'm not. But I'd like to be. For you. Maybe one day we can make this work."

Her voice trembled so he could scarcely understand the words. "One day. Perhaps."

Hale held her then, with all the force he could muster. His arms willed her to be bound eternally to him. For the tapestry was connected to both their hearts, he saw that now. And saw as well how it was colored by a billion shades his eyes could never see, nor his mind fathom. And all he could whisper was, "I'd like to try, Filly. If you'll let me. If you could ever forgive –"

She kissed him, her arms strong around him, even when she released him, even after she turned and walked away. He stood and watched her depart, perhaps forever, and felt all his weak points exposed, all the places he had striven his life long to protect from view and probing touch. Yet here he was, alone and bereft, his tattered armor in shards at his feet. All the lies, all the pains, all the unwanted memories, all laid bare in his moment of desolation. Standing there in all his naked shame.

Yet from his wretchedness there shone a beauty. And he did not mind the tear he shed as he watched the best thing in his entire life pass down the hall and out of view. The remnants of his being shouted to an uncaring world how sorry he was that he could not be a better man. For her.

* * *

The descent of night found Hale waxing his board. He had not surfed after dark since his wild angry days in Norfolk. But he had no desire to return just yet to Ryan's house. He could not explain it better than that. He simply was not ready.

The night was crisp and clear, the sky awash with stars. A ruddy moon hugged the horizon, impossibly large. Hale crossed the beachwalk at Sixteenth Street, and could not decide whether he was pleased or disappointed by the crowds. The walk and the sand were bustling with people waiting and watching northwards.

To his left, the Kennedy preserve curved seawards. At its zenith rose a pinnacle of light, where he could just make out the Titan rocket poised for launch. It was scheduled to fly from the Canaveral military pad in less than an hour. Hale decided the best course was simply to ignore the crowds entirely.

He crossed the beach and entered the warm water. He paddled through the reformed shorebreak, stroking hard, letting the waves hit and wash over him. He found he enjoyed the unexpected shocks, the rushing demand to pay attention and focus.

He made it outside, raised upon the board and sat there panting. Waves rose and crested, flickered with phosphorescent fairy dust. He let one set pass, then another. For the moment it was enough just to sit and listen. And settle.

He found himself drawn by the solitary moon. There was a powerful and lonely affinity between them, the water-bound surfer and the maker of tides. Lunar power rippled through his empty caverns, drawing him with a siren's song so lucid it melded perfectly with the music of the waves. It would be so easy to head seawards, paddling out to where his soul grew ready to leave body and earth behind. So easy.

Yet Philippa's absence kept him there, that and the yearning for something more, something new. Hale sat unmoving, rejecting the sad lunar melody. He found himself hearing a different refrain, one borne upon the memory of her, and the hope of further memories to come. Despite the void, the ache, the ton of regret, Hale found comfort in that hope. Enough to keep him there, tied to earth and to shore.

With a chest-crunching thunder, the Titan rocket ignited. The ocean before him turned a molten gold. Hale watched the torch blast upwards, until a wave rose in front of him. The liquid wall was a silhouette cut from the stars and the sea and the rising pillar of flame. Hale turned and pushed and felt himself lifted. He propelled himself onto his feet, sliding down the face of the wave, and accepted the ocean's momentary gift of wings.